Key to characters on cover

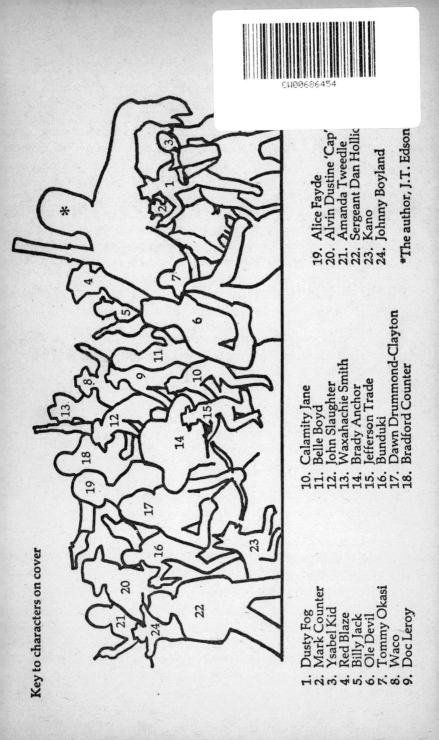

1. Dusty Fog
2. Mark Counter
3. Ysabel Kid
4. Red Blaze
5. Billy Jack
6. Ole Devil
7. Tommy Okasi
8. Waco
9. Doc Leroy
10. Calamity Jane
11. Belle Boyd
12. John Slaughter
13. Waxahachie Smith
14. Brady Anchor
15. Jefferson Trade
16. Bunduki
17. Dawn Drummond-Clayton
18. Bradford Counter
19. Alice Fayde
20. Alvin Dustine 'Cap'
21. Amanda Tweedle
22. Sergeant Dan Hollic
23. Kano
24. Johnny Boyland

*The author, J.T. Edson

'Waal now, seeing's how we're all so cosy and being real formal like, allow me to present us. I'm Loncey Dalton Ysabel. Thishere gent on the bloodbay's Mark Counter.' He paused for a couple of seconds to let the names sink in, noting the worry lines which were forming on two of the faces. 'Thishere,' he waved a hand towards the small rider, 'ain't nobody much at all. Happen you've never even *heard* of him.' He paused again, then:

'His name is Dusty Fog!'

With these words. J.T. Edson ended Chapter One of TRAIL BOSS, his first book, published in 1961. Since then, they have continued to flow in a steady stream. In time, Dusty Fog, Mark Counter and the Ysabel Kid were joined by other protagonists. Waco, Miss Martha 'Calamity Jane' Canary, General Jackson Baines 'Ole Devil' Hardin each wound up with a series of their own. The two Belles, Boyd and Starr, each deserved a series of her own, but somehow never made it. John Slaughter, Waxahachie Smith, Brady Anchor and Jefferson Trade all came into their own. So did Dusty's grandson, Alvin Dustine 'Cap' Fog and Mark's lookalike greatgrandsons, Deputy Sheriff Bradford Counter of Rockabye County and James Allenvale 'Bunduki' Gunn, with their female partners, Woman Deputy Alice Fayde and Dawn Drummond-Clayton. Not forgetting the beautiful 'school swot', Amanda Tweedle. Sergeant Dan Hollick and his big Doberman Pinscher, Kano, led the way for many other action-escapism-adventure series in the pages of the boys' paper, VICTOR and young Johnny Boyland's skill as a gunsmith was recorded in various editions of BOYS WORLD ANNUAL.

And here, gathered in one volume, they all are.

J. T.'s Hundredth

J. T. Edson

CORGI BOOKS
A DIVISION OF TRANSWORLD PUBLISHERS LTD

J.T.'s HUNDREDTH

A CORGI BOOK   0 552 10995 9

First publication in Great Britain

PRINTING HISTORY

Corgi edition published 1979
Corgi edition reprinted 1979

Acknowledgments:

The following are reproduced by kind permission of
D.C. Thomson and Company Ltd.: 'The Dogs of Kwang',
copyright © Victor 1962, and 'Johnny Orchid'', copyright © 1963.
The author also thanks The Hamlyn Publishing Group Ltd. for
permission to reproduce 'Johnny Boyland and the Quail Hunters'
(first published by Odhams Books), copyright © Boys' World
Annual 1971; and Brown Watson Ltd. for permission to reproduce
'The Joke', copyright Brown Watson Ltd. 1963.

This book is set in Linotype Times

Corgi Books are published by Transworld Publishers Ltd.,
Century House, 61–63 Uxbridge Road, Ealing, London, W5 5SA

Made and printed in Great Britain by
Richard Clay (The Chaucer Press), Ltd., Bungay, Suffolk

CONTENTS

*For all my readers, without whose
support there would not have been
any point in writing the first
ninety-nine.
My thanks to every one of you.*

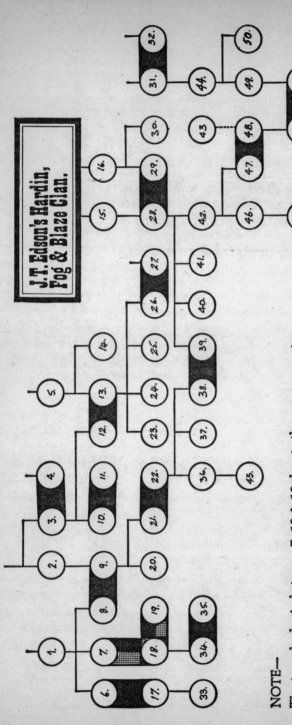

J.T. Edson's Hardin, Fog & Blaze Clan.

KEY
Married
Unmarried

NOTE—

The two shades in between 7, 18 & 19 denote the rumours as to General J.B. Hardin's (No. 7) marital status. The clan however has denounced these rumours as canards but there seems little chance of finding out the truth at so late a date.

On the Hardin, Fog & Blaze Clan there are several members of the family whose connections go back so far as to be virtually impossible to trace. Under this category come, Charles Goodnight, Shad Clements, Mannen Clements, Jubal Smith, and Tim Farron.

LEGEND

1. Capt Jerimiah Hardin
2. Edward Fog
3. Marsden Fog
4. Elizabeth Clements
5. Marsden Blaze
6. Joel Hardin
7. Jackson Baines Hardin (General T.L.C. — Ole Devil)
8. Elizabeth Mae Hardin
9. Hondo Fog (Sheriff)
10. Elizabeth Fog
11. John Slaughter
12. Georgina Mae Fog
13. Benjamin Blaze
14. Mannen Blaze
15. Rance Counter
16. Darby Sutherland
17. Eileen . . . . . (Died in childbirth)
18. See footnote please
19.
20. Daniel Jackson Fog (Died in 'A Town Called Yellowdog')
21. Dustine Edward Marsden Fog (Capt T.L.C.)
22. Lady Winifred Amelia Besgrave-Woodstole
23. Buck Blaze
24. Peter Blaze
25. Georgina Blaze
26. Charles Henry Blaze (Red)
27. Susan

28. Mark Counter
29. Dawn Sutherland
30. Vernon Sutherland
31. William Drummond
32. Venita Rutherford
33. John Wesley Hardin
34. Elizabeth (Betty) Hardin
35. Johnny Raybold
36. Jackson Marsden Fog
37. Winifred Belle Fog
38. Mark Loncey Fog
39. Dawn Belle Fog
40. Jane Alice Counter
41. Mark Rance Counter
42. Dustine Loncey Counter
43. Sir Henry Curtis ?
44. Roger Drummond
45. Alvine Dustine Fog (Capt Fog, Texas Rangers)
46. Andrew Mark Counter
47. Alison Dawn Counter (Tex)
48. Maj Roger Gunn
49. John Drummond-Clayton
50. Capt Hugh Drummond (Bulldog Drummond)
51. Bradford Mark Counter
52. James Allenvale Gunn (Bunduki)
53. Dawn Drummond Clayton

Author's note:

With the exception of 'The Joke' episode (which first appeared in the 1963 Brown Watson Ltd. 'Wagon Wheel Western' edition of *The Fastest Gun in Texas* but was deleted in the subsequent editions as it did not fit into the time-period of the other three episodes), *The Dogs of Kwang, Johnny Orchid* and *Johnny Boyland and the Quail Hunters*, all the stories in this volume are new and have not previously appeared in print in the United Kingdom.

Also, for the convenience of all new readers and to save my 'old hands' from repetition, I have included the backgrounds and special qualifications of my various heroes and heroines where necessary in the form of appendices.

INTRODUCTION

I am frequently asked, 'How can I become a writer?'

My usual replies are:

'*Don't!* There are too many of us at it already!'

Or:

'I wouldn't if I was you. It's a miserable, lonely, overworked, underpaid life.'

Actually, most of the latter response is a 'snow job'; but there is some truth in it.

Writing is hard work if you are going to do it properly. Not manual work, such as I did in a stone quarry before I was called into the Army, or as cold, wet and frequently unpleasant as being a postman.[1] It is a lonely life in the respect that, no matter how much you talk to other people about the various problems with

[1] This is a good place at which to clarify one point which has come to annoy me. Various newspaper and magazine articles have made a big thing about me being a 'postman turned author', apparently implying that no postman should have the intelligence, or the right, to make the transition. While I confess to having been a postman for three years, for two prior to that I had been a moderately—if not financially—successful full time writer. At that period, in addition to producing a number of Western novels, I was bringing out three or four short stories, or artist's scripts each week to appear in the D.C. Thomson & Co., Ltd.'s boys' paper, *Victor*. Furthermore, I was one of the very few writers to have had *three* series running at one time in any of Thomson's boys' papers and quite often had two running concurrently in *Victor*. So I hardly started writing while I was a postman. I became one because a change in editorial policy caused me to stop writing for the boys' papers and I could not live on the earnings from my novels. I also believed that neither I nor any other healthy person had the right to sponge off the tax payers by drawing unemployment benefits and National Assistance while waiting to break into the 'big time'. In addition, I hoped that the exercise I would be taking as a postman might help me solve a serious weight problem I had at that time (it did not). I realize, of course, that feature writers like to have pegs to hang people on; but wish that they would call me an 'ex-regular soldier turned author', which would be far more accurate.

15

whatever you are working on, in the final analysis the actual creative side of the finished product lies directly upon the writer's own shoulders. It is a miserable job on those occasions when no new ideas come, or something happens to disturb the creative flow, and you sit for hours at a time either staring blankly at the typewriter, or writing page after page only to have them wind up in the waste-paper bin.

On the other hand, writing does bring its benefits and I don't only mean on the financial side, although I'd be the last to deny that I like that too. Money might not buy friends, but it gives you a better class of enemies. There is the pleasure of creation and the knowledge that other people are enjoying, as well as taking an interest in the end products of your efforts. I have had ample evidence of this and have selected two examples. One of my lady readers wrote to tell me that on reading *The Drifter* and learning that Waco was on the verge of being married, she threw the book at the wall and gave me up for three months. I'm pleased to say that she has now come back into the fold. Another, who regrettably never sent his, or her—I'm inclined to think it was a lady, but that might be no more than my male chauvinist piggery— name and address (the letter however had a Bolton & Bury postmark) told me that after reading *Guns in the Night* and learning that her favourite member of the Floating Outfit, Mark Counter, had lost Belle Starr, while Dusty Fog and the Ysabel Kid were riding off into married bliss, she was very annoyed. In fact, she threatened to burn all her collection of my titles and start reading other Western authors if I didn't produce a nice girl for Mark to marry.[2]

Don't get me wrong. I'm not knocking the writers of the letters. As a working class ex-regular soldier, I know that in the final analysis it is the reader who makes a writer successful. Critical acclaim might help, although just about the only one of my books to have been granted the '*privilege*' of being reviewed by a critic, *Blonde Genius*, only sold a fraction of my average Western. Nor have I ever heard of a professional literary critic actually *buying*

[2] For the benefit of the anonymous letter-writer: Mark Counter married Dawn Sutherland, who he had first met in *Goodnight's Dream*. Don't forget, he has two great grandsons, Bradford Counter of Rockabye County and James Allenvale 'Bunduki' Gunn.

16

a book. What really counts where I'm concerned is the person who walks into the bookstore, takes out his or her money and *pays* for the book. In my opinion, it is they and they alone whose opinion of my work is worth considering.

Finally, with regard to the above two letters and all the others I have received either telling me how the books have been enjoyed, or asking questions, I love to receive them and every one is answered.[3] I think it is really great to be able to draw readers so closely into involvement with my characters that it produces such a response.

Now, having got that off my chest, I'd better get on with what the Introduction is all about and tell you something about my favourite subject—me ...

My entry into the writing field stemmed originally from a hatred of 'woodwork' classes at school. As I have two *left* hands, with six thumbs and no fingers on each, I was—and still am—absolutely helpless when it comes to tinkering with or making things.[4] Luckily, for my generation—when there was none of the current permissive 'please-yourself-whether-you-learn-anything-or-not', attitude in the classrooms—I had an exceptionally understanding teacher. Mr. 'Tommy' Dearnley, of the Shirebrook Selective Central School not only allowed me to write during the 'woodwork' periods, instead of wasting time botching up pieces of wood, but he allowed me to produce short stories and gave further encouragement by 'marking' them as he would have a standard text book type of essay. I must admit, however, that another master soberly warned my mother that I would never amount to anything by stuffing my head full of all that 'blood and thunder' nonsense. It's nice to know that some things never change, also that I've justified his pronouncement. One thing 'Tommy's' tolerance did

[3] The *J. T. Edson Appreciation Society* was formed to cope with readers' correspondence. Run by my very efficient secretary, Joan Coulter, it allows us to keep in touch via our bi-monthly Newsletters with those of our readers who join. We will still answer your letters if you don't join, but you will have more fun and get more information if you do. There is a small annual subscription, but until we are turned into a Nationalized Industry, we can't run at a complete loss. Our address is P.O. Box 13, Melton Mowbray, Leics.

[4] These days, my system of 'do it yourself' around the house consists of opening the 'yellow pages' of the telephone directory, finding a suitable specialist, arranging to have the job done and, finally, signing a cheque.

was allow me, at a very important period of my formative years, to develop the most valuable and vital asset for an action-escapism-adventure writer, imagination. He also instilled in me the idea that one must carry out research even if one is only writing 'cowboy' stories.

I was lucky too, in growing up between the Wars. I won't say *which* wars, other than to remark that the rumour claiming they could have been the Crimean and the Boer is something of an exaggeration. From then until the early 1960s was the vintage period for the good old action-escapist-adventure books, pulp magazines[5] and movies. In such works, authors wanted to *entertain* the public. If they had a 'message' they used a telephone, the telegraph services, or wrote letters instead of inflicting it upon the paying public. They also kept the cinemas filled with patrons who were willing and eager to return.

Have any of you been in a cinema recently?

I suppose, in retrospect, times weren't particularly good in the kind of small mining village where I grew up. However, unlike various people of around my age who are now active in the entertainment media, I can't remember feeling especially deprived or hard done by. Everybody in my circle was in the same general state, so I wasn't conscious of being down-trodden or persecuted by the Establishment. If it comes to a point, along with the majority of my generation and class, I'd never even heard there was such a thing until the 'intellectuals' started to ram it down our throats via the television.

At first hand, my memories of life only start shortly before the outbreak of World War Two. Times were grim from mid-1939 onwards. Britain was facing a threat to its existence and way of life which was—up to that time—unequalled. One thing which helped us through the war years, with its shortages, the ever present danger of being bombed—my home was hit early in 1940, but I wasn't there when it happened—and losses of relations and friends, was the escapist literature and movies of the day.

One of the most fortunate things to happen was being 'called up'

[5] The term 'pulp' originally meant that the book or magazine was printed on cheap 'pulp' paper, but has now been turned by 'intellectuals'—who realize that their ideas on entertainment will never be as popular with the mass audience—into meaning that the work itself is inferior.

in 1946[6] to do my National Service. In fact, I doubt whether I would have become a writer if this had not happened. Not only did it allow me to see that there was a great big world outside the village, but being in the Army encouraged me to think about and do things which would not otherwise have been possible.[7] When I was overseas, with no possibility of going home for the weekend or where it was unsafe to leave the barracks, I put my leisure time to good use by devouring books and attending movies at every opportunity. It was at this period I began my acquaintance with the work of the truly great escapist writers such as—in alphabetical order—Edgar Rice Burroughs, Robert McCaig, Nelson C. Nye[8] and Edgar Wallace. I also sat through hours of John Wayne, Randolph Scott, Errol Flynn and, later, my all time favourite, Audie Murphy, along with many other stars of the good old Hollywood 'pre-message' days of movies. I also began my first tentative steps at writing for publication. I don't know if any former members of the 1st Battalion, Rifle Brigade who served at Osnabrucke in 1947 remember the camp magazine, *Shufti*; but the immortal 'Hints On Self Preservation When Attacked By A War Dog' was the first appearance in print of Rifleman Edson, J. T., 14139362.

Excellent though I found the story lines of the good old action-escapism-adventure book and movies, I noticed that there was a lack of extensive detail in them. The hero would catch the 'baddie' cheating at cards, but there was only very rarely an explanation of how this was done. Or the villain would be on the point of shooting the hero in the back, when his gun would jam and, except

[6] This disproves the other canard that I was once charged in the Army with having a frayed string on my long bow under Robin Hood's command. However, I do think we should *never* have been made to change our Brown Bess muskets for the Baker rifle.

[7] One thing I did *not* learn to do in the Army was drive. I'm too modest to say that the Royal Army Veterinary Corps found my services as a dog trainer so invaluable I could not be spared for long enough to take a course of instruction. However, if any of my loyal readers wish to think that was so, I can't stop them.

[8] I finally met Robert McCaig and Nelson C. Nye at the 20th Annual Convention of Western Writers of America in Olympia, Washington State. When I asked Nels what was his deep inner compelling motive for writing *The Waddy From Roaring Fork*, he replied, 'For the money.' I was deeply shocked. I had always believed that, like myself, he had written to expose the evils of the Capitalist 'Establishment', or to expose the decadence of Western Society and had no interest in crass monetary gains.

19

on a few occasions, the cause was not described. Also, when watching a movie, I would find myself thinking of how I would have handled the plot. From those beginnings, I decided that if I wanted the kind of plot plus detail I would enjoy, I must follow the old Yorkshire adage, 'If you want a job doing properly, do it yourself.'

I also remembered 'Tommy' Dearnley's insistence upon research.

At that period in the Army, it seemed to be possible to find somebody who had knowledge on almost any subject which interested me. From a couple of armourers, I learned much about the mechanics of firearms. Western buffs themselves, they taught me ways in which the single action Colt, its contemporary handguns, or the toggle-link action of the Winchester could break down. I found out a few useful things about how to cheat at various forms of gambling from another serviceman. All these have been put to good use. With all undue lack of modesty, I can state that I have never been found at error in my references to the various firearms of the periods covered by my books.

My actual writing career might be said to have commenced one night in Hong Kong in the early 1950s. Playing Tombola—bingo to the younger generation—at the China Fleet Club, I won a 'line' worth two hundred and fifty (Hong Kong) dollars and purchased my first typewriter with some of them. Straight away, what had been a collection of somewhat illegible notes in exercise books took on a new and professional looking dimension. By the time my tour in 'Kong' was up, I had no less than ten 'Western' manuscripts completed, an early version of Bunduki had appeared (I regret I can't recollect his name) and I had also written the first of the short detective-type stories starring Waco.

When I left the Army, after serving for twelve and a half years as a dog trainer, I decided to try to sell my work. Having only the vaguest idea how to go about it, I took a correspondence course in short story writing. However, the people who ran it 'forgot' to mention until *after* they had taken my money, that there was *no* market for Western short stories in England. Almost the only benefit I had from the course was it taught me how to set out a manuscript for submission. There was also a 'market' section in their lessons, from which I learned that the publishing house of Brown Watson Ltd. were running a Literary Competition with a section for Westerns. So the thing was not an entire waste of time and money.

Sending along *Trail Boss*, which took second prize—I was never able to discover who won *first*—and two other manuscripts, which eventually appeared as *The Hard Riders* and *The Texan* instead of under my original titles, I had them accepted. The publishers also asked me to let them see any more I might write in the future.

And that is how it all began.

I produced forty-six books which were published and marketed by Brown Watson Ltd. Unlike some of my contemporaries in the British Western novel writing field, they are all written under my own name.[9] I'm not ashamed of being the author of action-escapism-adventure stories, nor do I think it is beneath my dignity to be involved in 'pulp' writing. If I did, I wouldn't do it. Generally, we had an amiable, good relationship, although they would change titles, or cut out passages which were not in accord with the editor's beliefs, without consulting me. Nor would they let me try any other style of novel. I fought for three years, at a time when my work was a major earning asset of the company, to put the Rockabye County stories on the bookstore shelves. However, I'm grateful to them. They took me at the beginning and built my sales to a point where the major publishing houses were interested.

Corgi Books have allowed me to expand my range of works, but no matter whether I'm working on a 'traditional' Western, an 'off beat'—i.e. a Western with a female chief protagonist like Calamity Jane—a 'Rockabye County', a 'Cap' Fog, a 'Bunduki' or a 'School Swot', the emphasis is *always* action-escapism-adventure. I have only one 'message' in my work. Read it, enjoy it, go out and buy more to help keep me in the manner to which I have become accustomed.

Well, I think that is about all. I've gone on for quite long enough about my favourite subject.

My modesty prevents me from expounding at length upon my

---

[9] Brown Watson Ltd. originally produced *Quiet Town* and *Arizona Ranger* under the names 'Chuck Nolan' and 'Rod Denver', without consulting me, but brought out the subsequent editions of each work under my own name.

second claim to fame, that I tell the worst jokes in Melton Mowbray.[10] So I'll just say thanks to all my readers for having put up with me through ninety-nine books previous to the present volume. It's been great fun writing them and I hope that there will be many more in all my categories in the future. In fact, I'm already thinking about what to say in the 'Introduction' for *J. T.'s Two Hundredth* when the time comes.

Best wishes, you-all,

J. T. Edson,
Active Member, Western Writers of America,
Honorary Admiral, Texas Navy,
Honorary Deputy Sheriff, Travis County, Texas,
Honorary Deputy Sheriff, Thurston County, Washington State.

P.S. I had better point out to all journalists, television interviewers and press photographers that I have *never* found it necessary to wear 'cowboy' clothes when writing my Westerns, any

[10] However, I consider I would not be doing myself justice if I fail to substantiate my claim and feel certain the following three examples ought to uphold it adequately.
(a) Robin Hood robbed a blind beggar and gave all the money to the lord of the manor. It's known as robbing the wretch to give to the peer!
(b) Needing money to finance another Crusade, King Richard the Lionheart tripled the country's taxes. In cases of non-payment, a lien was imposed which stripped the transgressor of everything he owned.
And proves the saying, 'I'm going to lien on him' is older than we imagined!
(c) A peasant caught trespassing upon the lord's domain had a lien placed upon him, taking all he possessed. Being caught trespassing again left him open to a second lien, but as he could not pay he was sentenced to be executed. Instead of fleeing to safety before the second lien could be enforced, he sat reading the Doomsday Book, was captured and put to death.
One should never read between the liens!
Which proves I'm too modest!
I should have said that I tell the worst jokes anywhere!

more than I need to dress in a loincloth when working on the Bunduki series. Nor did Peter Clawson and I put on 'drag' once while working on *Blonde Genius*: I've got the legs for it, but Peter hasn't. So, any time you want me to dress up for interviews or photographs, I've only one thing to say to you.
FORGET IT!

PART ONE

THE FLOATING OUTFIT SERIES

Dusty Fog in

THE JOKE

Dustine Edward Marsden 'Dusty' Fog started life as a tall, slim, yet powerful young man whose horse was startled by a car carrying two girls coming unexpectedly around a corner of the trail along which he was riding. His mount was a large paint stallion and he carried his handguns in cross draw holsters. However, as the story was set in Texas during World War Two, the weapons were a brace of Colt Government Model ·45 automatic pistols. At the time of writing, by long hand as I had not yet obtained my first typewriter, he was merely a drifting cowhand. The OD Connected ranch and the rest of the Hardin, Fog and Blaze clan had not been brought into being and he was one of the 'Three Sons of the Grande', partnered by Lon Dalton and Morgan Summers instead of Mark Counter and—although part of the name remained—the Ysabel Kid. The plot was later reworked into the book which I had called Guns on the Azul Rio, *but which appeared re-titled by Brown Watson Ltd. as* Rio Guns.*

When I arrived in Hong Kong and began to take up writing in earnest, I realized that the comparatively modern setting of the stories was unsuitable. During the War years, Roy Rogers, for one, had appeared in numerous 'singing cowboy' Western movies which had a hero, riding the range on a horse and handling a brace of Colt Peacemakers, being in contention with 'baddies' who wore contemporary suits, drove cars and operated night clubs, but this format did not appeal to me. Nor did I believe it would be saleable, although at that period I had no serious thoughts about submitting my work for publication. I had, however, seen and thoroughly enjoyed a movie called Duel at Silver Creek *while considering how to rework Dusty's image. It was my first contact* with Audie Murphy, although not his first movie, and I was most impressed. From that day on, Dusty became transformed into the small, insignificant-seeming perennial youngster who is overlooked until there is trouble or danger.

One problem I envisaged with having such a leading character was how he could take on and defeat larger, stronger and heavier men in bare-handed fights. The answer was to let him use ju-jitsu and karate, both being all but unknown in the Western Hemisphere at the period over which the stories were set. However, the solution created another problem. How could I explain away his possessing such little known knowledge. Tommy Okasi came into being, originally merely as General Jackson Baines 'Ole Devil' Hardin's valet and Dusty's instructor in the Japanese martial arts.

References to Dusty's participation in the War Between The States while writing Trail Boss, which was one of the earliest manuscripts I sold that had not had its inception in Hong Kong, led to a further expansion of his background and family. For him to have attained the rank of captain at seventeen, no matter how competent he proved and how merited the promotion might be, implied he was well connected. So first one and then others of the Hardin, Fog and Blaze clan came into being. In time, these included his wife, Lady Winifred Amelia, 'Freddie Woods' Besgrove Woodstole[1] and their grandson, Alvin Dustine 'Cap' Fog.[2]

The reasons I have selected The Joke for Dusty's contribution to the Floating Outfit Series section of this volume are that it will give the many readers who missed the story on its first appearance the opportunity to read it. Also, the plot portrays one of his most important character traits: that he does not look the kind of person a man with his reputation might be expected to be.

Audie Murphy died in an aeroplane crash on the 28th of May, 1971. Regrettably, we never met. Nor were we fortunate enough to see him appear on the screen as Dusty Fog, who I believe would have made an ideal character for him to play. Since his death, I have not seen any other actor who could portray Dusty to my satisfaction.

[1] The events leading up to the marriage are recorded in: *The Making Of A Lawman, The Trouble Busters* and *The Fortune Hunters.* Lady Winifred also makes 'guest appearances' in: *White Stallion, Red Mare* and *The Whip and the War Lance.*
[2] New readers, see Footnote 15, Appendix One.

26

During an interview with a reporter, I commented upon Dusty being a small man making good in a big man's world. When the piece appeared, there was a quote to the effect that 'This could also apply to Edson'. At the time, I was around five foot ten and weighed in the region of eighteen and a half stone (259 lbs). The writer was a young lady standing not more than five foot one and slender with it.

THE JOKE

Joe Lemp was a man who loved to play jokes. Almost everybody in Dodge City, Kansas, would agree to that and give testimony to the amount of amusement his jokes caused. The depth of feeling expressed depended largely upon the vocabulary of the teller and how he, or she, had been affected by a particular joke.

It was Lemp who had sold some dudes fresh off a train 'mining rights' and had them dig up a considerable portion of Military Avenue overnight in their search for the buried wealth. This had caused some considerable inconvenience and embarrassment to the City Fathers, who had arranged a parade along the Avenue as a prelude to a reception of welcome for a visiting senator.

On another occasion, Lemp had smuggled a monkey into the hotel room of a whiskey drummer who was sleeping off the effects of an excessive sampling of his wares and fastened it to the foot of the bed. When the drummer woke up, he did not scream he was seeing things or rush out to sign the pledge, as had been expected. Instead, he lay studying the animal for a short time and then reached a decision.

'Monkey,' the drummer said, taking a revolver from beneath his pillow and aligning its sights. 'If you're just imagination, you don't have a thing to worry about—— But, happen you're real, you're sure's hell out of luck.'

With that, the salesman squeezed the trigger. Passing through the unfortunate monkey and the wall of the room, the bullet ended its flight in the leg of one of Lemp's cronies who had gathered in the passage to hear and see the fun. This was regarded by Lemp as being the best part of the whole affair, which only goes to show what a fun-loving man he was.

Two later escapades might have resulted in some of the fun-loving being let out of Lemp permanently.

The first was when the joker advertised John H. 'Doc' Holliday as being a practising dentist. There was a quick result to the advertisement and that uncertain-tempered, irascible Southern gentleman found himself visited by a very large and determined Irish lady, who demanded treatment for her brood of ten children. Playing such a trick upon a gun fighter of Holliday's status and temperament might have brought dire consequences, but Lemp could be most elusive when anything of that nature threatened.

If anything, the second episode was even more dangerous and cost the good citizens of Dodge quite a large sum of money. It came about after Lemp had passed word down the trail to Texas that, by order of Town Marshal William Barclay 'Bat' Masterson, Mr. Clayton Allison must not bring any more cattle to the city's shipping pens. On being told, the Washita curly wolf rode north at the head of his 'wild onion' CA crew to expostulate with the supposed sender of the message and the joke began to go astray.

All might have been explained peacefully, but Masterson—whose reputation among the Texan visitors was far higher than that of most Kansas' peace officers—was out of town on the day Allison arrived. His absence so incensed the rancher that Dodge City was subjected to the 'hoorawing' of its existence by the rampaging cowhands. Faced with having to pay for the damage caused to their goods and property, the irate citizens sought to prove that Lemp was the instigator of the rumour. If they had done so, it was their announced intention to present him with a new suit—made from molasses and feathers—then transport him beyond the city limits on a rail.

Such a show of ingratitude by the fellow citizens he had tried to amuse would have driven a lesser man from joking. In fact, it had almost had that effect upon Lemp. However, although he had laid low for a time, another trail drive season was in full swing and the town was crowded with Texas cowhands newly arrived with their herds of the longhorn cattle which had helped to bring financial stability to their State.[1] It was a period of jollity and

[1] How this came about is told in: *Goodnight's Dream* (American title, *The Floating Outfit* and *From Hide and Horn*.

joviality. So Lemp felt the urge to resume his light-hearted creation of harmless—well, *fairly* harmless—amusement.

'Say, Daws,' Lemp boomed, as he stood with a crony outside the Birdcage Café and listened for the outcry when somebody found that they had exchange the contents of the salt and sugar containers on several tables. 'How about us pulling that old shoot-out joke we did late last year?'

'We ain't fooling around with Bat Masterson or Doc Holliday again, are we?' Daws asked and there was a note of anxiety in his voice.

'Naw!' Lemp assured his companion vehemently. There were limits to his love of joking. They were reached and passed when it was his own hide that could be endangered. 'Once like that is enough.'

'What've you got in mind, then?'

'I told you, the old shoot-out game.'

'What's that?'

'You remember,' Lemp declared, then shook his head. 'No, you don't. It wasn't you I pulled it with last time. But it's a sure-fired lalapalooza that'll have you tickled better than a goose-feather.' Pausing, he slapped his thigh and beamed in delight at the memory of that particular joke. Scanning the passing crowd of townspeople, railroad workers, buffalo hunters and a scattering of blue uniformed soldiers, he continued, 'This's how we played her last time. I was standing on the sidewalk down opposite the Buffalo House and, when this skin-hunter come along, I turned and bumped into him. Made out that I thought it was him who'd bumped me and done it deliberately, which'd riled me so bad I was all set to draw down on him. You should've seen his face, he looked real scared. He wasn't but a green dude, not long started hunting, and thought he'd got tangled with a real mean gun fighter. It sure was a pistol the way he stared and, to make it better, you should've seen the way everybody else around scattered and headed for cover when they saw us. They went out of sight like prairie-dogs down their holes when a chicken hawk flies over. That was's good a laugh's the rest of it.'

'What happened?' Daws inquired eagerly.

'Feller's was in it with me suddenly grabs me and says the skin-hunter's none other than Wyatt Earp,' Lemp elaborated. 'He wasn't of course, but I acted up like I thought he was and played real scared. I tell you, Daws, that jasper started to think he *was* Wyatt after we'd kept it up for a spell. Then, when I'd apologized and backed off, he headed over to the Buffalo House and got to telling them what'd happened. We let him do it for a spell, then went in and told them the truth. They laughed that feller clear out of town.'

'You aiming to try it now, Joe?'

'Sure.'

'There's not all that many skin-hunters around,' Daws pointed out.

'There're plenty of cowhands, though,' Lemp countered, having already foreseen this factor. 'We'll do it on one of them.'

'We'll have to watch's we don't pick the wrong one,' Daws warned. 'Some of those beef-heads[2] get touchy happen you rile 'em and he might not let you back off after you've apologized.'

While he could not be ranked among the world's great thinkers, Daws had hit the main snag of the joke. It could prove *very* dangerous if a poor selection of a victim was made. Lemp might sport the attire of a professional gambler and the rig of a real fast gun fighter, but he was far from being capable in the use of his holstered Colt.

However, Daws took comfort from the thought that it was still too early in the day for the victim to have been drinking. When sober, cowhands for the most part were amiable and friendly, with no desire to make trouble. It was only when the tide of whiskey ran high that tempers rose and then the Texans could become as unpredictable and dangerous as a stick-teased diamond rattle-snake.

'Naw, it won't come to that,' Lemp declared, a broad grin spreading across his florid and heavily moustached face. 'I'll pick a jasper who couldn't hit his leg through the bottom of his holster. The whole point is to pick the most unlikely cuss. The sort who'd give his eye-teeth to be the one you pretend to think he is. That's what makes the fun.'

[2] Beef-head: derogatory name for a Texan, arising out of their State's dependance upon the cattle industry.

'All right, let's give her a whirl,' Daws consented, satisfied that the joke was safe enough to play in the manner his companion had outlined. However, he foresaw another snag and raised it, knowing that the success of the joke could depend upon small things as well as large. 'There's one thing you've forgot, though.'

'What's that,' Lemp challenged.

'No *Texan*'d want to be mistook for *Wyatt Earp*,' Daws pointed out. 'Way they feel about him, they'd sooner you took them for a "hydrophoby" skunk.'

One of the reasons Lemp liked having Daws participate in a joke was that he took an active interest and helped with the planning. As on other occasions, he had detected a point that could have ruined the whole thing. It was certain that no self-respecting son of the Lone Star State, no matter how insignificant, would take kindly to being mistaken for Wyatt Earp. That pious-talking, bullying, Rebel-hating assistant deputy marshal was the epitome of everything that made the term 'Kansas lawman' one of opprobrium from the northern boundary of Oklahoma Territory to the Rio Grande.

However, selecting the right name for the deception posed a problem. The hero of one Texan was likely to be another's ideal picture of a double-dealing, murderous villain.

Then Lemp remembered the one man who might find favour with any Texas cowhand.

'I've got it!' the joker stated. 'He's the one we'll use!'

'Who,' asked Daws, having been unable to select anybody who would fill the bill.

'Dusty Fog!' Lemp explained. 'You've heard tell of *him*, haven't you,'

'I couldn't help but have heard,' Daws grunted. 'The trail hands talk like he's Wes Hardin, Clay Allison, Bad Bill Longley, Ben Thompson and King Fisher all rolled into one.[3] I've never seen him,[4] but I've heard he stands well over six foot tall, has got shoulders wider'n the front doors of the Texas House and's tougher than a thirty-year cavalry sergeant. Top of that, they allow

[3] New readers can find details pertaining to Dustine Edward Marsden 'Dusty' Fog's background and special qualifications in Appendix One.

[4] Neither Lemp nor Daws had been present at Dodge City when Dusty Fog paid the visit which is recorded in: *Trail Boss*.

32

nobody comes even close to being as fast as he is with a pair of guns.'

Noticing that his companion was no longer paying any attention to what he was saying, Daws stopped speaking. However, his momentary annoyance died away as he realized that Lemp was staring along the sidewalk like a bird-dog pointing at a quail.

'Damn it!' the joker ejaculated. 'I wish we'd got more time to make ready, but that's *him*. The very one we want!'

Following the direction in which the other was looking, at first Daws could not locate the person who had provoked the comment. In fact, for a moment he failed to see any cowhands among the people strolling along the sidewalk. Then the man who had caught his companion's eye came into his range of vision and a delighted grin creased his face. One thing was for certain, he told himself. Joe Lemp sure knew how to select a victim. They might have searched Dodge City from end to end without finding anybody better suited to their requirements.

The cowhand under consideration for a leading role in the joke was far from impressive in appearance. Even wearing tan coloured sharp toed, high heeled and expensive-looking boots,[5] he was not much more than five foot six inches in height. In fact, his low crowned, wide brimmed black Texas-style J.B. Stetson hat was only level with the chins of most of the people around him. His tanned, grey-eyed face was young and moderately handsome and his hair a dusty blond shade. Clad in the fashion of the Lone Star State's range country, his garments—like his made-to-measure footwear—were clean and of excellent quality. Yet he made them seem like somebody else's cast-offs. Around his waist was a finely made brown gunbelt. To Lemp's not over-discerning gaze, it looked new. He concluded that it had been bought since arriving at Dodge City, in the hope that the two white handled Colt Civilian Model Peacemakers[6] riding butt forward in the contoured cross-draw holsters might make onlookers imagine it was worn by a real hard-case gun fighter.

---

[5] The sharp toes of a cowhand's boots are an aid to slipping into and out of a stirrup-iron in a hurry and the high heels can be spiked into the ground for added security when roping on foot.

[6] New readers can find an explanation of the various types of Colt Model P 'Peacemaker' in Footnote 17, Appendix One.

Glancing at Daws, Lemp received a nod redolent of acquiescence and approbation. Proving that not only great minds think alike, each was drawing very much the same conclusions. Their proposed victim looked so young and insignificant that he was probably not even a fully fledged trail hand. More likely he was only a wrangler, night hawk,[7] or the cook's 'louse', performing such menial tasks as were considered beneath the dignity of the men who actually handled the half wild longhorn cattle.

Such a no-account member of rangeland society would fall hard once he believed that somebody was mistaking him for the Lone Star State's favourite son.

Blissfully unaware of what was in store for him, the small Texan ambled closer. He walked with the half awkward, somewhat slouching gait of a cowhand on foot. Obviously he was in no hurry. Taking his time, he was drinking in the sights of the Mecca for every Texas boy. The end of the long journey north and the greatest trail-end town of them all, Dodge City.

Watching the Texan approaching and gauging the distance between them, Lemp wished that there had been more time for him to teach Daws what to say and do. However, he consoled himself with the thought that the other had responded quickly and correctly without guidance on previous occasions when the opportunity for an impromptu joke had arisen.

Picking exactly the right moment, the joker turned and, bumping into the small Texan, caused him to stagger slightly.

'God-damn it, cow-nurse!' Lemp spat out, adopting a most convincingly tough and truculent tone. 'Why don't you watch where you're going? Do you want all the god-damned sidewalk?'

'Only part of it,' the victim of the joke replied, in a pleasant drawl a more discerning person than his antagonists could have identified as that of a well educated Southron.

'Only your share of it, huh?' Lemp growled, deliberately misquoting the other's comment and stepping back a pace.

Thrusting the side of his coat away from the low-tied Colt

[7] Night hawk: a man hired to look after the horses in the *remuda* while the rest of the trail drive, or round up, crew—except for the hands riding night herd on the cattle—were asleep. He replaced the wrangler, who carried out the duty in the daytime. The task was regarded by cowhands as even more menial than that of wrangler.

Artillery Model Peacemaker, the joker's right hand rose to hover above it. Fingers spread and crooked, thumb bent, they seemed eager to enfold the weapon's fancy Tiffany grips. Moving his feet slightly apart, he curved his knees a little as he had seen fast men stand when on the prod and hunting trouble.

To Daws' way of thinking, the pose was excellent. It was the correct stance for a gun fighter ready to draw and adopted so well that it might fool even experienced eyes.

There was nothing to suggest the small Texan came into *that* category.

'No more than my share,' the proposed victim answered, sounding mild if not frightened.

Taking in the sight, those pedestrians nearest to it backed off hurriedly to keep out of the possible line of fire. It was neither wise nor healthy to act inquisitive around what could develop into a corpse-and-cartridge affair. There was too much chance of a nosey onlooker catching a stray bullet. All of which, in the opinion of the perpetrators, was going to add to the merriment of the joke. What was more, there did not appear to be any other cowhands in the immediate vicinity who might butt in and spoil things.

To Lemp's way of thinking, only one thing more was required to achieve the best result. The small Texan was standing without any visible emotion. That was a pity. The buffalo hunter had at least tried to adopt a similar threatening posture to the joker's. If the Texan could be made to do so, it would add the final touch to the scene. However, perhaps because he was too afraid, he neither moved nor made more than the barest response to the questions being thrown his way.

'All right, damn it!' Lemp snarled, having darted a glance to let Daws know what was expected of him. 'If that's the way you want things, you'll be ready to fight for it. So fill your——!'

'Joe!' the second conspirator yelped. 'Hold it, for the Good Lord's sake! Don't you know who *he* is?'

'I don't know and I'm sure's hell not caring!' Lemp declared, oozing well simulated truculence.

'He's *Dusty Fog*!' Daws croaked.

No mean actor, the joker's assistant put just the right tone into his voice for one who had discovered that his friend was facing and about to challenge arguably the fastest gun in Texas to mortal combat.

What was more, Lemp demonstrated that he too was no slouch at simulating emotions. In fact, he possessed a talent which might have commanded good money in the theatre. Suddenly, his whole bearing was transformed in a manner that came close to being miraculous. The hard and tough air left him. All the bombast and threat faded into nothing. His face took on the kind of expression a hunter might display on chasing a whitetail deer into a cave and finding it had changed into a fully grown, starving grizzly bear. Fingers going limp, his hand fell clear of the Colt's butt and all his former arrogance departed.

Watching the cowhand intently, both of the jokers tried to decide how he was taking the latest development. What little they saw led each to assume he was relieved by not being forced into a gun fight and delighted at being mistaken for the great Dusty Fog. However, not much showed on the tanned young face and Lemp considered that the buffalo hunter had put on a much better exhibition.

For all that, the joker continued to play his part in a masterly fashion.

'S—Sorry, *Dusty*!' Lemp gasped, the words coming forth with a far different timbre from his previously bombastic and challenging manner of speaking. 'I didn't realize who *you* was, *Dusty*. Honest I didn't.'

'That's all right,' the small Texan replied, taking a step forward with the intention of going by the joker. 'We all make mistakes. No——.'

'We surely do at that, *Dusty*,' Lemp agreed, laying his left hand on the cowboy's right arm to stop him. There was a bulk of bicep beneath the shirt's sleeve which seemed out of keeping with the rest of the victim's appearance. Before the joker could draw any conclusions from the discovery—in fact, not even considering it in his eagerness to extract all the dregs from a vaguely unsatisfactory situation by continuing to plant the suggestion of the mistake in identity upon the other's mind—he went on with mock humility, 'Yes sir, *Dusty*. We all make mistakes. I should've re-

36

cognized you straight off, then this wouldn't've happened. I'm real sorry *I* bumped into and mean-mouthed *you* and I hope you've not taken offence over it. I'm surely real out and out sorry.'

'That's all right, mister,' the small Texan drawled, shrugging away the restraining grip with as casual a gesture as one might employ to remove a bothersome fly. Before Lemp could say any more, ignoring the right hand that had been extended to be shaken, he spoke over his shoulder as he set off across the street. 'Forget it. No harm's been done.'

The abrupt manner of the proposed victim's departure left Lemp with a feeling of anti-climax. Nor did the sight of the crowd resuming their interrupted activities, having decided that trouble would not be forthcoming, make him regard the matter in a happier light. The Texan had not responded as was required.

Thinking of the buffalo hunter's behaviour, the joker considered he had been an altogether more satisfactory selection. There had been no casual acceptance and walking away with him. Instead, he had continued to confront Lemp, drinking in the display of 'abject fear' until he had almost come to believe he *was* Wyatt Earp and expected Ned Buntline[8] to arrive at any moment with the present of a long barrelled Peacemaker.

Going by the way in which the small Texan had reacted, anyone would have thought that he went through his whole life having people mistake him for Dusty Fog.

'Whooee!' Daws enthused, clearly not sharing his companion's misgivings. Less perceptive and because he had not seen how the duped buffalo hunter responded, he felt that their efforts had been crowned with success. So he was delighted that the joke had gone off in such a smooth fashion and, with the kind of man they had selected, would be safe from future repercussions. 'His face when you kept calling him *"Dusty"* like you did. He'll have to use all his pay buying for the house when we let them know how he was took in and his crew'll never let him forget it.'

That having to spend all his hard earned wages might create hardship for the small Texan's family, or at least cause him humiliation and misery, never occurred to either of the towns-

[8] 'Ned Buntline': pen name of E. Z. C. Judson, journalist and author, whose books brought fame to William Frederick 'Buffalo Bill' Cody.

men. Nor would they have been particularly worried by the prospect if it had.

'I dunno,' Lemp objected, although he was catching some of his assistant's enthusiasm in spite of feeling something vital had been missing. 'He didn't seem to be playing along as well's he might have.'

'Let's give him time to think about it, huh?' Daws suggested. 'He didn't look any too smart and he's maybe slow at working things out, so hasn't realized all of what happened yet. Look, he's headed into the Texas House. Once it hits him what you kept saying, he'll soon start bragging about how he's been mistook for Dusty Fog.'

'I suppose he will,' Lemp said, but still with a slight doubt in his tone.

It had struck the joker while his companion was talking that he was unable to recollect a single instant when he could read anything from the small Texan's face or voice with certainty.

'Just imagine a short-growed runt like *that* thinking *anybody* would mistake him for *Dusty Fog*!' guffawed Daws, gazing with open admiration at the joker and puzzled by his attitude. 'Joe, if you ain't the living wonder. You couldn't have picked a better man for——'

'Mister, your *amigo* was lucky!'

Turning to find out who was addressing them in such a drawling, laconic and yet contemptuous fashion, the two men found themselves faced by a tall, lean, grizzled and elderly Texas cowhand. He was leaning his shoulder against the open door of the Birdcage Café, having stood just inside to watch and listen to what was taking place.

'What's that mean?' Lemp demanded, caring for neither the old man's words nor attitude.

'Thought you-all was concluding to draw down on that poor, dee-fenseless lil ole Texas boy just now,' the aged cowhand explained dryly. 'It'd've been foolish, *hombre*. Real out-'n'-back-again *foolish*.'

'Why?' challenged the joker, but a coldly frightening clairvoyant feeling assailed him.

'Well now, that lil ole Texas boy, he don't like two cents worth

38

of nothing at all,' the cowhand elaborated. 'Don't reckon's *you-all* might think he is, comes to that. But he was just about the best cavalry captain the South had in the War.[9] You-all couldn't tell it by just *looking,* but he's's good a cow-nurse's ever tossed a leg over the rough mount[10] of a ranch. Talking right truthful, he's the trail boss's brought in that big OD Connected herd last night. Comes right down to it, 'though it didn't look to faze *you-all* none, there's some's allows he's a regular lil ole snake at drawing and shooting them bone-handled Colts he carries.'

'Y—Y—You mean——?' Lemp gasped, the words emerging in a splutter from a face that was suddenly as white as a newly washed sheet. 'Y—You mean that *he* was——?'

'Why sure,' the old timer confirmed, having seen the changing of the salt and sugar as well as having guessed what was going on outside the café. 'You might even say's how you-all nearly called down *Dusty Fog!*'

[9] Details of Captain Dustine Edward Marsden 'Dusty' Fog's career whilst in command of Company 'C', Texas Light Cavalry, are given in the author's Civil War series.

[10] Rough mount: comprised of all the most difficult and recalcitrant horses of the *remuda.* As these required the greatest skill to handle, they were usually assigned to the top hand of the ranch. Unlike their contemporaries in the more northern cattle-raising States, Texas cowhands used the term 'mount' and not 'string' for the horses supplied by the ranch, or trail boss, to each man who was employed.

PART TWO

THE FLOATING OUTFIT SERIES

Mark Counter in

WE HANG HORSE THIEVES HIGH

Although Mark Counter is almost always listed second when there is any reference to the members of the OD Connected's float-ing outfit,[1] his character traits were demonstrated more slowly than those of Dusty Fog, the Ysabel Kid, or Waco. All three of them were to display the majority of their attributes from their first appearances in Trail Boss, *or in Waco's case, Part Five, 'The Hired Butcher', of* The Hard Riders—*not, as a number of the members of the* J. T. Edson Appreciation Society *assumed was the answer in one of our Competitions,* Trigger Fast, *although this is the title in which he first meets the others—but Mark's Herculean strength, ability as a roughhouse brawler and his at-traction for the ladies were not put into use to any great extent until he was given his first 'starring' role in Part One, 'The Bounty On Belle Starr's Scalp' of* Troubled Range.*

When I was re-thinking my ideas on the characters after dis-banding the 'Three Sons Of The Grande', I decided that Mark could serve as a counterpoint—no pun intended—for Dusty's small size and usually insignificant appearance. I realized that to make him a dandy dresser could only be acceptable if he had some other source of income beyond that of an ordinary working cowhand. This was overcome by making him the third son of a rich rancher and wealthy in his own right because of a bequest in an aunt's will which gave him financial independence.

At the time when I was beginning to appreciate that I was not utilizing Mark to his full potential, I had started seeing a number

---

[1] New readers can find an explanation of a 'floating outfit's' function and learn why Mark Counter elected to join the OD Connected instead of working on his father's ranch in Appendix Two.

of films which suggested how this could be done. They were the wonderful range of generally Italian-made action-escapism-adventure pseudo-epics with the 'Mr. Universe' type stars such as Steve Reeves, Gordon Scott, or my particular favourite, Brad Harris, playing 'Samson', 'Hercules', etc. Their efforts might not have appealed to intellectuals, but the vast majority of the audiences seemed to be sharing my enjoyment. In addition to these movies offering pleasurable relaxation—they suggested to me that Mark had the necessary physical attributes to perform similar feats of strength.

During the period of Mark's elevation to full 'starring' status, sexual prowess and success appeared to have become a must for every hero. Even the 'anti-heroes'—whatever they might be—possessed an unfailing ability to 'pull the birds' despite having no other worthwhile qualities. So, ever ready to follow a trend, I concluded that if an otherwise talentless, dull and boring 'anti-hero' could be successful, a man with Mark's looks and ability would be even more certain to succeed

One aspect more than any other in Mark's career which has aroused interest is his relationship with the lady outlaw, Belle Starr. A number of people have written to me over the years asking why the description I give of her does not tally with photographs they have seen. With the help of my friend and the world's foremost fictionist genealogist, Philip José Farmer,[2] I have solved the mystery. The lady about whom I have been writing is not the same person as the one whose photographs have appeared in other authors' works. However, although Phil and I have discovered the true identity of Mark's 'Belle Starr', we have been asked by the members of the Counter family to keep her name undisclosed and intend to honour the request.

One result of Mark's achievements with the ladies is that he was the first member of the floating outfit to have descendants follow him into print. However, more of them when I come to the sections in this volume devoted to Deputy Sheriff Bradford Counter and James Allenvale 'Bunduki' Gunn.

Here is Mark's participation in the saga. While other members

[2] Author of, in addition to many other books, the biographical works, *Tarzan Alive* and *Doc Savage, His Apocalyptic Life*.

of the floating outfit make 'guest appearances', I must ask all new readers to bear with the brief descriptions I have given of the Ysabel Kid and Waco. They will, of course, be fully covered in their respective sections.

WE HANG HORSE THIEVES HIGH

Mark Counter was in anything but an amiable frame of mind as he walked, leading a limping washy bay gelding, along the winding trail which traversed the wooded country a couple of miles east below the confluence of the Brazos and Navasota Rivers. Nor, justified as it might be under the circumstances, did the alarm displayed at the sight of him by the young woman he found himself approaching as he went around a blind curve improve his temper. She was standing alongside a neat fringe top Surrey,[1] gazing forlornly at the near side rear wheel which had parted company with its axle and lay on the ground at her feet. Considering her predicament, it might have been assumed that she would be grateful for his fortuitous arrival rather than perturbed. Of course, most members of her sex might have been disturbed by his appearance if he had come upon them while alone—as she seemed to be—at a considerable distance from the nearest human habitation.

Standing a good six foot three in height, Mark had the tanned, classically handsome features of an Adonis surmounting the tremendously wide shouldered, slim waisted and enormously muscled physique of a Hercules. Particularly when clad in his usual elegant fashion, there was nothing about his bearing or appearance—he was neither cumbersome, clumsy nor slow moving for all his great size—to cause any woman to feel it necessary to be wary of him; except perhaps a mother where her impressionable daughter was concerned and then only if she was not

[1] 'Fringe top Surrey': a four-wheel, four-seat, passenger vehicle similar to, but—being more luxuriously and comfortably equipped—regarded as superior to a buggy.

aware of his family background and excellent prospects.

While Mark's golden blond hair had been cut recently, circumstances beyond his control had caused him to be unshaven,[2] unkempt and looking more like a saddle-tramp than a normally somewhat dandified tophand member of Ole Devil Hardin's Floating Outfit; the elite of the great OD Connected ranch's highly respected and admired crew. Certainly his attire was of a far lower quality than that which he ordinarily wore.

The troubles which had resulted in the blond giant's lack of a shave, dishevelled appearance and ungracious demeanour had commenced several days earlier. Returning to the OD Connected from a trail drive, he had found a message asking him to go as quickly as possible to Daisetta, in Liberty County, East Texas, where a favourite aunt was dangerously ill and not expected to recover.

Even without needing to be asked, Ole Devil had told Mark to set off to Daisetta immediately and to stay as long as necessary. Doing so had posed a problem. The magnificent big bloodbay stallion he preferred to use when long and fast travelling was called for had been selected as a stud to help improve the strain of the OD Connected's *remuda*. The horse was his personal property and the rancher would have raised no objections to dispensing with its services, but along with the rest of his mount—which were equally up to carrying his weight for considerable periods— it had been worked hard recently and needed a rest. So he had borrowed a horse from the reserve in the *remuda*. Although it had been large enough to stand the strain of transporting him, it was not so well trained as those he employed regularly. Losing its footing while fording a creek which would have caused them no difficulty, it had succeeded in soaking him and all his belongings in the muddy water.

[2] The author suspects that the trend in movies and television series made since the early 1960's to portray cowhands as long haired and voluminously bearded stemmed less from the producer's desire for 'realism' than because such were the only kind of supporting players and extras available. In our extensive reference library, we cannot find a dozen photographs of cowboys—as opposed to mountain-men, Army scouts, or prospectors—who have long hair and bushy beards. In fact, our reading on the subject has led us to the belief that the term 'long hair' was one of opprobrium in the cattle raising States of the West then as it is today.

That had been the real start of the blond giant's problems.

On arriving at Caldwell, seat of Burlesden County, Mark had put up the horse at the livery barn and taken a room for the night in the best hotel. Having cleaned up his low crowned, wide brimmed J.B. Stetson hat, with its silver concha decorated band, himself and sent the remainder of his clothing, except for an old pair of Levi's pants, to a near by Chinese laundry, he had left his boots in his room to be polished and went to take a bath. As a basic precaution, he had taken his brown *buscadero* gunbelt, with the brace of ivory handled Colt Cavalry Model Peacemakers in its contoured fast draw holsters, to the bathroom. This had proved fortunate. Not only had his hat and boots disappeared out of the room he was renting, but the rest of his clothes were stolen from the laundry.

Having had his wallet in the Levi's, Mark had had sufficient money to make good the losses. However, his giant frame was not easy to supply from the limited range available in the small town. The only hat and pair of boots which would fit him were second hand. Despite being new, the dark red shirt, multicoloured cotton bandana and yellowish brown Nankeen trousers he procured did not have the excellent cut of the stolen garments, all of which had been specially tailored for him. Nor was that the end of his troubles. On arriving at the livery barn the following morning, he found his horse had contracted colic and was unfit to go any further. To make things worse, the only replacement was the washy bay and it had proved to be an even less satisfactory mount than the one he was compelled to leave behind.

Next, as if the fates wished to demonstrate literally that it never rained but it poured, there had been two thunder storms in quick succession as Mark continued his journey. The torrential downpours had not only saturated him, but they had made sleeping out in the open anything except a pleasant experience. Nor had he been able to make a fire and heat water with which to wash and shave. Finally, to add to his discomfort, the bay had thrown a shoe shortly after crossing the high-running combined Brazos and Navasota Rivers. Like every cowhand, the blond giant hated few things more than walking. His antipathy had not been diminished

45

by finding the boots he was wearing to be less well made and comfortable than the pair he had lost.

In spite of his present lack of enthusiasm for life in general, having a keen eye for members of the opposite sex, Mark decided the young woman was worth more than a second glance. About five foot seven inches and in her mid-twenties, she was a very attractive brunette with an eye-catching figure. She was wearing a light blue tailored two piece costume of the currently fashionable somewhat masculine line, which still showed off the contours of a curvaceous body, and had on an English 'pork pie' hat with a low, decorated crown and streamers dangling down her back. A dainty reticule swung by its loop from her left wrist and a matching furled parasol was on the rear seat of the Surrey. While her raiment was suitable for travelling, there was no baggage of any kind in the vehicle. Nor was there anything to suggest she might have had anybody with her.

'Howdy, ma'am,' the big blond greeted, coming to a halt and forcing himself to resume his normally polite and respectful tone of voice. 'It looks like you-all can use some help.'

'I most certainly could, sir,' the young woman admitted, her accent cultured and suggesting she came from the Middle West. 'But is there anything we can do? As you see, I'm all alone and I'm afraid I'm not strong enough to be of much assistance.'

'Shucks, I reckon I can handle things happen you can give just a mite of help,' Mark stated, releasing the split ended reins and causing the bay to come to a halt, a thing it was always willing to do. 'We'll give it a whirl, anyways.'

While speaking, the blond giant had been studying the situation and decided he could be optimistic about effecting a cure. Either only the fringes of the storms had struck on the eastern side of the river, or the sun had dried out the area quickly. Whatever the reason, the ground underfoot was firm and hard. The cause of the trouble was that the nut which should have retained the wheel on the axle had come unscrewed and lay in plain sight. Having lost its support, the Surrey's rear end was tilting slightly. However, the dainty blue roan harnessed to the vehicle was standing placidly and did not appear in the least alarmed by the incident. From appearances, the young woman had been equally unperturbed. At least, she showed no signs of having been thrown out when the accident occurred. What was more, she had had the presence of mind to attach the hitching rope with its heavy lead weight to the horse's headstall.

'Here we go,' Mark continued, picking up the wheel and placing it perpendicular at the side of the vacated axle. 'Reckon you-all can hold it there for a spell, ma'am?'

'I'll certainly try,' the woman promised and did as she was requested.

Hooking his hands under the bed of the Surrey, the big blond began to lift. Such was his enormous strength that he found no difficulty in raising the rear near side of the vehicle slightly above its horizontal line. Thinking of how much more difficult a task he had had on his first meeting with Calamity Jane—whose loaded freight wagon had needed a wheel raising from a hole into which it had sunk[3]—he took away his right hand without the burden sagging. Grasping the wheel by one of its spokes, he manoeuvred it into position. Breathing somewhat more heavily under the strain, he contrived to seat it on the axle once more. Still displaying good sense, the woman had retrieved the nut on being relieved of the burden and started to replace it without needing instructions.

'Looks like we licked her between us, ma'am,' Mark commented, stepping away from the Surrey and rubbing his hands on his Levi's legs.

'I'm sure I couldn't have without your help,' the woman replied, opening her reticule. 'You won't be offended if I——?'

'Shucks, there's no call for *that*,' Mark drawled, being in a better mood than on his arrival. 'I only *look* like a saddle-tramp——'

'Heavens!' the woman gasped, staring with what could have been wide-eyed and innocent near embarrassment. 'I hope I haven't——?'

'No, ma'am,' the big blond smiled. 'I *know* how I look and how I must look to you, but I'm not really such a mean and ornery cuss when you get to know me.'

'I never *really* thought you were,' the woman asserted, also

[3] For the benefit of new readers: the incident referred to is recorded in Part One, 'The Bounty On Belle Starr's Scalp', *Troubled Range*.

47

smiling. Then she swung her gaze to the washy bay and went on, 'Oh dear, your poor horse is hurt.'

'He's thrown a shoe is all,' Mark corrected, darting a malevolent scowl at the animal. 'But I sure wouldn't admire having folks think I own a worn-out, useless plug like that.'

'You don't *own* it?'

'Nope.'

'I see, it belongs to your employer?'

'Ole Devil wouldn't want to own it either.'

'Ole Devil?'

'General Hardin,' Mark elaborated. 'I ride for the OD Connected, but the horse I was using went down with colic at Caldwell and I picked that one up there.'

'I see!' the woman declared. 'But that means you can't ride it!'

'I can't,' Mark confirmed. 'Which's why I was walking when I first saw you. I'm taking him into Beckley to see the blacksmith.'

'But it's a good three miles!' the woman pointed out.

'So I figured,' the big blond admitted wryly.

'Then I can't let you walk,' the woman stated. 'I'll take you in the Surrey.'

'Well now, there's nothing I'd admire more,' Mark replied. 'But you're not going in that direction.'

'That's soon remedied,' the woman said cheerfully. 'I'm staying there on vacation and was just taking a drive to pass the time. In fact, I was thinking of turning back when the wheel came off and I'd enjoy your company.'

Removing the hitching rope, Mark placed it in the rear of the Surrey. Then, showing considerable driving skill, the woman turned the vehicle. He tied the bay's reins to the rear near support of the fringe decorated canopy and climbed into the front seat.

'We may as well introduce ourselves,' the woman remarked, as she set the Surrey into motion. 'I'm Arlette Brissac and my home is in Kansas City, Missouri.'

'Which's the best Kansas City to hail from,' the blond giant drawled, being aware that considerable rivalry existed between the town and its identically named neighbour at the other side of the Kansas border. 'I'm Mark Counter and, like I said, I ride for the OD Connected, although my home's over to the Big Bend country.'

48

'Are you going back to your ranch now?' Arlette inquired.

'Nope,' Mark replied, not surprised that his hostess was displaying a lack of knowledge concerning the geography of Texas. 'I'm headed down to Daisetta to see an aunt who's very sick, but that crowbait was slowing me down so much I reckon I'll see if I can get something better in Beckley.'

'I can understand why you would want to,' Arlette said sympathetically.

The drive continued in a pleasant fashion. From what she said, the young woman had come to Beckley to visit with an elderly aunt and uncle. Not only had she found nothing of interest or attraction in the town, they had little in common with her and she admitted to being disappointed, even bored. The impression Mark formed as he listened, then amused her with a graphic description of his trials and tribulations since leaving the OD Connected, was that she had come to Texas hoping for romantic adventures which had not yet materialized. Before long, he also concluded, she could be considering him as a potential supplier. Being honest and straightforward, he made it clear his stay in Beckley would be limited to that night provided he could either acquire a fresh horse or have the bay's missing shoe replaced. She declared that the position was understood, but hinted at her willingness to spend the evening in his company.

Knowing that his looks and appearance had frequently attracted members of the opposite sex in the past, the blond giant had also learned the wisdom of caution. His instincts warned that Arlette was less naive and unwordly than she pretended to be. With her hands being ungloved, he was able to see she wore no rings to indicate marital or even affianced status, which he knew proved nothing as they could have been removed easily enough. Considerable experience as a peace officer had taught him various ways by which unscrupluous women could make use of their sex to prey on gullible men, but he could not imagine she would regard him as a potentially lucrative victim. Unless she had some prior knowledge, she had only heard enough about him to assume he was a working cowhand. Taking everything into consideration, including his ability to protect himself with guns or bare hands if the need arose, he decided dalliance in her company would be a

49

welcome relaxation after the misfortunes of the journey. So he invited her to take dinner with him at whichever hotel he selected —not a difficult choice according to her as there were only two and one of them far from salubrious—and was accepted without hesitation.

By the time the arrangements were concluded, the Surrey was ascending a slope. On arriving at the rim, the horse was stopped for a breather and Mark was granted his first view of Beckley.

Before the blond giant's gaze reached the town, it was diverted by something closer at hand. Clearly having turned from the trail not far below the rim, a man was riding across the now fairly open country at a fast trot. If he had not been dressed in clothing more suited to an Eastern city than Texas, he would hardly have rated a second glance. Nor, apart from noticing that the only habitation in the direction towards which he was heading was a dilapidated ruin of a fair sized adobe cabin some distance beyond the edge of the town, was Mark particularly interested in him. What was more, the blond giant's interest was taken by his companion.

'There's Beckley, Mark!' Arlette said, almost urgently it seemed, grasping his left hand with her right and pointing. 'Did you *ever* see such a dreary little place?'

'Well, yes,' the big blond answered with a grin. 'I reckon I have, but maybe not more than one.'

Despite his comment, having turned his gaze from the man, Mark was willing to concede there was something to be said for the woman's point of view. Yet Beckley was neither better nor worse in general appearance than many other small communities scattered across the open range country west of the Big Muddy. There was only one street discernible as such, with the rest of the buildings scattered in a rough circle wherever the owners had felt like constructing. He had no trouble locating the hotel in which he hoped to spend the night, even if Arlette had not pointed it out to him. By far the biggest and most imposing place in the town, being the only one with a second floor, it appeared to offer the facilities of a saloon and livery barn as well as supplying accommodation for travellers. The barn was at the rear, alongside what was obviously a four hole backhouse.

Setting the horse into motion, Arlette continued to chatter with

50

an even greater intensity than during the earlier stages of the ride. However, as they were approaching a large cottonwood tree about fifty yards from the first building, Mark glanced around. The thickset man in the Eastern clothing was still travelling in the same direction and another, taller Easterner appeared at what had been a doorway of the roofless, badly damaged cabin.

'This is what I *hate* most about Beckley!' Arlene stated, with such vehemence that the big blond snapped his gaze back to her.

'What?'

'The sign on that tree. There's one on every trail into town.'

Looking in the direction indicated by the woman's pointing finger, Mark could sympathize with her. A poster in a tin-roofed wooden container designed to shelter it from the elements was fastened to the cottonwood's trunk in full view of anybody passing along the trail. It was clearly intended to be noticed, for its grim message was printed in large and glaring red letters.

YOU ARE NOW ENTERING BECKLEY,
THIS IS A CLEAN AND LAW-ABIDING TOWN
WE DON'T TOLERATE ROBBERS OF ANY KIND
AND WE HANG HORSE THIEVES HIGH!

***** *****

Although Mark woke up alone in the bed of the room he had rented at the Strawcross Hotel, he had not spent the night in such a solitary state.

As the blond giant had suspected, Arlette had proved far less innocent than she appeared on the surface. That had become increasingly apparent as the evening progressed. Joining him after he had had an opportunity to bathe, shave and generally tidy himself up, they had taken a good dinner in the hotel's dining room. She had then asked that he walk her home. However, on leaving, she had suggested instead that they returned secretly to his room. Her excuse that it would be unwise for them to go to her aunt and uncle's house, because the neighbours might see them and talk, had been acceptable as—from what she had told him—he doubted whether her kinfolk would approve of her entertaining a male visitor after dark in their absence.

Acting upon the suggestion, Mark and Arlette had contrived to carry it through without anybody else in the hotel being aware of her presence. With only a short period of preliminary love making, she had stated her willingness to climb into bed with him. Once this was done, he had soon learned that he was not the first of his sex to have had the privilege. Being tired after the three miserable days he had spent on the trail, he fell asleep more soundly than usual once they had sated their passion.

Habits instilled by several years caused the blond giant to wake up as the first red glow of dawn began to creep into the eastern sky. He was uncertain as to where he might be for a moment, then remembrance came flooding back. Becoming aware that he was now alone, an exploratory feel informed him that Arlette's portion of the bed was cold and a glance around established she was no longer in the room. He was aware that, if he had been his normal self, she could not have left the bed, dressed and taken her departure without having disturbed and aroused him.

Rolling from the bed and standing to stretch, Mark glanced about him. As far as he could see, only his erstwhile bed-mate and her possessions were missing. While he was not of a wildly suspicious nature, he checked his wallet and satisfied himself that the money it held was still intact. Reassured on that score, he started to dress. Yet, as he was donning his clothes, he found himself thinking about various facets concerning her which had been puzzling him.

That Arlette should have been recognized by the hostler in the barn and the hotel's staff, or asked if she had enjoyed her ride in the Surrey, was not surprising. A visitor in so small a town, especially one so attractive, could not avoid attracting attention and being noticed. Not only had she hired the vehicle from the livery barn, but she in all probability dined on occasion in the hotel.

Deciding that the woman had slipped away during the hours of darkness, so as to avoid being seen returning to the home of her kinfolk at an unseemly time, the blond giant felt no disappointment. Instead, he considered that everything had happened for the best. While the love making had been enjoyable, he wanted nothing more permanent to eventuate. Wishing to prevent this from happening, he concluded that he would be advised to take his departure as soon as possible.

Feeling an urge to relieve the pangs of nature as he was strapping on his gunbelt, Mark set off to do so. Leaving the hotel without seeing anybody, he went to the backhouse. From appearances, he concluded that his habit of early rising was not general practice in the town. He saw no other sign of human life either before nor after he came from the building. On the point of returning, he thought he might as well go to the barn and check on the bay. Having failed to obtain a replacement, he had had it shod the previous afternoon and wanted to satisfy himself that it would be all right to continue the journey.

Strolling into the barn, the big blond found it as devoid of human occupants as the hotel and street. Then he became aware of something which drove the thought from his mind. The bay was no longer in the stall where he had left it, but had been replaced by a fine *palomino* gelding. Thinking he *might* be looking in the wrong direction, a glance around assured him he was not. While some of the other stalls were occupied, his temporary mount was nowhere to be seen.

For a moment, Mark stood motionless. Then a feeling of irritation began to creep into him. He wondered if the *palomino*'s owner had been disinclined to leave it outside in the small pole corral and usurped the far less prepossessing bay's accommodation. On second thoughts, he concluded this was most unlikely. Not only were there vacant stalls in the barn, to remove another man's horse without asking permission could produce repercussions. There were, of course, genuine bullies or would be hardcases who might make the unauthorized substitution in the hope of stirring up trouble; but either would want to be present when the owner arrived to take advantage of his protests.

On the point of going to find out whether the bay had been taken to the small pole corral by the side of the barn, which hid it from view of the rim, Mark saw something that caused him to change his mind. He felt as if he was being touched by an ice cold hand as he read the garish red message on a poster similar to the one at the edge of the town which was displayed alongside the front entrance.

A thought began to nag at the blond giant's memory. Crossing to the stall, he studied the *palomino* with greater care. It was a fine looking creature, in the peak of physical health and showing no sign of injury. What was more, he felt sure he had seen it before. Unless he was mistaken, it had been hitched to the rail at the rear of the town marshal's office the previous afternoon. When he had commented upon it to the blacksmith prior to having the bay shod, he was informed that it was the peace officer's property, pride and joy. He had also been told that it was the cause of the final cryptic warning on the posters, having come close to being stolen on two separate occasions.

Among the other lessons Mark had received while serving as a peace officer under Dusty Fog was deductive reasoning. While he could not claim to have developed the skill Waco was capable of displaying,[4] he considered himself adequate enough for his own needs. Thinking fast, he began to appreciate the ramifications of his discovery and did not care for the speculations his conclusions began to arouse.

Firstly, if the marshal had been in the habit of leaving the *palomino* in that particular stall, the hostler would have at least commented upon it instead of allowing the bay to be placed there.

Secondly, if the horse merely resembled that belonging to the peace officer, its owner was unlikely to have exchanged it for the bay no matter how dire the need for such an action. It was far too superior in quality for that, particularly as it was apparently in good health and showed no signs of having been pushed hard recently.

The two factors raised the point of why the exchange had been made.

Hardly as a joke!

Mark could not envisage the most irresponsible practical joker perpetrating such a prank in a Western town, even one less demonstrably hostile to horse thieves than Beckley. Or in the highly unlikely event that one did, as in the case of the bully or trouble-causer, he would want to be present when the substitution was discovered. If not, the joke would be pointless.

Another contingency came to the blond giant's mind, aroused by the remembrance of the blacksmith's comments about the marshal's antipathy towards horse thieves and its cause. Yet he could not conceive anybody would be making a deliberate attempt

[4] New readers, see Part Six for information about Waco.

to have him accused of stealing the *palomino*. He had enemies who might care to take some form of revenge, but none of them would expect the peace officer to believe *he* was capable of such a heinous crime.

At which point, Mark realized he had only his own word regarding his identity. Possibly, with the exception of Arlette, nobody knew him in Beckley. He remembered that the hotel's clerk had looked somewhat dubious when he signed the register and he was willing to concede he was far from his usual dandified self. Furthermore, the woman could say that he had told her who he was and for whom he worked, but she could not substantiate the claim.

There was, Mark suddenly recollected with relief, one piece of proof he could offer. As a precaution, he had obtained a bill of sale for the bay. Not only was it made out in his name, it stated he had left the OD Connected's horse for collection on his return to Caldwell. Even if the marshal was disinclined to accept the document at its face value, being aware of the influence wielded by Ol Devil and the rancher's well deserved reputation for standing by employees or friends, he would at least check upon its validity before taking any drastic action.

More for reassurance than out of doubt, the big blond took out and opened his wallet. The ice cold sensation returned with greater intensity. Although the money was still in it, he had failed to notice earlier that the bill of sale was no longer there.

***** *****

Arlette Brissac possessed the faculty of being able to awake at any hour she selected. Opening her eyes about a quarter of an hour after Mark had arrived at the barn, she looked at the small watch on the bedside table. Satisfied, she rose and gave a contented sigh. Thinking of her experiences the previous evening, she wished there had been longer for her to enjoy the blond giant's company. She found herself comparing him to the other men with whom she had shared similar assignations in the past. None of them, particularly her current associates, had given her so much pleasure. Yet she had learned long since not to allow such considerations to interfere with business. She had work to do and felt no remorse over the realization that its successful conclusion would cause her most recent bed-mate to be killed.

After Arlette was dressed, she would visit the marshal to express her concern over having seen the big blond taking his *palomino* into the hotel's barn during the night. She would go on to claim her suspicions had been aroused by her passenger's comments as they were riding in the Surrey. Not only had he said he 'picked up' the horse in Caldwell, but he admitted he intended to replace it in Beckley and had shown great interest when he had seen the *palomino* tethered behind the jail house in passing.

From what she had seen of the peace officer, Arlette had formed a low opinion of his intelligence. He had, according to people with whom she talked, been given the appointment more for brawn and ability as a gun fighter than because of possessing a brilliant intellect. So she doubted whether he would wonder why, after having stolen the horse, the big blond would leave it in a place where it could so easily be found. In fact, by the time she had finished with him, she felt sure he would not allow the other man an opportunity to offer any explanation.

Although not of a philosophical nature as a rule, Arlette could not help thinking how everything had played into the hands of herself and her associates. Hired to prevent Mark Counter from reaching his aunt in Daisetta, they had been offered a substantial bonus if he could be stopped in a certain fashion. At first, none of them had believed they would be able to bring this about. Then a study of a map to establish the shortest route from the OD Connected ranch to his destination, along with hearing about the warning notices around Beckley, had suggested it might be possible.

Planning and not a modicum of good luck had played the big blond into the conspirators' hands. Employing a small-time thief who specialized in robbing hotels, they had caused him to lose his good clothes in Caldwell. Not only was he compelled to travel in far cheaper garments than was usual, but a noxious draught given to the horse he had been using ensured that he resumed the journey on a mount which had no connection with the ranch for which he worked.

There had been nothing fortuitous about Arlette's meeting with Mark, or the loss of the Surrey's wheel. Having remained in Caldwell long enough to ensure that the arrangements to make him continue his journey in the manner they required were effective, Howie—the leader of her party—had set out for Beckley riding a two horse relay. Doing so had allowed him to arrive ahead of the big blond and set the next part of the plan into operation. Estimating approximately when their victim would reach the vicinity, she had hired the Surrey and, accompanied by her cousin, Corin, went along the west-bound trail to wait for him.

Selecting a spot suitable for their purpose, Arlette had remained there while her companion kept watch. Having ascertained that their quarry was approaching, his being on foot had helped the preparations considerably, they had unscrewed the axle-nut and removed the wheel. Withdrawing to a position from which he could continue his observations, Corin was supposed to remain until she and the big blond went by. Instead, as soon as he was satisfied that the plot was going well, he had left to rejoin the others. As a result of his disregard for instructions, he had been in view when she and the big blond emerged from the woodland. However, she was confident that she had diverted her passenger's attention from him and, even if she had not, Mark attached no significance to seeing him.

Despite Corin's behaviour, Arlette had found no difficulty in continuing with the next phase of the scheme. The main problem she had envisaged did not arise. Fortunately, although she was asked if she had enjoyed her ride in the Surrey, nobody had mentioned she was residing in the hotel instead of elsewhere with a mythical aunt and uncle. For the rest, she had been helped by the big Texan being so tired. After a most enjoyable session of love making, he had fallen into such a deep sleep that she was able to rise unimpeded. Nor had he awakened while she was removing the bill of sale, which Howie had said he was carrying, from his wallet and, completing another precaution as instructed, collected her clothes so she could leave and return to her own quarters. Knowing her ability to wake at whatever hour she desired, she had decided to grab some sleep so as to be fresh and clear headed before going to see the marshal. She was hoping to time the visit so the peace officer found Mark up, dressed, armed and, for the best possible effect, just after he entered the barn.

Congratulating herself upon the way she had played her part, Arlette was on the point of removing her flimsy and figure-revealing nightdress when the key suddenly and inexplicably fell from the lock. Nor was she left for long in puzzlement over the phenomenon. The door opened and, although she caught a glimpse of two men wearing cowhand clothes standing in the hall, her main attention was directed at the person who stepped into the room.

There had been few women who had caused Arlette to consider herself at a disadvantage where sexual attraction was concerned, but the uninvited visitor who entered and closed the door was one who did.

An inch taller than Mark's betrayer, the newcomer was even more curvaceous. Nor, in spite of the nightdress's diaphanous material, was the fact concealed. The tartan shirt, Levi's pants and Kiowa moccasins she had on might look masculine rather than feminine, but they produced exactly the opposite effect. Although it showed lines of fatigue, her exceptionally beautiful face also expressed grim determination. Dropping the fringed buckskin jacket she had carried over her left arm, she removed and let fall her black Stetson, revealing a red head which Arlette suspected was dyed to that colour.

'The name's Belle Starr,' announced the newcomer, her voice that of a well educated Southron and underlaid with a resolution as threatening as her expression. 'I've come to stop what you're planning for Mark Counter.'

'You've come to do *what* for who?' Arlette demanded, wondering if her visitor really was the notorious female outlaw of whom she had frequently heard even before coming west of the Mississippi River and yet contriving to avoid showing the alarm which the other's words had aroused.

'Don't waste my time!' the newcomer warned, walking forward with all the feline grace combined with menace of a stalking cat. 'I was at Hofmeyer's when Chiggers brought in Mark's hat and gear——'

'I really don't know what——!' Arlette began, silently cursing the thief Howie had hired for having been so careless in disposing of the stolen clothing.

'Chiggers is as slick as they come, east or west of the Big

Muddy, at stealing from hotels and Chinese laundries,' Belle interrupted, halting and looking the other woman over from head to foot. 'But he's not brave. When Blue Duck and Sammy Crane out there asked him mean-like, he told us what you and Howie are up to.'

'I can't imagine what you're——!' Arlette bluffed, despite realizing that the thief must have overheard them discussing their plans as they had not intentionally made him privy to their affairs.

'Mark's a *very* good friend of mine!' the 'red head' stated remorselessly. 'So I'm not just going to *ask* you mean-like. I'm going to act it.'

With that, Belle swung her right hand. The flat palm caught Arlette's left cheek with an explosive 'splat!', snapped her head to one side and knocked her spinning across the room until she was brought to a halt by colliding against the wall. While the slap had been both unexpected and painful, she was far from incapacitated. As her assailant advanced, she thrust herself from the wall in a crouching posture which was not induced by fear. Rammed in the bosom by the lowered brunette head, Belle gave a croak of agony and was sent reeling to fall on the bed. She was only just in time to bring up and bend her legs as Arlette arrived with the intention of dropping on to her. With her feet against the brunette's chest, she thrust powerfully.

Returning to the wall involuntarily, Arlette bounced from it and dashed once more to the bed. Belle had already bounded up and regained her feet, but only just. Coming together, although each was conversant with more effective tactics, their hands instinctively dived into hair. Pulling and tugging with all their might, they spun around. Each was trying to kick at the other's shins, regardless of their respectively bare and moccasin covered feet being unsuitable. While doing so, their legs became entangled. Tripping, they fell to the floor, still locked and hair-tearing, rolling over and over without a pause. Nor, despite her earlier speculation, did the brunette notice that the locks she was jerking at so vigorously had roots of a much darker colour. Instead, all her attention was devoted to what she was doing and having done to her in return.

The door opened and, clearly having been attracted by the

squeals, cries and other sounds of feminine conflict which were rising, the two men looked in. Tall, lean, they had black hair and deeply tanned features indicative of a proportion of Indian blood. Their hats, shirts, vests and trousers might be of the kind cowhands wore, but they had moccasins on their feet. Each carried a revolver in a fast draw holster and a knife on his belt. In addition to that armament, the taller—by about an inch—held a Winchester Model of 1866 carbine negligently in his left hand.

'Looks like the gal wasn't obliging enough to say what Belle wants to know, Sammy,' the shorter and slightly older of the pair remarked in a matter of fact tone.

'Looks that way, Blue,' the other replied, showing no concern over their female companion being on the bottom at that moment and having her head banged on the floor. 'Hope they don't wake everybody up afore she gets to being sociable.'

'Best see they don't get "in—tee—rupted" happen they should,' suggested the man who went under the alias 'Blue Duck', as Belle toppled her assailant to assume the upper position and repay the punishment in kind, closing the door.

Considering what happened during the next ten minutes, it was fortunate that the owners of the hotel had had it built in a sturdy fashion and the rooms on either side of that occupied by Arlette were empty. Despite her proven ability in a feminine fracas,[5] Belle found herself contending against an anything but feeble opponent. In fact, the brunette's upbringing had been such as to instil in her a very sound knowledge of self protection when up against another member of her sex. She was also motivated by a realization of her peril if she should fail to subdue her assailant.

The fight raged all around the room. Standing, kneeling, or rolling on the floor with first one and then the other on top, the embattled pair traded slaps, punches, kicks, hair tearing, bites, or kneeings with equal abandon and verve. Not only had Belle's shirt been dragged so its flap was outside her trousers, all the buttons had been torn from it and it lost a sleeve sometime during the unceasing mill. Her flimsy underskirt suffered to such an

---

[5] For the benefit of new readers. Belle Starr's ability in bare handed combat is recorded in: Part One 'The Bounty On Belle Starr's Scalp' of *Troubled Range*; *The Bad Bunch*; *Hell in the Palo Duro*; *The Quest for Bowie's Blade* and Case One, 'The Set-Up' of *Sagebrush Sleuth*.

extent that both firm and full breasts were exposed to blows from fists, flat palms or clutching fingers. Not that Arlette's even less substantial attire escaped unscathed. Rather it suffered more. It soon was in tatters, then disintegrated completely. Yet, oblivious of being as naked as the day she was born, she fought on with undiminished fury.

At last, however, the Western girl's superior physical condition proved the deciding factor. In spite of having ridden hard and fast almost continuously since leaving Hofmeyer's Road House—a notorious gathering place for outlaws, particularly those with loot they wished to sell—on the outskirts of Caldwell, she began to gain the ascendancy.

Having rolled over the bed and on to the floor, Arlette's energy was nearly spent. Although she was barely able to continue fighting, she kept a tight grip on Belle's matted and sweat-sodden 'red' locks as if determined never to let go. Ignoring a sensation similar to the top of her head being on fire, Belle continued to rain slaps and punches upon her assailant. Perspiration was pouring from both of them, diluting the blood which was flowing from their nostrils and stinging the bites with which each had been inflicted, as the breath they could no longer expend on shrieking obscenities or yells of pain whistled gaspingly.

Even though Belle began to grow aware she was gaining the upper hand, she felt exhaustion welling over her. Urged on by the thought of what might happen to Mark, she found the strength to make a final desperate effort. Forcing herself erect without managing to dislodge the grip on her hair, she dragged Arlette with her. Up rose her left knee, ramming hard into the brunette's naked belly. Instantly, the tearing at her scalp ceased. Moaning in breathless torment, Arlette stumbled back a pace and folded at the waist with her hands clutching involuntarily at the stricken region. Instinct rather than conscious reasoning guided Belle's next action. As her left foot returned to the floor, she delivered a similar attack with her right leg.

In one respect, Arlette might have counted herself fortunate. Instead of meeting her descending face with the bone hard knee, it was Belle's thigh which made the contact. So, although the brunette was thrown over backwards on to the bed, she sustained less damage than would otherwise have been the case. Not that she was in any condition to appreciate the comparative good luck. Or to resist as Belle advanced to kneel and straddle her torso. What slight shred of consciousness remained was driven from her by the brief barrage of punches that were rained upon her unprotected face and bust by the other woman's fists in rotation.

At last, a realization that there was no cohesive or aggressive movement from the sweat-soddened body between her thighs penetrated Belle's mind. Slowly she forced herself to climb clear and stand up. Swaying on her feet and fighting to regain her breath, she saw the door being opened.

'Belle!' Blue Duck exclaimed, entering and halting to stare from the lady outlaw to her clearly defeated opponent and back. 'There's been some shooting out a ways. Could be it's Mark.'

'Y—You—b—best go—look,' Belle gasped, knowing the blond giant was not in his room as she had checked before coming to visit Arlette—whose location had also been revealed by an examination of the hotel's register. Waving a hand weakly to the naked shape sprawled motionless save for the heaving rise and fall of the bruised breasts, she went on, 'Sh—She won't—be—able to tell us if it is for a spell.'

*****   *****

'Good god, Howie!' Corin Hemel hissed, having chanced a glance through the window of the dilapidated adobe cabin in which he and his two male associates were waiting for Arlette to notify them of the success of their scheme. 'It's Counter and he's coming this way!'

'*What?*' Howard Fairweather spat out, going over to join his younger companion. 'Hell's fire, how——?'

'To hell with "how"!' growled the third man, his tones North Texas and his clothing that of a city dweller, if one of less affluent circumstances than either of his associates. 'Why's he coming here?'

'Looking for *that*, of course!' Hemel answered, always eager to leap to the obvious conclusion, pointing to the washy bay gelding which was standing in a corner of the cabin.

'I didn't reckon he was hunting for gold!' the third man corrected sarcastically. 'If I thought that god-damned gal——'

'Whether she did, or didn't, isn't important right now!' Fairweather interrupted in tones which brooked no argument. 'Taking care of him is our problem.'

'How can we do it and still make it look——?' Helm inquired, his thoughts on the bonus which had been promised if they could cause the blond giant's death to happen in a certain fashion.

'You'll get nothing but praise from that country hick marshal for shooting a horse thief,' Fairweather declared. 'So you pair go out there and do it while I take this damned thing where it won't be seen.'

'But what if Arl——?' Helm commenced.

'There's no time to argue!' Fairweather snarled, having no wish for Toby Fosten to be alerted to the possibility that their female accomplice had failed to carry out her instructions. 'Hold your guns cocked behind your backs and he won't have a chance.'

'Come on!' Fosten ordered, pulling the Remington Model 1861 Army revolver from his waistband and cocking its hammer. He was aware that Arlette had been ordered to exchange the bullets in the blond giant's revolvers for inert dummies and felt confident that the killing could be done without risk. 'Let's take him.'

Looking sulky and less assured, Helm nevertheless took his Colt Storekeeper Model Peacemaker from his jacket pocket. Pulling back its hammer with his thumb, he followed the other man towards what had been the door of the building. Keeping their weapons concealed as they had been instructed, they stepped out and looked to where, about thirty yards away, their intended victim had come to a halt.

'You looking for something, cow-nurse?' Fosten challenged, hoping to lure the blond giant closer.

'I've come for my bay,' Mark stated, hands dangling apparently loosely near the ivory butts of his Colts. 'That palomino you boys left at the barn's a touch fancy for my taste, even if he didn't belong to the marshal.'

'He knows!' Helm screeched, starting to bring the Storekeeper from behind his back. 'Get him!'

Letting out a low snarl of rage, Fosten began to duplicate his companion's action. Although he saw the big blond's hands commence moving with great rapidity, it was Helm who had provoked his wrath. Confident that Arlette had substituted the ammunition and there was no danger, he had not intended to open fire until his target was so close he would be unlikely to miss.

Fosten was to die before he could fully comprehend he had made a fatal mistake!

***** *****

Thinking of the message on the poster in conjunction with the presence of the marshal's *palomino* and the disappearance of the bill of sale, Mark had revised his opinion of what the incidents might portend. Unlikely as it had seemed before, he had concluded someone was trying to create the impression that he was a horse thief and, in Beckley, such a belief could cost him his life.

Having accepted the possibility, the big blond realized Arlette must be involved. Nobody else had had the opportunity to steal the bill of sale. She must also have accomplices.

Remembering how the woman had sought to divert his attention from the two men wearing Eastern clothing he had seen while coming into town, he felt they might qualify. What was more, they could still be in the ruined cabin. Even if they had stayed at the hotel, they would have left before the scheme was drawing towards its climax and taken their departure in such a manner they would be unlikely to have been mentioned in his hearing.

For a moment, Mark had thought of trying to get the truth out of the woman. He realized that she was lying about staying with kinfolk and, in all probability, could be found in the hotel. There was, he had decided, the danger that she might raise an outcry if he burst upon her. So he had concluded his wisest course would be to locate and capture her male associates, leaving her unaware that the scheme had gone wrong until she was confronted by the truth.

Taking the precaution of releasing the *palomino*, knowing it would return to its usual quarters, Mark had begun to visualize a further possibility. The idea was to have the marshal assume he was a horse thief and take the appropriate action. However, having gone to so much trouble to create the impression, he had doubted that they would leave the culmination so much to chance. There was a chance that, despite his being unable to produce proof of his identity on being arrested, the peace officer would refrain from carrying out the poster's warning until checking his assertion with the OD Connected. All of which had led to a disturbing conclusion. The affair had to be arranged so that he would not be granted an opportunity to announce his name. Yet it was unlikely that the conspirators had been ignorant of his prowess as a gun fighter. In which case, they could not be sure he would be killed by the marshal. It could go the other way.

Once again, the big blond had formed the correct deduction. An examination of the bullets in his Colt's cylinders had established they were inert. Fortunately, Arlette had not thought to change the twelve which were in the loops of his *buscadero* gunbelt. Having reloaded, he had set off by a circuitous route which prevented him from seeing Belle Starr and her companions riding into town. Arriving in the vicinity of the cabin, he had found his suspicions were correct. However he had seen only one of the pair who emerged the previous day. Before he could decide where the other might be, he was compelled to start defending himself.

Like Fosten, Mark would have preferred to be closer before having to open fire. Accepting that beggars could not be choosers, he swept the Colts from their holsters with the effortless-seeming rapidity which set the top gun fighter apart from the merely good. Swiftly as they emerged, his tactical sense warned against using them at waist level and by instinctive alignment. Ignoring a bullet from the Remington which missed him by a few inches, he carried up first the right and then the left hand weapon to shoulder height. Extending them at arm's length, he sighted along each seven and a half inch barrel in turn as he fired them alternately. On turning the third load from the right hand Colt, having felt the wind of two more close passing ·44 calibre balls which convinced him he was correct in his assumption of which man would be the more dangerous, he saw Fosten jolted backwards and, tossing aside the Remington involuntarily, sprawl face down on the ground.

Despite having brought his Storekeeper from its place of concealment, Helm made no attempt to use it. Instead, the instant his companion was hit, he turned and plunged into the shelter offered by the roofless walls of the cabin.

'Fosten's down, Howie!' Mark could hear the young man yelling as he disappeared into the building.

Studying the situation with an expert's eyes, the blond giant knew a frontal attack was out of the question. There were the two holes of former windows as well as the doorway from which the occupants could fire upon him. So he began to move around with the intention of closing the distance and seeking the most advantageous position from which to launch an offensive. He discarded the idea of waiting until the sound of shooting brought people from the town to investigate. If he did, Arlette might draw the correct conclusions and contrive to rescue her companions by having him killed before he could explain what he was doing.

Mark's reconnaissance informed him that the inner walls had collapsed, leaving just a single room; but it failed to establish where the two men might be in it. They had not left, of that he was certain. There was no cover they could have reached quickly enough for them to avoid being detected. Nor could he see any sign of either horses or any form of transport in the immediate vicinity upon which they might try to escape.[6]

Being aware that surprise was desirable under the circumstances, the big blond was alert for any chance to achieve it. After scanning the eastern side and rear of the building without being fired upon, he also was nowhere nearer to finding a solution. However, discovering that the western end had neither door nor windows, but there was a crack running from the top of the wall almost to the bottom, he decided it might offer an opportunity. Not one which would be taken if he had a choice, but still better than anything else he had seen.

*****   *****

'Where the hell has he got to?' Fairweather gritted, standing in the centre of the building with a cocked Remington New Line No. 3 revolver grasped by his right hand.

'Still around this side,' Helm answered, indicating the blank and—although neither he nor his companion noticed—cracked

---

[6] It was subsequently discovered that, having left Beckley on the pretence of going hunting along the Brazos River, the trio had left their horses and other belongings concealed in the woodland.

west wall. 'But he can't get at us——'

Even as the young man was making his pronouncement, it was shown to be incorrect!

Rapidly moving footsteps sounded very close to the indicated side of the building. Then the supposedly protective wall was burst asunder by a considerable impact from the outside.

Having rushed up and driven his left shoulder under the full propulsion of his two hundred and twenty pound, steel muscled body against the weakened portion, Mark smashed his way into the building. What was more, he entered with the Colts still held ready for instant use. His coming took the occupants unawares, but one glance told him that the affair was not yet concluded.

Stepping back unintentionally in his surprise, Fairweather still contrived to react with speed. Bringing up his Remington, he jerked at its trigger in a way which was not conducive to accuracy and missed. Against a man of Mark Counter's potential, such an error was not allowed to be repeated much less corrected. Turning apparently of its own volition, the right hand Cavalry Model Peacemaker thundered awesomely in the semi-confines of the cabin. Its ·45 bullet ripped into the Easterner's forehead, to burst out at the back of the skull and bring death instantaneously.

Stumbling away from one source of danger, although he had just sufficient presence of mind to start swinging the Storekeeper in the blond giant's direction, Helm inadvertently blundered into another. Squealing and bucking in protest at the commotion, the bay was displaying far more vigour and spirit than usual. One of its wildly lashing hind hooves caught the young man in the centre of the back just as he was squeezing the trigger to the point at which the sear of the mechanism disengaged the hammer. The weapon discharged, but its load flew harmlessly into a corner and he was knocked from his feet by the unexpected kick. As he landed on the floor, with the revolver flipping from his grasp, he realized that he was at the mercy of his party's intended victim and began to yell he was finished.

'*Gracias*, you slab-sided crowbait!' Mark drawled sardonically, glancing at the still plunging and kicking horse. 'Damned if I couldn't almost get to like you-all.'

***** *****

'They were hired by a cousin of your'n, Mr. Counter,' the town marshal of Beckley announced, having accepted the blond giant's invitation to join him and Belle Starr at their table in the hotel's dining room. 'Told me all about it, 'tween 'em.'

'Have some coffee and enlighten us, sir,' the lady outlaw requested.

Almost two hours had elapsed since the end of the brief gun battle at the ruined cabin. Belle's two companions had arrived before the marshal, but not soon enough for them to participate. All they had been able to do was inform Mark of her presence and what she had done at the hotel. As Helm had been too frightened to attempt a denial, the peace officer had accepted the big blond's explanation. His only question had been to ascertain the status of Blue Duck and Sammy Crane. Although he had not been told the truth, he had not questioned their assertion that they were hired by 'Belle Boyd' in her 'capacity' as an agent of the Pinkerton National Detective Agency.[7] The story had later been 'verified' by the lady outlaw producing an apparently genuine identification document.

Leaving the marshal to escort Helm to jail and collect Arlette from the hotel, Mark had joined Belle. By that time, she had recovered sufficiently to have cleaned up her appearance and changed into feminine costume from her warbag, which she had left in his room on finding he was not there. Apart from a blackened left eye and swollen top lip, she once more looked presentable and had managed to get her battered, barely conscious opponent attired sufficiently to be taken into custody.

'Seems like your aunt in Daisetta 'd disowned this cousin for wide-looping money and stuff from her,' the marshall continued, after receiving a cup of coffee. 'When he heard she was fixing to leave all she's got—which's considerable, what I can make out—to your side of the family 'cause they've allus been honest, he was some riled. When he got word she'd passed the word to you-all to come visit with her, he took on that bunch to stop you getting there. He told them that, happen they could do the killing, or get it done, so it looked like it was done 'cause you was up to no good, he'd give them extra. So they figured on getting you made wolf bait in a way it'd look like you got it for being a hoss thief. Not that *anybody*'d've believed it.'

'That'd be Cousin Cyrus, what I've heard tell of him,' Mark suggested, having heard something of the gang's motivation from Belle, but refraining from expressing his doubts over the peace officer's final assertion.

'What're you aiming to do about him?' the marshal inquired. 'Not that it's any of my never-mind, but I might be able to help.'

'I'll likely think of *something*, happen I come across him,' the big blond replied, far from displeased by the way the conversation was developing. 'Only, knowing him, he'll likely be harder to find than an unmelted snowball in hell. But I'll bear in mind what you-all said.'

'Thing I don't get, Miss Boyd,' the marshal went on, 'is why that gal allows you're Belle Starr.'

'She must have heard me wrongly,' the lady outlaw answered, but with such an aura of sincerity she might have been speaking the truth. 'I told her I'm Belle Boyd and work for the Pinkerton National Detective Agency, which was why she attacked me. As I explained to you earlier, we've been on the trail of her gang for some time. It's not their first try at this kind of thing and they're wanted.'

'Any rewards on 'em?' the marshal asked, an avaricious glint coming to his eyes, but he showed no sign of disbelieving what he had been told.

'No,' Belle replied.

'That being the case, they're going to have to stand trial here so's we can make an example of 'em!' the peace officer stated sourly. 'They stole my hoss——'

'That's true, marshal,' Mark put in, his voice taking on a warning note. 'Only this had better be *one* time you don't hang horse thieves high.'

Watching the response to the words and thinking of the peace officer's apparent eagerness to placate the big blond, Belle was willing to bet that the warning would be heeded. No matter what else happened to Arlette and Helm, they would not suffer such a fate.

PART THREE

THE FLOATING OUTFIT SERIES

The Ysabel Kid in

A WOLF'S A KNOWING CRITTER

Like Dusty Fog, the Ysabel Kid began to evolve during the early stages of my transitional writing period in Hong Kong. He too had commenced his existence as one of the 'Three Sons of the Grande', Lon Dalton, with the nickname, 'the Gunsmoke Kid—which I translated with the aid of an English–Spanish dictionary as el Cabrito de Huma del Escopeta[1]—and there was no mention of his ethnic origins. He was, however, tall, slim, black haired. dark and young looking. His armament consisted of two pearl handled Colt Peacemakers, a Winchester rifle, no type mentioned in either case, and a bowie knife. His clothing was all black[2] and he rode a large white horse.

When starting to consider marketable writing, I decided Lon needed changing if he was to be acceptable. At this point, I must make a confession. I have frequently claimed the Kid was modelled on Elvis Presley in Flaming Star, *but in fact he had his inception from seeing Jack Buetel in various roles, particularly as Billy the Kid in* The Outlaw *and the leading part in* The Half Breed (*not the same story as the one of that title in my*

---

[1] One of my readers, Reba Leon of Pacifica, California, informed me that in the current usage, the word '*Cabrito*' has come to mean 'Little Cuckold'. However, I would point out the connotation of words change over the years. During the period in which the stories of the Kid are set, 'Cabrito' was a literal translation in Spanish for a young goat, or kid. At that time, too, it was possible to call somebody 'gay' without hurting their feelings. Anyway, I'm grateful for the information as it will save me making an error in the Rockabye County series.

[2] I'm always amused when some people start airing their 'knowledge' of the movies by talking about the 'goodies' always wearing white hats and the 'baddies' black in Western films. I can remember numerous heroes—including William Boyd as Hopalong Cassidy—who wore black hats.

book The Half Breed*). However, there is much of Elvis's eternal youthful appearance of almost baby-faced innocence about the Kid. I'm not sure at this late date how the name 'Ysabel' came to be selected, probably I saw it somewhere and decided it had the correct kind of ring.*

Having decided that two revolvers, a rifle and a bowie knife were somewhat excessive when starting to produce Trail Boss, *I sought for an alternative. Remembering how few types of weapons appeared in the action-escapism-adventure Western stories which formed my inspiration, I began to buy reference books and learned that many companies had competed against Colt, Smith & Wesson, Remington, Winchester and Sharps (which were almost the only names I had seen mentioned) in the firearms' market. After considering several kinds, I settled on the big Colt 'Dragoon' Model of 1848 as his handgun, left him his James Black bowie knife and first a Winchester Model of 1866, then a 'One of a Thousand' Model of 1873 rifle.*

As the Kid was to carry out the Floating Outfit's scouting duties, I felt his expertise would be more acceptable if he had Indian blood. So his family began to grow. His Irish–Kentuckian father, his maternal grandfather, Chief Long Walker of the Pehnane *Comanche and his short lived French Creole–Comanche mother all eventually made their appearances. While on this subject, I would like to express my gratitude for the amount of detail I gathered from Ernest Wallace & E. Adamson Hoebel's definitive work,* The Comanches, Lords Of The South Plains. *This volume allowed me to elaborate upon the Indian side of the Kid's upbringing, including the phonetic spelling of many Comanche terms and supplied the legend of* Piamempits, *the Big Cannibal Owl, I introduced in* Comanche *along with the story of the Kid's birth and formative years. (Incidentally, the Brown Watson Ltd. Sabre Books edition in 1967 had one of the finest cover illustrations to appear on any of my books.)*

I think I should clarify one point. There is not and never has been any racial slur intended in having the Kid call his big white stallion 'Nigger'. Nor do I believe any of my readers believe there is. The name was selected as being something

71

which would appeal to the kind of dry, bantering humour in which the Kid indulges and which is characteristic of the Texas cowhand.[3]

Anyway, enough of this searching for deep inner motivation. I am writing this book for the enjoyment of my readers, who have bought it and for myself.

One thing which always used to surprise me was how many lady readers I have. Another is that the majority of them regard the Kid as their favourite character. Anyway, that is enough explanation, so I will start his part in the proceedings.

[3] My favourite examples of cowhand humour are as follows:
A rancher was served a rare steak in a café and sent it back with the advice, 'Get it cooked, ma'am. I had a steer on the ranch hurt a damned sight worse than that and it recovered!'

As the range had become infested with coyotes, the local ranchers decided to hold a big drive and thin them down. On hearing of this, a conservation freak asked a rancher why at the end of the drive, the coyotes could not be merely caught and castrated, as was done with cattle, instead of killed.
'I don't see what good *that* would do,' the rancher replied. 'The coyotes are *eating* our stock, not *raping* it.'

A WOLF'S A KNOWING CRITTER

'He's the fastest gun in Texas and the bravest of them all,
In the street you'd walk right by him 'cause he's not very tall,
Comes trouble he's the bravest, fights like a Comanche Dog,
He's from the Rio Hondo country and they call him Dusty Fog.'

Having successfully completed the descent of a high and fairly steep slope which a more prudent—or less skilful—rider would have avoided, the Ysabel Kid was relieving his boredom by raising his pleasant tenor voice in song. While he was making for a pre-arranged rendezvous with Dusty Fog and Mark Counter, he had no more pressing business than a desire to rejoin them and continue the return journey to the OD Connected ranch in their company. Aware that Nigger had done considerable hard travelling since circumstances had compelled him to part company with the blond giant a few days earlier,[1] he saw no reason to enforce a more rapid pace. So, once on level ground, he was allowing the huge, magnificent and, regardless of the saddle and bridle it bore being indications of domesticity, wild looking white stallion to set its own gait as they travelled in a south-easterly direction across the rolling, woodland dotted country of West Kansas.

There was not even the prospect of a night spent under a roof to cause the Kid to make his mount go faster. In spite of possessing exceptionally keen eyesight, he had seen no sign of human habitation from the top of the rim. However, he was sufficiently certain of the general direction of the town of Wide

[1] Why the Ysabel Kid had parted company with Mark Counter is told in: Part Two, 'Little Throat Cutter' of *Cuchilo*.

Creek for which he was heading to have taken the risky short cut instead of riding east or west in search of an easier and safer way down. Now, having reached the bottom, he was reconciled to using the sky for a roof and the ground as a mattress once again. It was not the first time he had slept in the open air, nor did he expect it would be the last.

Tall, whipcord lean in a way which suggested a wiry and practically tireless strength, the Kid had wavy hair as black as the wing of a Deep South crow. His Indian dark, handsome features seemed to express an almost babyish innocence, but there was something in his eyes that warned this could be more apparent than actual. Of a curious red-hazel colour, the reckless glint in them gave a warning of his true nature and that he was somewhat older than he appeared on the surface.

All the Kid's clothing, including the gunbelt which carried an old Colt First Model Dragoon revolver with its walnut handle turned forward for a low cavalry twist draw at the right and a massive, ivory hilted James Black bowie knife sheathed at the left, was black. Although he was fully competent in either's use and particularly at wielding the latter, the two weapons did not comprise his entire armament. A Winchester Model of 1866 rifle rode in the boot attached to the near side skirt of his low horned, double girthed range saddle, which also had a coiled rope strapped to its horn and his tarp-wrapped bed roll on the cantle. While his attire proclaimed his origins in the Lone Star State and implied he was a cowhand, his boots had low heels more suited to working on foot and, in fact, his duties for the OD Connected ranch were generally more concerned with scouting than actually handling the cattle. So, many of the tasks in which he became engaged called for walking if he was to perform them successfully.

With the song over, the Kid relapsed into silence. Yet, in spite of conveying the impression that he was almost asleep in the saddle, his eyes and ears were constantly seeking for any sight or sound which might herald danger for him. Although he had no reason to believe that there might be some malevolent presence lurking in the vicinity, the training he had received during his formative years and the habits of an event-filled lifetime demanded he maintained an unceasing vigilance. No man who had gained admittance into the famed Dog Soldier war lodge of the *Pehnane* Comanche band ever rode along, especially when traversing unfamiliar terrain, without remaining alert and watchful and, as a boy, he had attained that distinction.[2]

So, in spite of his slothful demeanour, little of what was happening around him escaped the Kid's notice as he continued his journey. Once he watched a swiftly plummeting prairie falcon stooping to take the last member of a covey of bobwhite quail which had been startled into flight by his passing. Further on, a coyote chasing a blacktailed jack rabbit held his attention until they disappeared. Shortly after a raccoon had waddled away rapidly to avoid his approach, his keen eyes detected a bobcat peering at him from what it obviously believed to be complete concealment beneath the foliage of a bush. A few feet away, he saw the scattered feathers and torn apart remains of a greater prairie chicken which had fallen victim to the crouching predator. He knew the interrupted meal would be resumed after he had passed by.

Being aware that various kinds of animals needed to prey on other living creatures in order to survive, the Kid saw no need to interfere in any of the various activities. Nor did he see anything in the predators' behaviour to disturb him from his apparent lethargy.

Something over a mile beyond where the Kid had seen the bobcat, a commotion arising from an area of woodland he was approaching caused him to devote his entire attention in that direction. For several seconds, he could see nothing, but the thudding of hooves and crackling of disturbed foliage grew louder. Then, clearly fleeing for its life, a buck Texas whitetail deer burst through the bushes and ran towards him.

Even before the reason for the buck's terror-induced flight came into view, the Kid had deduced what it would be and was discarding his somnolent posture. Apart from human beings, only three kinds of creature in Kansas had the size and strength

[2] For the benefit of new readers: how this came about is told in: *Comanche*. Details of the Ysabel Kid's background and special qualifications are given in Appendix Three. This also supplies explanations of various Comanche terms.

required to prey with any regularity upon a male of the species *Odocoileus Viginiansus Texanus*.[3] Of them, a black bear would only kill when presented with an opportunity which required little expenditure of energy and rarely offered to give chase. Designed and equipped to kill by springing from ambush, a mountain lion was not inclined to devote time and effort in trying to run down a healthy animal which escaped its initial charge.

Sure enough, the type of predator the Kid had anticipated emerged from the woodland. It was a good-sized, black-grizzled, light buff Great Plains buffalo wolf. What was more, at first neither it nor its intended quarry showed any sign of being aware of his presence. This was, in part, caused by his instinctive reactions to the deductions he was making with regard to the nature of the animal doing the hunting. A signal with his knees had brought the stallion to an immediate halt. Simultaneously, he had reached down and started to slide the rifle from its saddle-boot. While doing so, he was watching to find out how many more of the dog-like carnivores were present and was surprised when none appeared. Lacking the great strength and size of a black bear, or a mountain lion's better developed claws and fangs, wolves usually relied upon co-operation by several of their kind when trying to bring down such large and possibly dangerous prey as a mature buck whitetail deer.

Not until only about fifty yards was separating them did the rapidly moving ruminant discover it was confronted by another potential enemy. Swerving violently, it contrived to increase its speed to dash off at a tangent—tail erected to display the snow-white underside as a warning of danger—in a succession of bounds each covering at least twenty feet. Having been a short distance behind, the wolf was equally unaware of the Kid's presence until the buck's evasive action took place. Skidding to a stop instead of changing direction and continuing the pursuit, the predator stood and stared at the black dressed Texan.

Starting to bring the butt of the Winchester to his right shoulder, the Kid began to feel puzzled. His early training in all matters pertaining to range country survival had supplied

[3] While there is a separate sub-species of Kansas whitetail deer, *Odocoileus Virginiansus Macrourus*, it is confined to the eastern side of the State, with *O.V. Texanus* occupying the west.

him with an extensive knowledge of animal behaviour to which he had continued adding over the years by listening to the experiences of others and comparing what he was told against his own findings.

Everything the Kid had learned suggested that the wolf was behaving in a most uncharacteristic fashion. In the first place, it appeared to be alone. Secondly, it had halted and was standing motionless when it ought to have been taking the wise precaution of returning to the shelter of the bushes as a prelude to fleeing through the woodland. Yet it was not too old and infirm to have failed to detect he was a living and perhaps dangerous creature. It was, in fact, a big male in the prime of life and there were no visible physical defects to suggest a reason for its solitary state or lack of prudence. Living as it did in an area which was reasonably close to human habitations, it should have learned its kind had no more implacable enemies than men. The price of survival under such conditions entailed avoiding taking any unnecessary risks. Flight on sight was mandatory. Standing and looking, as it continued to do, was asking for an early death. The Indian-dark Texan was confident that he could oblige such a suicidal tendency.

The Kid's conclusion was inspired neither by blood-lust nor a sentimental desire to protect the 'pretty and defenceless' buck from the 'evil' savage beast which was chasing it. After all, he had felt no compulsion to intervene while watching other predators carrying out their natural functions. However, both as a fully trained Comanche warrior who was an initiated member of the *Pehnane* Dog Soldier war lodge and an employee in the cattle industry which had brought prosperity back to Texas after the impoverished years created by its support of the Confederate States, his behaviour was understandable.

As the Kid had not come under the influence of the professional 'conservationists' of a later generation, who would willingly distort the truth to serve their profit-motivated ends, he was aware of just how dangerous a wolf could be to domestic stock. Nor would its kind restrict their depredations to 'natural' prey if it was available, as would be claimed in the future by such 'authorities'. Like any carnivore, they sought for the easiest

77

and least dangerous prey. Domesticated animals, being in general less wary and less well equipped to defend themselves or escape, were more likely to fall victim if sought out and tackled. So they would be selected by preference no matter how many wild animals might be in the vicinity.

Conscious of these facts, the Kid's instincts as Indian warrior and ranch worker were to remove a possible menace. He was passing through mixed cattle and farming country, so felt he was performing a service to the community. Furthermore, considering how this particular member of the species *Canis Lupus Nubilis* was behaving, it had so little fear of man that its extermination was even more advisable. Its boldness could make it become a threat to human life.

With the big white stallion standing like a statue, the Winchester cradled at his shoulder ready for firing and a distance of less than seventy-five yards separating them, anybody who knew of the Kid's skill as a marksman would have given the wolf a life expectancy of only a very few more seconds.

***** *****

'Get that son-of-a-bitching rifle down, blast ye!' bawled a cracked and irascible masculine voice which suggested the speaker was of some age, as the black-dressed Texan's right forefinger was starting to draw back on the rifle's trigger. 'Whip, you god-damned fool critter, come on back here!'

'Sorry, mister,' the Kid apologized, restraining his finger's movement just in time as he saw the animal turn to lope back into the bushes. As a gesture of his good faith, he lowered the rifle and rested it across his knees with the barrel pointing sideways. Wondering if he had been mistaken in his identification and had almost shot the speaker's dog, he continued, 'I didn't figure it was anybody's pet.'

'Well he be!' the voice stated emphatically. 'Which he's still on *our* land and, no matter what you got told in Wide Creek, he ain't never been off it; nor pulled down nobody's god-damned cattle, not even when the fool critters've strayed over the river on to our range.'

'I wouldn't know about it,' the Kid replied, having located the speaker's position but unable to see him for the dense foliage of the bushes behind which he was standing. 'Fact being, I was headed for Wide Creek, not coming from there, and I didn't know that I'd come by it.'

'Ain't you-all been sent out to hunt down Whip here?' the voice inquired, its tone a trifle less hostile.

'I'm just a stranger passing through,' the Kid declared and, considering it was safe to do so, returned the Winchester to its boot. 'Happen I'd come across it, I was figuring on stopping by in Wide Creek for a spell to rest up ole Nigger here. But I've never afore been there and, way you're talking, seems like I've come by it somehow.'

'You-all ain't done no such thing,' the speaker corrected and, after a pause during which the Texan felt sure he could hear a second person whispering, went on, 'We'n's fixing to go in comes morning and, happen you're so minded, you could ride along of us.'

'Be obliged', the Kid accepted, being curious to see who he was addressing as they were still concealed by the bushes.

'You-all hungry?' the voice queried, again after receiving prompting in a whisper to make the suggestion.

'Some,' the Kid admitted. 'I've never took to cooking and don't have much food along was I minded to do any. That's another reason I was headed for Wide Creek.'

'Figured you-all wouldn't be no cooking man,' the speaker drawled, his accent that of the Kentucky hill country. 'Never yet comed across an Indian buck's was. What tribe be it, mister?'

'Comanche,' the Kid answered, a note of pride in his Texas drawling pleasant tenor voice, having noticed that the question had been posed in a friendly fashion. He had never felt ashamed of his birthright, so he continued, 'The *Pehnane* band.'

'I'd've reckoned the *Pahuraix*,[4] was I asked,' the speaker commented. 'Not one of ole Long Walker's bunch. You know him?'

_____

[4] Unlike most other Comanches, members of the *Pahuraix* (Water Horse) band tended to be tall and slim. They were noted as great runners, but also as compulsive gamblers. According to the legend, they attained their height through reaching so high when making their wagers. Also known as the *Par-Kee-Na-Um* (Water People), the names originated from their predilection for making camp near rivers or lakes.

'Some,' the Kid replied, realizing that the unseen man must possess considerable knowledge of the Comanche nation to have drawn such a conclusion even though it was erroneous. 'He's my grandpappy and I've got some of his ways. One of which's not taking to talking to somebody's I can't see.'

'You danged *Tshaoh* allus was touchy folks,' the speaker stated, but—in spite of employing the name the 'Enemy People' every other Indian tribe used to describe the Comanche nation—there was no hostility in his voice, rather the opposite, in fact. 'Come on, Zee.'

Followed by the animal which had been the cause of the conversation, two human beings emerged silently from among the bushes. Studying their appearance, the Kid could guess how they had acquired the necessary skill in such matters to have kept hidden from his well trained scutiny until satisfied it was safe for them to be seen. Each wore a high crowned black hat with a broad band decorated by Sioux medicine symbols, its style being much favoured by Indians—although neither showed any sign of being of mixed blood—a clean, if not new, fringed buckskin shirt, trousers of the same material and Pawnee moccasins with knee length leggings. For all the uniformity of their attire, he was in no doubt which of them had done all the talking to him.

Shortish, stocky, with snowy white hair cascading shoulder long from under his hat, the speaker was as old looking as he had sounded. What little that could be seen of his features among the bushy beard he sported was deeply tanned and leathery, but his blue eyes appeared keen. There was, moreover, nothing senile about the way in which he moved, or held a clearly well cared for Henry rifle with its barrel resting on his right shoulder. He had on a worn brown leather gunbelt with a walnut handled Colt 1860 Army revolver in a cross draw holster at the left and a bowie knife almost as massive as the Kid's was sheathed at the right.

Equalling the speaker in height, the second figure was much younger and a girl. No hair showed from beneath her hat, except for blonde eyebrows which contrasted with the tan of her pretty and cheerful looking face. While she had a buxom figure, the

ease with which she moved suggested little of its curvaceous—
although not blatantly displayed—weight was fat. She had a
Winchester Model of 1866 carbine in her hands. There was a
J. Russell and Co. 'Green River' knife at the right side of her
Indian-made waistbelt, but she showed no sign of being armed
with a handgun of any kind.

'Howdy, folks,' the Texan greeted, swinging from his saddle
and stepped forward, the stallion remaining motionless. He
halted as the animal he had intended to shoot let out a low
growl and, staring at it, exclaimed, 'God-damn it. That *is* a wolf.'

'I figured even a danged *Tshaoh*'d know it warn't no pussy-
cat,' the old man answered with a cackle of laugher. 'Or, happen
that's what you took it for, your Pappy Sam 'n' Long Walker
sure raised you wrong.'

'Hell, I figured it *was* a wolf until you-all called it back to
you,' the Kid protested. 'Anyways, like you-all've figured, the
name's Loncey Dalton Ysabel. Which's a mite fancy for most
folks 'n' they most time call me——'

'The Ysabel Kid,' the girl offered, her voice as suggestive of
the Kentucky hill country as that of her aged companion who
had been on point of suggesting '*Cabrito*', the Kid, as the black
dressed Texan was known to the Mexicans along the Rio
Grande, or the man-name '*Cuchilo*', the Knife, granted by the
Pehnane Comanche because of his skill in wielding that particular type of weapon.

'That's one brand they put on me,' the Kid conceded with a
grin. 'Only I was going to say, "Lon".'

'We've heard tell plenty about you, young feller, the old man
asserted, although nothing in his demeanour indicated whether or
not he approved of the information. 'Name's Jebediah Minns
'n' thishere's me granddaughter, Zerelda.'

'Which's sort of fancy, comes to that,' the girl went on amiably.
'So, happen you'll make it "Zee", I'll call you-all "Lon".'

'You-all've got a deal,' the Kid replied, as soberly as if concluding negotiations of great importance, but his gaze kept returning to the animal he now knew was not a dog.

***** *****

'Wolves ain't such all fired bad critters's most folks make

81

'em out to be,' Minns commented with a grin, glancing from the Indian-dark Texan to his big white stallion and back, concluding that neither of them was entirely reconciled to one part of the company they were keeping.

With the introductions performed, the Kid had been requested to accompany Zee and her grandfather to their cabin where he could eat and spend the night. From what they had said as they set off, they had been hunting in a way which they had found to be most productive. Having put up the buck, the big buffalo wolf had given chase with the intention of bringing it to bay so that they—in the capacity of the rest of the pack—could catch up to help to do the killing.

The old timer had next told how he and his granddaughter had settled on the land they were now traversing after having travelled 'some' following the death of her parents when she was a child. It was, he had claimed, large enough to supply them with all their simple needs. Although they had a few head of cattle, they made the majority of their living by hunting various animals for skins or meat and selling the results of their efforts to the people of the small town of Wide Creek.

Listening to the way in which Minns had referred to the near by community he had been seeking, the Kid was reminded of his father. Having had much the same kind of origins amongst the freedom-loving and self-reliant population of Kentucky's hill country, Big Sam Ysabel had shared the old timer's outspoken antipathy where the encroachment of civilization was concerned. Each had a similar abhorrence for its restrictions and regulations which led them to consider any area with other human occupants within fifty miles or so was becoming intolerably overcrowded.

There had been a defiant, almost challenging note in Minns' voice while he was delivering the explanation of his and his granddaughter's presence. However, before the Texan could think up a tactful way to ask questions, his obvious uneasiness over the continued proximity of the wolf had provoked the old timer's comment upon the species in general.

'They're not what most folks'd take to as house-pets, though,' the Kid countered. 'Fact being, I wouldn't've reckoned's anybody could get one tamed down even this much.'

82

While walking along and talking, the Texan had also given the wolf some of his attention. Neither he nor the white stallion were completely reconciled to having it at such close quarters. It had not offered to come near, nor had it displayed hostility or fear. Rather its behaviour had been similar to that of a big game hound which was used to the presence of human beings, but had not acquired the friendly affection exhibited by dogs kept purely as pets.

'Whip there ain't tamed down to being no house-pet,' Zee warned with a touch of indignation, confirming the estimation the Kid had made of the animal's character. 'He's never come inside our cabin, 'cepting when he was a pup too young to fend for hisself. He just reckons, there being no more wolves around, Gramps 'n' me're part of his pack. That's why he stays around us and wouldn't try to hurt us.'

'Nor nobody else, neither,' Minns inserted in tones of certainty. 'Only way he might'd be happen somebody come on him unexpected like 'n' he couldn't see no other way of getting by 'em. Which same ain't likely to happen. He knows right well to steer clear of folks most all of the time. He might've lived around Zee 'n' me ever since we come by him when he was a pup, but he's like his wild-running kin and figures other folks ain't to be trusted, so keeps well outen their way.'

'It's likely the first time he's ever come across anybody up this end of our range,' the girl supplemented. 'And, you pair being so still when he got his first look at you, he wasn't sure of just what you might be. Given just a couple more seconds, though, 'n' he'd've thought, "The hell with taking chances" and been up 'n' running for the trees faster'n a greased weasel chasing after a jack rabbit with its butt on fire.'

'You-all don't get too many folks around, huh?' the Kid inquired.

'We're lucky that way here on the Triangle,' Minns replied. 'Way we're fixed, we don't have too many borrowing neighbours coming to call.'

'The *Triangle*?' the Kid hinted.

'We don't go branding it on any of our stock,' the old timer obliged. 'But that's what we call our range on account of it's got the High Rim on the north end, with Wide Creek running down at the east until it joins with the Sand River coming along to the west. Makes this section look like what some fancy book-reading Eastern dude tells me's knowed as a triangle.'

'Looks like you're pretty well fenced off all 'round,' the Kid commented, remembering the difficulty he had experienced in descending what could only have been the 'High Rim'.

'Well enough,' Minns agreed. 'Not that we try to stop folks coming on 'n' passing through just so long's they don't bother us none. Doc Ginsberg, Deputy Jack Tremayne and a few more of the fellers from Wide Creek know's they're welcome to hunt the Triangle any time they want. But they know Whip 'n' wouldn't throw down on him was their paths to cross.'

'What you said, Zee, there's no other wolves hereabouts,' the Kid remarked. 'Now I'm not one for being nosy, but where'd he come from. What my daddy 'n' Grandpappy Long Walker allus told me, you had to have at least one momma and poppa of anything afore you got any young ones.'

'Wouldn't've figured either of 'em knowed that much,' Minns cackled, his attitude inferring that he was speaking about two men for whom he had considerable respect. 'Was a pack of the varmints around when we moved in, but we had to wipe 'em out when they took to living offen our stock 'stead of wild critters.'

'Whip come from off the Crossed Keys range, over the Sand River, though,' the girl went on. 'Dick Keys asked us to thin the wolves down on bounty and, when we started, we found's somebody else was cutting in—using poison. Anyways, Whip was the only one out of a litter's's momma had took some of it. I cottoned on to him straight off when I saw the way he chomped hold of Gramp's ankle.'

'Blasted women!' the old timer sniffed. 'Anyways, he's been around us ever since. And, like I said, he's never done nobody nor nothing any harm, 'cepting for wild critters he's hunted either with us or, was they little enough, by his-self.'

'Somebody been saying he has?' the Kid inquired, recollecting a comment which had been made before the couple had emerged to introduce themselves.

'It's been——!' Minns began.

'Gramps!' Zee yelled in alarm, pointing ahead. 'Look!'

Having found the conversation engrossing and, partially, because he was keeping an eye on the wolf, the Kid had been paying less attention to his surroundings than would usually have been the case. The girl's words and action brought an end to such lax behaviour. Looking in the direction she was indicating, he found they were approaching a large clearing. At the far side, a good quarter of a mile away, was what could only be the couple's home. Built close to a stream, it comprised a small, sturdily constructed log cabin with a lean-to at one end, a back-house and a pole corral occupied by half a dozen horses. Even from a distance, it looked to be a pleasantly situated, well maintained property. However, going by appearances, its condition was in danger of being changed drastically very soon.

The cause of Zee's consternation was a trio of men wearing cowhand style clothes. It was obvious that they were not merely paying a friendly, if unexpected, social visit. One of them was opening the corral's gate and, as they did not appear to have any horses with them, his motive might have been merely to acquire mounts if it had not been for what the other two were doing. While one of them was tossing liquid from a large can on to the wall of the cabin, the other was applying a lighted match to the end of a broken branch he held. The way in which flames gushed up indicated there was something of an exceptionally inflammable nature attached to it.

'What the——?' Minns yelled furiously, starting to bring the barrel of his Henry from its resting place on his shoulder. 'Stop them!' Although his granddaughter was already anticipating his order, he saw something which caused him to continue, 'Hey! What in hell're you doing?'

Without waiting to answer, the Kid went on with the actions which had provoked the question. After a glance at what was happening in the clearing, he had turned and shot out his right hand to grasp the low horn of the stallion's saddle. Instead of attempting to mount in the conventional fashion, he gave a single word of command which caused Nigger to quicken the tempo of the walking gait. Vaulting on to the white's back with no more apparent effort than if it was no higher than that of a donkey rather than a good seventeen hands at the withers, he had urged it to go even faster. Not only did he ignore the old timer's request for enlightenment, he paid no attention to a rage-filled suggestion that he got the hell out of the line of fire.

Possibly because he had no personal ties with the endangered building, the Kid was better able than either of his companions to see that starting to shoot from their present position and armed as they were would be a tactical error.

Unequalled at that period as hand-held weapons capable of sustained and very rapid fire as the Henry rifle and its successor —the Winchester Model of 1866 in rifle or carbine form— might be, the construction of their 'rimfire' cartridges of necessity restricted their effective range. To ensure that the firing pin could strike with sufficient force to ignite the priming charge, which was placed around the inside edge of the base's rim—as opposed to the later 'centre-fire' system wherein detonation was created via a centrally-inserted 'cap'—its metal could not be as thick as the walls of the case. This in turn required that, for safety's sake, the propellant charge must be limited.

Despite the Kid's rifle being equipped with a 'Sporting Leaf Sight' graduated from one to a thousand yards,[5] the 1,125 feet per second velocity produced by the twenty-eight grains powder charge could not send the two hundred grain bullet with accuracy for anywhere close to that distance. Its somewhat less sophisticated predecessor in Minns' hands and the shorter carbine held by the girl were even less adequate for the task their owners were expecting to carry out.

Conscious of the limitations of his party's weapons under the circumstances, the Kid was taking what he considered to be the best possible line of action. Having his horse instantly available, he would be able to close the distance until he could employ his Winchester to better advantage than the old timer's Henry or the girl's carbine. So, having made a flying mount as com-

[5] The manufacturers also offered the Winchester Model of 1866 rifle with a 'Musket Rear Sight' or a less complicated 'Sporting Rear Sight' graduated respectively for 100 to 900 and 50 to 300 yards. The carbine had only a two-position sight graduated more realistically from 50 to 300 yards.

petently as could have been performed by any Comanche brave heart, he continued to display his *Nemenuh*-trained skill by extracting the 'Old Yellowboy'—as the Model of 1866 was called because of its brass frame—from its saddleboot without needing to reduce the stallion's build up of speed in the slightest. By the time he was emerging from among the trees, he was holding the weapon in his hands. What was more, guiding the swiftly moving white by knee pressure alone, he turned it aside sufficiently on entering the clearing to carry out—if belatedly— the old timer's command.

Although none of the trio had shown any sign of having heard Zee or her grandfather, the Kid was certain that his own presence would not remain undetected for long. Sure enough, before he had covered thirty yards beyond the edge of the woodland, the man by the corral let out a warning yell and pointed towards him. Knowing there was no need to refrain now the alarm had been raised, the Texan responded with a ringing Comanche Dog Soldier's war-whoop and a signal from his heels that brought a further increase in the stallion's pace. Hearing the cracking of Minns' Henry intermingled with the lighter detonations from the girl's carbine from behind him, he saw nothing to suggest either's bullets were hitting their intended targets. However, the flying lead served one purpose.

Having delivered his warning, the speaker dropped the rail of the gate he had just drawn from its holder and, without attempting to either collect for use or drive out any of the horses from the corral, he turned to dart hurriedly for the shelter offered by the tree beyond it.

'Get out of here!' bellowed the torch-holder, throwing it at the side of the cabin to ignite the obviously inflammable liquid supplied by the third member of the party.

Ducking involuntarily as a bullet whistled by him, the last of the trio was discarding the can from which he had been tossing kerosene on to the wall even as his companion was speaking. Showing an equal disinclination to attempt to delay the rapidly approaching rider until the flames they had produced could take an unstoppable hold on the building, he followed the other member of the party's example by starting to run away. Acting

87

as if they had rehearsed together for months, the erstwhile holder of the torch accompanied him at the same instant.

For a moment as the Kid watched the trio taking flight, he was consumed by the eagerness of a *Pehnane* Dog Soldier to follow and count coup on one or more of them. Then he realized why he must restrain the impulse. As yet, the flames were only licking over the more readily inflammable liquid; but they would soon begin to eat into the summer-dried timber of the building. Once that happened, they might inflict irreparable damage before they could be quenched. So he turned his attention from the departing men and sought for the means by which he could fight the fire.

The search was not protracted. Close to the lean-to which housed an inverted V-shaped wooden 'burro' upon which saddles could be placed for safety when not in use, were several hides stretched on racks to be dried by the sun. Returning the rifle unfired to the saddleboot as he was approaching, the Texan quit the stallion's back while it was still moving at a gallop. Lighting down with an almost cat-footed agility, he brought himself to a halt by the pegged out skin of a whitetail deer. A quick wrench tore it free and, darting to the side of the cabin, he began to use it to beat at the flames.

Time after time the Kid swung the hide to strike at the blazing area, encouraged by the yells of Zee and her grandfather as they ran to help him. Just as he decided he was winning, he heard their cries turn to alarm and a warning snort burst from the stallion. A glance over his shoulder informed him of what had caused both. Not much over twenty-five yards away, the three men were returning from among the trees. Discovering that they had been detected, they skidded to a halt and each brought up to fire the revolver he was now holding.

Few white men could have saved themselves in a similar predicament, but—as always in times of great peril—the Kid reacted in the fashion of a *Pehnane* Dog Soldier; than which no better human fighting machine existed.

Dropping the smouldering hide, the black-dressed Texan went sideways in a rolling dive. While doing so, his right hand was turning palm out to close on the butt and twist the Colt Dragoon from its holster. He missed death by no more than a couple of inches as the three bullets fired at him passed through the space his body would still have been occupying if his reflexes had been less superbly attuned. Ending his evasive action on his knees, he grasped his right hand with the left for added support and thrust forward the already cocked revolver to arms' length. Sighting swiftly, he squeezed the trigger and the four pound one ounce old Dragoon's thumb-busting forty grains powder charge in the upper chamber of the cylinder was detonated. Ejected by a greater propellant force than could be attained by either the Henry or the Winchester '66 *rifles*, the ·44 calibre soft lead round ball struck the middle man of the trio in the centre of the chest and flung him backwards from his feet.

Rapidly as the Kid had responded, he had not removed the whole threat to his continued existence. Neither of the remaining men showed any sign of being deterred by their companion's fate. Instead, each was cocking his revolver with the intention of rectifying his previous inaccuracy. Before either could do so, they heard the savage squeal of an enraged stallion and the drumming of rapidly approaching hooves.

Jerking his gaze in the direction of the commotion, the man at the right let out a yell of alarm. Looking as menacing as a charging grizzly bear and only slightly less dangerous, the huge white stallion was rushing towards him. The sight was so awe-inspiring that he was numbed into immobility. Nor was he granted an opportunity to recover. Powerful jaws closed on his gun arm, the teeth grinding into flesh as effectively as if belonging to a carnivore rather than a grass-eater. A jerk of the head sent him sprawling over the body of the Kid's victim. Still screaming in fury, Nigger went after him to lash home kick after kick with iron shod hooves that did not stop landing even though the third killed him.

Horrified by the savagery of the white's attack, the last of the trio was also unable to continue the attempt at preventing the black-clad newcomer from being able to resume the dousing of the fire. He was, however, more fortunate than the other two. A bullet fired by Minns tore the hat from his head and, while it caused him no injury, served to put movement back into his

89

limbs. Already badly shaken by what had happened to the other two, he spun on his heel and fled once more into the woodland. This time he had no intention of returning, but was going to where they had left their horses and, taking all three with him, make good his escape.

Coming to his feet and returning the Colt to its holster, the Kid glanced around. As he went to gather up the hide, he yelled orders which caused the stallion to end its attack. Then he set about extinguishing the last of the flames.

*****　　　*****

'Do you know either of them?' the Kid inquired, after he and Minns had carried the two bodies beneath the lean-to and covered them with blankets.

'Never seed either of 'em afore,' the old timer replied, making a wry face. 'I know *what* they was, though.'

'And me,' the Kid declared, having drawn similar conclusions from his examination of the corpses. 'Thing being, who'd be hiring guns to burn you-all out?'

'I'm damned if I know,' Minns said, sounding more puzzled and worried than angry. 'We allus used to get on pretty good with folks hereabouts, even if we didn't sociable-ize all that much with 'em.'

'Only you're maybe not getting on so good with 'em right now, huh?' the Kid suggested, remembering the way in which he had been greeted.

'How'd you-all know about it?' Minns demanded, exuding suspicion.

'I sort of got some fool notion, from what's been said since we met until now,' the Kid explained calmly, 'that you'd not've sounded so surprised had it allus been that way 'tween you and them.'

'Sorry, young Ysabel,' Minns apologized with genuine contrition. 'What's just happened, coming on top of everything else just recent's getting me's jumpy as a good church-going maiden lady left alone in a room with the town's knowed womanizer.'

'Feel like telling me what's up?' the Kid inquired. 'Likely it won't do any good, but I don't reckon's how it'll do any harm, neither.'

90

'Like you say, it couldn't do no harm,' Minns admitted and something of his earlier amiability returned as he went on, 'You must've learned *something* from your pappy and Grandpappy Long Walker, only—what I remember of them pair of varmints— I shudders to think what it'll be. Let's go in and sit comfortable while we talk.'

Entering the cabin, the Kid found it to be clean and comfortably, if simply, furnished. It comprised a dining-cum-sitting room from which doors gave access to two small bedrooms and the kitchen. Still pallid from the shock of what had happened and the sight of the man killed by Nigger, Zee was already at work in the latter and from it emerged the mouth-watering smell of the food she was cooking. Bringing in a steaming coffeepot and cups, she placed them on the table as the men sat down. Then, remarking that some folks had more to do than spend their time jawing, she returned to her task.

'What's doing, Jebediah?' the Kid asked, rolling a cigarette filled with Bull Durham after refusing an invitation to help himself to the old timer's black shag tobacco.

'Like I said, I'm damned if I know,' Minns replied, lighting up his pipe. 'Zee 'n' me don't mix much with folks hereabouts. Never have, but we never had no fuss with anybody, neither. 'Cepting for fellers's come to do some hunting, the High Rim and the rivers keep folks from passing through or their stock straying over. So nobody ever used to worry about us having Whip around.'

'What's made 'em start?' the Kid inquired, glancing to where the wolf was laying outside the open front door showing no inclination to enter the building.

'There's been a couple of cows and a hoss or two pulled down just recent. Word has it, by a wolf.'

'Just *one* wolf?'

'That's the way the sign's read every time Jack Tremayne tells me.'

'Can he read it real good?' the Kid wanted to know, recollecting that the man in question was the deputy sheriff for the area and being aware of the skill which would be required to make such a pronouncement.

'Not's good's you-all, what I hear be true,' Minns replied. 'But he's been a hunting man for long enough to know the difference 'tween a wolf, b'ar, or cougar kill and he allows they warn't done by neither of the last two.'

'Why didn't he ask you-all to take a look?'

'He *did* at the last 'n' and I'd swear it was a wolf's work. But if there was a whole blasted pack, I sure's hell's for sinners couldn't cut their sign. Was only the one *big* son-of-a-bitch.'

'And you never saw hide nor hair of him?' the Kid guessed, looking at Whip once more and deciding he had rarely seen such a large representative of its species.

'Lost its trail on the stage trail,' Minns confessed. 'Which's what happened every time Jack Tremayne followed up after a killing.'

'Where at's this trail?' the Kid inquired, noticing the way in which the old timer had mentioned it.

'Just on t'other side of Wide Creek,' Minns replied, with a hint of defiance and challenge.

'Are there many wolves around?' the Kid asked, refraining from posing the question he sensed his host was expecting.

'Ain't been none hereabouts since Zee 'n' me cleaned out what of 'em's didn't get took by the poison along of Whip's momma,' Minns asserted. 'And, afore you ask, no there weren't no tracks from the trail to the Creek.'

'What I was going to ask is how's that rancher feel about losing his stock. Mean enough to maybe hire somebody to run you-all off and Whip along of you?'

'That wouldn't be Dick Keys' way, even was it his stock's's been took,' the old timer declared. 'They's been milk cows and harness hosses belonging to the sod-busters across Wide Creek. His range's over the Sand River and's not been touched. Which make the whole damned thing all the more pee-culiar. Maybe they ain't so close together they're farming fence to fence over there, but there's been enough of 'em around for years to've killed or run off every wolf and other kind of wild varmint way back. Fact being, 'cepting for coyotes 'n' chicken-hawks, this's the first trouble they've had from stock killers of any kind in a whole slew of years.'

'How're they taking it now it's started happening?'

'Some of 'em reckons it must be Whip's's doing it, him being the only wolf they *know* to be around, 'cording to what Jack says,' Minns answered, not troubling to conceal his anger. 'Damn it! He *never* goes off our range!'

'Not even when you and Zee go to town?' the Kid challenged.

'Not even then!' the old man stated emphatically. 'We taught him right off from the start to stay on this side of Wide Creek and Sand River where he's safe. Why, god damn it, more'n once he's been running so close behind a whitetail he could have licked its butt. But, when it took to swimming over one or t'other to get away, he quit and come back without needing telling. I tell you-all, young Ysabel, whatever damned wolf's doing the killing, it sure's hell isn't Whip.'

***** *****

'Well I'll be damned if I *believe* it!' ejaculated the burly young man clad in patched bib-overalls, but without a shirt. He was standing alongside a bale of hay in which was stuck a pitchfork and glaring truculently to where Zee Minns was entering through the side door of Sangster's Wide Creek Livery Barn accompanied by the Ysabel Kid. 'I'd never've thought's how even *you'd* have the son-of-a-bitching gall to come into town today of *all* "something" days.'[6]

'What do you mean, Tod Grinsgrave?' the girl inquired, her attitude showing she had no liking for the foul-mouthed speaker.

The time was almost twelve o'clock on the morning after the Kid's meeting with Zee, her grandfather and their unusual pet.

Although the girl and Minns had been inclined to doubt the Texan's suggestion that the mysterious killing of the farmers' stock might supply the motive for the attempted destruction of their property, they had agreed it was advisable to delay informing the local peace officer of the incident in case the dead men's companion should return with assistance and try to carry out the interrupted task. This had not happened and, after some

---

[6] The author realizes that in our present 'permissive' society, he could employ the exact obscenity. However, although some contemporary writers feel such usage is an aid to 'realism'—and, perhaps, a way in which to boost their sales—he can see no valid reason why *anybody* should consider it necessary to do so.

more inconclusive discussion, the evening had passed pleasantly with the old timer reminiscing about the days prior to the visitor's birth when he had known Big Sam Ysabel and Chief Long Walker. He had described so many humorously disreputable episodes that the Kid had stated it was now obvious why he had had to quit Texas.

Despite the night having passed without disturbance, Minns had taken the precaution of remaining to guard the cabin while the Kid was escorting his granddaughter to report the incident. The wolf had accompanied them on the first part of the journey, but the Texan had noticed it turned back without requiring orders on reaching the bank of Wide Creek. Announcing that there was no easier way to cross, the girl had led the way over. The water had been deep enough to make them remove their feet from the stirrup irons and raise their legs to horizontal, but their riding skill had allowed them to arrive on the other side without getting wet. Then, following the well used stagecoach trail upon which the stock killer's tracks had disappeared, they had made their way to the town. Instead of going in search of Tremayne immediately, they had stopped at the livery barn so Zee could deliver a message to its owner.

'You *something*-well know what I mean!' the young man stated. 'That god-damned wolf of your'n's been and close to killed Old Man Templer.'

'Whip *never* did!' Zee gasped.

'There ain't no other son-of-a-bitching wolf around!' Grinsgrave declared. 'And when we get through with the *something*——!'

'How about keeping your talk clean around the lady?' the Kid suggested in a polite voice. Although he had left the bed roll strapped to the stallion's saddle, he had drawn his rifle without thinking of it and now held it in both hands at arms' length in front of him. 'I don't reckon she's any too took by it.'

'Just who the *something* hell asked you to bill in?' Grinsgrave challenged, running his gaze at first warily over the black dressed Texan and then with growing contempt as he began to draw more than one erroneous conclusion.

Having acquired a reputation which gave him the opinion that he was irresistible to every member of the opposite sex, the young man had never forgotten nor forgiven Zee for the painful rebuff he received when he had tried to force his attentions upon her. Having heard she was approaching and hoping she would visit the barn, he had made preparations to give her a suitable reception. He had had momentary qualms on seeing she was not entering alone, but his examination of the Kid's youthful and apparently innocent appearance had led him to assume, despite the rifle, he had nothing to fear in that direction.

Grinsgrave believed that the Winchester was being carried merely to try to make its owner look older and tougher. What was more, there was an excellent reason why it could not be brought into use. Not only had two of his most reliable bosom companions brought the news that the girl was coming, they had expressed their willingness to help him teach her a lesson. On his orders, they had taken up positions on either side of the door through which she and the Texan entered and were now advancing silently so as to grab hold of the unsuspecting victims. While neither could match him in size, bulk or fighting ability, the instigator of the scheme was satisfied that they could do all that was necessary. Chuck would prevent the girl from escaping and Stymie could take care of the skinny 'cowhand' if he tried to intervene.

There were two major flaws to Grinsgrave's line of thinking. The Kid was not unaware of Chuck and Stymie's presence. Nor was he as harmless and unprepared as he appeared to be.

Ever alert, although he had given no sign, the black dressed Texan had noticed the lurking pair as he walked by. From their demeanour and the similarity between their clothing and that of Grinsgrave, he had deduced they were not there purely by chance. Nor was their approach as noiseless as they imagined and he was able to tell how close they were without needing to look around.

'She's billed in and staying there,' the Kid affirmed, sounding as meek and looking as angelically innocent as a freshly scrubbed choirboy hoping to get a prize for good behaviour when he knew his conduct did not merit it.

'We'll see about that!' Grinsgrave warned, nodding a signal

to his supporters.

Already in position, Chuck immediately caught Zee by the shoulders from behind. Just too late, he realized that Stymie had not moved as quickly and was still out of reaching distance of the Texan. Taking comfort in the thought that his friend was starting to rectify the situation, he noticed something which caused him to revise his plans.

Lunging forward so as to get to grips with what he believed to be an unsuspecting victim, Stymie received disillusionment and shock. The face which turned to confront him before his hands could take hold was no longer babyishly innocent. Rather he was reminded of paintings he had seen of blood-thirsty Indian warriors, such was the savagery acquired by the features which met his startled gaze. Even as his mind was trying to assimilate the change, the butt of the Winchester was swung to catch him in the *solar plexus* with considerable force. An agonized croak burst from him and, doubling over at the waist, he stumbled away to collapse winded and helpless.

Shoving the girl away from him, Chuck leapt towards his cousin's assailant. He met with no greater success. Turning and stepping to meet him, the Kid reversed the direction of the still horizontal rifle. Its muzzle took Chuck in the pit of the stomach to produce an identical effect to that inflicted upon Stymie.

Seeing first one and then the other of his supporters being felled, Grinsgrave had no doubt that he would be next to receive the attentions of their intended victim. Possessed of a bullying nature, he had also a strong sense of self-preservation. So, snatching up the pitchfork, he rushed across the barn in the manner of a soldier launching a bayonet charge. Coming into striking distance, he drove the double tines ahead, in an upwards swing aimed more by luck than intention for the Texan's throat.

Once again, the Kid responded like the Comanche warrior his face now resembled. Fetching up the rifle before him, he hooked it beneath and elevated the pitchfork with a surging heave. Disengaging it, he brought it around to propel the butt plate against the side of his attacker's jaw before any parry could be attempted. Changing direction under the impulsion of the blow, Grinsgrave was sent sprawling face down and barely conscious to the floor.

'Well now,' Zee commented, looking from one to the other recumbent figures. 'It couldn't've happened to three more deserving fellers.'

'Likely,' the Kid repeated. 'Only I reckon, what that foul-mouthed knob-head was saying, the sooner we find the deputy the better.'

*****   *****

'There's no doubt about it this time!' said the tallest and oldest of the men wearing the attire of farmers who were present as Zee and the Kid arrived at the open door of the town's small jail. 'It *was* a wolf!'

'I'm not gainsaying it,' Deputy Sheriff Jack Tremayne replied. 'This, or any of the other times.'

'Then when're you going to do something about it?' demanded another of the group and there was a general rumble of agreement.

'As soon as I can track it down,' the peace officer replied evenly, showing no concern over being confronted by an indignant deputation comprising influential members of the community and area for which he was responsible.

'You can easy enough do *that*!' the second speaker stated and, anticipating what was coming next, the Kid caught the girl by the arm to prevent her from entering. 'Just go over Wide Creek and call on the Minnses.'

Having seen and recognized Zee's dun gelding, the owner of the livery barn had come from his house to let her know the latest news. His only comment over the fate of the three young men had been that it was time somebody handed them their needings. Then he had warned her about the reaction of the local lodge of the Grange[7] to the latest attack. For the first time, a human being had been the victim and, as he was a member of the lodge, its leaders were in town to demand Tremayne took whatever steps were necessary to remove the menace. Leaving

[7] The Grange: the alternative name for the order of Patrons of Husbandry, a nation-wide association of farmers, founded in 1867, for the furtherance of agricultural interests.

their mounts in the owner's care and receiving his assurance that he would attend to the trio of trouble-causers, the girl and the Kid set off on foot to find out what was happening.

'And if you haven't a mind to there's those of us who *will*,' went on another farmer, whose facial resemblance stemmed from being Tod Grinsgrave's father and who possessed a similar nature.

'That would be *most* inadvisable, gentlemen,' a well-modulated voice with a Boston accent warned and every gaze turned to the speaker. Of medum height, inclined to corpulence and with bland, sun-reddened features, he was dressed in a brown suit of excellent style and cut, a white shirt and a flowing blue silk cravat embellished by a good-sized diamond stickpin. 'Doing so would constitute trespass and any attempt to injure Mr. Minns' person could legally be restricted by force.'

'It's all damned fine for you to go spouting the legal law at us, Councillor Netherhyde!' Joseph Grinsgrave protested, noticing that—although the speaker was a comparative newcomer to the area—the other men appeared to consider the comment was worth heeding. 'But it's us farmers's're suffering because of that god-damned wolf!'

'I own a farm, too,' the bland-faced man pointed out. 'And it was I who suffered the first loss, if you remember.'

'I mind that,' Grinsgrave conceded grudgingly, hearing his colleagues muttering concurrence. 'Only surely us folks've a legal right to defend our own?'

'You have,' the lawyer confirmed. 'But so has Mr. Minns.'

'That being so,' Grinsgrave growled, 'somebody ought to go out to his place and tell him he's got to get rid of that damned wolf, or else——'

'Somebody maybe had just that same notion yesterday,' the Kid announced, having contrived to keep the increasingly indignant girl quiet so far but knowing her temper was rapidly reaching boiling point. Releasing her arm, he strolled into the office continuing, 'Trouble was, they figured to do the "or else" without even telling him about it.'

All eyes turned to the Texan and there was suspicion, if not open antipathy, in most of them. To many members of the

Grange, anybody connected with the ranching business was an anathema and his appearance left little doubt that he came into that category. Being aware of this, he had considered it tactful to leave his rifle in its boot on the white's saddle.

'What do you mean?' Tremayne asked, studying the newcomer with a range-wise gaze and then darting a look at the clearly angry girl who was following him.

About five foot ten, lean, tanned and wearing range clothes, there was an air of calm, stand-no-nonsense, competence about the peace officer which appealed to the Kid. According to what Zee and her grandfather had said, he was liked and respected by the people in his jurisdiction. It was his firm and fair dealing which reduced friction between the local cowhands and farmers to a negligible level.

'Come on three *hombres* fixing to turn loose their hosses and set fire to their cabin,' the Texan drawled, coming to a halt in front of the deputy's desk and ignoring the scowls being directed at him by some of the office's other occupants. 'Two're still out there.'

'Dead?' Tremayne said, closer to a statement than a question.

'They wound up that way,' the Kid confirmed.

'Did that god-damned wolf kill 'em?' Grinsgrave demanded truculently.

'Did it?' the deputy repeated, when the Texan showed no sign of answering the farmer.

'Nope, I downed one,' the Kid replied. 'And, seeing the other was fixing to gun me down, my ole Nigger hoss did what he figured he had the legal right to do.'

'What'd that be?' Grinsgrave challenged, but a touch apprehensively, perturbed by the sardonic glint in the eyes of a face which he had at first thought to be young and innocently trying to impress those present with a non-existent toughness.

'Stomped him clean to death,' the Kid explained, with no more apparent concern than if he had been commenting upon the weather. 'What else?'

'Who were they, Zee?' Tremayne asked, paying no discernible attention to the startled exclamations which had been elicited by the Texan's unemotional sounding statement.

'I don't know,' the girl confessed, stiffening a trifle as she found herself the centre of attraction for the first time since coming into the office. 'But it wasn't nobody's I've seen here-abouts.'

'I couldn't go so far's to put a brand on any of them,' the Kid supplemented, having watched the various responses to his deliberately callous comment. 'Nor come up with any take-before-the-judge proof's Cap'n Dusty Fog expected to be given when I was wearing a deputy marshal's badge under him over at Mulrooney. But, was I asked, I'd have to come right out 'n' admit honest's I reckon they was all hired guns.'

'*Hired guns?*' Grinsgrave repeated, swinging his gaze around the other members of the Grange as if searching for some indication of who had been the employer.

'Seeing's how you wore a badge under Cap'n Fog,' Tremayne remarked, ignoring the farmer as was the Texan, 'I'd say's that'd make you the Ysabel Kid.'

'Shucks, that's not so hard to figure,' the Kid objected with a grin. 'I'd *have* to be. I'm better looking 'n' Mark Counter, older 'n' smarter 'n' Waco and don't reckon anybody'd take me for a professional gambling man, which I couldn't be Frank Der-ringer.'

'I don't suppose those two'd anything on 'em to say who they were hired by?' the deputy stated rather than asked, being aware —as was almost everybody else present—that the men whose names had been mentioned had also served as deputy town marshals under the Rio Hondo gun wizard in the trail end town of Mulrooney.

'They wasn't what I'd call first pick of the *remuda*,' the Kid replied. 'But they was good enough to've knowed better'n that. One who lit out was headed this way, 'cording to the sign he left, though.'

'How come you was with the Minnses?' Grinsgrave interjected, making the words sound like an accusation.

'I can't see your *badge*, mister,' the Kid remarked, in a decep-tively mild tone.

'I don't have one,' Grinsgrave pointed out, unsure certainly of what to make of the reply.

'Then wait until *after* you've been elected and given one,' the Texan said and there was no doubt that the words were an order. 'Which happens, I'll tell you.'

'How did it come about, Kid?' Tremayne inquired, as Grinsgrave took a hurried pace to rear away from the suddenly savage and dangerous looking young man.

'Was passing through the Triangle on my way here when I met up with Zee and her grandpappy,' the Texan obliged without hesitation, his attitude markedly different from when dealing with the farmer. 'And I'll swan if it didn't come out's how him 'n' my daddy used to be *amigoes* back 'fore I was born. So they asked me to visit a whiles with them. Only, when we got to their place, those three yahoos was already on hand and we concluded to stop 'em.' His gaze swung to the lawyer, who was still frowning in the puzzled fashion which had replaced the bland expression on hearing of how the stallion's victim had died. 'Happen you-all'll oblige, Councillor, did ole Nigger have the legal law's right to stomp that *hombre*'s was fixing to shoot me?'

'I can't bring a precedent to mind off hand,' Netherhyde admitted didactically, making a noticeable effort to compose his features as every eye turned towards him. 'But I doubt whether any court of law would demand the execution of an animal which killed a human being in defence of its owner. As long as there was proof that such an extreme measure was necessary that is.'

'Anybody's says there wasn't'd be a god-damned liar,' the Kid asserted, glancing at Grinsgrave and his attitude making it plain that he would take grave exception to such an implication. ' 'Nother thing. Whip couldn't've chomped that gent last night. He was moving around outside the cabin all the time.'

'Did you *see* him?' Tremayne inquired, showing no concern over the possibility that the question might be construed as doubting the declaration.

'More'n once,' the Texan answered, showing no offence. 'My ole Nigger hoss ain't used to have a buffalo wolf close by and woke me to let me know about it four or five times.'

'Then there must be another wolf around,' announced the man who had been speaking when Zee and the Kid arrived.

'Does it have to be a *wolf*?' the Texan drawled and, quietly as he spoke, the words brought to an end the various conversations which had started.

'What do you say, Jack?' the speaker asked, remembering how members of the Grange's Mulrooney lodge had frequently commented upon the ability and impartiality of Dusty Fog and his deputies. A fair minded man, he wanted to get at the truth and had never been entirely convinced that the Minns family's unconventional pet was the attacker of the animals and, most recently, a human being. 'Could it be something else?'

'Old Man Templer hasn't been able to talk yet,' the deputy replied. 'But the way he was chawed up makes it look that way. Why'd you reckon it wouldn't be, Kid?'

'Way I was allus taught, a wolf's a knowing critter,' the Texan explained and, apart from Grinsgrave's pretended indifference, he had the attention of every other person present. 'It knows it don't have the heft and strength of a bear, nor teeth 'n' claws's'll kill like a cougar's. So, unless it's got help, it don't go up against anything bigger'n itself. Which's how a harness hoss and even a tamed-down milk cow'd strike it's being.'

'Not even if it was *real* hungry?' Grinsgrave suggested, but realized as he was speaking that he might be weakening the point he was hoping to make.

'One'd have to get a whole slew hungrier than Whip ever did afore he'd go after anything big and then only was it hurt so bad it couldn't fight back,' the Kid countered and, although she had had the good sense to let him do all the talking, Zee nodded confirmation as he continued, 'Which, from all I've heard 'n' seen, they keep him fed real good.'

'But, if it *isn't* a wolf, young man,' Netherhyde put in, 'what *is* it?'

'That I wouldn't want to say, Councillor,' the Kid confessed, then went on in tones of grim determination, 'but, happen Deputy Tremayne and the rest of you gents don't object, I'm sure's sin's for sale in Cowtown[8] going to see if I can find out.'

*****   *****

[8] 'Cowtown': the colloquial name for Fort Worth, Tarrant County, Texas.

'Could be that's him,' the Texan remarked, as he stood in the darkness with the peace officer and Jebediah Minns, looking in the direction from which the howl of a wolf was originating.

Having gained permission for the Kid's offer to be accepted, Tremayne had brought the meeting to an end with a statement that he wanted to go and collect the two corpses. On the way to the livery barn, Zee had told him of the disturbance that had taken place there. Having had to warn Tod Grinsgrave previously for similar behaviour, he had promised to ensure there would be no attempts at reprisals. The three young men had not been present for this to be done, so he had accompanied the girl and the Kid to the Triangle without waiting to find them.

Despite feeling certain he had been told the truth, Tremayne had confirmed it by looking at the slightly charred wall of the cabin, the torch used to start the fire and the empty kerosene can. The latter bore a label which suggested it had been purchased in Mulrooney and not from the general store at Wide Creek, not that he had been surprised by the discovery. Being a conscientious peace officer, he always kept an eye open for strangers—especially those whose coming might presage trouble —in the area under his jurisdiction. On examining the two dead men, he had decided that he had never seen either of them before.

With the preliminaries attended to, the deputy had resumed the discussion of wolves and their habits he and the Kid had had during the journey. Finding that Minns confirmed the information he had received and supported the theory they had formulated, he had agreed to the plan for establishing Whip's innocence which was proposed by the Texan.

Leaving a clearly disappointed Zee to keep watch on the property, Minns had made the return journey with the Kid and Tremayne. They had timed their arrival in the vicinity of Wide Creek after night had fallen. The old timer had waited outside the town while his companions entered and no mention was made of his presence. Establishing that he intended to go in search of the wolf immediately, the Texan had rejoined Minns. Later, having given the impression that he meant to leave the hunting to the Kid, Tremayne had contrived to slip away unnoticed and completed the party. Although the darkness restricted their range of vision, they had waited on a hill which would have offered a view of a good section of the surrounding district during the daytime and hoped they would receive some indication of where to concentrate their efforts.

It had come at shortly after two o'clock in the morning.

'Out in the woodland back of Grinsgrave's place,' Tremayne estimated and, as Minns nodded agreement, went on, 'Only this's the first time I've heard the son-of-a-bitch howl.'

'Has to be a first time for *everything*,' the Kid drawled, sounding laconic to the point of disinterest. 'Anyways, it's given me a place to start looking. I just hope nobody else takes the notion to do it.'

'They won't,' Tremayne asserted. 'The Grange has passed word for everybody to leave it to you. They said you warned them you'd be likely to throw lead first and find out what at after, seeing it's already jumped one man.'

'I figured it's work,' the Kid answered, his teeth gleaming as he grinned. 'I'll be a mite more careful than that, but I don't reckon any of them'd expect it.'

'We could go all the way with you,' Minns hinted, although he was aware that this would be deviating from the plan they had conceived.

'It's a one man chore,' the Kid replied, swinging astride his stallion. 'That critter won't come near, is there more than one. Which's what I want him to do.'

'We'll play it your way,' the deputy promised and, being aware that the scheme might be the only chance of proving Whip was not to blame, the old timer did not argue as he continued, 'Let's get going.'

Riding in the direction from which the wolf was continuing to announce its presence, the trio arrived at the Grinsgrave farm just in time to see the father and son about to set off after it. Ordering them to return to their home, Tremayne ended their objections by telling them what he thought of Tod's behaviour at the livery barn the previous morning and warning that he would not overlook anything similar in the future.

Satisfied that the deputy could prevent any interference from the Grinsgraves, the Kid dismounted. He had concluded, from the description of the area he had been given on the way, that hunting on horseback would be impractical. What was more, he felt the rifle would be more of a liability than an asset under the circumstances. So, leaving it behind with the stallion, he walked off to put his theory to the test.

Before the Kid had gone a hundred yards into the woodland, in addition to noticing that the howling appeared to be coming from the same place, he considered he had made the right decision over the way he had elected to conduct the hunt. However, if any of the other members of the Floating Outfit had been present, they would have been surprised by his behaviour. Usually when after such a wary quarry as the wolf could be expected to be, he would have moved in almost complete silence despite the thickness of the undergrowth. Although he was far from noisy, he appeared to be less careful than the situation should have warranted. Not only did he brush against bushes and cause an audible rustling of the foliage on three occasions, once he stepped on a dry twig which broke with a sharp crack.

For all his apparent carelessness, the black dressed Texan was as alert as always. Even while the howling suggested that the wolf was some distance ahead, his eyes probed the gloom around him constantly and his ears never ceased seeking to pick up any warning sound however small it might be. What was more, as the distance decreased, he had taken out his Colt and, having eased the hammer back to fully cocked, was carrying it in his right hand ready to be used if the need arose.

Estimating that he was getting close to his quarry, although it had been silent for the past few minutes, the Kid found he was entering a small clearing. Once more, he had cause to be thankful for his keen and *Pehnane*-educated senses. Even as he thought he detected a slight movement the other side, they alerted him to something much closer. It was only a slight rustling from among the bushes to his left, but he guessed no small and harmless creature disturbed by his passing was the cause.

Swinging around rapidly, the Kid heard a sound such as might be made by blowing a puff of air into a bottle and felt something stick into the knot of his tightly rolled bandana without passing all the way through. There was no time for him to ponder on either. Bringing the Dragoon to waist level and pointing it by instinctive alignment, he grasped the butt in both hands to control the heavy recoil which he knew would come when he started firing. Closing his eyes to prevent himself from being dazzled by the muzzle blast, he began to shoot as swiftly as he could manage while turning the weapon slightly as each successive bullet left it.

After the third chamber's load was detonated, a human cry of pain gave testimony to how effective the Kid's tactics had proved. However, unable to prevent himself from firing again, he discovered that he had not removed the entire threat to his life. A voice from the other side of the clearing said something that sounded like, 'Angry',[9] the single word being followed first by a savage growl and then the sound of rapidly approaching animal and human feet.

The Kid's precaution of avoiding having his eyes subjected to the red glare emitted each time he fired paid a dividend. Turning and hoping he had inflicted an incapacitating wound on the person lurking in the bushes, there was sufficient light for him to be able to estimate the extent of his latest peril. Racing towards him was an enormous wolf-like creature. Behind it, moving less swiftly, came a big and burly man.

Faced with evidence of such danger, a less capable fighting man than the Kid might have made the mistake of trying to shoot the animal. He realized that to do so at such a comparatively small and fast moving target would be more likely to result in a miss than a hit. Either way, it would have the effect of destroying the night vision he had preserved while firing the four shots. So he let the Colt fall from his hands and sent the right flashing across to whip the knife from its sheath.

The conclusion had not been drawn and acted upon a moment too soon!

Already, giving an awesome roaring snarl, the big animal was leaving the ground in a spring which had the throat as its target.

Moving with lightning fast, yet unflustered speed, the Kid

[9] The author believes the word was '*angriff*', German for 'attack'.

106

took a long step to his left. Ignoring the click of the attacking animal's powerful jaws snapping together, he brought out the knife and swung it upwards to the right. Rotating his hands until the knuckles were directed downwards, he delivered a slash to the throat of the passing beast. What started as a yelp of agony was ended abruptly as the blade, no less sharp than many a barber's well-stropped razor, sliced without apparent effort through the windpipe, veins and arteries of the neck. Going down in a sprawling crash, the stricken animal thrashed spasmodically and briefly on the ground until claimed by death.

A bellow of rage rang out, giving the Kid an unneeded warning that the affair was not yet concluded. Sparing not so much as a backwards glance at the animal whose attack he had thwarted, he sprang to meet the third and, he hoped, last of his assailants. Nor did he consider the huge figure lumbering towards him would prove the least dangerous of them.

Spluttering what—although unable to understand the words —the Texan guessed to be curses, possibly in German, the man was reaching towards the waistband of his trousers with his right hand. Without waiting to discover what kind of weapon—or even if any—was there, the Kid set about countering the threat. In the heat of the moment, all traces of his white upbringing were gone and his response was that of a *Pehnane* Dog Soldier.

Out drove the huge knife in something approaching a classic fencing lunge. The clip point sank into the man's bulky body just above the hand that had grasped the butt of the Army Colt thrust into the trousers' waistband. Combined with his onwards momentum, the force with which the blow was struck sank the blade into his vital organs. Then it was ripped across and out.

'*Aieee!*' the Kid ejaculated instinctively, as he weaved aside to let his disembowelled would-be assailant blunder by to collapse across the body of the animal which had also fallen victim to his skill in wielding the James Black bowie knife.

Having given the traditional Comanche coup cry, 'I claim it', the Kid's instincts as a white man regained the upper hand. Reaching up, he felt at the slender piece of wood that was still sticking in the knot of the bandana. Guessing what it might be, he drew it out carefully. Dropping it near the two bodies, so

107

that he would be able to find it later, he walked towards where he could hear his first attacker groaning piteously amongst the bushes.

***** *****

Jasper Netherhyde, Attorney-At-Law, knew he was dying as he lay supine in the clearing not far from his two already dead accomplices. He had read his fate in the faces of the Ysabel Kid, who had been responsible for it, Jebediah Minns and Deputy Sheriff Tremayne as they were examining his wound in the light of the lanterns brought by the latter pair. So, as he was answering their questions, he was silently cursing the reason for his predicament.

Learning the route over which a spur line from the intercontinental railroad was to be built, Netherhyde had set out to make all the profit he could from his knowledge. Nor had he been content with the price which he could expect for the farm he had acquired. His examination of the region had convinced him that one of the most valuable properties would be the Triangle. Unfortunately, nothing he had seen and heard of the Minns family had led him to assume they would be willing to sell of their own volition. Nor would they be easy to compel and had a number of friends, including the local deputy sheriff, who would support them if conventional methods of inducement should be employed. However, the wolf they had as a pet had suggested a means by which they might be driven out. A client he had once defended sucessfully had what was needed to bring this about.

On being contacted, the man had arrived and secretly brought his large, well-trained and exceptionally savage German shepherd dog.[10] When told what was wanted of them, he had warned that—despite its size—the dog would have the greatest difficulty in pulling down and killing a full grown horse or cow. Not only had the lawyer anticipated this problem, he had the means and knowledge to deal with it. During a visit he had

---

[10] For the benefit of British readers, the German shepherd dog is what you call the Alsatian. The change of name was made when the breed began to grow popular in the 1920s as breeders believed the anti-German feelings aroused by World War 1 might have an adverse effect if 'German shepherd dog' was used.

108

made to Brazil a few years earlier, he had seen Indians using blowguns and poisonous darts. Manufacturing the necessary equipment, he had obtained a supply of *curare* from a criminal acquaintance who was sufficiently influential and deeply in his debt to procure it. When injected on the tip of the dart, the substance took effect quickly. Relaxing the 'end plates' between the nerves and muscles, it caused the victim to become lethargic as the heart and lungs were prevented from functioning. Before death from asphyxiation could result, the dog would be able to do sufficient damage to make it appear that the mauling was the cause.

Having satisfied himself that the scheme would work, by experimenting with one of his own cows, Netherhyde had put it into operation. After sending the dog in to attack its poisoned victim from a distance, the man had set out for the stagecoach trail and signalled for it to follow using a whistle pitched too high for it to be detected by the human ear. When the deaths of the animals failed to arouse public opinion sufficiently, the lawyer had decided to use human victims.

As the man had claimed his dog could easily cope with the first human being to be selected, Netherhyde had not used the poison. From what he had heard later, Old Man Templer had either fainted or been knocked unconscious and, when he became motionless, the dog had ceased to maul him. Although he had survived, it had at first seemed this would be advantageous as he was sure to state he had been attacked by a wolf when he was able to be questioned. Before this could happen, the Kid's arrival had produced a very disturbing element. Not only had he threatened the success of the scheme, by offering proof that the Minns family's pet was not the culprit and suggesting there was no wolf of any kind involved, his report on the attempted destruction of their property implied somebody else knew of the spur line and was trying to gain control of the Triangle.[11]

Impressed by the young Texan's acumen, the lawyer had

[11] Deputy Sheriff Tremayne's investigations subsequently established that Jasper Netherhyde's suspicions were correct and procured the arrest of the man who had hired the would-be arsonists. He was a senior employee of the railroad and also hoped to cash in on the information he had aquired.

decided he must be removed. On hearing that the hunt for the genuine culprit was to be commenced that night and believing it was to be carried out alone, Netherhyde had considered he was being offered an ideal opportunity to attain his ends. Knowing the terrain, he had selected what he had felt was the most suitable spot in which to lure his victim to be ambushed. Although the Kid had arrived there, everything else had gone completely wrong.

To add to the lawyer's mortification, he was to discover that the one ploy of which he had been especially proud, and had assumed it at least had worked properly, had actually failed as miserably as the rest. In fact, it had been a major contributory factor to the distaster which had befallen him.

'Shucks, I knowed from the start it wasn't no wolf, nor other kind of four-legged critter doing the howling,' the Kid declared, when Netherhyde finished boasting of the skilled impersonation which had 'lured' him to the clearing. 'You're pretty good, I'll grant, but I was raised and taught's a Comanche wolf scout and we signalled with them sort of calls all the time. First thing we learn is how to tell them from the real thing.'

'So you knew about me all along?' Netherhyde asked bitterly.

'Guessed what you was up to,' the Kid answered, 'but not who was behind it. Which we figured we could smoke out whoever it was.'

'And we did,' Minns went on. 'I'll tell you something else, Councillor. When that god-damned spur line comes, folks'll be swarming hereabouts like fleas to a hound dog. Neither Zee, me, nor Whip take kind to that. Happen you'd've come along all straightforward and honest 'n' told us, then made us a decent offer, we'd've sold you-all the Triangle without any of this needing to've happened.'

'You *would*?' the lawyer gasped, hardly able to believe his ears.

'Why sure,' the old man confirmed. 'Like Lon allowed, a wolf's a knowing critter. It knows when folks come in, it's time for him to get out. Zee 'n' me, we've been around Whip so long, we sort of figure the same way's him.'

PART FOUR

Ole Devil Hardin in

MR. COLT'S REVOLVING CYLINDER PISTOL

As I mentioned in the Introduction to Part One, supplying Dusty Fog with his background and specialized abilities called for the creation of various other members of the Hardin, Fog and Blaze clan, with Tommy Okasi being required to explain how he could have learned ju-jitsu *and* karate. *However, despite the important parts they played in making the small Texan such an effective fighting man and leader, neither General Jackson Baines 'Ole Devil' Hardin[1] nor his Japanese 'valet'[2] took any active part in the saga of the OD Connected's Floating Outfit until the series was well under way. They were merely mentioned in* Trail Boss *and made their first brief appearances in Part Two, 'Cousin Red's Big Chance' of* The Hard Riders. *Their earliest major contributions appeared in* The Fastest Gun in Texas, *of which Part Three ('The Paint') told how Ole Devil was crippled.*

Being confined to a wheelchair precluded the General from playing more than a supporting role in the Floating Outfit series, but his career began to gain impetus with the commencement of the Civil War series. Tommy had to wait even longer before he was allowed to come into his own. In fact, prior to the commencement of the Ole Devil Hardin series, his only brief active participation had been demonstrating his skill at tameshiwari—*breaking stone or wood with the bare hands and feet—in* Sidewinder.

Keeping up their tradition of finding me employment, various of my readers had asked for details of the General's and Tommy's

[1] For the benefit of new readers: details of General Jackson Baines 'Ole Devil' Hardin's background and special qualifications are given in Appendix Five.

[2] For the benefit of new readers: details of Tommy Okasi's background and special qualifications are given in Appendix Six.

young days. With that in mind, I began to do research into the Texians[3] struggle for independence from Mexican rule. As a further inducement, I had been involved in an abortive attempt to create a television series about an Englishman who was shipwrecked in Japan during the Seventeenth Century and became a samurai warrior. This had entailed gathering information about samurai fighting equipment and techniques which had subsequently been lying fallow.

As with what developed into the Calamity Jane series, I originally only planned the one volume, Young Ole Devil. *It was to have covered the collection of a consignment of caplock rifles and ammunition, the withdrawal of the Texians before the superior numbers of the Mexican armies and how the weapons helped turn the tide during the decisive Battle of San Jacinto. When I started writing, I found I had far too much material available for it all to fit into* Young Ole Devil. *For one thing, Tommy must at last be able to demonstrate various aspects of his samurai training which had hitherto gone unrecorded. So the plot expanded until there were five volumes in the series. I am now contemplating adding to it, but memories of* Doc Leroy, M.D. *(see the Introduction to Part Six,* Waco*) warn me not to go into further detail, particularly where mentioning the proposed title of the next episode is concerned.*

Thinking of the General's reaction to the report of Red Blaze's activities in Cousin Red's Big Chance *supplied me with the clue as to his character when younger. He was far from the uncompromising, hide-bound martinet he appeared on the surface during his later years. In fact, he could sympathize with Red as he had had his moments of impetuous recklessness in his youth. However, as he was older and more mature than Red during the Texas War Of Independence, the various scrapes in which he became involved were deliberately planned rather than occurring by accident. Tommy also displayed qualities far removed from the loyal, devoted valet and personal attendant he was portrayed as being in the Civil War and Floating Outfit series. So I explained*

---

[3] For the benefit of new readers: a Texian was an Anglo-U.S. born citizen of Texas, the 'i' being dropped from usage following the Mexican War of 1846–48

112

why he was willing to accept the pacific and comparatively minor role in later years instead of continuing his career as a fighting man. Doing this was attracting too much attention to him. With the ever increasing contact between the Western Hemisphere and his homeland—which he had been obliged to leave hurriedly—he had considered it advisable to seek the anonymity offered by acting in the capacity of a servant.

Here then is Ole Devil Hardin's and Tommy Okasi's participation in this volume.

MR. COLT'S REVOLVING CYLINDER PISTOL

Being roughly half way along the main trail from the United States' border to Austin, which had been selected as the capital city of what was now the Republic of Texas, the town of Henderson had grown by leaps and bounds. Not only had it an ever increasing population, there was a continuous flow of travellers passing through. Over a year had gone by since the Battle of San Jacinto's decisive victory had brought an end to rule by Mexico. Now a rapidly multiplying throng of people were arriving to take advantage of the enormous area of free land which was available for the taking.

Not all who came wished to settle upon and work the land. Some intended to establish themselves in their respective specialized businesses and trades, or to practise their learned professions. Others arrived in search of a fresh start, or merely out of curiosity. There were, of course, those who hoped to prey upon the more gullible or less well protected of the newcomers. Being aware of the need everyone had for relaxation and alert to the possibility of earning money from what they hoped would prove a less demanding and sophisticated audience than in more civilized regions, entertainers made their way to Texas. While the majority of them rendered the traditional fare of the theatres in which they had developed their acts, a few were more enterprising and offered diversion of a more novel nature. Yet few of the latter category could present such an unusual—almost bizarre— subject as was being advertised by the large and brightly coloured posters—the venue alone being handwritten—which were fastened in prominent positions throughout Henderson on that early June evening in 1837.

114

'NITROUS OXIDE GAS!
FOR LADIES AND GENTLEMEN!

The Celebrated Dr. S. Coult of New York, London and Calcutta, respectfully informs the Ladies and Gentlemen of your fair city that he will demonstrate the administration of NITROUS OXIDE, otherwise known as Exhilirating Gas, this evening in GLADWELL'S TAVERN, commencing at:

7 o'clock precisely.

The peculiar effects of this singular compound upon the animal system was first noticed by the celebrated English Chemist, Sir Humprhey Davis. He observed that, when inhaled into the lungs, it produced the most astonishing effects upon the nervous system: that some individuals were disposed to laugh, sing, or dance; others to recitation, or declamation; and that the greater number had an irresistible propensity to muscular exertion, such as wrestling, boxing, and with innumerable fantastic feats. In short, the sensations produced by it are highly pleasurable and are not followed by any form of debility.

As Dr. Coult is a practical chemist, no fears need be entertained of inhaling an impure gas and he is willing to submit his preparations for examination by scientific gentlemen.

Tickets 50 cents at the door on the evening of the exhibition. Each ticket will admit a Gentlemen, with or without a Lady.

Dr. Coult has exhibited the extraordinary powers of the Gas in many cities of the United States, to audiences composed of Ladies and Gentlemen of the highest respectability —and many Ladies have inhaled the Gas at select Exhibitions, suffering no ill effects. Those ladies who may be anxious of witnessing the Exhibition in Gladwell's Tavern may be assured that it now embraces every accommodation for their comfort and that not a shadow of impropriety attends the Exhibition to shock the most modest.

Dr. Coult will attend, on reasonable terms, to any application for private Demonstrations to select parties of Ladies and Gentlemen, if applications be made to him following

115

tonight's Exhibition.

Dr. Coult will likewise administer the Gas *to any Gentlemen wishing to inhale it privately between the hours of 8 and 11, at 50 cents per dose. All persons inhaling the* Gas *between these hours have the privilege of admitting two to witness the effects without charge.*
DOORS WILL OPEN AT HALF PAST SIX O'CLOCK.'

Standing on the small stage which Phineas Gladwell had had erected for the benefit of entertainers who appeared in the sizeable bar-room of his Tavern, the celebrated Dr. S. Coult ran a calculating gaze over the audience which was assembling. Although as yet there were no 'Ladies' present, they appeared to be a fairly representative cross-section of the town's permanent and transient populations. Their clothing ranged from attire in the latest style to have arrived from the United States, through homespun garments of the kind to be seen in any rural community of that country, to the buckskins of the frontier and clothing derived from that worn by Mexican *vaqueroes*. One thing the majority had in common, he noticed not without interest and satisfaction, was the wearing openly of either—or both—a knife and a pistol of some kind. Another point he observed with pleasure was that their numbers were sufficient to make the evening profitable. Even if he could not persuade suitable volunteers to come up and sample the '*Gas*', his three helpers, who were mingling with them, ought to arouse sufficient interest by their antics to ensure at least two more performances. Experience had taught him that word of mouth advertising was better than the garish posters when it came to drawing a crowd.

Dr. Coult appeared surprisingly young for one whose billing implied he had practised not only in New York, but in London, England and the Indian seaport of Calcutta. Tall, slim and good looking, with fashionably long curly brown hair, he had grown a neatly trimmed moustache in an attempt to make him look older. He had on a clean white smock, opened to exhibit a frilly bosomed white silk shirt, a black cravat of the same material and yellowish-brown Nankeen trousers from the legs of which emerged well polished Hersome gaiter boots. Set out upon the small table before him were a compact set of bottles and retorts holding the ingredients required for producing the nitrous oxide gas and the hose with a funnel to go over the mouth and nose by which it was administered. All could be packed away neatly into the polished wooden box which he had prepared and were designed for giving demonstrations where there were only limited facilities. Nor could anybody refute that, by making use of their qualities for easy transportation and manipulation, he had performed his exhibitions extensively throughout the United States.

Considerable experience in the past had taught Dr. Coult to assess the kind of crowd he would be entertaining. Looking around, he decided only one of them was sufficiently out of the ordinary to be worthy of a more prolonged examination.

Sitting with a companion at a table close to the stage, the man in question was about Dr. Coult's age. He was about the same height and build, with an erect carriage which suggested military training, but it was not his physique which attracted attention. Bare-headed, he had the kind of low crowned, wide brimmed black hat which young Texians preferred to the *sombrero* of the *vaquero*—because of its Mexican connections—hanging by its *barbiquejo* chinstrap on the square-set shoulders of his open necked fringed buckskin shirt. There was nothing out of the ordinary about the rest of his attire, or armament. A tightly rolled silk bandana which was a riot of multi-hued clashing colours was knotted around his throat. He had on fawn riding breeches which ended in black Hessian boots. At the left side of his broad black waist belt hung an ivory hilted, massive knife of the kind made by the Arkansas master cutler, James Black and known as a 'bowie' in honour of its designer. On the right, its barrel slipped through a wide, slanting leather loop and butt pointing forward to be accessible for either hand, rode a ·54 calibre Manton caplock pistol. What made him so noticeable, however, was his coal black hair and features. The former was combed so that it formed what looked like a small horn over each temple. Taken with a pair of eyebrows like inverted 'V's', lean tanned cheeks, an aquiline nose, a neatly trimmed moustache and short, sharp pointed chin beard, the protuberances made his face resemble the classic portrayal of the Devil.

Some three inches shorter and a few years older, the second man had wider shoulders and a blocky build which suggested power, yet also speed of movement and agility. Tanned and clean shaven, his strong features were ruggedly handsome. A hat similar to that of his companion was dangling on the back of his chair. He too wore a fringed buckskin shirt, but his riding breeches were black and he had on Indian-made moccasins with calf-high leggings. A bowie knife was sheathed at the left side of his brown waist belt, but his caplock pistol was thrust through instead of hanging on it.

Having noticed the deference shown to the pair by the waiters, Coult concluded they were of some influence in the community. The cut of their clothing and general demeanour implied wealth and the good breeding which also could mean social prominence or connections. If this should be the case, he felt they might be worth cultivating after the exhibition.

Seeing the big, jovial-featured proprietor of the Tavern staring pointedly at him brought Coult's attention back to his present affairs. Glancing at the clock on the wall behind the bar, which had been closed at his request as a concession to the feelings of any 'Ladies' who chose to attend, he saw it was time for him to commence the exhibition. What was more, the still all male audience was showing signs of growing restless. They could be served drinks by the waiters, but not quickly enough to suit all their requirements.

One group in particular were becoming increasingly vociferous in their dissatisfaction. Six in number, they were well armed, hard faced, dirty and unshaven, wearing grubby collarless shirts and with trousers thrust hit-and-miss into the legs of heavy low heeled boots. Having studied them when they first began to grow rowdy, Coult had been puzzled by their presence. None of them had struck him as being the kind of man who would be sufficiently interested to pay out a whole fifty cents, or even a lesser sum, to attend; particularly when his posters stressed the propriety and gentility of the exhibition.

Throwing a precautionary look into the small polished mahogany box which shared the table with the equipment he would be using in the demonstration, Coult raised his hands in a signal for silence. Slowly the rumble of conversations died away and, at last, he was satisfied that he had the attention of his audience.

'Good evening, ladies and gentlemen!' Coult greeted, his voice that of a trained entertainer who was used to making himself heard throughout a large room without any artificial aids. 'It is with pleasure and pride that I see so many citizens of this fair metropolis assembled here tonight. There would not be so much interest evinced in matters scientific in less enlightened communities, but I expected nothing else from a city of Henderson's known standards of taste, culture and refinement.'

'You saying Austin don't have any taste, culture and refinement?' challenged the largest of the recalcitrant six, his hard New York accent suggesting a reasonably good education, as he came to his feet.

'I certainly am not, sir,' Coult declared hurriedly, being aware that playing upon the audience's civic pride could become a two-edged weapon if members of it were visiting from a rival community. 'Although I have yet to visit there, I have heard nothing but the most glowing reports of your Republic's capital city.'

From all appearances, the attempt at being tactful was not having the desired effect. Followed by his companions, the burly man started to stalk towards the stage. Coult swung his gaze quickly to where, dressed in diverse fashions to prevent any suggestion of colluding with him, his three assistants were seated at separate tables. If necessary, they would come to his aid and, hopefully, they could create sufficient of a diversion for him to pack away his equipment before it was broken. While he was looking, his right hand went towards the open mahogany box. Having to produce its contents, he decided, could prove a mixed blessing.

'You saying's Austin's——?' the burly man commenced, but his words died away with the question unfinished.

The two young men who had attracted Coult's attention and speculation earlier had shoved back their chairs. Coming to their feet, they moved until standing in the path of the advancing sextet.

'We've all paid our money to see the good Doctor's exhibition,

119

Mr. Bully Rathers,' the shorter of the pair announced, his voice that of a well-educated Southron. 'Not to have you cause a ruckus for Cole Turtle's benefit.'

Recognizing the speaker and his Satanic-featured companion, the burly man came to a halt in addition to stopping speaking. Sharing his knowledge, the other five duplicated his cessation of movement and awaited his guidance in what action they should take. Considering what had been said to him, he was uncertain of how to respond for the best. The comment had implied an understanding of motives which should have been kept secret, particularly from the man who had made it.

As Rathers and his companions were aware, Samuel Hamilton Walker was a captain in the Texas Rangers, which meant he was not a man to go up against, particularly when supported by Jackson Baines 'Ole Devil' Hardin, even with the odds a favourable six to two. While the force had originally been organized to provide a means of combating raids by hostile Indians it was already developing a formidable reputation for participating in matters pertaining to law enforcement. This being the case, it was not surprising—if disturbing—that Walker would be taking an interest in anything concerning Cole Turtle, who had ambitions to become the leading member of the Republic of Texas's criminal faction.[1]

'I dunno what you're talking about, Wal—Cap'n Walker,' Rathers protested sullenly. 'All we——'

'Could be I was misinformed,' the Texas Ranger interrupted. 'But I heard Cole Turtle was trying to persuade people like Mr. Gladwell there that they need him as a full-shares partner in their places.'

'It's a lie!' Rathers declared, but without any great aura of conviction. 'Somebody's been joshing you—Cap'n.'

'That's the trouble these days,' Walker answered, almost gently. 'Everybody's a practical joker. Anyway, as you-all don't

---

[1] Some details of Cole Turtle's criminal career are given in: *Ole Devil and the Caplocks*. He achieved his ambition and, as is told in *Set Texas Back on Her Feet*, *The Quest for Bowie's Blade*, *Beguinage* and *Beguinage is Dead!*, also by inference in *'Cap' Fog, Texas Ranger, Meet Mr. J. G. Reeder*, his family have continued to maintain the tradition in the law breaking circles of Texas up to the present day.

seem interested in watching the Doctor's exhibition, I reckon he'll be willing to give you your entrance fee back on your way out.'

'*Out?*' Rathers repeated, conscious that everybody in the room was taking in all that was being said.

'I *could* be wrong,' Walker drawled. 'But I thought you were leaving.'

Despite the still gentle-sounding way in which the words were being addressed to him, Rathers knew he was being ordered from the Tavern. What was more, it was equally apparent to every other occupant of the bar-room. So he had to decide—and quickly—whether to accept or refuse the challenge. To yield would entail a loss of face, but to stand firm meant fighting and there was a better than fair chance he would become the first casualty. Nor did he believe that Walker, being aware of his true character, would hesitate over killing him if given an excuse.

While Hardin was not a member of the Texas Rangers, he had gained a reputation during the struggle for independence of being a bone tough and deadly efficient fighting man. If it came to trouble, he could be counted upon to supply Walker with very capable and effective support. In fact, his expression—which put Rathers in mind of how he believed Old Nick might look when prodding sinners into Hell's fiery furnaces—suggested he was ready, willing and eager to demonstrate his prowess if trouble started.

Conscious of his men moving a trifle restlessly behind him, Rathers knew he could not prolong avoiding taking a decision. He had two other supporters, as yet unsuspected as such by Walker and Hardin, but drew little satisfaction from the fact. Not only might the pair have companions just as close by, but Gladwell—being aware of his purpose in the bar-room—would rally assistance to come to their aid. Trying to carry out Cole Turtle's orders was one thing, but getting killed in an attempt that was almost certainly doomed to failure was a horse of a *very* different colour. That would neither serve his boss's purpose, nor his own.

'Come on!' Rathers snarled, spitting out the words as if they tasted bitter and turning on his heel. 'Let's go some place where we can have us some *real* fun!'

Shoving between his companions, the burly man strode away from the stage. Nor did he find any reluctance among the others towards making what, despite his comment, was clearly a tail-between-the-legs retreat. He saw delighted grins coming to the faces of various onlookers who had cause to enjoy his humiliation. Despite the anger which assailed him, he did not offer to turn aside and try to re-instil the respect—or rather fear of the consequences—he desired to be felt by the smirking members of the crowd. He knew that, for the moment at any rate, his days of superiority in the Henderson area were over. It would take effort to regain his former position of prominence.

Effort—and letting it be known vengeance had been wreaked upon the two men chiefly responsible for the fall from power!

*****   *****

Just as Rathers was nearing the front doors, he saw somebody was entering upon whom he felt sure he could vent his pent up wrath without arousing the animosity or objections of the crowd. What was more, past experiences suggested that he could do so without risk to himself from the recipient of his attentions. Although he was aware that they could be dangerous when numerical superiority and circumstances favoured them, no single Chinaman he had met during his extensive travels as a sailor had ever displayed courage or aggression. Nor was one, being regarded as a 'foreigner' and a 'heathen Chinee' likely to arouse any sympathy no matter how he might be mistreated. Even if either Walker or Hardin felt inclined to intervene, they were likely to turn public opinion against them by doing so.

If Rathers had been of a discerning nature, or less wrapped in fury, he might have observed that the newcomer—while undoubtedly of Oriental extraction—differed in several respects from the Chinese merchants and coolies with whom he had previously been in contact.

Not quite five foot six inches in height, the newcomer was in his mid-twenties. His almond-eyed, cheerful yellowish features were those of an Oriental, but his close cropped black hair lacked the long pigtail by which tradition claimed a member of the Chinese race expected to be drawn to the Celestial Paradise on

122

dying. His garments consisted of a loose fitting and wide sleeved black cotton shirt hanging outside trousers of the same material which were tucked into black Hessian boots he wore instead of sandals or being bare foot as was generally the case among his supposed race. Although he had a sash of scarlet silk around his waist, he did not appear to be armed in any way; but this was in no way surprising. Few of his kind carried weapons openly. It was, however, in his demeanour that he showed the greatest difference. He walked in a free-striding manner and not with the usual short, shuffling steps to which Rathers was accustomed and his arms swung instead of the hands being tucked subserviently into the opposite sleeves.

'Get out of my way, you heathen son-of-a-bitch!' Rathers bellowed.

Without waiting to find out whether the command would be obeyed and oblivious of the fact that he might be making an error in his summation of his intended victim's nationality, the burly man swung his right hand around as soon as he finished speaking. The blow he was meaning to deliver to the side of the newcomer's head had almost sufficient power to fell an ox. However, for it to achieve any effect whatsoever, it had to strike the person at whom it was being directed.

Rathers never settled in his mind exactly what went wrong. In fact, his memory of the next few seconds always remained blurred. All he knew for certain was that fingers which seemed to have the strength of a closing bear-trap caught hold of his wrist. He had a vague sensation of the trapped limb being pulled at and twisted, while the 'Chinaman' bobbed below it instead of allowing the blow to land. Then his feet left the floor and he found himself turning a half somersault that carried him through the doors to alight supine on the sidewalk with an impact which jolted all the wind and wits from him.

For a moment, Rathers' companions were shocked into immobility. They could hardly believe that they had seen him tossed over the small 'Chinaman's' shoulder with no more apparent effort than if he had been a tiny child rather than a large and heavy man. Recovering from their surprise, the two hardcases who were in the lead began to move forward with the intention of avenging their leader. Brought from a state of shock by seeing them doing so, the other three prepared to follow their example.

Much to the amazement of the quintet, instead of taking what might have been considered to be the sensible precaution of returning as quickly as possible from the bar-room, the little Oriental literally bounded to meet them. Rising into the air, he contrived to deliver a thrusting kick with his right foot to the chest of one of the foremost pair. At the same time, he lashed a blow with his left arm at the other. He did not clench his fist in the Occidental fashion, keeping the fingers extended together and thumb bent across the palm, but his attack was none the less effective because of the deliberate omission. The edge of his hand chopped against the second man's throat with considerable force, provoking a strangled croak of anguish which testified to its potential as a means of offence. Both would-be assailants were sent reeling and, passing through the gap created by their involuntary departure, their attacker landed among the other three.

Startled by the second unexpected turn of events, the trio fell back a couple of steps as the 'Chinaman' alighted. Then the hard-case to the left lunged forward driving out a punch. Before it reached its destination, the little Oriental caught his wrist and jerked him closer to be kicked in the ribs. Nor, coming in from the right, was the second man's attempt to deliver a blow any more successful. His fist was deflected by a chopping motion of the Oriental's right hand and he too received a kick to the body which drove him into retreat. Advancing from the rear, the last of the three hoped to reap the benefit of the distractions created by his companions. However, his out-thrusting knuckles passed harmlessly over their proposed target as the 'Chinaman's' torso bent to carry him below them. Shot behind him in a continuation of the kick to the second attacker, his right boot's sole took the third in the ribs and sent him staggering.

When Ole Devil Hardin had seen what was happening at the front doors of the bar-room, he had known Rathers was falling into a not infrequent error. Tommy Okasi was not Chinese, but came from the group of islands which comprised the Empire of Japan. What was more, unlike the coolies and merchants of China with whom most Occidentals came into contact, he was far from being meek and defenceless. Having been trained as a *samurai* warrior, he possessed fighting skills and unarmed combat techniques which more than offset his lack of size.

However, despite being aware of how well the little Oriental could defend himself with his bare hands, the Mephistophelian-featured Texian thought he might require assistance. Nor did the apparent ease with which he was coping against his larger would be assailants cause Ole Devil to revise the summation. While he had done remarkably well so far, Tommy was up against five hard-cases well versed in rough-house fighting. So far, with the possible exception of their leader, none showed signs of having been rendered *hors-de-combat*. Now the element of surprise had been lost and they had learned that they were dealing with an exceptionally competent antagonist, they would prove a vastly more dangerous proposition.

'Come on!' Ole Devil snapped, moving forward as he watched the three men starting to launch their attacks.

Wanting to resume his exhibition now the interruption was over, Coult knew there was no point in doing so as long as the audience's interest was being directed elsewhere. Seeing the trouble developing at the door, the concern which had ebbed away began to return. The two Texians were setting off to assist the little Oriental, which meant the danger to his equipment which he had considered to be over still existed.

Then Coult noticed something which diverted his attention from his rescuers. From all appearances, two men occupying another of the tables nearest to the stage were preparing to become involved. What was more, although they were dressed in a different and more costly style than that of Rathers' party, their behaviour implied they were not intending to support his rescuers. Going by the surreptitious way in which each was drawing a pistol from beneath his broadcloth coat, they had exactly the opposite in mind.

Despite realizing that he might be doing the pair at the table an injustice, Coult also appreciated there was no time to be spared while making sure. Nor did he believe calling a warning to his rescuers would serve any useful purpose. Neither was holding a

125

weapon and they were facing away from the potential danger. If the two men were in cahoots with Rathers, they would be able to open fire before either Texian could turn and arm himself. Having drawn his conclusions, Coult dipped his right hand into the open mahogany box before him.

Easing back the hammer of his pistol, the larger of Rathers' supporters fixed his gaze on the middle of Walker's back. He knew his companion was aware of his intentions and could be relied upon to take care of Ole Devil Hardin. So, confident that he was unobserved and no warning would be given, he began to raise his weapon. Before it had moved more than a couple of inches, there was the crack of a light calibre pistol shot from his rear and the schooner of beer by his side shattered as the bullet passed through and into the top of the table.

Startled exclamations burst from the pair and, although they saw their intended victims starting to turn, neither could prevent himself from looking in the direction from which the intervention had come. They found Coult was pointing a strangely shaped pistol towards them. Smoke was rising from its muzzle, indicating that he had fired, but he was cocking the hammer with his thumb and, still taking sight along it, moved the barrel slightly. Then his forefinger tightened on the trigger, which had no guard around it.

To each man's amazement, although there only appeared to be a single barrel, Coult's weapon discharged a second time and splinters erupted from the table in front of the shorter of them.

'Drop the pistols!' the young man on the stage commanded, once again drawing back the hammer and keeping the weapon raised ready for further use.

Prudence demanded that the order was obeyed. Similar thoughts were passing through each of the pair's heads. They had seen multi-barrelled 'pepperbox' pistols capable of firing several shots in succession and at first believed Coult was using one. Then they realized that, although there was a cylindrical protuberance bored with holes below the hammer, it differed from every 'pepperbox' they had ever seen in that the latter's barrels were always the same length and rotated together. While the cylinder turned as the hammer was cocked, the long barrel remained motionless. Yet the bullets still passed along it from the holes in the cylinder. Neither man had previously come into contact with a weapon capable of performing such a feat. However, no matter how it was done, Coult's actions showed he was aware it could continue to discharge bullets and he handled it with a competence which demanded obedience to his wishes. With that in mind, they let their weapons fall on to the table and raised their hands in a sign of submission.

While swinging around rapidly to investigate the disturbance to their rear, Ole Devil demonstrated the advantages gained by carrying the Manton pistol as he did. Turning palm outwards, his right hand closed around the butt. Then, employing a technique which would be used by a later generation's gun fighters when performing what became known as the 'high cavalry twist' draw,[2] he slid the barrel from its retaining loop far more swiftly than Walker—who was turning with an equal alacrity—could extract the pistol tucked through his belt. What was more, coming across, the heel of the Satanic-faced Texian's left hand met and drew back the hammer with a similar practised ease. However, on completing his turn ready to take whatever action might prove necessary he discovered that none would be and the situation was now well in hand.

'Go and help the "Chinaman",' Coult suggested, making a slight emphatic gesture with the pistol. 'I'll take care of these two.'

Deciding that the young man on the stage was capable of carrying out the promise, Ole Devil and Walker turned towards the front doors. Before they had taken more than a couple of steps, it was obvious that there would be no further need of effort on their part in that direction. The sound of shooting had caused Rathers' hard-cases to refrain from resuming the attack upon Tommy. A glance informed them that it had not been done by their companions. Seeing the Texians were not only approaching once more, but now each was holding a pistol, they reached a mutual—if unspoken—conclusion that discretion was the better part of valour. So, of one accord, they turned and dashed from the barroom. Such was their eagerness to vacate what they suspected

---

[2] A description of the later method of performing the 'high cavalry twist' draw is given in: *Slip Gun*. The main differences are that the revolver was generally carried in a holster and, unless possessing a double action mechanism which removed the need, the hammer could be cocked with the thumb of the shooting hand.

would be a *very* unhealthy locality that they trampled over their still recumbent and barely conscious leader in their haste. Deserting him to his fate, they scattered and fled as fast as their legs would carry them.

'Why didn't you follow Rathers when you threw him through the door, Tommy?' Walker inquired, after the trio had looked around outside to make sure no further hostilities were being contemplated and having left the man in question lying on the sidewalk.

'Spirits of illustrious *samurai* ancestors would not be happy if they saw unworthy self retreating,' the little Oriental explained in a sing-song tone. 'But, more important, I knew the others would come after unworthy self.'

'Unworthy self ought to have had more sense than to jump into the middle of them the way he did,' Ole Devil commented dryly, his accent suggesting he had a similar background to that of Walker.

'Very ancient and wise Nipponese saying,' Tommy answered, with the air of one who was imparting important information. 'When threatened by attack from many enemies, do something which they are not expecting—But make sure you have friends close by who can come to your aid very quickly.'

'Is that really an old Nipponese saying?' Walker asked, as he and his companions were strolling back towards the stage, knowing 'Nippon' was another name for the little Oriental's homeland.

'It may come to be in the future,' Tommy replied with a grin and reverting to his more usual way of speaking English. 'But not yet. I only just made it up.'

'It wasn't particularly wise, either,' Ole Devil supplemented, his tone showing he was commenting about a liked and respected friend. 'Which *none* of those ancient and wise Nipponese sayings he keeps making up ever are.'

'I'm too cagey to say so to a feller who knows such fancy fighting tricks,' Walker admitted, exhibiting a similar regard for the little Oriental. 'But I'm inclined to agree.'

Leaving the Texas Ranger to deal with the two men at the table, Ole Devil and Tommy went to the stage. While Walker was listening to an explanation that the pistols had only been drawn in case he should need help to stop the fight, the Satanic-faced Texian thanked Coult for the assistance.

'The pleasure was all mine,' Coult declared, retaining the weapon in his right hand. 'After all, this equipment is fragile and your intervention kept it from being damaged if a fight had started. In fact, to show my gratitude, I hope you will be my guests for supper after the Exhibition.'

'All *three* of us?' Ole Devil challenged and, despite his eagerness to make a closer examination of what he realized was a most unusual pistol, his attitude warned that a refusal to include Tommy would produce a negative response.

'Of course, sir,' Coult assented, watching Walker dismissing the two men with orders to keep out of his way and take Rathers with them. 'Now, if you'll all be seated, I will continue with the Exhibition.'

***** *****

'To tell the truth, gentlemen—although I wouldn't want it spreading around at this point—I'm not a qualified doctor and my name isn't "Coult",' the young man introduced, as he and his three guests sat in the Tavern's small dining room waiting for the meal they had ordered to arrive. 'I'm Samuel Colt, lately of Paterson, New Jersey. However, I have spent reasonable periods in New York, London, England and Calcutta.'

Despite the contretemps which had delayed it starting, the demonstration of the nitrous oxide gas's effects had gone off without a hitch. 'Doctor Coult' had proved a competent showman and an entertaining speaker. The 'antics' of his three assistants had not only been amusing, but encouraged a couple of genuine members of the audience to participate. At the conclusion, in addition to receiving considerable applause, he had had a few bookings for private inhalations, three requests for exhibitions in people's homes and a number of assurances that satisfied customers would return the following evening bringing their wives and families.

With so much going on, the time was just after eleven before 'Coult' had been at liberty to join his guests for the promised meal. They had not been idle while waiting. Making a search to ensure that Rathers and his men were not contemplating trying to take revenge against them, they had found out all had left the town. However, from what had been said as they were conducting the search, Ole Devil had deducted that Walker—not unexpectedly— shared his interest in the weapon used by their host-to-be when preventing them from being shot in the back. They had been pleased to see, on joining him, that he was carrying the mahogany case into which he had placed it before commencing the exhibition.

'Would you mind showing us that gun of yours?' Walker requested.

'Certainly not,' Colt declared and went on frankly as he raised the lid to display the contents, 'I was hoping you'd ask. In fact, if you hadn't I'd have suggested it myself. These are the real reason I'm visiting Texas.'

The case proved to contain not one but two pistols. Each was finished in a dark charcoal blue colour covering all the metal parts. There were silver bands inlaid around the muzzle, behind the small front sight of the seven and a half inch barrel, on the upper part of the barrel lug curves, on the top of the barrel breech and in the recoil shield. An oval silver plaque bearing the initials 'S.C.' was set into the back-strap. Made from two pieces of finely checked walnut glued together, the grips were large with flared curves. The cylinder, bored for five shots, had an engraving of a stagecoach hold-up scene. However, there was no sign of either a trigger or its guard.

Like the cylinders and grips of the pistols, a spare cylinder for each and what was clearly a specially designed powder flask rested in recesses made in the dark blue cloth which covered the inside of the case. The rest of the accessories—a watch-like device for carrying and dispensing percussion caps, a bullet mould and a multi-purpose tool of a kind neither Texian had seen before— were held in place by wire guides.

Removing the pistols, Colt handed one to each of the Texians. Then he sat back and watched for their reactions with a mixture of pride, eagerness, anticipation and a little apprehension. He felt sure either would be able to give him a competent fighting man's assessment of them as practical weapons and particularly as to their suitability for use in the conditions which prevailed on the still untamed frontier country of Texas.

'I've only come across a Collier Repeating Pistol[3] which looked anything like this,' Ole Devil remarked, turning the weapon over slowly and discovering that its trigger was reposing in a slot under the frame. 'But that was a flintlock and nowhere near as compact as this beauty.'

'They're far less complicated,' Colt replied. 'For one thing, despite the cylinder being turned mechanically instead of by hand, they have less than three dozen separate parts and that *includes* the screws connecting the rest.'

'That *is* an improvement,' Ole Devil admitted, knowing the Collier Repeating Pistol had more than forty separate parts in the lock alone, to which had to be added the lock-plate, attaching screws, stock and barrel cylinder pin. 'What do they call this?'

'The Colt Revolving Cylinder Pistol,' the young Easterner answered, with more than a touch of pride in his tone.

'Your family make them, huh?' Walker asked, having conducted a similar scrutiny of the weapon he had been handed.

'It's *my* design,' Colt declared, trying without any success to detect any sign of disbelief—or other emotion come to that—on the faces of his small audience. 'These are what I call my "Holster Pistol". I've got my factory up in Paterson making them and lighter "Belt" and "Pocket" models. They can all be had in different barrel lengths, but every one of them has a five shot cylinder.'

'Bore looks a mite small,' Walker commented, having become accustomed to the ·45 and up sizes of single shot, muzzle-loading pistols.

'It's point thirty-six of an inch,' Colt replied, deciding against

[3] Invented in 1813 by Elisha H. Collier at Boston, Massachusetts, the Repeating Pistol was an early and moderately successful attempt to create a single barrel firearm capable of discharging several successive shots without reloading each individually and in turn. Lack of production facilities in the United States caused him to cross the Atlantic Ocean and manufacture the pistols in England. A number of them were purchased for use by the British Army serving in the Colonies. Although there is no evidence to substantiate the claim, it has been suggested by some authorities that—having seen examples while aboard a ship which visited Calcutta, then a part of the British Empire—Samuel Colt used the Collier Repeating Pistol as the basis for the mechanism for the first of his 'revolving cylinder' firearms.

131

mentioning that his smaller models had even smaller calibres.[4]
'I had to keep the ball around that size to prevent the cylinder from becoming too bulky or reducing the number of shots.' Wanting to change the line of the conversation, he reached into the case and went on hurriedly, 'This is a combined powder and ball flask I designed to help speed up reloading the cylinders. You insert the five nozzles on top into the chambers of the cylinder and twist the revolving band to place the correct charge into each one simultaneously. Turn it around and the lower end supplies each chamber with its ball from separate tiers which each hold enough for five complete reloadings.'

'That's *real* handy,' Ole Devil stated, knowing no such device existed for use with multi-barrelled 'pepperboxes' and thinking that the position of the cap nipples on the pistols' cylinders should counter a very bad fault which affected such of the other weapons as were percussion fired.[5]

'It speeds reloading considerably,' Colt asserted, demonstrating how the brass bands around the cylindrical copper flask sprang back into the closed position when released after dispensing their charges. Replacing it, he extracted the unusual tool. 'I'm particularly proud of this. It combines the services of a screw-driver, nipple wrench, wedge or key-mallet and loading lever.'

Swiftly the Easterner explained and exhibited the various purposes of the ingeniously designed implement. It was made in two parts, the knob unscrewing to expose the four-pronged wrench and pick for removing the cylinder's cap nipples. Taking up a spare cylinder, he described and demonstrated the use of the loading lever. The plunger's concave face was placed upon it, to seat the balls after the powder charge had been inserted. Then the tool's pointed end was fitted into the cylinder's key slot. This allowed the plunger to be thrust through a narrowly confined arc, pressing the ball below the lip of the chamber.

'You can do everything you need with this, even take the pistol

---

[4] The other calibres were, ·28—only in the 'Pocket Model'—·31 and ·34. Barrel lengths in all three Models, which became collectively known as Colt Paterson revolvers, ranged from two and a half to twelve inches; those up to six inches being restricted to the 'Pocket' and 'Belt' models.

[5] What the fault was and how dangerous it could be is described in: *Ole Devil and the Caplocks*.

completely to pieces, the screw-driver fits all of its screws,' Colt finished, returning the multi-purpose tool to the case and replacing it with the round 'capping box'. He continued, sounding almost ashamed of having to make such an admission, 'I can't claim to have made any special improvements on either the bullet mould, or the "capper" here, but they both do their work satisfactorily.'

Made of brass and about one and seven-eighths of an inch in diameter, like the pocket watch it resembled, the latter device had a ring on its edge—similar to the one on the knob of the multi-purpose tool—to which a thong could be attached as an aid to preventing it being lost when carried outside the case. Its lid, bearing an embossed rearing horse with the butt of a knight's broken lance between the forelegs and the pointed end gripped in the mouth[6] above a pair of crossed pistols, was hinged and fastened by a spring catch. The internal mechanism consisted of an arc, actuated by a spring, which pressed the percussion caps automatically into the feeding cycle and ejected them one at a time. Surrounding the figures on the lid, within circular border lines, was the inscription, *Patent Arms Man'g. Co. Paterson, N.J. Colt's Patent*. There was also a number which, later examination found, did not conform to either of the pistols in the case.[7]

'It handles mighty nicely, Sam,' Ole Devil commented, testing the balance of the pistol in his right hand (it would not be for some time that the word 'revolver' was coined and brought into use). He noticed that the shape of the butt allowed more instinctive pointing than was possible with the weapon in the loop on his belt. 'Weighs a heap lighter than my Manton, too.'

'Something tells me you just might have a few of these for sale, *amigo*,' Walker suggested, concurring with his companion's summation and interested despite his reservations where the small calibre of the pistol was concerned.

[6] This, of course, became the 'rampant colt' insignia which is the trademark of the Colt's Patent Fire-Arms Manufacturing Company of Hartford, Connecticut.

[7] According to James E. Serven's definitive work, *Colt Firearms, 1836–1959* (Serven Books, Santa Ana, California, 1959 edition) although no reason is given, a similar discrepancy between the serial numbers on 'capping boxes' and the pistols with which they were issued was the rule rather than the exception.

133

'I have indeed,' Colt confirmed, delighted by the possibility that his arms had found favour with the two knowledgeable young men. 'What is more, I'll let each of you have a cased pair of the "Holster Model" with all accessories at a reduced price if you will promise to write down your comments about them after you've used them for a while and send them to me.'

'You've got yourself a deal!' Walker declared without a moment's hesitation, or asking the price.

Much to his satisfaction, Colt saw that the Satanic-featured Texian was nodding in agreement.

*****   *****

'Yes sir, *amigo*,' Ole Devil enthused, as he completed reloading the second of his Colt Revolving Cylinder Pistols after having emptied them in succession and to his entire satisfaction into the man-sized and -shaped chalk outline he had drawn on the massive trunk of a cottonwood tree some thirty feet from where he was standing. 'Sam Colt sure knows how to make a tolerable straight shooting gun. Are you sure you don't want your pair?'

'Unworthy self not trust inventions of foreign devils,' Tommy Okasi answered, in the tone he adopted when preparing to deliver one of his newly made up 'ancient and wise Nipponese sayings'. 'Know he can rely upon weapons of honourable *samurai* ancestors and would rather use them.'

There was some truth in the comment.

The little Oriental knew how to handle firearms and could shoot quite well, but he preferred to place his reliance upon the more primitive—yet far from ineffective in his hands—weapons, which were almost all the property he had brought away from his homeland. He had his bow and arrows with different types of points designed for various purposes to be used at long range. When fighting at close quarters, he had a *daisho*, two long hilted slightly curved swords with small circular guards. The *tachi* had a thirty inch blade and the *wakizashi* was about half that length. The bow was not strung at that moment and was suspended by two loops on the left skirt of his double girth saddle with the quiver of arrows hanging from its low horn. He was carrying the *daisho* in their bamboo sheaths attached either side of the black

134

leather belt he was wearing over his sash,[8] the *tachi* at the left.

Four days had elapsed since the weapons had come into Ole Devil's possession, but the family business which had brought him to Henderson had kept him too busy for him to try firing them earlier. Sam Walker had already left to commence the investigations which, although failing to convict and put Cole Turtle out of business permanently, at least curtailed his activities to some extent. After having spent two profitable and successful days in and around the town, Colt too had taken his departure. He was, he had informed Ole Devil, making for Austin where he hoped to arrange with the Republic of Texas's government for a contract to supply the army and recently formed navy with his revolving cylinder pistols, rifles and carbines.

The pistols might have remained unfired until that afternoon, but Ole Devil did not consider the delay had been a waste of time. He had taken every opportunity to learn how to strip, clean and reassemble them as well as becoming acquainted with their handling qualities. Covering the nipples of the cylinders with dead percussion caps to protect them, he had taught himself to draw back the hammer with the hand which was holding the weapon instead of using the other's heel as was necessary with the Manton, practising until he was equally deft with the left and the right. However, although he had not mentioned the matter to Colt as he had wondered whether he would change his mind when he had grown accustomed to it, he was not enamoured of the folding trigger. He felt the pistol's effectiveness would be increased by one which was permanently exposed and shielded by a conventional guard.

At last, having time on his hands and wanting to conduct his first shooting tests in private, Ole Devil had ridden out of Henderson. Accompanied by Tommy, he had found a valley in some woodland about three miles from the town which was ideal for his purpose. Having removed the saddles and bridles, then fitted hobbles, they had allowed their mounts to graze. It was fortunate that neither animal was afraid of gun shots. Another way of pass-

[8] For the benefit of new readers: Tommy Okasi's weapons are described at greater length in Appendix Six.

135

ing the time, in which they had both participated, had been the moulding of bullets. They had been able to bring along a hundred of the ·36 calibre soft lead balls, ninety of which were already expended, and a sufficiency of powder.

The Texian had found the pistols easy to control, the recoil kick being mild compared with that of the Manton. His natural manual dexterity, aided by the dry-firing training in which he had participated, had allowed him to master firing rapidly with either or both hands. He had found the weapons were accurate, but limited in this by their extremely rudimentary sights; the one at the rear being no more than a notch cut into the lip of the hammer. To their credit, however, they pointed instinctively as well as he had anticipated and he considered this compensated in some measure for their poor deliberate aiming qualities. They would, he felt, be at their best as defensive arms where there would rarely be an opportunity for them to be aimed deliberately.

Reloading, which had been carried out by Tommy as well as Ole Devil, had posed problems. While the combined powder and ball flask was useful under some conditions, the barrel had to be removed before it could be used to charge the cylinder on the pistol. What was more, each chamber's load still had to be rammed home individually. Then grease had to be applied, Colt had stated, with the dual purpose of holding the ball in place and preventing any flames which leaked through the tiny gap between the face of the cylinder and the barrel's breach igniting the powder in the other chambers prematurely. So employing the combined flask was not much faster then loading the chambers one at a time by more conventional methods. Of course, having spare cylinders ready charged speeded up the reloading process as they were interchangeable and taking off the barrel to make the substitution was not difficult. Thinking about the matter, the Texian had concluded that the pistol's efficiency could be improved by attaching a rammer to it permanently. The multi-purpose tool to which one was fitted could easily be lost although having the means for securing it with a thong.

Despite his misgivings, Ole Devil considered that the Colt Revolving Cylinder Pistols had great potential. They were strongly and well made, simple to maintain and operate. Further developments along the lines he had been contemplating would make later models even more effective. In fact, if the improvements he intended to suggest could be made, he was convinced they would render all single shot, muzzle-loading pistols and even 'pepper-boxes' obsolete.

'Are you ready to eat yet?' Tommy inquired, after delivering his pronouncement upon the matter of armament.

'I reckon so,' Ole Devil replied. 'Those were the last ten balls I just loaded and I might find something to use them on while we're going back to town.'

'I've put the food on the rocks by the stream,' Tommy remarked.

'*Bueno*,' Ole Devil drawled and, carrying the pistols and reloading equipment, followed his companion.

The Texian found that the little Oriental had selected a pleasant and convenient spot for them to have their meal. The food was set upon a flat rock which could serve as both seat and table. It was so close to the small stream that flowed along the bottom of the valley that clear, clean drinking water was readily available. Sitting down on the rock, they ate in a leisurely fashion while discussing the merits and disadvantages of the pistols which lay between them. Without either of them realizing it, close to half an hour had gone by before the meal was over.

As Ole Devil was bending down, meaning to rinse his hands in the stream, a bullet hissed just over his head. Fired from the trees lining the top of the valley down which he and his companion had come, it caused both of them to twist around and, starting to rise, look in that direction. Their movements saved their lives. Three more bullets followed in the wake of the first, passing through the spaces their bodies had just vacated. Nor were they kept for long in suspense before discovering who was shooting at them.

Accompanied by eight villainous looking Indians and Mexicans, Bully Rathers appeared on the rim.

***** *****

After the failure of his attempt to demonstrate to Gladwell the kind of trouble which was to become a frequent occurrence if Cole Turtle was not accepted as a silent—but profit-sharing—equal partner, Bully Rathers had known he had forfeited his employer's favour. He had also concluded, not without satisfaction as he had a bitter and vengeful nature, that the only way he would regain it would be to prove he had taken revenge upon at least some of the men directly responsible for the débâcle. There had, however, been a major snag to his carrying out his intentions. He had found himself completely deserted by his party of supporters. Deciding he would not take kindly to their having left him behind when fleeing from the Tavern and being aware of his vicious malevolence when crossed, they had all decided it would be unsafe to remain in his vicinity. So they had gone their various ways before he recovered sufficiently to impose his will, or vent his ire, upon them. Nor, as the news had spread through the town of what had happened and who was involved, had he been able to recruit the assistance he required there.

One quality which nobody could claim Rathers lacked was persistence. While he had accepted it was prudent to follow his erstwhile supporters' example and leave Henderson that night, he had only gone as far as the small property owned by a man who dare not refuse to offer hospitality or a means of remaining in communication with the town. Nor had he been deterred when he discovered he was unable to persuade, or bully, any of the local criminal element into helping him. His luck had been variable from then on.

Sam Walker had gone before Rathers could arrange for any assistance in the quest for revenge. Although he had subsequently enlisted the aid of all that remained of José Gomez's band of *Comancheros*, the rest having been killed or scattered during a confrontation with a company of Texas Rangers, 'Dr. Coult' had set off for Austin in the company of a larger party than he had felt his new recruits could deal with.

Finally Rathers had learned that the last pair of the men responsible for his downfall had left Henderson on horseback and alone. Apparently, as they were not carrying bed-rolls or other noticeable property, they were merely paying a visit somewhere near by rather than taking their departure. Deciding to make the most of the opportunity, he had given the order to follow them. By the time the news had reached him, they had about two hours start, but fortunately he had the services of a good tracker. Even with this advantage, the pursuit had been so slow that he had come upon the Texian and 'Chinaman' too late to discover the reason for them being in the valley. The sound of the pistols being fired, much quieter than the discharge from heavier calibre weapons, had been muffled to such an extent by the side of the valley and surrounding woodland that it had gone unnoticed by him and his men as they were approaching.

By the time the tracker had received his first view of his quarry and signalled to the rest of the party—who were following at a distance—to join him on foot, they were sitting on the rock at the conclusion of the meal. Wanting to take no chances of them escaping, Rathers had ordered the only four *Comancheros* who had rifles to shoot them from the rim. Even with the not too accurate smoothbore, flintlock 'trade guns' which was all they possessed, he had felt at least some of them would make a hit. Regrettably, Hardin's movement had coincided with one man firing prematurely and caused them all to miss. On the other hand, neither the Satanic-featured Texian nor the little 'Chinaman' had a rifle readily accessible with which to fight back. In fact, while wearing a foreign-looking knife and sword, the latter did not appear to have a firearm of any kind on his person. Although he had noticed them, Rathers did not attach any special importance to the two Colt Revolving Cylinder Pistols lying on the rock. He had neither seen nor been told about the exhibition of their special qualities in the bar-room of the Tavern, so believed them to be no more than ordinary single shot weapons.

Even as Rathers was drawing his comforting summations and deciding that the situation could be far worse, something happened which he considered made it a foregone conclusion.

Instinct had caused Ole Devil to twist the Manton from its belt loop and cock the hammer instead of picking up the Colts. Then he noticed that only four of the men on the top of the slope held rifles, the smoke rising from the muzzles of which indicated all had been fired. Thinking as swiftly as always in an emergency, he saw he might be able to turn his involuntary actions to his advantage. Raising the Manton to shoulder height, he took a rapid sight and squeezed the trigger. Not unexpectedly, the range being a good two hundred and fifty yards, he missed.

'Come on!' Rathers bellowed, snatching the double barrelled pistol from his belt and bounding forward. Hoping that none of his companions had observed the two weapons on the rock, he continued with the intention of preventing them from doing so, 'Get the bastards before they can reload or grab their horses!'

Eager for loot, even those *Comancheros* who had noticed the Colts needed no urging believing them to be no more than conventional single shot weapons. Discarding their empty rifles with reckless abandon, the four who had fired drew whichever kinds of sidearms they were carrying as their companions were also doing. No matter whether holding a pistol, knife, tomahawk, or any two in combination, they all rushed forward goaded by the knowledge that the first to arrive would have the pick of the loot. So they vied with one another for the distinction. None of them gave any thought to why Rathers, who was equally aware of how the spoils would be divided, allowed them to pass him.

Moderately elated by the success of his ploy, Ole Devil warned himself silently that the affair was far from over. Nor, he went on while twirling the Manton's barrel back into the belt loop, was it any sinecure. Everything depended upon whether his confidence in Samuel Colt's inventive genius was justified. Furthermore, even if it was, there could still be desperate fighting ahead. No band of starved-looking and poorly armed *Comancheros* who had clearly fallen upon hard times recently were going to be deterred or easily frightened away. Not when they saw an opportunity to collect horses, firearms and possibly other valuable property. They would count the loss of a few lives a small price to pay, particularly when the deaths would increase the share of the loot for those who survived.

Tommy had duplicated his companion's estimation of the situation. Yet, despite knowing something of the Colts' potential and guessing how Ole Devil was hoping to utilize them, he was disinclined to put his trust in them alone. Not only were they untried in the demanding conditions of mortal combat, he still retained something of the trained *samurai* warrior's disdain for firearms as a means of fighting; particularly when in contention with men who were not armed in that fashion. So, as the pistols were being scooped up by the Texian, he went into action after the fashion of his ancestors.

'*Banzai!*' the little Oriental bellowed, leaping forward without waiting to draw either of his *daisho*.

Enfolding the butts of the Colts in his hands, Ole Devil pulled back their hammers with his thumbs and his forefingers found the triggers as the cocking action exposed them. Having expected such a response from Tommy, he too hurdled the rock. On landing beyond it, he set off at an angle from his companion with the intention of splitting their attackers into two groups. He met with success, but not of a kind many men would have welcomed. Three Mexicans, each armed with a pistol and a knife, accompanied by two Indians who had no firearms, showed signs of selecting him as their objective. So did Rathers, but he was lagging behind and clearly meant to let them bear the brunt of the fighting. The other two Indians waving a knife and tomahawk apiece and the last of the Mexicans, carrying their party's solitary pistol as well as a knife, kept going towards the little Oriental.

Advancing until less than fifty yards separated him from the nearest of the *Comancheros* who were making for him, Ole Devil prepared to stake his life on the Eastern inventor's ingenuity and his own ability to handle the still not entirely familiar weapons. Coming to a halt on spread apart feet and standing squarely towards the enemy, he brought up the right hand pistol to fire and miss. It was, he realized, vitally important for him to remember exactly how many of the ten loads he had discharged.

'One!' the Texian counted audibly, raising the left hand weapon to fire while lowering and cocking its mate's hammer. He continued as he once more failed to make a hit, 'Two!'

On the second attempt with the right hand Colt, the head of the foremost assailant—a gaunt and evil-looking Mexican—jerked as a small hole appeared in the centre of his eyes. Casting aside his unfired pistol, he spun helplessly and sprawled lifeless to the ground.

'Three!' Ole Devil scored with satisfaction.

To the trio converging with Tommy, it seemed that they had made the safer choice for a victim. While a sword and what they took to be a long knife swung in scabbards from his belt, the strange looking little foreigner was making no attempt to draw either. Instead, it appeared that he intended to tackle them with his bare hands. In which case, neither of the Indians—having left the shorter and more thickset Mexican a short distance behind them—had the slightest doubts over the outcome. Spreading apart and raising their tomahawks, they prepared to launch their attacks and each was hoping the other would hold the foreigner's attention until he could deliver the coup counting blow.

Annoyed rather than alarmed at coming under fire, the two remaining Mexicans returned it. The difference was that they cut loose with their single barrelled pistols while still running, which was far less conducive to accuracy than when standing still and using the sights. For all that, one of the balls sent the black hat spinning from Ole Devil's head without touching him. The other bullet came nowhere near. Ignoring the damage to the hat, he continued to count the shots he was sending at the rapidly approaching quartet.

Not until the right hand Colt was discharging another bullet, which took the leading Indian in the right shoulder after the left had sent its second load to carve a groove across one of the Mexican's filthy necks, eliciting a yelp of pain, did any of the four men realize they might be up against something unusual in the way of weapons. They were conversant with double-barrelled pistols, but had never seen nor heard of even a 'pepperbox' which had the capability of firing more than twice without reloading. So the full potential of the Colts was something beyond their comprehension. It struck, in fact, at their inborn belief in the supernatural. The sensation of awe was further augmented by the appearance Ole Devil now presented.

Losing the hat had brought the horn-like tufts of hair over the Texian's temples into plain view. Taken with the other Mephistophelian aspects of his features and the way in which the clearly single barrelled pistols continued to spit flames and lead when such a thing should have been impossible, he looked like the very Devil with whose wrath all *Comancheros* had been threatened by priests at one time or another. When yet another Mexican was struck down by a bullet entering his left breast and puncturing

142

his heart, the remainder came close to panic. Then something else happened which added to the growing suspicion that they were up against beings with supernatural powers. They had begun to slow down on coming under the mysterious repeated fire. So the other group had drawn ahead and were in sight. What they saw take place, despite the majority of their attention being on the Satanic-looking figure confronting them, proved to be their breaking point.

With the two Indians bearing down on him, Tommy showed that he was at no disadvantage by having left his *daisho* sheathed. In addition to lulling the attackers into a sense of over-confidence, he had the ability to arm himself at great speed. Like every *samurai*, he had been taught and gained proficiency in *laijitsu*, the very rapid withdrawal of the longer sword. Measuring the distances carefully with his eyes, he prepared to put the training to use.

Giving the traditional cry of self-assertion, *'Kiai!'*, the little Oriental increased the pace at which he was moving. While doing so, he sent his right hand across to grasp the long hilt of the *tachi*. Bringing its blade free and around to the right in a smoothly whip-like striking motion, he slashed the last couple of inches of the blade into the throat of the man at that side. Blood spurted from the severed jugular vein as the stricken Indian allowed the tomahawk to slip from his fingers and he staggered away.

Swiftly reversing the *tachi*'s direction and turning his hand so the knuckles pointed towards the ground, Tommy struck at his second would-be assailant. By sheer coincidence, this one was left handed, so there was nothing to stop the blade reaching the side of his neck. What was more, he had come closer than his companion and was brought into contact with the centre of the cutting surface. Such was the power behind the blow and the excellent temper of the steel that the razor-sharp weapon cut onwards to pass through the neck's bone. Unsupported except by a narrow strip of flesh, the Indian's head tilted sideways. Although killed instantly, reflex actions kept him running until he passed his assailant in the fashion of a decapitated chicken.

Cries of horror burst from the men confronting Ole Devil as they watched the apparently headless figure keep moving. Nor did its collapse after a few steps do anything to alleviate their terror.

Emitting close to screams of fright, they discarded their weapons and turned to flee. Some twenty feet away, Rathers saw what was happening; but he was made of sterner stuff. Snarling in fury, he lumbered onwards and the left hand barrel of his pistol belched fire. Feeling the wind of the close passing bullet, Ole Devil sighted and sent one out of his right hand Colt in return. He saw it hit the burly man in the right side. Such an injury delivered by a ·54 calibre ball from the Manton would, while not fatal, have knocked the recipient from his feet. The far lighter ball, propelled by a smaller powder charge, did not have the same effect. Despite wincing in pain, Rathers kept his feet and, halting, he grasped the pistol's butt in both hands to help him make certain of his aim.

Watching the fate which was befalling the two Indians, the stocky Mexican came to a stop. It was, he concluded, no time to be relying upon the knife in his left hand. Having disposed of them, the little foreigner was coming his way without as much as a pause to make sure they were rendered *hors-de-combat*. Alarmed by the prospect of being attacked by a warrior of such terrifying skill, he was trying to raise the firearm into alignment.

Alert to the danger, Tommy changed his rush into a rolling plunge. Passing underneath the bullet sent at him by a scant couple of inches, he ended on his knees and lunged with the *tachi*. Although far from ideal for thrusting, the reverse-Wharncliffe point[9] impaled the Mexican just below the breast-bone and emerged behind him. A startled and anguished cry broke from him. Stumbling backwards, he helped his assailant's tug to withdraw the blade as he fell dying.

Knowing that Rathers intended to kill him if possible, Ole Devil began to take advantage of the Colts' facility to be fired rapidly. Left, right, left, right, he sent the bullets from the smoking muzzles until—as he had no longer offered to try to keep count—the hammers fell on empty caps. Through the swirling white cloud of gas created by ignited powder, he saw the burly man

[9] For the benefit of new readers: a reverse-Wharncliffe point has the main cutting edge of the blade joining the back in a convex arc. The normal Wharncliffe, also called a 'beak point', is said to have been developed by the Earl of Wharncliffe in the sixteenth century although variations of it have been in use since at least Roman times. It is mainly used for pocket-knives. So the back of its blade describes a convex arc to the cutting edge.

reeling. For a moment Rathers contrived to remain on his feet, attempting to lift the pistol despite the blood which oozed from three more wounds. Then a glazed expression came to his eyes and his legs began to buckle. The weapon's barrel sagged groundwards and he crumpled at the knees to collapse face down.

'Are you all right, Devil-san?' Tommy called.

'Why sure,' the Mephistophelian-faced Texian replied, watching the remaining *Comancheros* continuing to flee up the slope. 'But I'll tell you one thing, *amigo*. Sam Walker was right, these guns of Colts don't have a heavy enough calibre.'[10]

---

[10] Ole Devil Hardin and Samuel Walker reached almost identical conclusions with regards to the faults of the 'Paterson' Colt. Although production was delayed and the first of the weapons embodying the suggested improvements did not appear until 1847, they had an attached rammer, a permanently exposed and guarded trigger, the calibre was increased to ·44, the chambers given the capacity to take a larger powder charge and increased to six per cylinder. At the time of marketing, Walker's name was more prominent than Ole Devil's. So the publicity-conscious maker began to call them the 'Walker Colts'.

PART FIVE

THE CIVIL WAR SERIES

A TIME FOR IMPROVISATION, MR BLAZE

Having established in Trail Boss *that Dusty Fog had been a captain in the Confederate States' Army and was acknowledged as an expert in handling a company of light cavalry in what has come to be known as 'commando' raids,*[1] *I realized that I had left the way open to produce books which covered his career during the War Between The States.*[2] *When I started my research into the period, various books—particularly* Arms and Equipment of the Civil War, *by Jack Coggins (Doubleday & Company, Inc., New York)—I became aware of just what a tremendous scope was offered.*

In many ways, the conflict between the North and the South— lasting from 1860–64—was the first of the modern 'total' wars. The period was in an era of great technical development. As is always the case, much of this was devoted to producing improved methods of killing. Although repeaters were not manufactured in sufficient numbers—or sufficiently popular with the General Staff of either side—to have any major effect, breech-loading offered an increased rate of fire in rifles. Self-contained metallic cartridges made possible simple forms of 'machine' guns such as the Gatling[3] *or—as was used in* The Devil Gun—*the Agar Coffeemill, but again, the top brass did not favour their utilization to any great*

[1] The term 'commando' originated out of the respect formed by the British Army for the tactics employed against them by the semi-irregular South African raiding 'commandos' during the Boer War.

[2] Although many people in the South prefer the name the 'War Between The States' and I employ it in the books, the words 'The Civil War series' are less unwieldy on the list of titles in chronological order.

[3] The designer, Dr. Richard Jordan Gatling (1818–1903), had pro-Confederate sympathies; but allowed it to be manufactured in the Union because he believed possession of such a potent weapon might persuade the South to sue for peace.

extent. Using observation balloons presaged aerial warfare. There were the first successful attempts at underwater attacks, albeit—with one exception—carried out by submersibles, which increased their draught until very little showed above the surface of the water as they approached to ram an enemy vessel with the explosive warhead of the long spar extending from the bow.[4] Siege warfare had such refinements as shells filled with an incendiary compound. There were even primitive and barely understood delvings into bacteriological warfare, dropping dead bodies into wells to pollute the water supply. The blockading of the Confederate States' coastline by the United States' Navy led to the development of mines, known as 'torpedoes', of great ingenuity for the protection of southern harbours and to the building of very fast ships for the express purpose of blockade running, bringing both essential supplies and luxury goods from Europe or the West Indies. Many of these blockade runners were not only made in British shipyards, but were commanded by Royal Navy officers supplementing their half pay incomes.[5] Telegraph, for speeding up communications and photography were given great impetus by the needs of the war. Trains were employed to move large bodies of men swiftly from place to place.

Despite all the above, chivalry was not forgotten in the War Between The States. The Southron officers in particular maintained a code of honour regardless of anything present day 'liberals' might try to prove to the contrary.

---

[4] The one exception was the Confederate States' Navy's *Hunley*. This was a genuine submarine, although its motive power was supplied only by eight men operating cranks to the propeller. After serious teething troubles, the *Hunley* rammed and sank the Federal corvette *Housatanic*, which was blockading the harbour at Charleston, South Carolina on the 17th of February—my birthday, incidentally, although I doubt whether *that* had any effect on the issue—1864, going down itself at the same time.

[5] For the benefit of new readers: this participation was to help bring costly repercussions. In 1872, an international committee sitting in judgement on what became known as the 'Alabama' Arbitration Tribunal, over protests levelled by the United States of America at Great Britain's conduct during the War Between The States, ruled in favour of the complainants. For allowing vessels of the Confederate States' Navy—particularly the efficient commerce-raiding cruisers *Alabama*, *Florida* and *Shenandoah*—to not only be built in, but operate from its ports and being involved in blockade running and other activities detrimental to the Union's cause, the Government of Great Britain and Ireland were ordered to pay compensation to the sum of £15,500,000.

However, beyond pointing out that the slavery issue was only one factor and not the primary cause of the War Between The States,[6] I did not attempt to discuss the pros and cons of the political situation which brought it about. My only concern was to use the period as the setting for action-escapism-adventure stories, not to try to prove one side was completely in the right and the other entirely in the wrong.[7] I was amused to read an interview about me in the TV Times *a few years ago. One part said, after a dramatic pause, 'All my heroes are Confederates'. Knowing the 'liberal' mentality, I suspect an unspoken accusation against my politics—whatever they might be—was being made.*

Once again, enough of this searching for 'deep inner motivations'. Here is the story from the Civil War series. In response to many requests, the action takes place shortly before the events recorded in You're in Command Now, Mr Fog. *However, I must warn that I have no plans to write anything more about the early lives of Dusty, or Mark Counter, in the foreseeable future.*

[6] Friends in the United States with Southron sympathies have commented that the slavery issue was exploited by the Federal Government to give the Northern enlisted men a more easily understandable reason for fighting—setting free the 'poor, down-trodden slaves—than the major issue. This was the Northern States' refusal to accept that, as was laid down in the Constitution, any State had the right to secede from the Union if it found its policies were incompatible with those of the Federal Government.

[7] An offer was once made to film Part One, 'The Futility Of War', *The Fastest Gun In Texas.* However, the producer wanted to change the plot so that, although Dusty Fog's testimony at a court martial exonerated a Union Army officer who was falsely accused of cowardice and desertion, he was still found guilty and executed. This, it was explained, would draw attention to America's conduct in Vietnam. When I suggested we changed the plot still further and had a German officer exonerating a Russian with the same effect in World War II, the offer was rejected. Apparently it is perfectly all right to malign the Armed Forces of the Free World, but one must not level the slightest criticism at our Communist 'allies'.

A TIME FOR IMPROVISATION, MR BLAZE

Word had been going out across the South and West Texas range country for weeks that recruits were required for service with the Army of the Confederate States. It had also been announced that any volunteers who arrived in Polveroso City would have the opportunity of trying to qualify for acceptance in the Texas Light Cavalry. Privately established, equipped and financed by the Hardin, Fog and Blaze clan, this regiment had acquired a well deserved reputation for ensuring its personnel had the best money could buy, or ingenuity supply. It was also known to have been highly successful in all its actions against the 'Yankees'.

Many hopeful candidates had gathered in the town which was the seat of the Rio Hondo County. Knowing that not all who came would be fortunate enough to enter the Texas Light Cavalry's ranks, the Confederate States' high command had sent Major Septimus Stone to try to persuade those who failed to enlist in other outfits which had an even greater need for men. Watching the latest group to have been examined being taken away for a meal, he felt that he had not made the long journey in vain. While the cream of those who had come—some travelling very long distances—had attained their goal, the remainder would make good recruits for the regiments which received them and few who had failed to make the grade had refused to take service elsewhere. Having seen them ride and shoot, he knew they needed little training in either. Which, as there was little time to provide it, was an advantage.

Of just over medium height, lean, clean shaven, tanned, and in his late forties, the major bore himself with the stiff backed, yet somewhat swaggering posture of a regular, long serving cavalryman despite having a permanent limp by courtesy of a 'Yankee' bullet at the climax of the Second Battle of Bull Run.[1] His white Burnside-style campaign hat tilted jauntily. Decorated by the single gold star which denoted his rank, the stand-up collar of his double-breasted cadet-grey tunic—which had two rows of buttons, seven to the row, and a skirt extending halfway between hip and knee, as required by the Manual of Dress Regulations—was closed regardless of the heat. Like the stripe along the outside seams of his reinforced light blue trousers' legs, the collar and cuffs of the tunic were yellow to indicate the branch of the Army in which he served.[2] There was a matching silk sash around his waist, over which was buckled a black leather weapon belt carrying a revolver in a closed top holster on the right and a sabre hung by its scabbard's slings at the left.

A grunt of what could have been relief, or satisfaction, broke from the man standing at Stone's side as he too looked after the departing volunteers. Apart from wearing a *kepi*, having a colonel's three stars on his collar and buff facings on his uniform —although as 'field' officers above the rank of captain, each sported the same three gold wire strands forming the 'chicken guts' Austrian knot insignia of rank on their sleeves—he was dressed in the same fashion, but was not armed. A good six foot two in height, although bulky he was not fat and gave the impression of being exceptionally fit for one of his fairly advanced years and apparent corpulence. His sun reddened features bore an expression which might imply a choleric disposition if there had not been a hint of humour in the dark eyes which peered from beneath bushy white brows and his thick 'walrus' moustache could not entirely conceal the grin quirks at the corners of his mouth.

'Is that all of them, Mannen?' Stone inquired.

'It is,' Judge Mannen Blaze replied. 'Now perhaps we can go and take a dr——'

The words were brought to a halt by a ringing Rebel yell and the

---

[1] The battles were fought on and around Bull Run Creek, near the town of Manassas, North-East Virginia on 21st of July, 1861 and the 29th–30th of August, 1862. Both ended in victories for the Confederate States of America.

[2] For the benefit of new readers: the colours were, Cavalry, yellow; Infantry, blue, Artillery, red; Medical, black; Staff and Engineers, buff.

drumming of swiftly moving hooves. Turning their gaze in the direction from which the sounds originated, the major and the judge saw two riders emerge from a clump of cottonwood trees about a quarter of a mile away. Despite being the youngest to have appeared so far, the newcomers were at least the equal of any Stone had seen at riding. Handling their horses as if born in the saddle, which was not surprising as in all probability they had ridden for most of their lives, they began to carry out a variety of tricks with all the aplomb of experienced circus performers. With no reduction to the rapid pace at which they were moving, they stood on, hung alongside, dropped to the ground at the left and, retaining a grip on the saddles' low horns, vaulted over to alight on the right and rebound until astride once more. Having run through other tricks with an equal skill, they brought the animals to a rump-scraping halt in front of the onlookers. Almost before their mounts had ceased to move, they had quit the saddles and approached the older men as smartly as two thirty-year veterans marching in review before the President of the Confederate States.

Running his gaze over the pair, Stone decided they would be at most sixteen years old. For all that, he liked what he saw. Bareheaded, their low crowned, wide brimmed hats having been dislodged to dangle by the *barbiquejo* chinstraps on their backs, they wore the attire of working cowhands, Although they had not been introduced to him, he remembered having seen them while paying a brief visit to the OD Connected ranch's main house as he was passing on his way to Polveroso City.

One of the pair was close to six foot tall, with an already powerful build. An untidy mop of fiery red, curly hair topped a freckled, happy-looking pugnaciously handsome face. He carried himself with an air of jaunty self confidence, although there was also a suggestion of worry as he avoided meeting Judge Blaze's stern gaze. A gunbelt with two walnut handled Colt 1860 Army revolvers, their butts turned forward for a low cavalry twist draw, encircled his waist and, despite his youth, Stone felt it was anything but a mere piece of ostentatious decoration.

Lacking a good six inches of the other's height, the second youngster had dusty blond hair and his tanned face was good looking, if not in an eye-catching way. Small he might be and giving his good quality clothes the appearance of being somebody else's cast-offs when they had clearly been tailored for him, but Stone observed that there was the physique of a miniature Hercules under them. Unlike his companion, he met the judge's scrutiny squarely and yet without any suggestion of defiance. There was nothing of the bombast and arrogance which a person of diminutive stature but possessing influential family connections might be expected to display. Nor did he give the impression that he had strapped on his excellently designed gunbelt hoping that the two bone handled Army Colts in its cross draw holsters would make him appear a bigger, more mature and aggressive person.

'Well ridden, gentlemen,' Stone praised, eliciting a sniff which might have expressed disapproval from the man at his side. He noticed that each horse bore the OD brand which signified they were the property of General Jackson Baines 'Ole Devil' Hardin's OD Connected ranch.

'You *could* say that,' Judge Blaze growled. His outer appearance and tone implied more criticism than approval. Nor did it change as he went on, 'These are my nephews, Septimus. Dustine Edward Marsden Fog and Charles William Henry Blaze.'

'You'll be Hondo's boy, then?' Stone suggested, offering his right hand to the taller of the youngsters.

'No, sir,' the red head replied and nodded to his companion while shaking hands with a firm grip. 'That's Cousin Dusty, not me.'

'I tend to favour momma's side of the family, sir,' Dusty Fog explained, his voice having an easy Texas drawl which suggested he had had a good education as did that of his cousin, showing no annoyance over the mistake in identity.

'I suppose you intend to join the Army,' Stone remarked, after shaking hands with the blond and noticing there was a surprising strength which was not applied in a desire to establish its possession.

'We've been training to do just that at Un—Judge Blaze's military academy here in Polveroso City, sir,' the red head stated. 'Fact being, we've just recently graduated and are counting on going to join the Texas Light Cavalry real soon.'

'I suppose *that* was your idea, Mr Blaze?' the judge challenged,

152

nodding towards the two horses.

'Yes, sir,' the red head confessed, looking a trifle embarrassed.

'We *both* thought the major would want to see us, sir,' Dusty declared, standing ramrod straight and speaking with quiet respect.

'That's the spirit,' Stone drawled, having no doubt the idea had been the red head's in the first place and pleased the blond was willing to share in the responsibility for it. He was aware that the small establishment run by the judge had already turned out several very capable officers and considered he was looking at two more to add to its roll of honour. Glancing downwards at their gunbelts, he continued with the intention of changing what was obviously a subject the youngsters would rather avoid, 'You ride well. How are you with your Colts?'

'With your permission, sir?' Dusty requested.

'Go ahead, Mr. Fog,' Blaze authorized, in an anything but encouraging manner.

'You first, Cousin Red?' Dusty inquired, nodding to the man-sized and shaped metal target which had been set up about thirty feet from where they were standing and had been used to test the other candidates' abilities with handguns. 'Or me?'

'I'll give her a whirl, Cousin Dusty,' Red Blaze answered. 'Then you-all see what you can do.'

Glancing at the judge as the two youngsters made a smart about face and began to walk forward, Stone deduced from the twinkle in his eyes—even though the rest of the florid features appeared to imply the opposite—that their conduct was being regarded with greater approval than appeared on the surface. Satisfied on that point, the major returned his attention to the pair. He wondered whether they could exhibit a skill at shooting to match their ability as horsemen, but considered it unlikely.

The question was not long unanswered!

After having taken only a couple of strides forward, Dusty and Red came to a halt. Each stood with his feet about a shoulder's width apart and looked comfortably relaxed.

Then, flexing his knees a trifle, the red head turned his right palm outwards. Grasping the forward pointing butt of the offside Colt with the second, third and fourth fingers, but keeping the forefinger extended outside the triggerguard, he curled the web of his thumb around the hammer's spur. Lifting with the twisting motion which had given the kind of draw he was using its name, he raised the weapon from its well designed holster to demonstrate one advantage offered by the method. The action of turning the muzzle forward also caused the hammer to be drawn to the rear without any further effort upon his part being required. He fired so quickly after raising the weapon to eye-level that Stone decided he must have taken aim along the barrel after the fashion of a shotgun rather than employing the sights. For all that, his bullet struck the target—which had been whitewashed by a Mexican hired hand to conceal the marks of the earlier shooting and had already been dried by the heat of the early afternoon sun—in the centre of the chest. As he was discharging the right side Colt, his left hand repeated the draw with its mate and he scored a second hit in the same region.

'By cracky!' Stone ejaculated, more impressed by the—what to him was remarkable—speed at which the first Colt had been fired than the two hits. 'That was damned good shooting.'

'Not bad,' the judge admitted in an off-hand tone which continued until the last two words as he went on, 'Not bad at all—*Mr. Fog*!'

Returning his eyes to the youngsters as the last two words were snapped out, Stone found he was only just in time. He also could hardly credit the sight which greeted them.

The small blond had looked to be lounging almost, with hands dangling at his sides. On hearing his name mentioned, they rose to cross and disappear in front of his body as he adopted a similar bent knee posture to that of the red head when drawing the first Colt. There were, however, two major differences.

Firstly, both revolvers left their holsters almost simultaneously and, turning forward, roared at practically the same instant!

Secondly, the small blond had only taken about half the far from lengthy time Red had required to get off a single shot!

Despite the latter and the fact that the Colts were held at waist level, which meant the alignment of the barrels must have been done by instinct rather than taking formal aim, the target clanged and vibrated. What was more, the two patches which appeared on the whitewashed surface were no more than a hand's width apart and on the left side where, in a human being, both bullets would have entered to pierce the heart.

'Well I'm damned!' Stone gasped, turning a now clearly astonished face to Blaze. 'I *saw* it, but I can hardly *believe* I did.'

'The boy's had good teachers,' the judge answered, still apparently impassive in spite of the inner amusement he felt at the display of emotion from a man who was usually taciturn in the extreme. 'And it helps, of course, that he is completely ambidextrous. Has been ever since he was born.'

'I can see how all that would help,' the major conceded.

Yet, even as he was speaking, Stone realized the matter went far beyond the explanation he was given.

Such skill could not have been acquired merely as a result of teaching, no matter how competently carried out. Other, more experienced, men would have demonstrated the way in which to perform the various movements of the draw. Much thought, top quality materials and superlative craftsmanship had undoubtedly gone into the production of a belt and holsters which would permit such remarkable speed. Sufficient powder, bullets and percussion caps had obviously been made available for him to have developed so high a standard of ability in handling the Army Colts.

Yet there were things which only the small, almost insignificant looking blond youngster could have supplied!

The superb reflexes which created the near perfect co-ordination between the mind, eyes, hands, for instance. While he might have been educated and given all the facilities by which to utilize them to their best advantage, they must have been born in him. Nor could his ambidextrous prowess have been entirely taught, although training would be necessary to bring it to such a pitch of excellence.

No matter what Judge Blaze had said, Stone was aware that only great effort and much hard work on Dusty Fog's part could have produced such a fine display of gun handling. It went far beyond anything the major, having been born and raised in Virginia, had ever seen or—as the techniques and skills of Western trained gun fighters had not yet received the widespread publicity they would attain in later years—would have believed

155

was possible.

'How are they with sabres?' Stone asked, making an effort and regaining his composure, as the blond was returning the Colts to their holsters.

'Mr. Blaze is reasonable, although there are times when it looks as if he thinks he's beating a carpet rather than fencing,' the judge replied. 'But Beau Amesley says Mr. Fog is the most promising youngster he's come across in a long time.'

'*That* good, huh?' Stone breathed, knowing the man in question had been acknowledged as one of the South's finest fencing masters before the War and who was now serving in the same capacity with the Texas Light Cavalry despite having been lamed, like himself, in battle during the early days of the conflict.[3]

'*That* good,' Blaze confirmed and, for a moment, allowed the pride he felt to show. It remained only briefly. Then, glaring to where Dusty and Red were still standing at their places on the firing point, he barked gruffly, 'Well, *young gentlemen*, don't you-all *think* it might be *advisable* to walk around and cool down those unfortunate animals you've ridden into a muck-sweat while displaying what *you* obviously imagine has impressed Major Stone as being excellent horsemanship?'

'Yo!' the youngsters responded in unison, giving the traditional cavalry acquiescence to what was clearly a command no matter how it had been worded.

Stone noticed that neither youngster appeared abashed, or perturbed, by their uncle's apparent irascibility. Nor, a quick glance informed the visitor, was there any reason for them to be on this occasion. Being in the peak of condition, the horses were showing no signs of having suffered from their exertions during the brief period they had been required to gallop. They were far from being in the distressed condition implied by the judge and would be no worse for the strenuous exercise.

'You know something, Septimus,' Blaze commented with a grin, after his nephews had led away the horses and were beyond earshot. 'There are times when I wonder whether I'm terrifying those two as much as they pretend.'

[3] Some details of Major Beauregard Amesley's career are given in: *The Colt and the Sabre*. How he met his death is told in: *The Bad Bunch*.

156

'Could be they know you too well,' Stone answered, also smiling.

'Could be,' Blaze agreed. 'Anyway, that is the *last*, unless the Misses Betty Hardin and Georgina Blaze decide *they* should give you a demonstration of how well they can ride, to prove they're capable of taking an active part in the War.'[4]

'They were hinting on those lines to me,' Stone admitted, having met the two high spirited girls on his arrival and found them to be pleasant company.

'I hope you didn't give them *any* encouragement,' Blaze sniffed. 'Come on, let's get out of the sun and sample some of Abel Wallace's Jack County moonshine.[5] That's *one* thing the War hasn't changed. It's still the best around.'

Accompanying his host towards the town, Stone studied the two youngsters who were walking a short distance ahead and considered their potential as members, officers in all probability, of a fighting regiment which would almost certainly be the Texas Light Cavalry. Aided by past experience, he had developed his skill at assessing character during the months he had spent helping to gather recruits. He considered that he had the ability to estimate a man's worth as a soldier with considerable accuracy.

Although he had no doubt that Red possessed courage, was an excellent horseman and a competent pistol shot, the major had misgivings. In spite of his cousin's acceptance of a share in the responsibility, it had clearly been by his instigation that the display of trick riding was given. He looked as if he might have a quick temper which frequently led him into scrapes or trouble. Possibly he possessed an irresponsible streak which would make him more of a liability than an asset in action against the enemy. Taking everything into consideration, Stone did not think he was sufficiently mature as yet to make an officer with men's lives dependant upon his judgement and wondered if he ever would be.

There was no such uncertainty in the major's mind where the

[4] The tragic results which accrued when such a demonstration was attempted are described in: *Kill Dusty Fog!*

[5] More information about Abel Wallace's moonshining activities is given in: Part Three, 'The Trouble With Wearing Boots' of *The Floating Outfit*. This is the Transworld Publisher's edition. The Bantam Books, New York, edition of *Goodnight's Dream* was re-titled *The Floating Outfit* by them.

young blond was concerned. Perhaps because he was comparatively short himself, he found it easy to look beyond Dusty's stature and make an accurate summation of what lay below the surface. For all his inability to show off clothes to their best advantage, which created an impression of insignificance, there was a budding strength of personality to be discerned which transcended his looks and lack of height. In spite of being smaller than most of his generation, Stone was willing to bet he would swiftly become the leader in any group of them.

Taken all in all, if Dusty Fog did not make a name for himself, the major would be *very* surprised.

'I suppose the boys will be going to join Ole Devil and the Texas Light?' Stone remarked, the words being more of a statement than a question.

'As soon as I'm satisfied that they're ready,' the judge replied and, inadvertently, went on to confirm at least some of the visitor's summations. 'And, as far as Dustine at least is concerned, that day's not too far away.'

*****   *****

'It's not *fair*, is it, Cousin Betty?' Georgina Blaze complained petulantly, having listened to Red Blaze describing his and Dusty Fog's activities earlier that afternoon. 'Menfolks have all the excitement and fun.'

'Go-on, Georgie-gal!' the red head grinned, throwing a glance at the small blond and making the first words sound like, 'Gwan', as they were escorting two of their female cousins along the main street of Polveroso City. 'Way you-all take on about it, you'll be saying next that women could maybe do something useful in the War.'

'I've heard that Belle Boyd and Rose Greenhow are doing plenty,'[6] remarked the girl to whom Georgina's complaint had been made. 'And, unless I'm mistaken, *they* are women.'

Despite being the same age as her three companions and the smallest of them, Betty Hardin conveyed an impression of being somewhat older and more mature. Bare headed, with shoulder long black hair gathered at the back of her neck in what a later generation would call a 'pony tail', she was petite and very beauti-

[6] See Appendix Seven.

158

ful. There was a suggestion of command and intelligence about her face and she carried herself with all the assured composure that might be expected of one who was descended from Ole Devil Hardin. Yet, for all that she was the 'granddaughter' of the head of the powerful Hardin, Fog and Blaze clan,[7] there was nothing arrogant or snobbish about her. Rather, as in Dusty's case, her demeanour was of competent, yet unassertive unless the need arose, self-confidence.

'Why sure,' Red conceded, being too wise to tease Betty unless there was a clear avenue of escape. Like Dusty, she had had a thorough training in the remarkably effective barehanded fighting methods which Ole Devil's Japanese valet, Tommy Okasi still used to good advantage on occasion. 'Thing being, they're a mite older than you.'

'I'm three weeks older than you-all, Red Blaze!' protested Georgina. About Dusty's height, clad in a gingham dress, buxom without being fat, she was a blonde with a pretty and expressive face that looked meant for laughter, but now displayed righteous indignation. 'But you still think *you're* old enough to go and fight the Yankees.'

'Fighting's men's work,' Red pointed out.

Before any more could be said, four burly youths between one and three years older than the quartet came from an alley. They wore untidy cowhand style clothing, but were not armed and there was a distinct family resemblance about their unprepossessing features, which were adorned with stubble intended to make them look older and fiercer. Although they came from across the county line in Jack County, Dusty's party recognized them as Burt Rothero and his cousins, Willie, Trace and Hobie Benedict, the latter being twins of seventeen. What was more, as the blond and Red were aware, while they had all enlisted in the Army earlier that day, none had gained acceptance in the Texas Light Cavalry.

'Well, well, well!' Rothero exclaimed, coming to a halt and glowering at the approaching quartet. He noticed that, as was usual when in town, neither Dusty nor Red was wearing a gunbelt. 'Will you-all just take a look who's coming along here.'

'It's some of them high-toned 'n' fancy Hardin, Fog 'n' Blaze

[7] See Note 1 of the Hardin, Fog and Blaze clan's family tree. Pages 10–11.

crowd,' identified the younger twin, Hobie, as he and his brothers halted so they and their cousin spread across the sidewalk. 'Strolling along so head-in-the-air and prideful like they must reckon they own the whole god-damned town.'

'Don't tell me you-all haven't heard?' demanded the oldest of the three Benedicts, Willie, also speaking sufficiently loudly to make sure his mocking words would be heard by the youngsters at whom they were directed. 'They's going to be *officers*, no less.'

'*Officers?*' Trace Benedict exclaimed in tones of incredulity. 'I thought *officers* had to be grown men?'

'Not when you've been to a fancy school for soldiers run by a red-faced, whiskey-swilling old goat's calls himself a judge when he can't even judge good moonshine,' Rothero explained, having heard his father—a prominent Jack County politician with shares in one of the illicit stills which abounded in the area—frequently make the charge because its products were not considered worth buying by the Judge. 'Or if you're kin to a skinny-gutted old hardhead who's meaner than the Devil he's named after and runs him his own private army.'

'Easy, Red!' Dusty warned, *sotto voce*, hearing his cousin let out a hiss of indignation and annoyance. 'We don't want any trouble.'

'*They* do,' Betty stated, just as quietly.

'Hey though!' Trace ejaculated, watching the girls and their escort walking closer. 'Seeing's how we 'n's going to be soldiers, will we have to salute them two?'

'I've heard tell that be the case,' Rothero declared. 'Only you-all won't have to let it worry you none, Cousin Trace. We won't be running across 'em, seeing's how we 'n's joining a *fighting* outfit.'

'*Red!*' Dusty hissed, his tone bearing a note of urgent command as he sensed rather than saw his cousin was on the point of rushing forward.

'God damn it, Dus——!' the red head began furiously, but he restrained his impulse to launch an attack upon their tormentors.

'We don't want any of *that* sort of fuss!' the blond cautioned, without taking his eyes from the four youths.

'Uncle Mannen wouldn't like it!' Betty supplemented.

Even while making his pronouncement, it was obvious to Dusty that trouble might be difficult to avoid. Everything about the quartet from Jack County implied they were bent on mischief. Resentful at having failed to obtain admission into the ranks of the Texas Light Cavalry, they were intending to take out their spleen upon the two members of the family they blamed for their rejection with whom fate had brought them into contact. For all his summation, the small blond did not want his impulsive and quick tempered cousin to make the hostile gesture which would start the fight he felt sure was inevitable.

Showing an equally shrewd assessment of the situation, Betty caught Georgina's eye and they slowed to let their cousins move ahead of them. Betty looked around, hoping to see the elderly—but competent—peace officer who was acting as town marshal in the absence of Dusty's father, but the street was devoid of any human beings other than her party and their four antagonists. Knowing Georgina to be almost as impulsive as Red, Betty darted a warning glance in her direction then gave her attention to what was being said and done.

'Excuse me, *gentlemen*,' Dusty said, with an icy politeness his cousins recognized as the calm before a storm, coming to a halt while a few feet still separated him from the quartet. 'You're blocking the sidewalk.'

'Then you-all get off it 'n' walk 'round us!' Rothero suggested truculently, but he deliberately refrained from making anything which witnesses might consider was a threatening gesture. He was aware that, although the town was owned almost entirely by members of the Hardin, Fog and Blaze clan, the law was administered fairly. So he wanted to provoke either Dusty or, more likely in his opinion, Red into hitting out and giving his party an excuse for what could pass as fighting back against aggression.

'Like h——!' the red head commenced, having halted at the blond's side, bristling with indignation and willing to do as the Jack County youth wanted.

'Easy!' Dusty drawled in a placating fashion, throwing a look pregnant with admonition at his cousin. Then, having made a gesture indicating the other would remain, he stepped forward a couple of paces and resumed addressing the quartet. 'Now *that's* a thing no gentleman would ask a lady to do.'

'You-all ain't *ladies*,' Willie Benedict pointed out, guessing what Rothero was hoping to achieve and sharing the desire to make sure all the blame for what they were trying to make happen would fall upon their two local victims.

'We've ladies with us,' Dusty countered mildly, sounding like a 'good' little boy explaining to the preacher that his boots were clean.

'Them two?' Hobie scoffed, nodding disdainfully in the direction of Betty and Georgina. By far the least intelligent of the quartet, he could not understand why his oldest brother and cousin were wasting time talking instead of jumping the two local boys who had been selected to be taught the superiority of Jack County's residents. For the moment, however, he was content to follow their lead. 'They ain't nothing but a couple of no-account, nose-wiping, scent-sniffing, doll-playing *gals*.'

'Hold hard, hot-head!' Betty commanded quietly, catching her blonde cousin by the arm as she was on the point of darting forward and announcing her objections to the description which had been given of them. 'Leave it to Dusty!'

'They're still ladies as far as Cousin Red and I are concerned,' the small blond declared, hearing the comment from behind him and, guessing what had provoked it, pleased that Betty was showing her customary forethought. 'So we'd be obliged if you'll let us pass.'

'You would, would you?' Hobie snorted, finding the continuing discussion growing irksome and wanting to bring about some more positive response. 'Well, if there *was* any for-real ladies in this god-damned one-hoss town, or the whole stinking Rio Hondo County——'

'No, Red!' Dusty snapped, twisting his torso so he could place the palm of his left hand on his cousin's chest. Such was his strength that he halted the other's proposed advance. His gaze, however, remained on the quartet. Although still out of reaching distance, they were gradually edging closer. Without removing the hand, but reverting to speaking as gently as the soft murmuring of a summer's breeze, he went on, 'I think you should rephrase your last remark, sir.'

'Oh you do, do you?' Hobie answered, clenching his fists and, faced with what he considered to be a far from manly attitude, finding it increasingly hard to control his eagerness to start fighting. 'Well I ain't a-going to, see. So what're *you-all* fixing to do about it?'

'I'll——!' Red growled, pushing against Dusty's restrictive palm.

'You'll *what*?' Hobie challenged, unable to restrain himself any longer and, spitting on the sidewalk, took a step forward.

'I'll show y——!' Red began to promise heatedly, but—in spite of still shoving against the constraint of the palm on his chest—realizing the small blond had something in mind while apparently refusing to be goaded by the insults and threatening behaviour to which they were being subjected.

'You're always too quick to temper, Cousin Red, so calm down,' Dusty requested, showing no sign of noticing the spittle which had landed near his feet and swinging around until he was facing the other male member of the clan without removing his hand from its prohibitive position. Yet there was a growing hardness underlying the almost pleading tone which was recognizable to anybody who knew him well as he went on, 'I *know* he's being insulting and *you* feel that *somebody* should remonstrate with him. But *you-all* aren't going to be the one to do it—*I* am!'

With that, the small blond reversed his direction rapidly!

Having been lulled into a sense of over-confidence by Dusty's meek and placid behaviour, also having no idea what the word 'remonstrate' meant, Hobie was caught completely unawares. There was more to cause him consternation, however, than merely discovering that a more aggressive course than had been suggested was being contemplated.

In the past, returning bruised and sorry for themselves from marauding visits to Polveroso City, other boys from Jack County had invariably laid the blame for their misfortunes up on the fighting skill of Dusty Fog. According to the various explanations, not only was he of enormous size and strength, but he possessed such a knowledge of wrestling tricks, punching and kicking that he had hardly needed any support to attain victory no matter how many assailants were against him.

Like his brothers and cousin, all of whom were making their first foray into Rio Hondo County, Hobie had been unable to reconcile the description with what they had seen. Certainly the short-growed cuss who had been pointed out to them as Dusty Fog had not impressed him as being dangerous. Exactly the opposite, in fact. Nor, having made closer contact, had he seen fit to revise his supposition that the vanquished boys had lied about the cause of their defeats for some reason. So the sight which confronted him caused him to forget his hostile intentions and stare in amazement when he should have been devoting all his attention to protecting himself.

Suddenly and inexplicably, as far as Hobie was concerned, the blond had stopped seeming to be small and harmless!

Such was the strength of Dusty's personality that he appeared to have taken on size until he gave the impression to the Jack County youth of being the largest person on the sidewalk.

Before Hobie could decide what to make of the remarkable transformation, the blond's knotted right fist was swinging around with a speed which defied his belated attempt to block it. Hard knuckles took him on the side of the jaw, sending him spinning until he collided with the hitching rail.

Having been behind Hobie, neither his brothers nor cousin had been subjected to the change which appeared to come over Dusty when launching the attack. While they were taken as unprepared as the youngest of the Benedicts by the change from passive to active, they responded with commendable rapidity to the sight of him being knocked across the sidewalk. Leaping forward, Willie and Trace each grabbed one of the small blond's arms. Before Rothero could take advantage of their teamwork, he found his attention would be required elsewhere.

Seething with annoyance though he might have been, Red knew Dusty too well to have been fooled by appearances. He was aware that the insults to the uncles they both respected and admired, and to their cousins, and to home town and county, were not being ignored by the blond any more than by him. Which was why he had been content to await developments. As he anticipated, they commenced with the kind of devastating effectiveness he had come to expect from his *big* cousin.

164

Red had long since ceased to think of Dusty in mere feet and inches. In fact, he found it surprising when less knowledgeable people referred to the blond as being small.

Concluding that his cousin was now ready for him to take action, the red head sprang forward. While he saw the brothers grabbing Dusty, he considered Rothero to be the more urgent target. So he went at the burly youth with eagerness, but not in a blindly reckless fashion. That was one thing about Red which few people other than Dusty and Betty appreciated. Easy as he undoubtedly was to provoke, once he started to fight he became calm and far from rashly incautious.

Instead of meeting the bull-like rush of the somewhat heavier Rothero, Red side-stepped the reaching hands at the last moment and sent his left fist into the other's stomach. A croak left the recipient of the blow and, folding at the waist, he was unable to halt his charge. He blundered by, but was fortunate. Before Red could complete the turn which should have been the prelude to following up the attack, Hobie came from the hitching rail to pinion his arms to his side.

Although Willie and Trace had obtained their holds on Dusty, Red's intervention was preventing their cousin from taking advantage of his indisposition. What was more, the brothers rapidly became aware that they were in a similar condition to the man who caught a tiger by the tail and realized, too late, that the consequences of letting go could prove extremely unpleasant. They might not be the quickest of thinkers, but each was very soon aware of the great strength packed in their intended victim's small frame.

Seeking a way to liberate himself, Dusty saw how it might be offered. In their attempts to control him, the brothers had swung until they were facing the building in front of which the conversation had taken place. Swinging up his feet, the blond took a couple of steps against the wall to help him turn a back somersault. While the actions were unexpected, neither Willie nor Trace lost his hold. Finding himself still grasped, but feeling his captors were unbalanced, Dusty gave a surging heave with his arms. Demonstrating his strength in no uncertain fashion, he hurled both of the heavier youths from him and stepped to the rear as they released him. Then, as Willie struck and rebounded from the wall, the blond interlaced the fingers of both hands to drive them between his shoulders and knock him into it once more. However, as Dusty was starting forward to render the oldest brother *hors-de-combat*, Trace, who had contrived to prevent the collision with the wall from being too severe, plunged forward to tackle him around the waist.

Rubbing his stomach as he came to a halt, Rothero swung around. A snarl of satisfaction burst from him as he saw how Red was being held. Although he also noticed what was happening to his other two cousins, he left them to their own devices. Clenching his fists, he began to move towards the trapped red head. So intent upon his purpose was he that he ignored the patter of light footsteps coming from his rear. His first intimation that all was not as well as he believed came when his hat was knocked off and two sets of fingers dug in to pull hard at his hair.

Giving a howl of pain, Rothero pivoted and flailed around with his right arm. It caught Georgina in the side an instant after she, sensing the danger, had let go of his hair, and sent her staggering into the side of the building. Deciding to teach her not to meddle in men's affairs, he took a step in her direction and began to draw back his left fist. As he did so, he saw the smaller girl approaching him in a clearly hostile fashion. Thrusting out his right hand, meaning to put its palm against her face and shove her away, he had no doubt that he could accomplish this without difficulty.

Which proved to be a mistake. One which was inspired by ignorance, maybe, but none the less surprising and painful for that.

Rothero had never seen or heard of Ole Devil Hardin's Japanese valet. So he could not be expected to know Tommy Okasi had taught Betty a number of highly effective tricks from his *ju jitsu* and *karate* repertoire. How well she had benefited from this unconvential education was soon demonstrated. Catching the youth's reaching hands in both of hers, so the palms were across its back and her thumbs wrapped around his wrist, she turned it upwards and outwards. Despite being much heavier and stronger than her, the speed with which she responded and the leverage her hold put on his limb rendered him incapable of resisting. Instead, he

166

found he was being tilted backwards and off balance. Swinging her right leg to strike him behind his already bending right knee, she completely ruined his equilibrium. With that achieved, she removed her hands. Stepping clear, she watched him topple help-lessly to land supine on the sidewalk.

'I think we'd better leave the rest of it to Dusty and Red,' Betty commented to Georgina.

'It's like I said,' the blonde replied, thinking regretfully of the days—not too long gone by—when she would have plunged into the fray as willingly as any boy. 'Men have all the fun.'

Brought down on his back, with Trace straddling him and see-ing Willie lumbering in their direction, Dusty might have argued with Georgina's notions of what constituted fun. What was more, as Red was still being held from behind by Hobie, he knew he could not count on help from that direction. His first problem, he realized as a wild yet still painful punch thudded against his right cheek was to remove the younger brother from him before the elder arrived. There would not be much time in which to bring this about.

Fortunately for Dusty, he had acquired an even more extensive knowledge of *ju jitsu* and *karate* than Betty

He had found that this knowledge and being ambidextrous was the greatest help in offsetting his small size when in contention against larger and heavier antagonists. He hoped it would prove equally effective in this case.

Bringing up his left hand, the blond made no attempt to hit in the conventional Occidental manner. Cupping it slightly instead of forming a clenched fist, he thrust its heel under Trace's lightly bristled chin. Delivered from such a restricted position, the attack could not develop its full potency. For all that, it was able to serve at least part of its purpose. The impact jolted back his assailant's head and, despite failing to stun him completely, dazed him momentarily. His bewildered condition lasted long enough for Dusty, bracing shoulders and feet against the ground, to jerk up-wards and dislodge him, but *not* sufficiently quickly to prevent his brother from coming close enough to drive a kick into the small blond's ribs.

Trying without success to burst free from the arms which were wrapped around him at elbow level, Red concluded he must employ other means. What was more, he had an urgent need to do so as quickly as possible. Georgina and Betty might have removed the threat of an attack by Rothero, even if the latter was unlikely to put him out of the fight completely, but Dusty was in dire need of assistance. With that thought in mind, the red head used all his strength to shove himself and his captor backwards. He heard the thud as Hobie was rammed into the hitching rail, but the hold on him did not weaken.

Gritting his teeth, Red surged forward a stride, dragging the Jack County youth after him. Then he reversed direction with even more vehemence and propelled Hobie's already suffering spine into the unyielding timber of the sturdy rail once more. This time he felt the constriction weakening slightly. It was enough. Shoving his previously pinioned arms away from his sides, he forced the encircling grip to loosen still more. Then, inspired by the urgency which he saw was necessary where Dusty was concerned, he propelled first the left and then the right elbow to the rear. Each struck Hobie's solar plexus with some force and caused him to go into an agonized retreat.

In spite of having set himself free, the red head discovered he was going to be too late to intervene on his cousin's behalf.

Grunting in pain as he subsided on to his back, Dusty saw Willie was preparing to deliver a kick with the other foot. Rolling slightly on to his left side, he delivered a blocking swing with his left arm to the approaching right shin. His right hand, displaying the same kind of co-operation that had been in evidence when he was drawing his two Colts, grasped his attacker by the ankle. Drawing the captured limb above him, he snapped a kick with his right leg. Against an opponent of his own size, the toe of his boot would have reached the groin to produce an excruciating and incapacitating effect. As it was, he struck the back of the knee and caused Willie to stumble against the hitching rail. Certain that the affair was still far from over, he then wasted no time in bounding to his feet.

Dusty's summation proved correct. In fact, considering the youth of the contenders, the audience which gathered—including the marshal, who saw no need to interfere as no weapons were being used—were later to declare the subsequent fight was as good as they had ever seen.

During the twenty minutes the fracas continued, while the blond and the red head were not only more skilful but fought as a team, the other four made up for any lack of training and co-operation by weight, numbers and dogged determination. Furthermore, Dusty was hampered by the restrictions such a conflict placed upon him. Being aware that many of the *ju jitsu* and, more particularly, *karate* moves he had been taught might cripple permanently, or even kill, he could not bring all of his training into use. For all that, there were moments when only his knowledge stood between himself, Red and defeat. Not that his cousin was entirely dependant upon him, proving very adept and, on occasion, saving Dusty from a precarious situation. It was, however, Dusty who, using a *yoko geri* thrusting side kick to the jaw, put Willie Benedict out of the action and paved the way for their eventual victory.

The end came when, sprawling on the street—bloody, bruised and aching—trying to rise, Rothero saw a lump of jagged rock under the sidewalk. Above him, Dusty and Red had swung and crashed the other two Benedict boys back to back. Seeing they were preparing to launch what he could tell would be knockout punches, he reached for and grasped the weapon he hoped would turn the fight his way. If he had glanced over his shoulder, he would have noticed his actions had not gone unnoticed. Darting forward, her face flushed with excitement and the exertion she had put into yelling encouragement to her cousins, Georgina planted a hard kick to his butt. Sent forward by this unexpected attack, his head struck the edge of the sidewalk and he collapsed as Trace and Hobie too were being felled.

'Whooee, Cousin Dusty!' Red gasped, looking from one to another of their opponents' recumbent bodies. Sucking in breaths between the words, he continued, 'Looks like we sure remonstrated with them.'

'Why sure,' the small blond agreed, grinning at the reminder of the way he had acted and spoken while lulling the quartet into a sense of false security. He too was gasping for breath as he went

169

on, 'Thing being, what's Uncle Mannen going to have to say about it?'

***** *****

'Well, Mr. Blaze!' the Judge growled balefully at his taller nephew. 'Why did you start it *this* time?'

The time was nine o'clock in the morning of the day after the fight. Apart from a blackened eye and swollen lip apiece, there was no indication that Dusty and Red were stiff, sore and still feeling the after-effects of their strenuous activities. Dressed in cadet-grey uniforms, with the white Burnside-style campaign hats they hoped would soon bear the silver five-pointed star-in-a-circle badge of the Texas Light Cavalry under their left arms, they stood rigidly at attention before the mahogany desk in the study of the mansion which served as Judge Blaze's small military academy. Each kept his eyes to the front, looking over their uncle's head. Although they had seen Major Stone sitting in a comfortable leather armchair by the window as they entered, neither gave the slightest indication of knowing he was there.

'With respect, sir,' Dusty said, before Red could reply. 'It was I who started the fight, not Mr. Blaze.'

'*You*, Mr. Fog?' Blaze challenged, although he had been given a thorough verbal report of what had happened, sounding as if unable to believe his ears. 'But Marshal Sutcliffe told me you were having to hold Mr. Blaze back.'

'I wouldn't go so far as to say *that*, sir,' Dusty objected, being aware that the elderly peace officer had seen the trouble brewing, but could not get there quickly enough to prevent it. 'It was *I* who struck the first blow.'

'And what made *you* do it?' Blaze demanded, despite having already been told by Betty and Georgina.

'I considered the situation called for me to do so, sir.'

'In what way?'

'They were clearly trying to provoke a fight by making derogatory remarks, sir.'

'Such as?'

'Well, sir,' the blond replied, in a neutral tone. 'They referred to you as a "red-faced, whiskey-swilling old goat" and cast doubts on your ability as a judge of anything, especially moonshine whis-

170

key. The General was described as a "skinny-gutted old hard head who is meaner than the Devil he's named after".'

'And that was why you hit him,' Blaze suggested.

'No, sir,' Dusty corrected. 'I doubted whether the General or yourself would want a brawl started because of a few ill-advised words.'

'You *did*, did you?' the Judge barked, face reddening and taking a glance which informed him that his guest was smiling. 'Was that all they said?'

'No, sir. They called Cousins Betty and Georgina a couple of no-account, nose-wiping, scent-sniffing, doll-playing girls.'

'So you hit him for *that*?'

'No, sir. While I might have argued over the "no-account", I couldn't in all truth say they don't wipe their noses, sniff at scent occasionally and may still play with dolls.'

'Who else did they insult?' Blaze demanded.

'They called Polveroso City a god-damned one horse town and implied the whole of Rio Hondo not only stank, but did not have any ladies,' Dusty continued.

'That was cause enough for you to hit him,' Blaze stated judicially.

'Yes, sir,' the blond conceded. 'But it wasn't why I hit him.'

'Then *why* did you, by Jupiter?' the Judge almost bellowed.

'He spat on the sidewalk, sir,' Dusty explained, in a tone which suggested nothing further need be said on the matter.

'He *spat* on the sidewalk?' Blaze repeated.

'Deliberately, sir,' Dusty declared, sounding as if such an act completely vindicated his behaviour in his opinion.

'Let me understand what you are saying, Mr. Fog!' the Judge commanded. 'You allowed him to make derogatory remarks about your home town and county, your cousins, the General and myself without considering you should take some form of punitive action?'

'Yes, sir,' Dusty confirmed. 'As I said, I felt you are all big enough not to let such a thing worry you. Or to want a fight starting because of it.'

'But you still *started* one!' Blaze pointed out, his moustache bristling with what might have been anger and was clearly caused by some strong emotion.

'I'm afraid I did, sir,' Dusty apologized. 'But, as I said, he spat on the sidewalk and as I've always been told that was a dirty habit——'

'I don't think I want to hear *any* more, Mr. Fog!' the Judge interrupted firmly. 'Now I don't know how you and Mr. Blaze regard it, but I think the whole affair was not only disgraceful, but conduct unbecoming *men* who aspire to become officers in the Army of the Confederate States. Certainly General Hardin would not consider either of you is fit to lead soldiers under his command——'

'Cous—Mr. Fog only hit that feller to stop m——!' Red began, too honest to allow his cousin to suffer for what he knew had been an attempt to prevent him from being the one who started the trouble.

'You're at attention, Mr. Blaze!' the Judge barked. 'What I've said still applies, no matter *who* struck the first blow. Now I'll thank you both to leave and you can forget any notion of joining the Texas Light Cavalry just *yet*. You'll stay here until I'm satisfied you can comport yourself as *officers*. You are dismissed, *gentlemen*.'

'You were a little rough on them, weren't you?' Stone remarked, crossing to the desk after the cousins had saluted and marched from the room.

'I can never remember irascible old senior officers being particularly worried over whether they hurt my feelings or not, can you?' Blaze answered, a broad smile coming to his face. It turned into an appreciative chuckle as he continued, 'What a tactician young Dustine will make. He knew there was no way of avoiding a fight, so wanted the right excuse to do it. No matter what the cause, or whoever started it, he knew I'd have to take some kind of punitive action against the pair of them. You know what blasted politicians are like. Cuthbert Rothero's already going to be riled because we wouldn't let his son and nephews join the Texas Light Cavalry and he'll put it about that I'm showing favouritism if I was to let the boys go now, no matter who started the trouble.'

'There were few who would blame either for taking exception to the remarks made to them,' Stone protested. 'If anybody had said anything like it about my kin, or home town, I'd have started hitting.'

'That's not how Rothero will see it,' the Judge answered, rising and crossing to a large cupboard in the corner of the study. 'And Dustine knew it. So he picked the spitting on the sidewalk to give me my excuse.'

'Didn't he also know that causing his enrolment to be delayed will affect his seniority?' the major inquired.

'I'd be surprised if he *didn't*,' Blaze declared. 'But he wouldn't have let it stop him even if he intended making the Army his career. He's done *me* a service, too.'

'In what way?'

'Their mothers insist they're still too young to go just yet and, ready as they are, this gives me an excuse to keep the womenfolk happy by holding them back for a while longer.'

'You think they're *both* ready to go?' Stone asked.

'I do,' the Judge stated, opening the cupboard's door and reaching inside. 'The way Charles William Henry spoke up to take the blame convinced me of that.' Taking out a pair of well made sabres, one slightly shorter than the other, which the major readily identified as made by L. Haiman & Brother of Columbus, Georgia —arguably the makers of the best blades in the Confederate States, he continued. 'So as soon as this affair's blown over and they give me an excuse to rescind my "decision", I'll give them these and send them to join Ole Devil.'

*****   *****

Cradling the butt of the Hawken rifle against her right shoulder, Betty Hardin lay prone and lined its sights carefully down the slope. She was aiming so that the bullet would break the neck of the big buck whitetail deer which stood at the edge of the winding trail about a hundred and fifty yards from where she was hiding. Also lying in concealment at the top of the rim, Georgina, Dusty and Red watched and waited expectantly. Although they all had rifles in the hands, they were leaving whatever shooting had to be done to her. It had been she who first saw the animal, so the privilege of taking the trophy belonged to her and, in accordance with the rules which they had been taught, she alone must make the attempt.

173

Almost two weeks had gone by since the interview with Judge Blaze. All traces of the fight had left the youngsters' faces and they showed no sign of having suffered any after effects. Although they still had not been given any indication of their uncle's true feelings regarding the incident, he had raised no objections when they had requested to be allowed to accompany the girls for a day's hunting.

Having decided that an area in the vicinity of the Jack County border line might offer the most opportunities, the party had ridden in that direction. Leaving their horses in the corral of a line cabin belonging to the Blaze family's Double BB ranch and close to the edge of the woodland which fringed the Rio Hondo, they had set out on foot, After having covered no more than a mile, it had appeared that their choice was correct. Being in the lead, having won the draw to decide who should have the first shot, Betty had sighted the buck as she was approaching the rim of a slope overlooking the trail which ran from Diggers Wells—seat of Jack County—to Polveroso City.

With her forefinger starting to tighten on the trigger, Betty was annoyed to see the buck throwing back its head in obvious alarm. She realized this could not have been caused by it having discovered the presence of her party. It gazed for a moment in an easterly direction along the winding trail. Then, before she could either correct her aim or complete the pressure on the trigger, it took off with a bound which carried it over a nearby clump of flowering dogwood bushes.

'Blast the luck!' Betty ejaculated.

'I'll see if I can——!' Georgina began, meaning to suggest she should try to shoot the buck before it disappeared and starting to rise.

'Stay down!' Dusty commanded urgently.

'Why?' the blonde girl asked, obeying nevertheless.

'Something spooked that buck,' Dusty pointed out. 'And it wasn't us. So I want to know what—or *who*—it was!'

The small blond's curiosity was not to be denied an explanation for very long. What was more, his caution proved to be justified.

Eight villainous looking Mexicans appeared around the bend in the trail towards which the buck had stared before taking its hurried departure. All were armed with knives, revolvers and shoulder arms of various kinds. They had on expensive, if garish, but dirty and neglected clothing. Following them, his horse being rein-led by the rearmost member of the party, was Burt Rothero. There was, the watchers concluded, good cause for his clearly dejected attitude. Not only were his hands bound behind his back, but blood still ran from a cut on the side of his forehead. Although he was swaying from the effects of the blow which produced it, he was prevented from falling from his mount by having his ankles fastened to the stirrup irons. Furthermore, if he had been inclined to throw himself from the saddle and contrived to do so in spite of his bonds, his position would not have been greatly improved; if at all. There was a rope, secured by a 'hangman's' knot around his neck and secured to the low, massive horn of his escort's saddle.

'Shall I down the jasper leading his horse?' Red suggested in a whisper, moving his rifle into the firing position. 'Or will you?'

'Neither of us!' Dusty replied, his tone and bearing suggesting he would brook no argument. 'Let them go by!'

'I don't like that surly son-of-a-b—gun either,' Red commented, after the party had been allowed to pass out of sight and hearing without any action being taken against them. The alteration to pungent description had been caused by a timely remembrance that the two girls were present. 'But I don't cotton to leaving them bunch have him.'

'Neither do I,' Dusty answered, coming to his feet. 'Thing being though, there're but four of us and eight of them. Which, counting we all put down one apiece, that will still leave four to make wolf bait of him.'

'Shucks,' Red sniffed, but he was beginning to see the difficulties which his proposal would have created and which his cousin had already envisaged. 'The ones who weren't hit'd've lit out like the Devil splashed with Holy Water.'

'Likely,' the small blond conceded. 'Only, knowing them, they wouldn't have left him behind. Not alive, anyways.'

'Do you know who they are?' Georgina inquired, still puzzled by Dusty's insistence upon passive behaviour.

'Not so's I could go up and say, "Howdy, you-all, *Senor* Something-Or-Other," ' Dusty admitted. 'But I'm sure as hell's for sinners know *what* they are.'

'*Bandidos*,' Betty suggested.

'*Bandidos*,' Dusty confirmed, gazing along the trail down which the riders had disappeared. 'Which I know we haven't had any of them around Rio Hondo County, no matter what's been happening elsewhere since so many of the menfolk have gone to fight the Yankees. But, like they do say, there's a first time for *everything*.'

'I reckon there's still enough men around here to hand eight of them their needings,' Red declared.

'I'm not gainsaying it,' Dusty replied. 'But there's likely to be a whole heap more than just the eight of them. Could be they've been sent on ahead as scouts to find out if there's easy pickings around here for the rest to come after.'

'Which being,' the red head commented grimly, 'seems like to me it'd be a right good thing was any that's left of them take back word there aren't.'

'There's something in what you say,' Dusty drawled, adopting the quiet manner of speaking his cousins knew presaged action. 'Thing being, how do we do it?'

'Use all those fancy tactics Uncle Mannen's been teaching us,' Red offered. 'Sneak up close and cut loose at them. I reckon we could put down four with the first volley——'

'We could've done that as they rode by,' Dusty pointed out. 'Only we'd've got Burt Rothero killed by doing it.'

'Get close enough so you and me can drop the rifles, then start throwing down on the rest with our Colts,' Red supplemented, although he had a feeling that he was missing some important fact.

'How?' the small blond challenged.

'Like I said,' Red replied. 'Sneak up close, then start popping caps and burning powder. That ought to do it.'

'Why sure,' Dusty drawled. 'Except that sneaking up on them, while they're riding or after they've made camp, won't be easy. One wrong move and Rothero's as good as dead.'

'That's something to think on,' the red head conceded. 'Have *you* any ideas?'

The final words were less of a question than a statement.

176

What was more, Dusty was already prepared to justify his cousin's faith in him.

Ever since the *bandidos* had come into view, appreciating the threat their presence could pose to the local people, the small blond had been devoting an inborn flair for tactics—which had been strengthened by the lessons on the subject he had received at Judge Blaze's hands—to solving the problem. He had realized that it was desirable to inflict such a lesson that any who survived and escaped would spread the word to others of their kind that Rio Hondo County was a region to be avoided. The question was how to bring this about, particularly without causing the captive to be killed in the process.

There were, Dusty had concluded, a few factors which were in his party's favour. The Mexicans were unaware that they were in the vicinity and, providing they could continue to avoid being detected, the element of surprise was with them. Not only had Red and he exchanged their boots for moccasins as an aid to silent movement while hunting, they had on their cowhand clothes and gunbelts. Neither girl had a revolver with her, but each carried a small, single shot Henry Deringer's Pocket Pistol on her person. Furthermore, to permit greater freedom of movement than would be allowed by their usual attire, they were defying convention by wearing masculine hats, jackets, shirts and lightweight boots. For all that, he had qualms over the scheme which he was contemplating if an opportunity should be presented for its employment. Carrying it out might offer the Jack County youth a chance of survival, but putting it into operation would entail placing Betty and Georgina in very grave peril.

'Some,' Dusty admitted, reaching a decision with the speed which was to make him the excellent light cavalry fighting leader he became. 'What we have to do is to take them by surprise and tackle them in such a way that they'll be too occupied with us to think of killing Rothero.'

'Sounds reasonable,' Red conceded dubiously. 'Only I'm damned if I can see how we can bring it off.'

'Conventional tactics would be for us to follow them until they make camp for the night,' Dusty elaborated. 'Then, utilizing all our resources, we'd surround them, close in while a diversion was being caused and attack.'

'That's be fine,' Red declared. 'Excepting that we're a mite short of resources.'

'We are, but it's like Uncle Mannen's been teaching us,' Dusty answered and his tone became that of the Judge when delivering a lecture. 'When conventional tactics are no use, it's time for improvisation, Mr. Blaze.'

'I don't know about you, Cousin Georgina,' Betty remarked, turning her attention from the small blond to the other girl. 'But I didn't care for the way he looked at *us* when he said that.'

'Or me,' Georgina seconded, although her doubts were for a different reason to those of her more perceptive cousin. 'Something tells me that, whatever he's got in mind, I'm *not* going to like it.'

*****   *****

Lying where he had been toppled from his horse after his ankles were cut free, Burt Rothero looked with growing horror at the two riders who were entering the clearing in which his captors had elected to make camp for the night. Although the sun was going down and the surrounding woodland was already growing gloomy, there was still sufficient light for him to identify them as Betty Hardin and Georgina Blaze in spite of the way in which they were dressed. What was more, he judged that neither realized she was being most injudicious and had placed herself into a position of even greater jeopardy than his own.

Having been on his way to Polveroso City with a message for Judge Blaze, Rothero had found himself surrounded by the Mexicans. Although dazed and knocked to the ground by the blow from the barrel of their leader's pistol, he had had his wits sufficiently about him to save his life by stating his father was wealthy and would willingly pay a ransom for his safe return. Instead of taking him back to Diggers Wells and commencing negotiations, they had ridden into Rio Hondo County. As far as he could make out with his not too extensive knowledge of Spanish, they intended to check the prospects of acquiring loot from what had previously been regarded as a most unsafe area in which to attempt depredations. He was under the impression that his future depended upon the result.

178

To give Rothero credit, regardless of remembering how the girls had helped bring about the defeat he and his cousins had suffered in Polveroso City, he did not hesitate over before trying to alert them to their peril.

'Look out——!' the youngster yelled, beginning to thrust himself into a sitting position, but was prevented from finishing the warning by the nearest *bandido* turning and sending a kick to his chest which flung him on his back once more.

Even as he was going down, Rothero concluded he had spoken too late.

'What do you think you're doing?' Betty demanded in English, as a man sprang to grab her horse's reins.

'How dare you?' Georgina yelled indignantly, also in her native tongue, as her mount was snatched by another of the *bandidos*.

'Hey, Cruz!' the man holding Betty's horse whooped in Spanish. 'This's a little girl, not a boy!'

'And mine,' the other captor seconded, showing an equal delight.

'Bring them over here and let's take a look!' commanded the big, burly leader of the band.

'Let go of me!' Betty shrieked, struggling weakly as the gaunt *bandido* dropped the reins to grab her by the left arm and leg, then drag her from the saddle.

'Take your hands off!' Georgina screeched, sounding equally alarmed and behaving in a similar fashion as she too was seized and hauled from her mount.

Watching from the concealment of a couple of trees at the edge of the clearing, Dusty and Red had their rifles at their shoulders. Despite his scheme having progressed satisfactorily so far, the small blond felt a sense of apprehension as he was aligning his sights.

On hearing that she and Betty were to collect the horses, Georgina had stated she did not intend to be restricted to nothing more than going for help. She had discovered this was not to be her participation in certain eventualities. Instead, while they were bringing up the animals, their cousins were to follow the *bandidos* on foot until able to ride. This had been done and the pursuit accomplished without their quarry learning it was taking place.

They had been helped by the Mexicans travelling at a leisurely pace and deciding to halt reasonably early in the afternoon.

Making a reconnaissance of the *bandidos'* proposed camp ground alone, Dusty had needed only a cursory study to realize he must employ the means he had hoped to avoid. There was too much risk in waiting until after nightfall before attempting the rescue. To do so would have entailed approaching through the woodland in the darkness. Capable though they all might be at stalking wary game in the daytime, doing so after dark and with another human being's life at stake was a vastly different proposition and one he did not wish to chance trying.

Rejoining the others, Dusty had told them how he proposed to deal with the situation. Allowing their cousins sufficient time to get into position on foot, the girls were to ride into the clearing as if unaware of the danger. How the attempt to capture them was made would dictate their next actions. If more than one man came towards both—or either—of them, they were to set their horses running immediately. Despite having had no illusions as to the danger they would be facing, Betty and Georgina had agreed to play the parts to which they were assigned.

As each girl was contending with only a single would-be captor, they were going along with their alternative instructions. Everything now depended upon whether they could justify the small blond's faith in them being able to produce the required diversion.

Allowing herself to be pulled to the ground without resisting, Betty contrived to land on her feet and face her captor. He was taller and heavier than herself, but she felt confident that the lessons she had received from Tommy Okasi would allow her to overcome the discrepancy; particularly as what she intended to do would come as a complete surprise after her apparently passive acquiescence.

'Hey!' the man said, releasing her arm and leg to place his hands on her shoulders and leering into the little girl's beautiful face. 'You're not bad for a *grin*——!'

Thrusting up her hands between the Mexican's arms, Betty grabbed his ears between her thumbs and forefingers. Digging them in, she caused sufficient pain to bring his words to a halt and make him jerk back his head to add to it. As he tilted his torso

180

to the rear in an attempt to free himself, she sent up her left leg with all the force she could muster to impact against his testicles. A strangled croak of unadulterated torment burst from him and, clutching at the stricken area, he stumbled away to collapse retching violently on to his knees.

Lacking Betty's aptitude and extensive training in unarmed self defence, Georgina had had no intention of trying to escape by such means. As she was being hauled from her horse, she reached with her right hand to enfold the butt of the Deringer in her jacket's outside right pocket. Before she could extract it, her captor had transferred his left hand from her thigh to her right bicep. There was, she realized, only one thing she could do. Turning the barrel forward as best she could and thanking providence for Dusty having had the foresight to insist she cocked the hammer before setting off, she squeezed the trigger. A look of amazement mingled with agony twisted at the man's face as the little pistol cracked and, having ripped through the cloth of her jacket, the ·43 calibre ball[8] ploughed into his left thigh. As in the case of Betty's victim, he lost his hold and tottered away to fall down.

Waiting until he could see how successful the girls were in defending themselves and satisfied they were drawing the rest of the *bandidos'* attention to them, Dusty used his rifle's only available load to send its bullet at the man who had kicked Rothero. Caught in the head, the Mexican spun around and went down dead. Before his body struck the ground, confident that the most immediate threat to the Jack County youth was removed, the small blond was tossing aside the empty weapon and, sweeping out the matched brace of bone handled Army Colts, sprang forward.

Ready to fire if Georgina needed help, having been positioned so he could cope with such a contingency, Red changed his point of aim as soon as it became obvious that she would not. With the sound of his cousin's rifle going off ringing in his ears, he snapped off his shot in the hope of putting down the man he had deduced to be the *bandidos'* leader. In his haste, he failed to achieve his purpose. Without wasting time in futile recriminations, he too

[8] As all Henry Deringer Pocket Pistols were hand-made, there was considerable variations in their calibre although all were of comparatively large size.

181

discarded the rifle which would have required reloading before it could once more be employed as a firearm. Drawing his revolvers, he charged towards the enemy a couple of seconds after his cousin had burst from concealment.

The distance from the nearest cover to the centre of the clearing was too great for anything but slow and deliberate shooting with a handgun. So Dusty had had the girls take the risk of entering in the hope they could create enough of a diversion to allow himself and Red to close the range. He noticed, not without considerable relief, that—despite the rifles' shots suggesting help was in the offing—they appeared to be doing what was needed. Not until he and his cousin were several vital strides nearer to their objective did any of the *bandidos* show any indication of knowing they were coming. What was more, not one of the Mexicans was holding a weapon. Letting out yells of alarm and turning, they began belatedly to try to rectify the omission.

Left!

Right!

Left!

Right!

Firing on the run, Dusty's ambidextrous prowess allowed him to send the ·44 calibre bullets with devastating effect.

The leader of the *bandidos* died with his revolver half drawn. Another man went over backwards, a hole in the centre of his forehead and the base of his skull shattered as the bullet emerged. Neither of the other shots produced such a lethal effect, but one ripped off a *sombrero* and stunned its wearer while the other took a Mexican in and cost him the use of his left arm for the remainder of his life.

Nor was Red's participation to be disclaimed. He too had practised sighting and firing a Colt while on the move. Although he was only capable of employing one revolver at a time under such conditions, his first shot tumbled lifeless the *bandido* who was closest to duplicating the leader's speed. Fired before he could prevent himself, the second inflicted what was to prove a mortal wound for the man Dusty's third shot had knocked unconscious.

Finding himself left without support, the solitary uninjured member of the band forgot his original intention of fighting. Ignoring his partially drawn revolver as it fell over the lip of his holster on being released, he twirled about and raced to his party's tethered and disturbed horses. Managing to catch hold of one horse's mane as it was breaking free, he also contrived to vault astride its bare back. Clinging on with a skill born of desperation, he sent the animal bounding forward.

To his great relief, the *bandido* made the gloomy shelter offered by the trees without feeling lead driving into him. Urged on by thoughts of how at least a dozen enormous and ferocious Texans had burst from nowhere upon them, each firing two big revolvers with terrifying accuracy, he kept the horse running regardless of how dangerous travelling at such speed through the woodland might be.[9]

'We did it!' Red enthused, as the escaping *bandido* disappeared from sight.

'Why sure,' Dusty replied, hoping he sounded more convinced that the scheme was certain to succeed that he had been.

'Like Uncle Mannen tells us,' the red head went on, all his early apprehension departed; 'it sometimes pays to improvise.'

***** *****

'Are you telling me, *Mr.* Fog, that despite realizing the danger you allowed your Cousin Betty and Cousin Georgina to take part in your hare-brained scheme?'

Standing in uniform and at attention before Judge Blaze's desk, Dusty had just concluded a description of the previous day's events.

After disarming and securing those of the *bandidos* who might have been able to continue hostilities on recovering, Dusty and Red had liberated Rothero. Then, while his cousin started to attend to the injured, the small blond had asked the no longer objecting Georgina to accompany Betty to Polveroso City and send back assistance. The bodies had been left where they lay, but the survivors of the gang had been collected to be lodged in the town's jail until their fate could be determined. Not unexpectedly, Dusty and Red had been ordered to report to Judge Blaze's office at noon the following day. Arriving they had dis-

[9] The result of the Mexican being allowed to escape is told in: Part Four, 'It's Our Turn To Improvise, Miss Blaze' of *J.T'S Ladies.*

covered that, although uninvited, the girls were present and went in with them. Strangely, considering his views on such matters, their uncle had raised no objections.

'I did, sir,' the small blonde admitted, in answer to the furious-sounding question Blaze had hurled at him.

'You *did*, sir?' the Judge repeated. 'And didn't it occur to you, *sir*, that it might be injudicious to put them in such grave peril?'

'Yes, sir,' Dusty confessed, having no doubt that Georgina's mother and others of the clan's ladies had already expressed similar views. 'But I couldn't see any other way of doing it and avoiding getting Burt Rothero killed.'

'Dusty warned us it would be dangerous,' the blonde put in, looking as if she expected her intervention would cause lightning to strike. 'But we insisted on helping.'

'Are you in the habit, *Mr*. Fog, of allowing mere chits of girls to dictate your decisions?' Blaze demanded, having directed a glare which caused Georgina to back away hurriedly. 'Because, *sir*, if you are, I can only——'

The words ended abruptly as the Judge found himself confronted by a furious looking little female figure which bounded to the front of his desk.

'Uncle Mannen!' Betty snapped, slapping her hands on the mahogany top. 'There are times when I think you are developing into an old curmudgeon!'

'A *curmudgeon*, young miss?' the Judge thundered, also banging the top of the desk with his palms.

'Yes, sir!' Betty confirmed, but with something less than her original ferocity. For all her realization that she was overstepping the bounds which her relationship with Ole Devil allowed, she forced herself to continue, 'I'm not sure exactly what one is, but that is how you're acting. Dusty *knew* the risks and warned us of them. If there had been *any* other way, he would have used it. He even tried to refuse as it was, but Georgina and I wouldn't let him.'

'Have you *quite* finished, ma'am?' Blaze challenged, leaning forward and glowering as if ready to explode.

'Y—Yes!' Betty gulped, now thoroughly alarmed at her temerity and wondering if it had made things worse instead of better for her cousins.

'Then have the kindness to leave!' the Judge ordered. '*Both* of you!'

'Yes, sir!' Betty assented and, with Georgina preceding her, took her departure as quickly as her legs would carry her.

'*Curmudgeon*!' Blaze repeated, in closer to a chuckle than a snort, sitting down after the girls had left and closed the door. There was more than a hint of amusement in his eyes, although his tone did not change too much, as he continued, 'Let that be a lesson to you, gentlemen. *Never* let the womenfolk become involved in your affairs. They've no control over their emotions.'

'Yes, sir!' Dusty and Red promised in the same breath, sensing their activities might have met with more approval than appeared on the surface.

'Blast it, I've had Cousin Georgina-Mae abusing me as if it was *my* fault you'd put her gal in danger and asking what I mean to do about it,' the Judge went on indignantly. 'And look what happens when I try to remonstrate with you in a perfectly amiable fashion. I have the pair of "defenceless" little darlings on my neck like a pair of cornered bobcats. There's no pleasing females, I tell you, gentlemen.'

'I'm sorry about it, sir,' Dusty apologized and the red head nodded agreement.

'And so you *should* be,' Blaze declared, walking towards the cupboard instead of resuming his seat. Opening it and taking out the two Haiman sabres, he continued without his voice suggesting any change of attitude as he turned around, 'Anyway, I suppose I'll have to do *something* to keep Cousin Georgina-Mae happy. So I'm going to punish the pair of you. You'll each carry one of these all the way until you report to the Texas Light Cavalry at the end of the week. What's more, seeing that you saved his son's neck, I think Cuthbert Rothero will think that's punishment enough.'

Author's note: The events which followed those recorded herein are told in: *You're in Command Now, Mr. Fog.*

PART SIX

Waco in

KEEP GOOD TEMPER ALIVE

'He'd been born to the sound of war-screams, the crack of weapons, the soggy thud as Waco Indian arrows sank into white flesh. Two minutes after his mother gave birth to him, she was a widow. Half an hour later, he was left an orphan by the same means which killed his father.'

These were the first words to be printed about Waco!

Some time ago, a Mini-Competition in a Newsletter of the J. T. Edson Appreciation Society *asked for the name of the book in which Waco made his first appearance. To my surprise, the majority of the entrants—who usually exhibit a far greater recollection of what took place in earlier titles than I have without actually checking on the volume concerned—fell into the same error and said it had been in* Trigger Fast.[1] *While this was the book which explained how he became a member of the Floating Outfit, he had already been in print several times before it was published. In fact he was introduced, along with Doc Leroy, in what became* The Hard Riders, *the second of the three titles I submitted to Brown Watson Ltd. for entry in their Literary Competition's Western category.*

However, Waco had been born long before that. He first appeared, written in longhand on a notebook—my typewriter being with the majority of my belongings in the hold—while I was returning in a troopship from Hong Kong to the United Kingdom at the end of my three year tour in the Far East. Being the

---

[1] I submitted the manuscript under the title, *Trigger Fast and Up from Texas*, but it was abbreviated for some reason I have never been able to discover by Brown Watson Ltd.

only member of the Royal Army Veterinary Corps aboard and a corporal, which excused me from most fatigues and duties, I found time was hanging heavily on my hands during the eight weeks' voyage. So, procuring a notebook, I started writing the stories which eventually formed the nucleus of Sagebrush Sleuth *and* Arizona Ranger.

Waco underwent far fewer changes than any of the characters I had created during my years in the Army when the time came to prepare him for publication. From the beginning he had always been the youngster left an orphan by an Indian attack and saved by his meeting with Dusty Fog from turning bad. I selected him to be the main protagonist in the basically deductive type detective stories written during the voyage as he seemed to be the one best suited to play the part. I was able to have him acquire knowledge of various subjects from the other members of the Floating Outfit. This paved the way for books such as The Making of a Lawman, *which told how he received his training in the work of a peace officer. He was the first of my characters to attain the status of a separate series. In addition, he has two other firsts to his credit. At the end of* The Drifter, *he is on the verge of being married— before such an event is being contemplated by Dusty, Mark or the Kid—and he is the only one whose adventures in later life have as yet been recorded, appearing as a middle-aged U.S. Marshal in* Hound Dog Man.[2]

Doc Leroy became Waco's partner in the Arizona Rangers because of a plot I have in mind for a book which will tell what happens when his former employer, Stone Hart, gives up driving trail herds on contract and takes a ranch of his own. I don't have the full details of this story settled as yet, but I do know that his original 'sidekick', Rusty Willis marries at the end of it. This gives Doc an excuse to move on and explains how he appears as a member of the Floating Outfit in The Small Texan *and* The Town Tamers. *I never realized how popular he was becoming until* Doc Leroy, M.D. *was mentioned as being 'In Preparation' on my*

[2] A reference to Dusty Fog having married Freddie Woods and settled down to run the OD Connected ranch was deleted from *Hound Dog Man* by the editor of Brown Watson Ltd. on the grounds that the readers might object to any suggestion that he had reached middle-age.

187

earlier list of titles in chronological order.[3] *Not only was this book frequently requested in mail from readers, many of whom overlooked the* + *symbol indicating it was 'In Preparation' and not yet even with the publishers, but members of what we came to call the Doc Leroy, M.D. syndrome appeared at every autograph party or signing session I attended demanding to be informed when it would be available. After it finally appeared, attention was switched to* The Whip and the War Lance. *As this is also now available, we are wondering which will be the next title to be requested.*

Well, that's enough of an introduction. Here goes with Waco's participation in the volume.

[3] To avoid similar confusion, our policy now is to list only those titles which have already been published, or are completed and held by Transworld Publishers Ltd. pending publication.

188

KEEP GOOD TEMPER ALIVE

Gliding on silent wings through the woodland, the common night-hawk paid no attention to the four horses—a large paint stallion, an equally big black gelding and a pair of somewhat smaller coyote-duns—which were standing hobbled on the banks of the small stream at the western edge of the fire-lit clearing. Yet, despite the abundance of moths and other night-flying insects attracted by the flickering flames, it would have avoided the area if there had been any sign of movement from the four shapes, each completely concealed by a blanket, which were lying on the up-wind side of the fire. Satisfied that the motionless mounds posed no threat to its continued existence, the bird swooped eagerly towards the unexpected bounty. On the point of engulfing the first of its winged prey with a wide mouth ideally suited for such a purpose, it discovered that it was not the only being intent upon taking other creatures' lives in the vicinity.

Coming from the darkness of the trees at the northern edge of the clearing with the noiseless and deadly manner of any predatory beast, three figures darted swiftly towards the fire. Of medium height, thickset without being cumbersome, their savage coppery brown features and shoulder length black hair would have informed anybody with experience of Arizona Territory that they were Apache Indians. Their attire was a mixture of traditional tribal costume and cast-off, or looted, white men's garments, but this did nothing to lessen the menace of their demeanour, nor their murderous purpose.

Each of the young men, none would be far past his teens, was carrying a weapon ready for instant use. One held a short, yet powerful bow with an arrow nocked to its string. The second grasped a Winchester Model of 1873 carbine with medicine symbols made of brass tacks glinting from its wooden foregrip and butt. On the surface, the third might have been less efficiently —even inadequately—armed. He had a feather decorated, brightly painted nine foot long war lance held in the position white soldiers indulging in bayonet fighting practice called the 'high port'. While his companions had weapons which offered a greater effective range, any brave-heart who elected to use a war lance was expected to press home an attack and strike down an enemy regardless of how dangerous the attempt might be.

Fanning out as they sped forward, the trio were clearly timing their approach so as to launch their attacks simultaneously. Nor did the braves with the bow and the carbine intend to take any chance of missing. Neither halted until he was so close to his proposed victim that there was little danger of his aim being anything other than true.

After a glance to ensure his companions were in position, the lance carrier gave vent to an awesome war whoop and, raising the weapon, he plunged its head into the blanket shrouded mound at his feet. The blow was struck so it would impale the chest of the sleeper. The yell was echoed by the hiss of the bow as its string was released and the sharp crack of the carbine. Both discharged their missiles with an equal accuracy. Propelled by a velocity capable of sinking it fletching deep into the chest cavity of a fast running bull buffalo when loosed from the back of a pursuing horse, the arrow almost disappeared into the mound at which it had been directed. Struck by the flat-nosed ·44 calibre bullet emitted from the Winchester, the third blanket jerked sharply at the point of impact.

Although, on the face of it, the attack had been launched successfully, doubts began to assail the trio. Experienced braves, if young, each had taken human life on other occasions. So they were puzzled by the complete lack of response from their victims. Usually, even if death was as nearly instantaneous as could be achieved, there would be some slight movement to show life was fleeing. Still more curious, the fourth blanket covered shape remained just as motionless. Yet the person they assumed it to be had had an Apache's education in the matter of waking promptly if disturbed by sounds far less noisy than those which had just been made.

'Dog shit!'

Even as the appreciation that all might not be well was starting to assail the trio, a voice from the blackness at the opposite side of the clearing to their point of entry made the brief, pungently coarse comment. While the words were spoken in their native tongue, the person who said them did not have the accent of an Apache.

Which was not surprising!

Like another of the four people who were advancing into the firelight as rapidly and otherwise silently as the trio, the speaker was a white man. Just over six foot in height, with a powerful young physique filling out to manhood, he was a tanned, handsome blue eyed blond dressed after the fashion of a Texas cowhand. Around his waist was a brown *buscadero* gunbelt with a brace of Colt Artillery Model Peacemakers in its contoured, tied-down holsters. Nor were they his only armament. In his hands was a Winchester Model of 1876 rifle, its barrel slanting as if drawn by magnetism and at waist level towards the lance carrier as he came to a halt.

Also armed with the latest product from Oliver F. Winchester's factory at New Haven, Connecticut, the second white man was a fraction shorter and more slender. He too wore the attire of a Texas' cowhand, but his face had a tan-resisting pallor and—although the three braves did not recognize it as such—a somewhat studious expression. Unlike his companion, who sported only a brown and white calfskin vest, he had on a brown jacket with its right side stitched back to leave clear access to the ivory handle of the Colt Civilian Model Peacemaker in the fast draw holster of his exceptionally well made gunbelt. Again differing from the blond, he was bringing the butt of the rifle to his right shoulder as he came to a stop and his target was the warrior holding the carbine.

The male Indian with the Texans had a similar build to that of his would-be assailants, but his hair—held back by the red head band of an Apache chief—had turned grey with age even though he was moving with a similar speed and precision. Despite retaining something of the amiability responsible for his man-name 'Good Temper', his face was set in hard and angry lines. He wore a buckskin shirt, blue breech clout, moccasins and fringed knee-high leggings. A knife hung sheathed on the left side of his belt and he was carrying a Winchester Model of 1866 rifle which might be described as the grandfather of the shoulder-arms in the two white men's possession.

Slightly taller and slimmer, the woman at the chief's left side was much younger. She was beautiful by any race's standards and moved with a feline grace. Nor could her loose-fitting, multi-hued blouse and ankle-length skirt conceal that she had an eye-catching figure. Although her features implied she was an Apache, they also hinted she might have a proportion of Mexican blood.

'Die, white-eye!' the lance carrier screeched, recovering from his surprise more quickly than the other two and springing to the attack as was expected of one who had elected to carry the medicine weapon.

Instantly, the young blond's rifle barked an answer to the challenge. Its ·45 bullet, driven by gasses created by the ignition of seventy-five grains of prime du Pont black powder, took the brave in the centre of the chest. There was a crack like the sound of a stepped-on twig snapping as his breastbone was broken and he pitched backwards. Nor were his companions any more fortunate when they attempted to resume hostilities.

For all his slender build and studious demeanour, the second Texan proved equally capable of defending himself. Settling into a position which allowed a careful aim to be taken, his rifle thundered as the carbine was pointed in his direction. Caught between the eyes, the second brave was flung from his feet and he was entering the Land of Good Hunting before his lifeless body struck the ground.

Nor did the chief lack ability and he did not allow himself to be deterred by the fact that he was in contention with members of his own race. His rifle's crack was somewhat lighter in timbre than those of his allies, being powered by a mere twenty-eight grains of powder, but he had no cause to complain about the result. Flying true, the ·44 calibre bullet ripped through the archer's skull as he was drawing another arrow from the quiver on his back and brought his desire to continue the attack to an abrupt end.

Three right hands operated levers, ejecting empty cases and sending live ammunition from the tubular magazines to the rifles' chambers. It was obvious, however, that the precaution of reloading was needless. None of the trio who had arrived bent upon murder had survived the trap sprung upon them by their intended victims.

'Do you-all know any of them, Chief Good Temper?' the taller and younger white man inquired in English, his drawl confirming his origins were in Texas rather than Arizona.

'I know them!' the male Apache answered, sounding bitter and speaking the same language with only a trace of an accent. 'They are some who——!'

Before the sentence could be concluded, the girl shouted a couple of words in her native tongue and jumped to give the chief a push. As he went staggering aside, a shot crashed from a different point to that at which the original attackers had emerged. Although she contrived to prevent him from being hit, she had placed herself in jeopardy. Struck in the right side by the bullet fired by the as yet unseen assailant, she cried in pain and, after spinning a few paces, sprawled to the ground.

Raising their rifles shoulderwards, the slender Texan having started to lower his, the three men spun rapidly towards the new source of danger. Taking sight equally swiftly, they commenced to fire with the speed only a Winchester's lever action mechanism permitted when being manipulated by such obviously competent hands. A veritable hail of lead tore into the night darkened woodland from which the latest attacker had shot, to elicit the harsh screech of a man in mortal pain and a brief thrashing of foliage being agitated violently.

'See to Clear Eyes, Doc!' the younger of the Texans snapped, lowering the rifle to the ground and substituting it with his right hand Colt, then starting to stride forward without waiting to see whether the other accepted what had been more of an order than a suggestion.

'Watch what you're doing, *amigo*,' the recipient of the command answered, showing no resentment.

After throwing a glance at the departing Texan, Good Temper was too experienced a warrior to attempt to follow him. If their fourth attacker should only be feigning an injury, or have companions, the young blond would not want to have to keep remembering he had an ally in the vicinity while searching through the darkness of the woodland. So the chief turned his gaze to the wounded girl. While his features were not given to expressing emotions as a general rule, he showed deep concern. Nor was he kept long in ignorance of the latest assailant's identity. After only a brief absence, the Texan returned. His Colt was back in its holster and he was dragging the limp body of an elderly Apache by its left ankle.

'How about this one, chief?' the blond asked, releasing the limb.

'I know *him*!' Good Temper declared, the bitterness even more noticeable. 'We rode many war trails together.'

'Only you-all had the good sense to know when the time came to quit,' the blond stated.

'I thought *he* had too,' the chief growled, then brought his attention to where the second white man was kneeling by the injured girl. 'My daughter——'

'Leave Doc to 'tend to her,' the blond suggested. 'He knows right well what he's doing when it comes to fixing gun shot wounds.'

'Very well.' Good Temper asserted, any reluctance he might have felt being replaced by acquiescence as he watched the competent manner in which the studious-faced young man was using his daughter's knife to cut away clothing and expose the wound. 'Do what you have to, but save her, Doc Leroy.'

'Count on it,' the slender Texan promised. 'Go get my bag, *amigo*.'

'Yo!' the blond assented, accepting the change from giver to taker of orders with as little objection as the other had shown when obeying him.

'The lead hasn't gone in, Clear Eyes,' Doc announced, before the youngster whose only name was Waco had done more than turn to carry out his instructions. 'But it's left a bad cut and may have broken a rib. I'm going to have to stitch up the cut, if you know what that means?'

'I understand,' the girl admitted, speaking English as fluently as her father. 'If you bring the small buckskin medicine pouch which you will find in my left saddlebag, Waco, it has something that will lessen the pain. If you don't object to such things, Doc?'

'I'd've used something of mine if you didn't have any pain killer to hand,' the slender Texan answered with a smile. 'Letting yourself get hurt when there's no call to doesn't show you're brave, just stupid.' His gaze lifted to where Waco had done as requested and was standing with the chief, his tone becoming less amiable as he continued, 'Which I work better without an audience standing breathing down my neck.'

'He's allus a mite tetchy when he's got work to do, chief,' the blond commented, handing over the bags he had collected. 'And worse than that when it's doctoring he's facing. Let's move off a spell so's he can get to doing it.'

'Many of our medicine men and women are the same,' Good Temper replied. 'I think the reason they don't want us to watch is in case we learn they aren't as clever as they would have us believe they are.'

'I've allus thought that self-same thing,' Waco admitted grinning and walking, accompanied by the chief, to where he had left the fourth body. 'It's right lucky you saw their dust on the back trail late this afternoon and we found a place this good for us to wait and let them figure they were taking us unawares when they caught up.'

'You saw it too,' Good Temper pointed out.

'It was you-all who knew how to find this clearing,' the blond repeated, far from displeased by the comment. 'If we'd've seen how many of them were after us, we could have saved Clear Eyes from being hurt. Do you reckon there'll be any more coming?'

'Not now we're so far from the border,' the chief answered, stolidly refusing to look at what was happening to his daughter. 'We thought we had shaken them off before we met you, but they managed to stay on our trail.' Indicating the man who had been dragged from the woodland, he went on, 'This one could always read sign better than any other, but I did not know his true heart on the peace making and was not expecting it would be he who followed.'

'It's always hard to lose a friend, even one who has turned against you,' Waco said sympathetically. 'And I'm sorry I didn't show him more respect when I brought him out to let you look him over.'

'You didn't know he was a friend,' Good Temper replied, concluding—not for the first time—that the young Texan had learned well Indian ways from *Cuchilo*, grandson of his old colleague, Long Walker, war leader of the *Pehnane* Comanche band's Dog Soldier lodge. 'I think there might also be those of your people who will try to stop the peace being made.'

'There could be,' Waco conceded, in a tone which suggested he considered the possibility to be likely. 'Leastwise, Cap'n Bert said we should watch out for it being tried.'

While Waco and Doc dressed like the Texas cowhands they had been for most of their young lives,[1] they were currently employed as members of the Arizona Rangers. It said much for their ability that their commanding officer, Captain Bertram Mosehan, had given them their present very responsible assignment.

After having been forced by the continued harassment of the United States Cavalry to cross into Mexico, the San Pedro River Apaches were now desirous of making peace and being allowed to return. As their leading Old Man chief, Good Temper had been elected to conduct the negotiations. Although they had fought against each other in the past, such was the respect he felt that he had stipulated he would only visit the town of Guernsey—which had been nominated as the rendezvous—if Mosehan took charge of the arrangements. This had proved most fortuitous under the circumstances.

Mosehan's new capacity (he had been manager of the great Hashknife ranch when in contention with the chief's raiding parties) allowed him to devote all of his attention and resources to the task. A shrewd man, he contrived to keep in touch with

[1] For the benefit of new readers: details of Waco's background and special qualifications are given in Appendix Four. Information pertaining to his association with Marvin Eldridge 'Doc' Leroy is given mainly in the volumes of the Waco series.

public sentiment throughout the whole of Arizona despite the distances and comparatively primitive means of communication involved. On this occasion, he had concluded that a peaceful return was favoured by the majority of the white population. They realized that there would be a danger of further raiding and suffering as long as the San Pedro River Apaches remained south of the border. People who had seen the horrors of such expeditions were in general eager to see the threat removed.

There were, of course, others who opposed the arrangement. Some, whose hatred was aroused by losses of families, friends, or property at the hands of the Apaches, failed to see why a peaceful solution rather than total annihilation should be the Government's aim regardless of which band had been responsible for their sufferings. Being based on political or business interests, the motives of a second faction were less laudable.

According to Mosehan's information, while the majority of dissidents in the first category would only make their objections known if chance brought them on to the scene, the latter group were more determined to ensure no peace treaty would be ratified. As yet, he had not been able to learn their identities or more than that they were men with the wealth and means to enforce their opposition. So he concluded it would be inadvisable to offer them opportunities which could be avoided.

While Mosehan and several Rangers were escorting the Apache scout, Johnny No-Legs[2] and his wife—posing as Good Temper and Clear Eyes—by the most direct route to Guernsey and acting as decoys, the two Texans were following a more circuitous trail to the rendezvous. Having great faith in Mosehan, the chief had accepted the arrangement without argument. Nor had he harboured doubts about their abilities for long. Their questions about the feelings of his people towards the peace treaty had quickly established they were intelligent and competent. What was more, he had been impressed by learning from whom Waco had acquired a sound knowledge of Indian ways and put the lessons to good use. The latter had been demonstrated in the careful watch the

[2] Johnny No-Legs, Apache scout, appears in Case Two, 'A Rope For Johnny No-Legs, of *Sagebrush Sleuth* and Chapter One, 'The Campaigner' of *Waco Rides In.*

197

blond had kept and how he had detected the far from obvious signs of pursuit during the afternoon. Although the chief's knowledge of the country they were traversing had suggested the place which offered the best opportunity of dealing with whoever was following, Waco had proposed how they should protect themselves. Both he and Doc had further gained Good Temper's approbation by maintaining a silence worthy of an Apache warrior while waiting for the attack to commence.

'Anyways,' the blond drawled, glancing around. 'We shouldn't be having any more trouble tonight and, from now on in, it'll likely be the white-eyes instead of your people who'll be giving it.'

*****   *****

'Hello, the fire!' Waco called, standing with the sturdy trunk of a cottonwood tree between himself and the men he was addressing even though he was also shielded by the shadowy darkness of the woodland.

Having spent the remainder of their disturbed night sleeping in the clearing, the quartet had moved on at dawn. It said much for Doc Leroy's skill in medical matters and Clear Eyes' fortitude that she was able to ride in spite of his diagnosis with regards to a rib having been broken proving correct. Her wound had been cleaned, stitched and dressed. So it was far less painful and dangerous than it would have been if capable aid had not been available. Although the pace had not been fast, she was able to avoid delaying the journey.

The party had travelled all day exhibiting a wary alertness, but without seeing anything to disturb them until coming across the tracks of several shod horses which had been recently made shortly before sundown. Leaving his companions to come after him at a more leisurely pace, Waco had followed the sign. Just as the last of the light was going, he had seen the glow of a fire which had clearly been lit in a position intended to avoid being seen. Leaving the big paint ground hitched by its dangling reins, he had resumed his advance on foot. Despite having no liking for what he had seen on approaching the red glow, he had considered a closer inspection might be fruitful if it could be managed.

Dressed in cowhand clothing, the four men seated around the fire were unshaven and well armed. Unless Waco was mistaken, they had little legitimate association with the cattle industry. While he could not recollect having seen their pictures or read any of their descriptions on wanted posters, he considered this was not because they had led law abiding and blameless lives. Nor did their response to his words lead him to correct his summation. Anybody would be startled by hearing an unexpected voice from the darkness, but honest people were not likely to exhibit such obvious suspicion even if they did rise hurriedly and reach for their guns.

'Who're you?' demanded the tallest and best looking of the quartet, which did not make him a thing of beauty, his voice hinting at birth in Illinois.

'Name's Billy-Bob Thomson from out Bisbee way,' Waco lied. 'Left my hoss down the trail a ways after it throwed a shoe and I'd admire to come rest by your fire.'

'Let him do it, Storky!' called a drawling voice from the darkness at the other side of the fire, after there had been no reply for a few seconds. 'Where's your Yank' hospitality gone?'

'You know him, Bill?' the spokesman inquired, his tone tinged with grudging respect.

'I know him,' confirmed the voice. 'Come ahead—"Billy-Bob Thomson".'

Watching the man who strolled into the firelight as he was resuming his advance, Waco felt a sense of relief. Tall, wide shouldered, ruggedly handsome with an expression of reckless bravado, his attire was also that of a cowhand and the gunbelt he wore suggested he was exceedingly competent in the use of the ivory handled Colts in its holsters. In spite of that, he was far more prepossessing than any of the others around the fire and the blond was pleased to see him.

Some people might have thought such a reaction from a peace officer was strange. Even though he was not wanted for any legal infraction at that time, Curly Bill Brocius was a notorious law breaker. However, various circumstances had given them mutual respect which was without favouritism on Waco's part.[3] What was

[3] Details of Waco's earlier meetings with Curly Bill Brocius are recorded in Case Five, 'Statute of Limitations' of *Sagebrush Sleuth*, Chapter Two, 'The Juggler and the Lady, and Chapter Three, 'The Petition' of *Waco Rides In.*

more, Brocius was aware of this. So the Texan assumed he possessed a sufficiently clear conscience to be able to extend the invitation.

Although three of the quartet by the fire showed signs of relaxing on hearing the newcomer vouched for by Brocius, the last seemed less certain. Thickset and the shortest, his surly face was set in a puzzled frown and he made no attempt to sit down as his companions were doing. Instead, he remained on his feet and his right hand continued to dangle close to the low-tied Colt as he subjected the approaching Texan to a suspicious scrutiny.

'Hey!' the man yelped. 'Last time I saw you, you was with that damned Bert Mosehan!'

'Why sure,' Waco agreed, exhibiting not the slightest embarrassment or alarm at what was clearly intended as a damning accusation. 'I ride for Cap'n Bert.'

'Ride,' the first speaker growled, also starting to exude suspicion. 'Or *rode*?'

'Both,' Waco admitted, halting about fifteen feet from the fire and, despite apparently being at ease, the other men knew he was as ready as a sidewinder coiled for a strike.

'*Both!*' the challenger repeated and, after a moment, his puzzlement was replaced by realization. 'Then you're a god-damned Ranger!'

'*I* wouldn't've put it just *that* way,' Waco drawled, seemingly in a laconic fashion, yet his whole bearing conveyed a warning. 'But you-all called it right. Does it bother *you* that I'm a lawman?'

'*Me?*' the standing man ejaculated, concluding the challenge was directed at him personally and having an uncomfortable feeling that his companions were content to let it stay that way. 'Naw! Of course it don't! I ain't wanted for nothing and ain't never done nothing bad. Have I, Bill?'

'Well now,' Brocius answered sardonically, reaching up his left hand to run its fingers through the short curly black hair which had given him his sobriquet. 'I'm not one for lying, nor for being a snitch. So I'll just let that one ride.'

'You and your damned sense of humour, Bill,' Waco growled, without taking his attention from the man with whom he was conversing. 'Take it easy, *hombre*. I'm not hunting for you-all, or anybody else, tonight.'

'What're you after then?' Storky wanted to know.

'I don't mind you-all *asking*,' Waco declared, almost amiably. 'Just so long's you don't mind me *not* answering.'

'Could be I do mi——!' Storky commenced, but the word and his suggestion of rising ended as the right side Colt left the Texan's gunbelt in a flickering blur of motion and, while its barrel dangled towards the ground, the hammer had been cocked the instant it cleared its holster.

'Reckon *that's* a right smart answer, Storky-boy,' Brocius remarked with a wolfish grin. 'You concluding to debate it?'

'It ain't none of my never-mind what he's here for,' the discomfitured man mumbled, darting a baleful glare at the mocking-faced outlaw. 'We've done nothing to make us need to worry happen we run up against a lawman.'

'*Bueno*,' Waco said, returning the Colt almost as rapidly as it had appeared. 'You-all feel like coming with me to collect my horse, Bill?'

'Why not,' Brocius assented. 'It's sort of dark 'n' spooky out there.'

'You-all with those yahoos?' Waco inquired, after he and the outlaw were beyond the hearing of the quartet.

'*They're* with *me*,' Brocius corrected.

'You-all wouldn't be doing some Injun hunting,' Waco suggested. 'Now would you?'

'Injun hunt——?' Brocius began, then a tone of enlightenment came to his voice. 'So *you're* riding herd on ole Chief Good Temper, huh?'

'We're riding herd on him.'

'Just you 'n' Doc Leroy?'

'Isn't that enough?'

'I figured Cap'n Bert'd be pulling something slick when I read's how him and all his Rangers'd be riding with the chief from the border,' Brocius declared. 'You run into any trouble?'

'Few of the chief's bucks figured on stopping us last night,' Waco admitted, feeling sure that more than idle curiosity had prompted the question. 'But we talked 'em out of it. Did you allow's we'd be running into some sort of fuss?'

'Didn't give it a thought,' Brocius stated. 'About *them*, I mean.'

'You heard tell of somebody else who might have the same notion?'

'There's them around who don't reckon how Apaches should be given nothing 'cepting the chance to be made wolf bait. And there's others who figure there's money to be made out them stopping on the war path. And the last're the more likely to see if they can keep their wantings happening.'

'Would that be *anybody* in particular?'

'Are *you* asking me to be a snitch now?'

'I just might be at that,' Waco replied, noticing the other's tone was more amiable than when addressing a similar remark to the man in the clearing.

'Then I've got to 'fess up all truthful that I don't know,' Brocius answered, glancing ahead to where the big paint stallion was standing under a tree. 'Tell you, though. Word has it that Buckskin Bartrop's been sent for. Do you know him?'

'I can't say I do,' Waco drawled.

'I've never come across him myself,' Brocius confessed. 'But they do say he's at least as good as ole Sharpshooter Schindler used to be afore he got done to death by that fancy European hired killer down in Texas.'[4]

'I'll keep it in mind,' Waco promised, realizing how the man in question must carry out any killings he was hired to perform. Gathering up the split ended reins, he swung on to the saddle. '*Gracias amigo.* What'll you-all tell those jaspers when you go back without lil ole me?'

'That your hoss's done had a miracle and got his shoe back on, so you've rid off about your business,' Brocius replied. 'Which I reckon they'll be wanting to do the same.'

'Would their business be likely to become *my* business?' the Texan asked.

'Not what they wanted me to come in on with 'em,' Brocius stated. 'I don't want fuss with you blasted Rangers. One thing, though. What I've heard, Buckskin Bartrop got his name 'cause that's the way he allus dresses when he goes after somebody. Hope that helps.'

[4] How Sharpshooter Schindler was killed is told in: *Beguinage.*

'It's worth knowing,' Waco stated, preparing to set his mount into motion. '*Gracias* again, *amigo*. See you-all down the trail.'

*****　　*****

'It can't be *this* easy!' Doc Leroy declared, looking at the brand on the rump of a fine paint gelding occupying one of the stalls in Sweeney's livery barn.

'Likely not,' Waco conceded, also studying the letters 'BB' burned into the horse's hide as a mark of ownership. 'But, if not, it's sure as hell a big coincidence. Let's ask the hostler who owns it, happen he's around.'

Three days had elapsed since the meeting with Brocius, but they had been completely uneventful as far as Waco's party were concerned. Out of consideration for the information he had received, they had been even more watchful as they were travelling. They had tried to avoid crossing a skyline. When this had been necessary, they had subjected the surrounding terrain to a careful scrutiny before advancing. At all times, they had scanned every distant rim for any trace of lurking human beings, but knowing something of the man who might already have been seeking them caused them to pay an even greater attention to their surroundings. With Clear Eyes injured, taking the added precautions had not caused any noticeable reduction to the speed at which they were able to move. Nor, although nothing untoward happened, did they regret having displayed so much care.

On arriving at the appointed rendezvous in the vicinity of Guernsey, the party had found another Ranger waiting for them and he was not alone. He had brought the small covered wagon belonging to the town's Chinese laundry with him. It was being driven by its owner and the Ranger explained the reason for its presence. Having learned that there was likely to be an attempt to assassinate Chief Good Temper, although not how or by whom it would be made, Mosehan was resorting to further subterfuge. The Apache, his daughter and the Ranger were to complete the journey inside the vehicle with its flaps closed. While they were being delivered to the rear entrance of the Grand Hotel and taken to the rooms which were reserved for them, Waco and Doc were to remain outside the town until night had fallen.

Satisfied that their superior had the situation under control, the two young Texans had continued to carry out their instructions. Waiting until after dark, they had ridden into Guernsey and taking the Apaches' horses as well as their own, made for Sweeney's livery barn. It was the largest establishment of its kind in the town. Although there had been no human occupants when they entered, there were sufficient empty stalls for their needs and they found something they considered worthy of investigation.

'Howdy, gents,' greeted the tall, lean man of middle age, wearing a collarless shirt and bib overalls, who emerged from a door at the rear of the barn in answer to a shout from Waco. 'Them stalls's all took——'

'We're them's they've been taken for,' the blond replied, extracting a small wallet from his vest's inside pocket and flipping it open.

'Rangers, huh?' the man grunted, studying the badge of office which was exposed to his view. 'Put 'em in anywhere you've a mind, gents.'

'Who-all owns the paint here?' Waco inquired, indicating the horse which had aroused his and Doc's interest instead of doing as requested.

'Never seed him afore,' the man admitted. 'Which I'd not've been likely to forget him happen I had.'

'How come?' Doc asked.

'He was sure one fancy dressing dude,' the man explained in a derisive tone. 'Tall, well made, shoulder long black hair and handlebar moustache. Got on just about the prettiest buckskin jacket I've ever seen. Danged if he wasn't toting a Sharps buffalo gun along with a pearl handled, nickel plated revolver. If I didn't know's how good old Wild Bill Hickok was done to death up to Deadwood back in 'Seventy-Six,[5] I'd've reckoned it was him.'

'When did he get here?' Waco asked, darting a glance at Doc.

'Just afore sundown,' the man replied, sensing the urgency behind the young blond's quietly spoken question and wondering what might be causing it. 'Looked like he'd come a fair ways and hadn't took much time doing it.'

'Do you-all know where he's staying?' Waco went on, being aware that hostlers ranked with barbers as gatherers and spread-

[5] See Part Seven, *Deadwood, August 2nd, 1876* of this volume

ers of information.

'Asked me where the best hotel in town is,' the man replied. 'I told him it's the Grand, but he wasn't likely to get in there what with all the high mucky-mucks 'n' such who's either here or coming to say howdy to ole Chief Good Temper.'

'What'd he say to that?' Doc wanted to know.

'Said he'd heard tell the chief was coming,' the hostler answered. 'And asked if he'd got here yet. Well now, seeing's how I figured Cap'n Mosehan wouldn't want it spread about promiscuous-like after all the trouble he'd took to get Good Temper here without folks knowing, I was fixing to say "no"; but one of them mission fathers's'd come in to see if we'd any stalls for their hosses told him's he'd got to the Grand Hotel safe 'n' sound.'

'Which mission fathers are they?' Waco asked, as there was no such establishment in the vicinity of Guernsey.

'Bunch from over Casa Grande way. They got here a couple of days back. Reckon they're going to ask Good Temper to let them set up a mission on his reservation so's they can show his heathen bucks the light. Come wanting to leave their hosses here, but we'd already had all the spares took ready for the high mucky-mucks 'n' such's'd be on hand for the peace treaty signing. Fact being, that fancy dressed jasper wouldn't've been able to leave his hoss here if a feller hadn't've pulled out as he got here 'n' left an empty stall.'

'So you don't know where he went after he left here?' Waco challenged.

'I told him to try Mrs. Grange's rooming house,' the hostler replied. 'But I don't know if he went there. Reckon he might, though. He left his saddle in the backroom.'

'With all his gear on it?' the blond challenged.

'Nope,' the hostler answered. 'Toted along his war bag 'n' rifle.'

' 'Tend to the horses while I go take a look, will you, Doc?' Waco requested. 'It's likely nothing, but I'd sooner be sure than sorry.'

'Trust you-all to get the notion first!' the studious-featured Texan sniffed, but the words were directed at his companion's departing back.

'What's up?' the hostler asked, watching the blond striding

swiftly towards the front entrance and considering that only a matter of great importance would cause him to leave the attending to his mount's needs to even a close friend.

'Maybe nothing, like he said,' Doc answered. 'Can you-all see to the two duns while I take care of my horse and the paint?'

'I was just going to suggest that,' the hostler admitted, being a shrewd judge of animals and having formed an accurate conclusion as to how the blond's mount would react to the ministrations of a stranger. 'Let's get 'em all bedded down.'

Leaving the barn and hurrying towards the Grand Hotel, Waco wondered if he might be worrying unnecessarily. It seemed most unlikely that a competent professional killer would display clues to his identity so blatantly even if he did believe his coming was not expected. Yet doing so might be in the nature of a double bluff. The very manner of his arrival might lull Good Temper's guardians into a sense of false security by causing them to assume anybody with evil intentions would take the precaution of being less noticeable and easily identifiable. However, no matter what the answer might be, the youngster was disinclined to leave the matter uninvestigated.

'What's up, *amigo*?' asked Billy Speed—the Ranger who had been with the laundry wagon—needing only one glance, as the blond youngster arrived in the hotel's lobby, to sense something was wrong. He discarded his pose of lounging in a chair as if waiting for a visitor.

'Has a jasper with long hair and dressed in a fancy buckskin jacket been in?' Waco inquired. 'He'd likely be toting a war bag and carrying a Sharps buffalo gun.'

'Ain't seen him, and, dressed like that, I'd likely've noticed him if he had,' Speed declared. 'Specially after you——'

'Where-at's Good Temper 'n' Clear Eyes?' the youngster interrupted.

'In a room at the back, upstairs,' Speed replied.

'Come on!' Waco ordered, but swinging around and making for the door through which he had entered instead of crossing to the stairs. 'Go 'round to the left and I'll take the right.'

'Yo!' assented the Ranger, concluding that the situation might be too urgent for him to waste time in asking further questions.

Walking swiftly in the direction he had indicated, Waco contrived to pass silently along the dimly lit alley at the side of the hotel. On arriving at the rear end, he peered cautiously around the corner. Even as he was starting to feel relief at finding the street behind the building deserted, he became aware of movement at the other side. Leaving the shadows, a tall, well built man with long hair and wearing an elaborately decorated fringed buckskin jacket advanced. Although he was not carrying a rifle, his whole attitude was redolent of stealth.

On the point of moving forward, Waco saw that to do so at that moment might be inadvisable. Remembering the deductions he had made regarding the method of killing employed by Buckskin Bartrop, he considered it possible that reconnaissance rather than murder was intended. He might merely wish to see and ensure he could identify his proposed victim so as to avoid making a mistake when conditions were more suitable, in which case, there was little to be gained by intercepting him.

Waco realized that he had no way of proving the man's identity or intentions. Nor would an experienced hired killer be likely to carry anything which would betray his purpose, particularly if he was merely on a scouting mission. If challenged, he would merely produce some reasonable explanation for his presence behind the hotel and there would be no legitimate cause for the Rangers to arrest him. Or, if they should, it was unlikely he would remain in custody for long. His employers were likely to have a lawyer in the vicinity who could procure his release. Even if they or he should decide against his continuing with the assignment, they might be able to hire a replacement. In any case, he would be at liberty to leave Guernsey and carry on his murderous career elsewhere.

While the youngster was forming these conclusions, the man came to a halt. After glancing around furtively without discovering he was under observation, he turned his gaze upwards and swung his right hand in a throwing motion. Whatever left it merely pattered against and did not break the pane of a first floor window.

'Hold it right there, *hombre*!' Waco shouted, springing from his place of concealment, his right hand Colt leaping from its holster and the hammer clicking back to the fully cocked position.

'Like he says!' Billy Speed supplemented, stepping from the alley at the other end of the hotel, having waited to discover how his companion intended to handle the situation, and arriving on the street holding a Colt just as ready as Waco's for use.

'Wha——?' the man gasped, looking first in Waco's and then the other Ranger's direction, his left hand opening to allow several small pieces of gravel to fall from it. 'Wh——?'

'Get those hands high, *hombre*!' Waco ordered. 'We're Arizona Rangers!'

'Arizona Rangers?' the man repeated, raising his hands hurriedly above his head. However, his voice showed more relief than alarm as he continued, 'Take it easy, gents. I don't mean any harm!'

'Well now,' Waco said dryly, glancing upwards to where the window was being opened cautiously. 'I don't know how it is where you-all come from, *hombre*, but down here in Arizona we call trying to kill somebody doing harm.'

'Trying to *kill* somebody?' the man almost yelped. 'Is *that* what you reckon I've come to do?'

'You might've come figuring to elope with your sweet loving gal who's momma and poppa won't let you marry her right and proper,' Waco answered. 'But, happen that's it, you got the wrong window.'

'That's closer to what I'm doing than trying to kill somebody,' the man stated, clearly recovering from the surprise he had been given. 'Only I got to the right window for what I'm after.'

'And what'd that be?' Waco challenged.

'I was wanting to talk with Chief Good Temper,' the man explained. 'As soon as Buffalo Bill got word he was coming in, he sent me here to try to put him under contract to appear in our show.'

'*Buffalo Bill?*' the youngster growled. 'Do you mean Buffalo Bill Cody?'

'There's only one Buffalo Bill,' the man asserted, lowering his hands slowly and looking relieved. 'And I'm one of his talent scouts. That's why I look and dress the way I do. It's expected of us.'

***** *****

'*Steak!* Holy Mother! Is it forgetting you are that today's Friday, Father?'

Delivered in a rich feminine Irish brogue, the words caused Waco to glance around as he was entering the Grand Hotel's dining room on the morning following his arrival in Guernsey. The speaker was a plump, motherly looking waitress and she was gazing in near horror at the burliest of four men clad in the hooded brown robes of mission brothers who were occupying a table near to the door which connected with the entrance lobby.

'Yes,' the tall and slim man at the offending brother's left agreed, before the other could reply. 'It was an oversight. Brother Boski has a healthy appetite which sometimes runs away with him. He will have eggs and grits like the rest of us.'

Idle curiosity led the blond youngster to look at the quartet as he went by on his way to join Doc Leroy, Captain Mosehan and Billy Speed for breakfast. He noticed that their features were suggestive of Northern or Mid-European rather than Hispanic origins, but found nothing out of the ordinary in that. Since Arizona had become a part of the United States, the various missions were no longer occupied solely by Spanish brothers. The one who had answered the waitress looked to be in his early forties and was the oldest. Like his companions, he was clean shaven. However, in Brother Boski's case, it appeared he had only recently removed a beard as his cheeks and chin were reddened instead of tanned brown like his forehead and big hands. They all had the look of spending much time out of doors, which was not surprising. Many missions were virtually self sufficient and the occupants worked at tasks more suited to dirt farmers than men of the cloth.

'Morning,' Mosehan greeted, diverting Waco's thoughts from the quartet. 'Oh should I say "good afternoon"?'

The head of the Arizona Rangers was a tall, wide shouldered, sun bronzed man in his late thirties and dressed after the fashion of a well-to-do working rancher. He had a good looking face which showed strength of will and yet its grimness was softened by the grin quirks at the corners of his mouth, suggesting correctly that

209

he had a sound sense of humour. His blue eyes twinkled as he looked at the youngster who was proving to be one of his best officers and he made the comment wondering what the answer would be.

'It's all Doc's fault,' Waco replied, drawing out a chair and sitting down. 'He used up all the hot water and I had to wait for some more to be sent up.'

'You're getting too much luxury,' Mosehan stated. 'When I was your age, I was expected to shave in cold water.'

'That's what they call progress, sir,' the youngster pointed out and looked around for a waitress.

'I ordered for you,' Doc announced.

'*Bueno*,' the youngster accepted. 'I reckon it's too early to have gotten a reply back about that jasper, isn't it, Cap'n Bert?'

'Some,' Mosehan confirmed.

On being questioned further the previous night, the man in the buckskin jacket had produced documents to substantiate his claim to work for Buffalo Bill Cody. He declared that he had intended to visit Good Temper openly, but he saw a man he believed to be a talent scout for a rival Wild West Show in the hotel's lobby. Wanting to avoid being discovered, he had withdrawn unnoticed. Circling the building, he had waited in an alley at the opposite side of the street until seeing the chief in the upstairs room. He had gathered a couple of handfuls of gravel with which to attract the other's attention, but was prevented from achieving his purpose by the two Rangers' intervention. Questioned about the Sharps buffalo rifle, which he had left with his war bag at the rooming house, he had stated it was part of the costume which went with his job and which he had never fired.

Although an examination of the lobby had failed to locate the rival talent scout, the Rangers had been inclined to accept the man's story. Certainly the rifle showed no sign of having been fired recently, nor did it have the telescopic sight which was likely to prove a necessity for the way in which Buckskin Bartrop carried out assassinations. However, in addition to telling the man he could not see Good Temper until after the negotiations were concluded, Mosehan had sent a telegraph message to the chief of police where Cody's show was appearing asking for verification, and had arranged for the town marshal's deputies to keep him under observation.

'*Gracias*, ma'am,' Waco drawled, as the Irish waitress delivered the breakfast which Doc had ordered for him. Waiting until she had withdrawn, he once more addressed his superior. 'Have you-all talked that jasper from the Indian Affairs Bureau into changing his mind on that fool notion of his?'

'Nope,' Mosehan admitted. 'He says that as the mayor's been good enough to offer his office for the chief to meet the newspaper-men who've come to see him, and as he's used the good tax-paying citizens' money to buy fancy food 'n' liquor for them, it's only right we should go there instead of doing it here.'

'Even though that means walking Good Temper along the main street at noon?' Speed growled indignantly.

'He allows *that's* partly his notion,' Mosehan explained. 'Says it'll let people see the chief's just an ordinary human being, instead of being some kind of devil complete with horns and a pointed tail.'

'And puts him right out in the open where that jasper, Bartrop, can draw a bead on him,' Speed pointed out, despite feeling sure the danger had not escaped his superior's attention.

'Not from the kind of distance he usually works over,' Mosehan stated, justifying the Ranger's confidence. 'The street's curved, so there's no chance of Bartrop laying a sight on him along it from either end and the mayor's office's on this side of the plaza and we don't need to cross it. The four of us'll be around him and we'll be walking too fast for aim to be taken between any of the buildings as we go by.'

'How about from *inside* one of the buildings?' Doc wanted to know.

'Pete, the rest of our boys and some fellers I can trust'll be covering us,' Mosehan replied, referring to his second in command, Sergeant Glendon. 'They're working in pairs, one with a rifle and the other using a pair of field glasses to watch the windows. Nope, I reckon Good Temper's going to be safe enough the way I've got things arranged.'

'Well, at least he let Good Temper and Clear Eyes have their breakfasts taken up to the room,' Doc remarked, with the air of one conferring a favour. His gaze swept around the other occupants and he went on, 'Which I don't reckon anybody here's fixing to try and jump him as he came in.

Although Waco was listening to the conversation, he was too preoccupied to take any further part in it. An ill-defined thought at the back of his mind was disturbing him. He had no idea of what it might be, but it continued to nag while struggling to take form. In the past, he had had a similar experience on other occasions when he had seen or heard something the full significance of which had temporarily eluded him. Experience had taught him that he could not force through the recollection. Instead, he must wait until a full appreciation could be triggered off by a word, or incident. So he concentrated upon eating his food and listening to what was being said by his companions. The discussion went on until breakfast was finished and they rose to go about their business, passing the four brown-robed men who were still seated at the table by the door.

'God-damn it!' Brother Boski growled softly, after the Rangers had left the dining room. 'He didn't come down!'

'That's the way it goes,' answered the eldest of the quartet, showing no surprise over the way in which his companion prefaced the comment. 'We'll just have to wait a while longer before we get a chance to show our Indian brother the light.'

*****   *****

'Looks like the word's spread wide, thick and hip deep about the get-together down at the mayor's office,' Waco remarked, looking at the street from Mosehan's room on the first floor at the front of the Grand Hotel. 'I'll bet near on everybody in Guernsey County and their drinking kin've turned out to watch Good Temper going to it.'

'Be a right miserable shame to disappoint them, then,' the head of the Rangers replied. 'And, anyways, it's what we figured on happening. They'll help stop Bartrop drawing a bead on him through an alley from way outside town, happen he's around, else make him use either an upstairs window or try from a roof-top. And there aren't many of the last will suit his needs and all that are're being watched.'

'How about somebody jumping out on us from among the

212

crowd?' Doc asked, standing by the blond and assessing various other possibilities.

'Could happen, so we'll have to be ready for it,' Mosehan admitted. 'Which's one reason why I picked you three to help ride herd on him during the walk. The range is likely to be too short for us to chance using rifles and there're too many folks around for us to start spraying buckshot from scatters, which'd've been my first choice happen I'd first pick at the *remuda*, and you're the best I've got when it comes to handling your belt-guns.'

'One thing, though,' Waco drawled, trying to hide the satisfaction aroused by his superior's summation. 'There're enough folks on each side for any would-be killers to have to either be at the front or chance shoving through. No matter which, it'll give us a chance of seeing them in good time. There's sure to be more than one of them in it, too. And, tried from so close, no matter how many or few, they'll need to have horses close by ready to light out on when it's done.'

'And they'll have to count on the crowd scattering to let them through,' Billy Speed supplemented, having noticed that the marshal had carried out Mosehan's instructions by clearing all the horses from the hitching rails between the hotel and the building which housed the mayor's office. 'I reckon most folks will have the good sense to do it, but some of them're sure to take cards and side with us and that means getting away's not going to be any tight drawn cinch.'

'The last thing I want is for *everybody* to cut in!' the captain stated emphatically. 'Lead that's being thrown by some well-meaning citizen can kill you as dead as if it comes from an owl-hoot cutting loose your way.'

'It's worse, even,' Speed declared, with considerable vehemence. 'You can't shoot back at an honest, law-abiding, tax-paying citizen.'

'I should think not, for shame!' Mosehan answered, confident that he could rely upon each of the trio to behave sensibly and avoid endangering lives unnecessarily if there should be gun play on the street. 'Clear Eyes being wounded helps us, though. Not even Mr. Indian Affairs Commissioner Gusset could expect her to attend the get-together, hurt as she is.' He drew a watch from the pocket of his vest, consulted and replaced it, continuing, 'Well, it's time for us to be going. I'll check that everything's all right outside while you boys fetch him down.'

By the time the three Rangers had collected the stocky, grey-haired Apache from his room and reached the top of the stairs, their superior had already left the hotel. Unlike the street, its lobby was sparsely occupied. In fact, the only occupants were the desk clerk and the four mission brothers. The latter were no longer gathered in a group. Their leader and the shortest of them were at the desk. While Brother Boski was by the door to the dining room, the last member of the quartet had crossed to take up a similar position near the entrance to the bar room which had been kept closed that morning at Mosehan's request. They were standing with their heads bowed forward and hands behind their backs, as if in meditation or prayer. At each person's feet were the plain leather bags which Waco had noticed beneath their chairs in the dining room.

Seeing that Mosehan was being kept talking by a prosperous looking man, the party started down the stairs. Waco and Doc took the lead, with the Apache four steps behind them and Billy Speed brought up the rear from a similar distance. As the Texans were passing the half way point, the two brothers turned from the desk. Slipping their hands into the voluminous sleeves of their brown robes, they started to walk in the direction of the stairs.

Watching the pair approaching, Waco decided that they intended to speak with the Apache about the possibility of trying to convert the San Pedro River band when the reservation was established. More from habit than any other reason, he studied them. The first thing to strike him was their footwear, which had been hidden by the dining room's table earlier. While every other mission brother he had seen wore sandals, they had on sturdy boots. Of course, remembering what he had been told about their asking if they could leave their horses at the livery barn, this could be explained by their needing something more substantial than sandals when riding. For all that, the blond felt himself growing uneasy. The position of their hands seemed more suitable to Chinese in ceremonial costume than members of a Christian religious order. In fact, if it had been anybody else who was coming up with concealed——

Suddenly, the thought which had struggled to express itself earlier, leapt into focus and took on a clarity which was alarming in its implications!

What Waco had noticed in the dining room without fully appreciating it was that all the quartet had soft well kept hands. Despite the suggestions that all of them spent much time in the open, none had shown the roughening which would have resulted from the hard manual toil which is frequently the lot of mission incumbents. Taken with the recollection that Brother Boski had asked for a steak on the day of the week when the Catholic creed enjoined eating only fish—an omission a man of the cloth would be unlikely to make in public, even if he was more lax in private—and the discovery that the quartet wore boots instead of the customary sandals, the soft hands created a sinister suspicion.

'Watch them!' the youngster yelled, hands leaping towards the staghorn butts of his holstered Colts. 'They're hired guns!'

Startled and furious exclamations burst from the two brown-robed men's lips as they realized their purpose had been detected. Although they had intended to move closer before doing so, each started to free the short barrelled Merwin & Hulbert Army Pocket revolver he carried in a spring retention holster strapped to his left forearm. Echoing their far from religious comments, the other two discarded the postures of meditation and began to bring to the front the sawed-off shotguns which had been concealed behind them after being removed from the leather bags.

The ambush had been well thought out, but Waco's flash of realization came just before its instigator had intended it to be sprung. Although his warning took the quartet unawares his companions responded with the alacrity which had been acquired during a lifetime spent in perilous situations and where the possession of lightning fast reactions spelled the difference between staying alive or being killed.

Flashing from the contoured holsters of the *buscadero* gun-belt, Waco's Colts lined at waist level and thundered almost simultaneously an instant before the oldest of the bogus brothers could get the Merwin & Hulbert into action. Hit by the two bullets—either of which would have proved fatal—in the left breast, he was knocked in a staggering, sprawling spin away from the foot of the stairs. Nor did he go alone.

There was a flickering white movement as Doc Leroy plucked the ivory handled revolver from its holster so rapidly that it appeared to meet his thin, boneless seeming hand in mid-air. Flame gushed from its muzzle and, hit in the right side, the shortest of the would-be killers let his weapon fall as he too was twirled around before going down.

Snarling curses, 'Brother Boski' grabbed for the foregrip of the shotgun as his right hand brought it into view. He had his eyes on the Apache, being responsible for that aspect of the affair while his companions dealt with the escort. However, he received a second surprise to add to the confusion caused by discovering that their disguise had been penetrated and purpose detected.

Displaying a remarkable agility for one so apparently well advanced in years, the proposed victim turned in 'Boski's' direction. With a wild war whoop, he vaulted over the banister of the stairs. While still in mid-air, he was plucking the knife from its sheath on the left side of his belt. Alighting, he rose and whipped down his right arm. Leaving his grasp, the weapon flashed across the intervening space to bury itself almost hilt deep in 'Boski's' throat. With a cry of pain, the stricken man dropped the unfired shotgun and reeled through the door of the dining room. Rising involuntarily, his hands tugged the knife from his throat. It was followed by the blood which gushed from the severed jugular vein and he collapsed, dying without discovering that he and his companions had not been alone in creating a deception.

Going forward in a rolling dive, the Apache snatched up 'Brother Boski's' discarded shotgun in passing. Such was the energy he put into his movements that the grey 'hair' and chief's head band were dislodged. They fell away to reveal the black hair of a much younger man. Returning to his feet with deft ease, he flattened himself against the wall prior to twisting through the dining room door with the intention of taking any further action that might prove necessary.

For all that he had been taken by surprise, Billy Speed proved no less adept than the other three. Sweeping out his Colt, he deduced from their actions where he must devote his efforts. Turn-

216

ing the revolver to where the man by the bar-room's door was bringing up the shotgun, but wavering in indecision as to which of the party on the stairs posed the greatest threat, he fired. Hit in the head before reaching a conclusion, much less acting upon it, the man reeled. Although a reflex action caused the shotgun to fire, its load struck the side of the staircase without causing any more serious damage or injury.

'Are you all right, Johnny?' Waco called, glancing around as Mosehan burst through the front entrance holding a Colt.

'Sure am,' the Apache replied, strolling out of the dining room having satisfied himself he had nothing to fear from that direction. 'But, if this is what happens to a chief, I'm pleased I'm not one. It gets dangerous.'

***** *****

'Well, that ends the danger to the chief,' Herbert Gusset declared complacently, as Mosehan concluded a description of the abortive attempt at the Grand Hotel. 'But it is a pity you couldn't have taken them prisoners so they could be questioned.'

'Land's sakes, sir,' Waco put in, addressing the tall, bulky, grey-haired and pompous-looking Commissioner of Indian Affairs with what sounded like polite respect. 'Had we known that's what you-all wanted, we'd've let 'em shoot a couple of us so's the other two could wrassle them down.'

'One of them was still alive when the smoke cleared,' Mosehan went on, being aware that the youngster's behaviour was less innocuous that it appeared although Gusset was clearly taking it at face value. 'He told us who had hired them before he died.'[6]

'Who was it?' the Commissioner inquired eagerly, but his attitude was more suggestive of a desire to acquire a juicy piece of gossip, than of an official seeking enlightenment upon an important issue.

'Well now,' Mosehan replied. 'We've only *his* word and the

[6] In addition to informing upon his employers, the dying man had said his party meant to kill Chief Good Temper in the dining room that morning. When he had not appeared, they set up the ambush in the lobby and had horses waiting near by for their escape. The man blamed their failure upon 'Brother Boski', who he believed had been recognized by Waco despite having shaved off the beard worn when they had last come into contact. He had died without revealing when the earlier meeting had taken place.

217

names he gave are men well known in political and social circles——'

'Perhaps it would be as well if you kept their names to yourself until you've carried out an investigation!' Gusset interrupted, as all of the Rangers had anticipated he might, realizing that the possession of such details could be damaging to his career and might even prove dangerous. 'After all, we don't want *anything* to jeopardize your chances of bringing them to justice.'

'I reckon you could be right about that,' Mosehan declared, contriving to sound as sincere and grateful as Waco had seemed to be respectful. 'Here comes the chief now, from the sound of things.'

Although the ruin of the attempted ambush had suggested the danger might be ended for the time being, the captain had ordered the continuation of the plan. Donning the wig and head band, Johnny No-Legs had resumed his role of decoy. While he was walking along the main street, Good Temper was being taken in the laundry wagon by a circuitous route to the mayor's office. The wound sustained by Clear Eyes had been helpful to the deception, removing the need for the scout's squaw—who was smaller and plumper—to be endangered by accompanying him as the chief's daughter. The sound of a horse-drawn vehicle halting at the rear of the building announced that the real guest of honour had at last arrived.

'Good, good!' Gusset gushed, rubbing his plump hands. 'Now all we have to do is introduce him to the newspapermen and complete the arrangements. For example, where he wants the signing ceremony to take place?'

'I'd say his room at the hotel would be the safest place,' Doc suggested.

'We can't hold the ceremony there,' Gusset protested, as Waco and Billy Speed nodded their concurrence. 'It's traditional among the San Pedro River Apaches that all such major issues are conducted out in the open where everybody can see them taking place.'

'I'd say this's one time a change should be made,' Speed commented.

'Can't do it,' Johnny No-Legs stated, before anybody else could speak. 'You have signing inside and word gets back to San Pedro people, them bad-hat bucks who don't want peace going to say it not made proper and the others'll most likely listen.'

'He's right!' Gusset supported, although he was motivated by a desire to have the ceremony take place as publicly as possible to add to the acclaim he was sure he would receive for organizing it. The possibility suggested by the scout had not occurred to him. 'Besides, now you've killed those four men, the danger to the chief is over.'

'Maybe not,' Waco warned. 'There's still Buckskin Bartrop to take cards.'

'But you said the man you thought was him turned out to work for Buffalo Bill Cody's Wild West Show,' the Commissioner objected.

'That's what he tells us and there's nothing to show he's lying,' the blond conceded. 'But it doesn't mean Bartrop isn't around and waiting his chance.'

'Would you say the man who told you about him is reliable?' Gusset challenged, then looked at the captain without waiting for a reply. 'I have heard that criminals sometimes sell bogus information to young lawmen.'

'He didn't ask to be paid for telling me,' Waco growled. 'And he'd no cause to lie either, comes to that.'

'You can count on it he was reliable,' Mosehan put in hurriedly, knowing the youngster's temper was fraying thin and having been told the informant's identity although it had not been divulged to the Commissioner.

'But you haven't *seen* anything of this Bartrop,' Gusset asked, a slight note of alarm entering his voice as he went on, 'have you?'

'Well now,' the youngster answered, hard put to prevent his annoyance from showing in something more than the mildly sarcastic note which was creeping into his previously even drawl. 'Seeing's how I don't know what he looks like, excepting that I'm not counting on him walking around dressed all in buckskins no matter how he got his name, I'd be hard put to say "yes", or "*no*" to that.'

'So, for all you know, he may not be here in Guernsey?' Gusset snapped, having the kind of nature which disapproved of disrespect from those he considered to be his inferiors.

'He may not——!' Waco began coldly, but noticed and obeyed the negative shake of his superior's head and let the rest of his intended comment go unsaid.

'But he *may* be,' Mosehan went on. 'With the chief's life at stake, it's something we've *all* got to consider.'

'Of course and *I'd* be the last to want to influence you against your wishes, captain,' Gusset replied, taking a warning from the emphasis placed upon the word 'all'. But his bearing suggested that to do so was his intention. 'But the making of peace with the San Pedro River Apaches is considered a matter of national importance. The Governor of Arizona and the President himself have both announced their wish that it should be done. So I feel we must make *every* effort to ensure it is. And that it is done in a way which cannot be refuted as improper by *anybody* at a later date.'

'And you're saying that the ceremony has to take place out in the open?' Mosehan inquired, guessing what was coming.

'I'm not *ordering* it to be done,' Gusset corrected, glancing around to make sure that point was understood by all the assembled men. 'As I've been instructed to take your advice on such matters, I'll yield to your decision. All I will say is that, if it is at all possible, I believe we should carry out the ceremony in the open. Whether you decide to do this or not is up to you.' Seeing the way in which his audience was regarding him and deducing they were aware of his motives, he was relieved when a knock on the door heralded the arrival of the man whose welfare they were discussing. Bringing a politician's smile to his face, he walked forward as it opened saying, 'Ah, Chief Good Temper, I'm so pleased you've arrived safely. If you will come with me, please, there are some gentlemen who wish to speak with you.'

***** *****

Thrusting the point of the specially designed forked stick into the ground, the man who called himself 'Buckskin Bartrop' gave a sigh of satisfaction. In spite of his earlier doubts, he was confident that he could carry out his current assignment as he rested the round barrel of his Sharps Model 1878 'Long Range' rifle in the U-shaped notch at the top of the stick. Although the Arizona

220

Rangers had taken precautions which prevented him from doing so earlier and clearly believed this was still the case, they had left the means by which his superlative skill at shooting could strike down the victim he was being well paid to kill.

When deciding to take up the most lucrative work which had eventually caused the death of his uncle, Oscar 'Sharpshooter' Schindler, Bartrop had been determined to avoid a similar fate. One of his precautions had been that he never allowed even his employers to become aware of his true identity. During his meetings to negotiate with them and while carrying out the actual assassinations, he always had on a shoulder length wig of reddish brown hair, a matching bushy false beard which concealed almost all of his features and wore the buckskin garments that had been fashionable among the mountainmen of an earlier generation.

The disguise had always been successful. Nor did Bartrop consider it would be less effective on this occasion. None of the men responsible for protecting Chief Good Temper had shown any indication of being suspicious of the tall, pallid, be-spectacled Eastern newspaper photographer who had taken such an interest in the arrangements they were making for protecting the Apache during the ceremony for signing the peace treaty. With that vital information acquired, he had donned his disguise and set out to reconnoitre the surrounding district. He had found only two spots which satisfied his needs by providing the necessary concealment and allowed him to align his powerful rifle's telescopic sight upon his victim. Wanting to make sure of what he knew would be his only chance, he selected the position closest to the town. It was still almost three-quarters of a mile away, but he had hit his mark at distances in excess of that on other occasions and knew the cartridge would provide sufficent velocity to kill when the bullet reached its destination.

Satisfied with his arrangements, Bartrop sat down and positioned his legs on either side of the forked stick. His hands grasped the checkered fore end and pistol grip as he settled the butt's shaped, hard rubber heelplate against his right shoulder. Then he peered into the telescopic sight, moving the rifle until he was able to see through the narrow gap between two buildings which at any point a few inches to either side concealed the canopy-covered table on the far edge of the plaza. The various dignitaries were already assembled. He could see the fat, pompous Indian Affairs Commissioner Gusset, Captain Mosehan—whose precautions had so far prevented him from earning his pay—two senior U.S. Army officers in full dress uniforms and various civilian dignitaries, including a man belonging to the faction who had hired him.

However, as yet Bartrop was not being offered a clear shot at his intended target that he required. That was absolutely necessary. While he was in no doubt that he could escape even if he missed, he was equally positive he would not be given a second chance. One thing more than any other he had learned during his career as a professional killer was patience. So he sat on the edge of the woodland overlooking the town, his rifle alongside the thick trunk of the post oak tree which concealed him, waiting for the chief to step forward and stand still while signing the peace treaty. When that happened, he would tighten his right forefinger on the trigger and earn the balance of the money he had been promised.

'Doc'll swear I picked here on purpose,' a drawling voice remarked. 'Which I did.'

Even before the second part of the comment was concluded, Bartrop had released the rifle and started to turn in the speaker's direction. Although he had not heard a single warning sound, the tall, blond Arizona Ranger he had seen with Mosehan was now standing within a few feet of his position and lining a cocked Colt unwaveringly at his head.

'What——!' Bartrop croaked in alarm, but refraining from trying to draw the revolver for which he had been reaching. 'How——?'

'Easy enough,' Waco replied. 'I've had most of Friday and yesterday to look around and pick a place for the table which would only let you-all have two hidey-holes where you could draw a bead on it.' He raised his voice in a yell, going on, 'Hey Doc! You-all picked wrong. He's down here.'

Being aware that there was justification in Gusset's insistence that the ceremony took place in the open as Apache tradition demanded, Mosehan would still have insisted it was cancelled if he had not been sure Chief Good Temper could be saved from

222

assassination. His examination of the plaza and its immediate surroundings had convinced him he could prevent an attempt from the immediate vicinity. Making a thorough reconnaissance beyond the town, but taking care to remove all traces of his passing, Waco had located the most suitable position for the table to be set up. It was so shielded by buildings that there were only two possible positions from which a would-be killer could take a shot at it and only then if armed with a rifle capable of firing accurately at long distances.

Wanting to bring an end to Buckskin Bartrop's career, Mosehan had—with Good Temper's agreement—agreed to let the ceremony go on. At a second meeting with the newspapermen, he had informed them not only where it was to take place, but explained for the benefit of the photographers who were present the exact position of the table upon which the signing was to be carried out. Leaving Guernsey before daybreak on Sunday morning, Waco and Doc Leroy had concealed themselves close enough to the selected firing points to be able to intervene should the killer put in an appearance.

'Damned if you didn't pick lucky again!' the pallid featured Texan protested, on strolling up with a black doctor's bag in his left hand. 'He told you who hired him?'

'Not yet,' Waco replied, having used the interval before his *amigo*'s arrival to make his captive remove and throw aside the revolver. 'How about it, Mr. Bartrop?'

'I don't know what you mean,' the hired killer answered, hoping he sounded more confident than he felt despite believing his employers would save him now he had been apprehended by peace officers.

'Wonder if he'll feel the same way about it after I've got through fixing his wound?' Doc asked, exuding a chilling menace despite the mild way in which he was speaking, as he opened the bag to take out a vicious-looking scalpel and a long-nosed plier.

'*Wound?*' Bartrop repeated, puzzlement and growing concern plain in his voice. 'I don't have a wound!'

'Do you-all want to shoot him, *amigo*?' Doc inquired, with the air of one who was conferring a favour. 'Or shall I?'

'*Me!*' Waco accepted eagerly. 'You-all have the fun of digging

223

around and hauling the bullet out.' Turning his gaze to the now alarmed hired killer, he gestured with the Colt and his voice hardened. 'Who did you-all say hired you, *hombre*?'

'Y—You wouldn't just shoot me in cold blood!' Bartrop muttered, trying to convince himself rather than his captors.

'Shucks,' Waco drawled and began to line the revolver at the killer's right knee. 'Happen anybody asks, we'll say you got it resisting arrest.'

'You using town loads, *amigo*?' Doc said, more as a statement than a question, referring to the frequent practice among top gunfighters to reload their own cartridges and select a powder charge suitable for the task it was to perform.

'Fed the shells just enough so's the bullets'll go in, but not all the way through and out the other side,' Waco confirmed.

'Then put one into his right side,' Doc requested, as casually as if remarking about the weather. 'I've not had to dig a bullet out of there for a spell now and might's well learn something while I'm at it.'

Swinging his gaze from one young Texan to the other, Bartrop sought for any hint that they might merely be bluffing. All he read was grim determination from the blond as the muzzle of the revolver turned in the required direction, and what he took to be sadistic anticipation on the pallid face of the second man. Although he had not previously operated in Arizona, he had followed his usual habit of learning all he could about the peace officers against whom he might come into contention. Nothing he had been told about Waco led him to assume he could expect any mercy. What was more, his informants claimed Doc Leroy had ambitions to become a qualified physician and already possessed a thorough knowledge of how to remove bullets. In which case, he would also know how to do so in the most painful manner.

From the beginning of his career, Bartrop had wondered how it would feel to be captured by peace officers. He had also repeatedly consoled himself with the thought that, operating as he did at such a long distance from his victim, it would never happen. Continued success had made him over confident and careless, causing him to forget to take the precaution of ensuring he was alone in the area from which he would shoot.

224

Suddenly the killer realized that the location had been forced upon him. Clearly the Arizona Rangers must be very determined to capture him, or his employers, if they were willing to gamble the life of the man they were guarding to bring it about. So there were not likely to be any embarrassing questions asked over the means by which information was extracted from him. Nor might he be in any condition to complain when the torture was over.

There was, Bartrop told himself, only one chance. He would make up names and rely upon his real employers to extract him from his predicament as the price for his silence where they were concerned.

'Happen you're figuring on being all sneaky and lying,' Waco remarked, as the solution came to the killer. 'You go ahead and do it. Only, afore the real jaspers you're working for can show how grateful they are by prying you loose, Doc and me'll be taking you somewheres they'll not know how to reach you.'

'And on the way,' the pallid-featured Texan continued, almost with relish, 'you'll just happen to get shot trying to escape.'

'All right!' Bartrop gasped. 'I'll tell you who hired me.'

Having been told the names, Waco handcuffed the killer and bent to look through the rifle's telescopic sight. He found that the signing ceremony was just being completed. Straightening up, he gave a contented sigh. No matter whether or not Bartrop's evidence would be sufficient to bring the men who hired him before a court of law, the blond felt there was cause for satisfaction. He and Doc had succeeded in the main part of their current assignment by helping to keep Good Temper alive.

PART SEVEN

Calamity Jane in

DEADWOOD, AUGUST 2ND, 1876

Over the years, I have seen several movies employing versions of Calamity Jane. Among others, they include The Plainsman *(Jean Arthur),* The Paleface *(Jane Russell),* Calamity Jane *(Doris Day),* Calamity Jane and Sam Bass *(Yvonne de Carlo) and* The Raiders *(Judi Meredith). In none of them did I consider the film makers were utilizing her character traits to their full potential. Possibly Jean Arthur came the closest to the actual Calamity in her portrayal, appearing as a whip-toting freight wagon driver. Jane Russell and Yvonne de Carlo each presented her as being at odds with the law and this she never was in real life. Either of them, however, had the looks, figure and temperament to have been ideal for my version of Calamity. So would Judi Meredith have been, although she appeared to have been brought in merely to supply a touch of glamour to an otherwise stark, if fast paced, movie. Of course, Doris Day's portrayal was aimed at a light-hearted musical. While she did have something of the requisite tomboy outlook and at least a modicum of skill with a bull whip, I cannot really see her as the kind of Calamity who Mark Counter knew so well.*[1]

There was something else I noticed in the 'Calamity Jane' films. To quote from William K. Everson's excellent The Bad Guys, A Pictorial History Of The Movie Villain, *Page 221:*

'Westerns, (*The Old Chisholm Trail* is a good example) occasionally used female villains too. They had a special advantage in

---

[1] The first 1968 Corgi Books' edition of *Calamity Spells Trouble* had a Doris Day style 'Calam' on the cover. I heartily disliked it and, as this feeling was apparently shared by my readers, a second edition in the same year had an improvement in its artwork. However, until Mike Codd's superlative illustration for the 1978 Corgi Books' edition of *The Whip and the War Lance*, the best Calamity appeared on the 1969 Bantam Books' edition of *The Bull Whip Breed*.

226

the Old West, and they knew it. They could rustle the hero's cattle and he, as a kind of composite Knight and Boy Scout, could do little about it. (Fortunately, he usually had an athletic leading lady who *could* take on the villainess in a climactic fist-fight!'

This was true enough. Destry Rides Again (*Marlene Dietrich vs Una Merkel*), Destry (*Mari Blanchard vs Mary Wickes*), The Woman They Almost Lynched (*Joan Leslie vs Audrey Totter*) Go West, Young Lady (*Penny Singleton, of Blondie and Dagwood fame, vs Ann Miller*), Jesse James' Women (*Peggy Castle vs Joyce Rhedd*), The Legend of Frenchie King (*Brigitte Bardot vs Claudia Cardinale*) *are examples which spring to mind. Yet Calamity Jane, one person who might appear most suited by character and temperament to take on the villainess in a brawl, never has to the best of my knowledge.*[2]

As always when such a situation arises, I started to think how much better a job I could make of Calamity Jane.[3] *I decided she would be a kind of pre-Women's Lib liberated woman, if less inclined to over-react than some of her present day counterparts, and ready, willing and able to compete with men on their own terms in what was basically a masculine-orientated world. There was, of course, only one person in whose company I could introduce her. However, as authors don't function like human beings, I had already brought Calam into print as a* very *good friend of Mark Counter before I wrote the story of their first meeting.*

The episode in which Calamity made her first appearance was based on fact. She was beaten in a fist fight by Madame Bulldog, although the end was recorded as being somewhat different than in my version.[4] *Nor had it ever been proved to my satisfaction*

[2] The same applies to the lady outlaw, Belle Starr, who has been portrayed by Gene Tierney (*Belle Starr*), Isabel Jewell (*Badman's Territory*) and Jane Russell (*Montana Belle*) without any of them having been called upon to 'lock horns' with a villainess. However, Annie Oakley—who hardly qualifies as an Old West personality—fought in the Three Stooges' *The Outlaws is Coming* (Nancy Kovack vs Sally Starr) and *Carry on Cowboy* (Angela Douglas vs Joan Sims and a supporting actress).

[3] For the benefit of new readers: details of Martha 'Calamity Jane' Canary's background and special qualifications are in Appendix Eight.

[4] The researches of fictionist genealogist Philip José Farmer, q.v., suggest that the version upon which I based Part One 'Better Than Calamity', The Wildcats, might have been circulated deliberately at Calamity's instigation to prevent the truth—that her mother was engaged in a somewhat unsavoury occupation—being made public. We believe mine to be correct.

227

that Calamity did not help to rescue a young Army officer who had been captured by Indians as I described in her first 'starring' title, Trouble Trail.

The Calamity Jane series grew out of what was originally intended as a six episode anthology. However, when I started working on the manuscript, I found the first story was stretching beyond my expectations. So I decided to turn it into a complete book and produce a four part anthology. The same thing happened to the second story, which became The Bull Whip Breed *and the third,* The Cow Thieves, *after which instead of writing the anthology, I finished up with a series.*

White Stallion, Red Mare *was one of the books which ran into title problems. I wanted to name it* Call Me Calamity, *but Corgi Books' Sales Department said they did not like the idea of emphasizing a woman as the leading character. This was also their original objection to having Calamity on the covers. I next suggested* The Owner of the Water, *as being what the basis of the plot was all about, but this too failed to find favour and we finally settled for the title it was given.*

Until Calamity made her appearance the field of action-escapism-adventure literature had been almost exclusively a masculine domain. Despite that, much to my relief, she caught on.

Anyway, here is Calamity Jane's participation. Again, as is confirmed in Eugene Cunningham's Triggernometry, *it is based on an actual incident.*

DEADWOOD, AUGUST 2ND, 1876

'Who the hell does Wild Bill Hickok think he is?'

Shouted loudly in a Kentucky accent which was slurred through too much hard liquor, the question caused an uneasy silence to descend over the busy bar-room of the Silver Wheel Saloon. Teetering on his heels drunkenly at the bar and waving an almost full bottle of whiskey, the speaker was far from an impressive specimen of manhood. Perhaps twenty-five years of age, he was not much over five foot eight in height and scrawny rather than brawny of build. Having the optical condition known as *strabismus*, which prevented his eyes from being simultaneously focused on the same spot,[1] and a broken nose, did nothing to improve his sallow and weak-chinned features. A battered black Burnside campaign hat with an eagle feather stuck into its band was tilted on the back of his lank, greasy dark hair. He had on a smoke-blackened fringed buckskin jacket, a grimy tartan shirt, dirty U.S. Cavalry breeches and Osage moccasins with leggins extending to knee level. A massive bowie knife hung on the left side of his belt and he had a Colt Civilian Model Peacemaker which showed signs of neglect tucked into his breeches' waist-band.

'God damn it!' the man went on, swinging his off-centre gaze about him as if seeking an answer, or disappointed because none had been forthcoming. 'He's only been here a few son-of-a-bitching days and he's already started threatening 'n' abusing honest, law-abiding folks. Well, there's plenty of us say he ain't being let get away with it. Deadwood City ain't no stinking, flea-bit Kansas

---

[1] When one, or both, eyes of a sufferer from *strabismus* are turned inward, the condition is called 'cross-eyed'. If they point outwards, the term is 'wall-eyed'.

railroad town and we ain't fixing to have no bribe-taking fighting pimp wearing the marshal's badge here.'

'Jerry!' Thomas Braskey hissed urgently. 'We've got to have that drunken, stupid son-of-a-bitch shut up before he says too much!'

'Yeah!' Jeremiah Verity agreed. 'The cross-eyed bastard'll be coming to *us* next.'

As co-owners of the saloon and being involved in various illicit activities, the two men had a more valid reason than the speaker for being disinclined to see James Butler 'Wild Bill' Hickok offered the position as town marshal of Deadwood, Dakota Territory. In fact, apart from having been stirred by them to hatred of the famous gun fighter, Jack McCall had no cause to feel concerned over the issue. He was neither a resident of the town, nor had he been present during the 'threatening and abusing' incident to which he referred.[2] Furthermore, his reporting of the affair was far from accurate. None of the participants could be regarded, even by the most tolerant person, as deserving the classification, 'honest, law-abiding folks'.

However, while the pair had been responsible for McCall's animosity towards Hickok and arranged for him to be supplied with the liquor needed to keep up his spurious courage, they had no desire to let it be known they had any connection with him. They had been commissioned, at their own suggestion and with the promise of a sizeable financial remuneration, to ensure that Deadwood was allowed to continue in its present state of non-existent law enforcement. The people who had hired them were all too aware that such a state would end if the portion of the community less enamoured of it had any say in the matter. Even before it was learned that Hickok had arrived, announcing he and his companion, 'Colorado Charley' Utter were only interested in staking a claim at the 'diggings', there had been rumours of the more law abiding citizens' intention to bring in professional

[2] On hearing that a bunch of hard-cases were issuing threats where he was concerned, Wild Bill Hickok confronted them and said, 'I understand some of you two-by-four gladiators have been making remarks about me. So I came to tell you that if I hear any more talk about what you're going to do to Wild Bill Hickok, this camp is going to have the biggest bunch of cheap funerals ever seen in the West. Line up, all of you! I'll take charge of your artillery.' With that, he proceeded to disarm them.

peace officers capable of cleaning up what was rapidly gaining the reputation of being the most lawless of lawless mining camps. As Hickok had proved in the Kansas trail-end towns of Hays City and Abilene, he was a man who might be considered capable of repeating the process.

Having an all too healthy respect for Hickok's proficiency as a gun fighter, neither Braskey nor Verity had had the slightest intention of attempting the dissuasion personally. When they had made tentative suggestions to the local hard-cases, they had found an equal reluctance to perform the task. Hickok might have been in the East play-acting with Buffalo Bill Cody for the past few years and was now rumoured to be a married man whose eyesight was failing, but his reputation had lost little with the passing of time. Nor, as he had demonstrated since his arrival, had he lost his nerve. His shooting was as swiftly accurate as ever. Hints that he could be removed by other than a face to face confrontation had failed to yield the required result. There was a major deterrent against killing him from ambush. He had a number of friends among the fast drawing fraternity who would be willing to travel far and expend effort in avenging him.

A possible solution to the pair's dilemma had presented itself. Jack McCall, a former and far from successful buffalo hunter, had arrived in Deadwood. It was soon apparent that he was a drunken braggard who craved the benefits offered by possessing the reputation of being a fast draw killer. While he would have less chance than a snowball in hell of surviving in a fair fight against Hickok, they had felt sure he could be persuaded that an equal fame would accrue no matter how he gunned the other down. However, his loud mouthed talk was starting to alarm them.

Little about the conspirators' appearances suggested they were partners. Tall, slim, clean shaven and good looking, Verity was dressed after the fashion of a successful professional gambler. Matching him in height, but bulky to the point of corpulence, Braskey had sun reddened and ugly heavily moustached features. He dressed like a prosperous town dwelling businessman. Shrewd and unscrupulous, between them they made a force to be reckoned with. They knew that, apart from the monetary benefits, they would have a much enhanced status in the town if they could

231

prevent Hickok from becoming the marshal. The last thing they wanted was to have their intentions betrayed by the inebriated babbling of their irresponsible dupe.

'The hell with Hickok!' McCall bellowed, stepping from the bar with his eyes turning to the two men. Much to their consternation, he raised the bottle over his head and began to walk in their direction, declaiming just as loudly: 'Come on, let's have a drink to that long haired son-of-a-bitch getting what's——!'

Two new arrivals had entered the saloon while the drunken words were being uttered. It was hard to decide which of them looked the most out of place as they came to a halt and listened to what was being said.

Of medium height and in his early thirties, the newcomer at the right had a Texas-style J.B. Stetson hat tilted back on rusty red hair. Despite a luxuriant moustache and solemn expression, his face had a rugged attraction. His stocky, powerful frame was clothed in a sober black suit, plain white shirt and dark tie such as a member of one of the more strict religious sects might wear. However, riding slightly higher than was normal on a stiff, two and a half inch-wide belt, and in an open fronted spring retention holster of unusual design, was a Rogers & Spencer Army Model revolver with bell-shaped, square bottomed black walnut grips. Furthermore, he wore a pair of high heeled, sharp toed cowhand boots.

Normally the inconsistencies in the man's appearance would have caused him to be the object of speculation. On this occasion, if McCall had not been the centre of attraction, his companion would have diverted attention from him. Despite the attire being masculine, what was inside left no doubt that the wearer was feminine. A battered U.S. cavalry kepi perched jauntily on a mop of shortish curly hair. Her freckled, tanned, pretty face had sparkling blue eyes, a slightly snub nose and a full lipped mouth with grin quirks at the corners, but it had lost its smile on hearing McCall's words. The fringed buckskin shirt clung like a second skin to her torso, the swell of her full bosom causing its open neck to spread sufficiently to indicate she did not consider underclothing a necessity and the sleeves were rolled up to show strong brown biceps. Her waist trimmed down without the aid of a corset, widening to curvaceous hips and shapely, powerful legs emphasized rather than concealed by buckskin trousers which—like the shirt—appeared to have been bought a size too small, or to have shrunk in washing. She wore no female adornment, her ensemble being completed by a pair of Pawnee moccasins and a brown gunbelt slanting down from her left hip to the ivory handled Colt 1851 Navy revolver riding butt forward in the low cavalry twist holster on her right thigh. On the left side of her waistbelt, its handle thrust through a broad leather loop, was suspended a long lashed, coiled bull whip which looked far more functional than decorative.

A look of anger came to the girl's face as McCall began to propose his toast. Crossing swiftly, her right hand grasped and slid free the whip. Seeming to take on a life of its own, the lash curled behind her. Then, as her arm swung forward, it reversed its direction. Moving almost too quickly for the human eye to follow, the three inch solid leather 'popper' attached to the tapered lash struck and shattered the upraised bottle with a crack like a pistol shot.

A screech of alarm and rage burst from McCall as fragments of disintegrated glass and a deluge of whiskey sprayed over his head. Swinging around with such violence that he sent his hat flying, his never pleasant features were rendered even more ugly by an expression of anger and fright. Although the shock had increased his condition of *strabismus*, it did not prevent him from sending his right hand in a spasmodic, yet fairly fast, grab at the walnut handle of his Colt.

Swiftly as her victim was moving, the girl's response was even more rapid. An almost casual appearing swing of her arm caused the whip's lash to return and she sent it forward once more with the deft ease that told of considerable practice. How well she had absorbed her lessons in its use showed when, in a continuous motion which hardly seemed to have allowed opportunity to change the point of aim, much less for such control to be attained, the plaited leather coiled around McCall's neck and tightened without cutting into the flesh. Nor did his misfortune end there. Not only did he find himself suddenly and unexpectedly being choked, he was subjected to a jerk that propelled him forward.

233

He was so startled that he lost his hold on the revolver and it fell to join his hat on the floor. Having disarmed him, she liberated the lash in the same apparently effortless manner and, acting almost as if of its own volition, it retired to a position of readiness behind her.

If he had not been drinking, McCall would have been too cowardly to take the matter further. In his present condition, he was imbued with a courage that would have been lacking if he was sober. On being released, ignoring the Colt he had dropped, he gave vent to a squawl of fury and rushed towards his assailant. As he advanced, he reached for the hilt of the bowie knife. However, his belief that his menacing demeanour would terrify the girl and her 'preacher' companion into a state of immobility was soon disillusioned.

Declining to stand in quaking terror, or to turn and flee (the only other alternative envisaged by her would-be assailant) the red head sprang to meet him. While her companion remained motionless, there was nothing in his bearing to indicate fear was causing him to do so. Instead of employing the whip's lash, the girl allowed its handle to advance through her fingers until she was grasping it at the top. Stepping aside an instant before McCall reached her, she whipped around her arm and drove the counter-weighted butt to the top of his head as he blundered involuntarily by. Crumpling like a steer struck by a pole-axe, he sprawled face down at the black-attired male newcomer's feet.

'The name's Calamity Jane, ladies and gents,' the girl announced, looking around the bar-room in a challenging fashion and without as much as a glance to make sure her attacker was rendered *hors-de-combat*, while coiling the whip. However, she did not return the handle to the loop on her waistbelt, but continued, 'Should *anybody* have notions of drinking that son-of-a-bitching toast he was making, you'd best know now that Wild Bill's a *real* good friend of mine and I don't take to hearing folks mean-mouthing him.'

'Which're my sentiments all the way from here to there and back the long way,' the man supplemented, his Texas drawl as solemn as he looked. 'Like it says in the Good Book, brothers and

234

sisters, "Speak not evil against one in his absence lest he hath *bueno amigos* on hand ready to stand up for him".'

Even the few present who had sufficient knowledge of the Bible to doubt if the quotation came from it made no attempt to raise the point. Every eye was on the girl who had introduced herself as the already legendary Calamity Jane. Nor, after the masterful display of whip handling, did anybody doubt she was speaking the truth. Her audience were equally aware that she was on friendly terms with Hickok and would be ready, willing and fully able to back up her challenge even if she was alone. Studying her companion, those with knowledge of such matters—which meant almost everybody—would have been willing to bet he was fully competent in matters *pistolero* to be able to support her against any opposition.

'One thing's for sure, Reverend Wisdom,' Calamity declared, replacing the whip when it was obvious nobody intended to pick up the metaphorical gauntlet she had cast before them and directing a look of disgust at her stunned victim. 'We'll not find Bill in here. This booze-rotted son-of-a-bitch wouldn't have been spouting off that ways if he was.'

'You'll not get any argument from me about that, sister,' the man intoned, sounding like a particularly doleful preacher delivering a sermon to a congregation of unrepentant sinners. 'As the crackling of thorns under the campfire's skillet, so do mealy-mouthed no-accounts talk big and brave when it's safe to do it. We must seek Brother Hickok elsewhere.'

'Maybe somebody here'd be right neighbourly 'n' tell us where we might find him?' the red head suggested. 'How's about it, folks?'

'Try at the Fullerton Hotel,' a somewhat surly voice called.

'Thanks,' the girl said dryly. 'Let's do just that, shall we, Reverend?'

'Now that's what I call lucky,' Verity commented, after he had watched the couple leave, turning his gaze to where McCall was already showing signs of regaining consciousness.

'*Lucky?*' Braskey repeated incredulously. 'She could've bust his head in.'

'She never aimed to, or he'd be lying there with it bust,' Verity declared. 'But she sure as hell stopped him saying too much.'

'How's her being here going to affect——?' Braskey began, then glanced around to ensure nobody had overheard his incautious words.

'It's not,' Verity stated. 'Except that she's likely to save us the trouble of killing McCall if he pulls it off. It's that son-of-a-bitch who's with her that's puzzling me.'

'*Him?*' Braskey snorted disdainfully. 'No matter he's toting a gun, it's too high for him to get it out fast even if he wasn't just a circuit riding preacher. He's nothing for us to be worried over. Fact being, he could be useful to read over Hickok during the funeral.'

*****   *****

'Howdy there, Bill,' Calamity greeted, as she and the man she had addressed as 'Reverend Wisdom' crossed the dining room of the Fullerton Hotel. 'You're looking fit as a flea.'

'*Calam!*' Wild Bill Hickok responded, rising from the chair which allowed him to follow his long established habit of sitting with his back against something solid enough to halt a bullet. His gaze flickered briefly to the girl's companion as he went on, 'Aren't you a sight for sore eyes?'

While approaching the famous gun fighter's table, Calamity had studied him. They had not met since he left for the East and she could see changes which might not be noticeable to a casual acquaintance, but worried her.

Despite Hickok's six foot odd of wide shouldered height being as erect and powerful as the girl remembered, there was now a tinge of grey in the shoulder long light brown hair and heavy moustache. His face had regained its tan and the strength was still there, but his eyes seemed somewhat less keen and penetrating. As usual, he had on a well tailored black cutaway coat, frilly bosomed white silk shirt with a black satin cravat fastened in the form of a bowtie, yellowish-brown Nankeen trousers and black boots more suitable for walking than riding a horse. She noticed that he still carried his two ivory handled Colt Model of 1851 Navy revolvers thrust butt forward into the scarlet silk sash around his waist and did not doubt he had other weapons con-

236

cealed upon his person.[3]

'Damned if I wasn't going to say the same about you,' Calamity enthused with a grin, shaking hands and holding back a wince at the strength with which she was gripped. 'Hey, do you know Sol —Solomon Wisdom here?'

'We've met, back a spell,' Hickok admitted, releasing the red head and extending his hand to the other man. 'Howdy, Solly. What brings *you* to Deadwood?'

'Same thing's takes me most places, Bill,' Wisdom replied. 'I was told it might be a good place for me to come and bring the "word". And, from what I've seen so far, I reckon it's all of that.'

'It's *all* of that, and more,' Hickok confirmed, waving a hand to the empty chairs. 'Rest your butts a spell.'

'Solly's offered to buy me a meal,' Calamity remarked, glancing at the Texan. 'Happen the food's good, here'll be's good a place's any to take it.'

'You'll not do better in Deadwood,' Hickok declared and, after his guests were seated, went on, 'I've got me a poker game down to Mann & Lewis's Number Ten Saloon at two o'clock, but there's plenty of time for me to sit and visit a spell, unless you pair want to come and play?'

'I've got some chores to see to for Dobe[4] first,' Calamity replied. 'But as soon's I get through, I'll drop by and teach you how she's played.'

'I can't come straight off either,' Wisdom apologized. 'Like the Good Book says, "Consider that I work my butt off not for myself only, but for all them good tax-paying folks's help pay me".'

'One day I'm fixing to read the Bible and find out if *any* of those sayings you keep spouting're really in it,' Hickok threatened amiably.

'Happen you find one, holler "keno",' Calamity suggested. 'Saw Agnes's I come through Cheyenne, Bill. Said to give you her love and tell you to mind what she told you afore you 'n' Colorado set

---

[3] The concealed weapons proved to be two small, compact pistols; a four-barrelled ·32 C. Sharps' Triumph and a single-shot Hammond Bull-dog firing the Tyler B. Henry ·44-28—having a calibre of ·44 and taking a twenty-eight grain black powder charge rifle bullet.

[4] For the benefit of new readers, Cecil 'Dobe' Killem was the owner of a freight wagon outfit and Calamity Jane's employer.

off. And, what happened last time I met her,[5] I'd say she's a gal who bears listening to.'

'I'll mind it,' Hickok promised.

'So you should, for shame,' the red head grinned and looked up as a waitress came to the table. After she and Wisdom had ordered meals, she continued more soberly, 'Anyways, a feller with a right nice wife to home'd be *loco* to take on as John-Law in a wide open town like this.'

'Is *that* what I'm fixing on doing?' the gun fighter inquired.

'There's them around's thinks so,' Calamity warned.

'Who's doing the thinking?' Hickok wanted to know.

'Without being nosey, even though I am, Bill,' Wisdom drawled, when he had finished describing the incident at the Silver Wheel Saloon. 'But are you-all figuring to take on as marshal?'

'I've been asked,' Hickok conceded, showing no resentment over the interest in his private affairs. 'But I've not decided one way or t'other. Like Calam knows, my lil lady don't cotton to me doing it.'

'This sin-hole needs a good man wearing the badge,' Wisdom commented, drawing a baleful glare from the red head. 'Anyways, there'll be time enough to talk about it while we're eating.'

'It'll have to be after the game,' Hickok corrected, glancing at the clock on the wall and shoving back his chair. Taking his wide brimmed, low crowned black hat from the table, he rose and concluded, 'Happen you'll excuse me, I'll have to be getting down to it. I'll see you there later on.'

'I don't know about the Reverend here,' Calamity answered. 'But you'll sure's sin's for sale in Cheyenne be seeing me.'

'And me,' Wisdom seconded, making the words emerge almost as a threat. 'You owe me some from the last time we played, Bill.'

*****   *****

'God damn it all ways!' Hickok protested, but without rancour, watching the pot in which he had just participated unsuccessfully being gathered up by the winner. 'I *knew* I should've been in *that* seat.'

'Why do you reckon I snuck in early and took it?' asked the man who was sitting on the chair usually occupied by the gun

[5] What happened is told in Part Six, 'Mrs. Wild Bill', of *J.T.'S Ladies.*

238

fighter, drawing the money he had won towards him. 'You've been so lucky using it all week that we figured it was time somebody else walked out a winner.'

Ever since the occasion in Hays City when Hickok had only escaped being shot from behind because he had caught sight of Jack Strawhan's actions reflected in a fortuitous bar mirror, he had always avoided sitting with his back to people in public places. Nor had he considered Deadwood to be a suitable community in which to forgo the precaution. So he had seated himself accordingly, even when among friends.

However, on his arrival at the No. 10 Saloon two hours earlier, Hickok had discovered that a joke was being played on him. With the exception of Colorado Charlie Utter, whose chair had been moved, the rest of the regular participants were already seated; but the only vacant position was on the outside of the circular table. Tall, handsome, well dressed and armed gambler-gun fighter Charlie Rich was seated in the place Hickok usually occupied. The grins on the faces of Rich, and of beefy and jovial Charles Mann (one of the proprietors), and of thickset and white haired Frank Massey (whose attire proclaimed he was the captain of a riverboat), and of the bartender, Harry Young, implied the change in the seating arrangements was deliberate.

In any other place, or with less trustworthy and reliable company, Hickok would have demanded his usual seat or withdrawn from the game. Assured in his own mind that he was at the only saloon in Deadwood where he could do so safely, albeit protesting as he knew it was expected of him, he had allowed himself to be talked into occupying a chair which would leave his back exposed to anybody coming through the front batwing doors.

Considering how he had fared since starting to play, Hickok wondered if surrendering what his companions referred to as his 'pet superstition' was clouding his judgement. On three occasions he had stayed in a pot when cold mathematical chances enjoined that he should fold. Furthermore, twice he had continued to raise, then call, instead of taking the sensible course of cutting his losses and withdrawing. Competing against the class of opposition around him, such errors could prove costly—and had done so.

Warning himself to concentrate solely upon what he was doing, Hickok gathered up the five cards he had been dealt while thinking. He knew there was no need for such a precaution where the men around the table were concerned, but he cupped them in his big hands to prevent anyone other than himself from having the opportunity to discover their value.

'Ace of clubs,' the gun fighter read silently and without allowing the slightest trace of emotion to show on his face. Then he fanned the other four cards out one at a time, continuing, 'Queen of hearts, eight of spades—huh, that's *no* help—eight of clubs—that's better—*ace* of spades, *that's* better still!'

Despite the hand being completed by what tradition claimed was the 'death card', the famous gun fighter was elated at the sight of it. It gave him a potentially powerful force with which to contend for the pot. In fact, with the chances of receiving such a combination on the deal being one in 21.03—when, as was the case, no 'wild cards' which could be given any value were allowed —the odds were greatly in his favour that he held the best hand at this stage of the proceedings. The problem was deciding how it could be utilized most advantageously. Taking a single card on the draw gave a one in 11.75 opportunity of acquiring an ace or an eight to complete a full house, as well as possibly misleading the other players into assuming he was hoping to fill either a straight or a flush.[6] On the other hand, to discard the two eights and the queen for three fresh cards offered the same odds for improvement as would playing a single pair from the beginning.[7] He did not even contemplate the possibility of tossing back the lower pair and retaining the queen as a 'kicker' for the aces.[8]

There was, Hickok realized, one ploy which might serve his needs. He could stand pat and, by refraining from drawing further cards, hope to delude his opponents into believing he had been

[6] An explanation of the various poker hands and their respective values is given in: *Two Miles to the Border*.

[7] The chances of improving a pair with a draw of three cards are: any improved hand, 1–3.48; two pairs, 1–6.25; three of a kind, 1–8.7; full house, 1–98; four of a kind, 1–360.

[8] The chances of improving a pair and a 'kicker' with a draw of two cards are: any improved hand, 1–3.86; two pairs, 1–5.9; three of a kind, 12.9; full house, 1–120; four of a kind, 1–1,081. Improving three of a kind with a 'kicker' gives odds of: any improved hand, 1–11.8; full house, 1–15.7; four of a kind, 1–47.

dealt a straight, flush, full house, four of a kind, or a straight flush. As he had not employed that particular tactic so far today, he decided he would do so. It called for shrewd play designed to make the opposition uncertain whether he was betting on a genuine pat hand, bluffing, or running a double bluff.[9]

'I'll see your fifty and raise it seventy-five,' Hickok declared confidently, when his turn to bet arrived.

Wanting to establish the requisite mood, the famous gun fighter had eyes only for his immediate surroundings. Being equally proficient poker players, the other three men were also giving the game their full attention. So none of them, nor the bartender—an eager spectator with a very thorough knowledge of poker—noticed that Jack McCall was about to come through the front doors.

As at the Fullerton Hotel's dining room, there was a clock on the wall. Its hands showed the time to be almost ten minutes past four.

A calendar was hanging alongside the clock.

The date was August the 2nd, 1876!

***** *****

'Why the hell have those two come here?' Thomas Braskey growled worriedly, having watched Solomon Wisdom go by the table at which he and Verity were sitting to join Calamity Jane at the bar of the Silver Wheel Saloon.

The time was just after five minutes past four and the partners were awaiting the results, if any, of their plotting.

Having reached the conclusion that there was no cause for alarm over the visit by the red head and her sombre-looking companion, Verity had arranged for McCall to be brought to his private office without any of the other customers learning of it. Finding their dupe somewhat sobered by what had happened to him, the partners had set about reviving his ire by claiming his misfortunes were the result of Hickok having sent Calamity to assault him. Accepting the story, aided by a couple of drinks, he had gradually returned to his earlier state of truculence. The arrival of a man hired by Verity, bringing news of the joke that was being played on the gun fighter at the No. 10 Saloon had

[9] How effective such a ploy can be is described in: *Beguinage*.

struck all three of them as a heaven-sent opportunity and McCall was dispatched to make the most of it. In spite of wishing him good luck and assuring him of their support no matter how the affair ended, the pair had respectively expressed a silent hope that he would not be alive when it was over regardless of the result. From what he had said while they were awaiting the watcher's arrival, he was not only aware of the deal they had made to prevent Hickok from becoming town marshal, but he had learned the names of several of their principals.

'I don't know,' Verity answered. 'But you'd best go tell Slocum to be ready in case they're hunting trouble.'

While his partner crossed the room to deliver the message to one of the hired killers they had tried without success to interest in removing Hickok, Verity took out a deck of cards. He intended to start playing patience, which was known as a sign that he had no desire for company, as he kept the couple under observation. If he had not been so engrossed in them, he might have noticed two men outside. Glancing through the open batwing doors, the taller—who was well built and dressed after the fashion of a professional gambler—paused and, saying something to his small, far less affluent looking companion, turned to enter alone. Instead of walking on, the other man remained standing at the edge of the sidewalk.

A low spoken oath burst from Verity as the newcomer strode swiftly towards the bar. There was an urgency in his movements which filled the conspirator with a sense of foreboding. It was not like Colorado Charlie Utter to display such obvious agitation.

'Have you seen Bill?' the newcomer inquired, without any preliminary greeting, coming to a halt before Calamity and Wisdom.

'Not for a couple of hours,' the red head replied, drawing a similar conclusion to that arrived at by Verity. 'He told us he was going to the Number Ten to——'

'Did he ask you to come *here*?' Utter interrupted, once more acting out of character although he seemed a trifle relieved by the news.

'Nope,' Calamity answered. 'We figured it might be a smart notion to drop by——'

'What's wrong, Charlie?' Wisdom put in, being equally perceptive.

'I've just been told a jasper called McCall's been liquored and primed to go gunning for Bill,' the gambler explained.

'*McCall?*' Wisdom repeated. 'He was the yahoo you-all whomped on the head, Calam.'

'Which being, I don't reckon's Bill's got a whole heap to worry over,' the girl declared, being aware that her companion had intended to find out the identity of the man with whom she had dealt and having cause to know how competent he could be in such matters. 'He could whip half a dozen of that kind one handed, leftie at that.'

'Not if they'd been told it didn't make no never mind how they went after him,' Utter pointed out, reaching over with his right hand to scratch at his stomach close to the ivory butt of the Colt Civilian Model Peacemaker in its cross draw holster on the left side of his belt. 'Which's what McCall's been told.'

'And that's what made you think we'd come here about?' Wisdom drawled, dipping his left hand into his jacket's inside breast pocket and removing something which he kept concealed in his palm, while the words sounded more of a statement than a question.

'Huh huh!' Utter agreed, showing no surprise over the shrewd deduction. He was facing the couple, but could see the room behind him reflected in the bar mirror. 'Verity, that gambling man sitting alone by the door's one who's in i——!'

'Charlie!' the gambler's short, rat-faced companion—who Wisdom recognized as an informer going by the name of 'Mousey'[10] —shouted from the sidewalk in a tone redolent of alarm. 'McCall's going into the Number Ten holding a gun behind his back!'

'Come on!' Calamity snapped, thrusting herself away from the bar. She realized that Hickok's speed on the draw might be insufficient to offset such an advantage, particularly if—feeling himself secure in a saloon owned by friends—he should be taken

[10] Other examples of 'Mousey's' penchant for informing are given in: *The Town Tamers* and, although his name is not mentioned, *The Making of a Lawman*.

243

unawares. Or the former buffalo hunter might be taking part in a planned and concerted attack involving other assailants. 'Bill might need help!'

'Stop them!' Verity yelled, throwing over his chair in his haste to rise and grabbing for his holstered revolver.

Swinging around as the red head and Wisdom began to move forward, Utter had anticipated some such reaction on the part of the saloonkeeper. That was why he had taken the precaution of surreptitiously positioning his right hand close to the Colt's butt. On hearing Mousey shout his name, he had commenced his draw without waiting for the rest of the message and he completed his turn with the weapon in his hand. For all that, he realized that the position was anything but a sinecure. There would be, he discovered, more than just Verity to contend with.

Despite having noticed Mousey waiting outside as Utter entered, Braskey was just as taken aback as his partner by the betrayal of McCall. He had thought the little man had merely been trying to panhandle the price of a few drinks from the gambler and would never have expected such a warning, which implied an unhealthy knowledge of what should have been a private affair. Alarmed at the possibilities aroused by the last point, as well as goaded by Verity's words and actions, he too reached for his gun. At his side, the surly, hard-faced 'honest, law abiding' citizen started to draw the revolver bought to replace the one surrendered to Hickok on the memorable occasion a few days earlier.

'Stairs, Solly!' Utter yelled, wanting to alert the solemn-looking man to the presence of Verity's partner (which Mousey's yell had prevented him from mentioning) as he was preparing to go into action himself.

While the gambler had not attained a notoriety as high as Hickok's in such matters, he proved he was a competent gun handler with a shrewd judgement of how to cope with the situation with which he was confronted. Despite the distance separating him from Verity being at least fifty feet, he did not take the extra moment needed to raise his Colt high enough for him to make use of the sights. Instead, tucking his right elbow tight against his side, he aligned the barrel instinctively and at waist level, using his left hand to fan the hammer. There was no faster way by which a single action revolver, needing cocking manually for each successive shot, could be fired and, turning it slightly between every detonation, he spread the bullets like the spokes of a wheel.

Even before Wisdom heard Utter's brief warning, he had been aware of the possible danger. While making inquiries about the incident in which he and Calamity had been involved earlier, he had learned that the Silver Wheel was owned by two partners and obtained their descriptions. On meeting Calamity, who had suggested they stopped by to find out if McCall was still on the premises before going to join the poker game at the No. 10 Saloon, he had had no difficulty in identifying the owners. Nor had he missed what had happened when Utter arrived and he had been keeping Braskey under observation.

Swivelling towards the stairs, Wisdom dipped his right hand to the black butt of the Rogers & Spencer in a rapid motion. What happened next disproved Braskey's theory with regards to his holster being unsuitable for fast draw work. Instead of lifting the revolver above the lip, he thrust it through the slit at the front and began to tilt it upwards as his thumb drew back the hammer and his forefinger entered the triggerguard in a way which warned he was well versed in such matters.

Instead of waiting to find out what her companions intended to do, Calamity continued to run towards the front door. She heard the thunder of shots from behind and either side of her, but neither turned nor looked. Instead, watching Verity caught and knocked backwards by what she deduced to be Utter's bullets, she started to twist her Navy Colt from its holster. Before it was out, a man ahead of her started to rise with the intention of carrying out the saloonkeeper's orders. Then, studying the expression on her face, he thought better of it and flopped back on to his chair. Darting glances around, she saw others were showing signs of contemplating intervention. She did not halt, but left her two companions to take care of any further hostile intentions.

Shock twisted at the faces of Braskey and Slocum, neither of whom had expected—or could match—the speed with which the solemn featured 'preacher' was moving. The Rogers & Spencer

245

thundered three times in rapid succession, its hammer thumb-cocked. The direction in which the ·44 calibre muzzle pointed changed during each successive recoil kick. Flying across the room, the first bullet took Slocum high in the right shoulder and ended his participation before it fully began. Splinters erupted as the second finished its flight in the stairs. Even as Braskey's gun was clearing leather, the third ploughed into his left breast and ripped apart his heart.

'Hold hard, all of you!' the solemn-featured man bellowed, raising his left hand above his head and displaying the shield-shaped peace officer's badge he had taken from his pocket. 'The name's Solomon Wisdom Cole.[11] I'm a U.S. Marshal!'

*****　　*****

Wild with elation, which was only slightly marred by the remembrance that the smoking Colt in his right hand had misfired when he threw down on the bartender who had started to leap over the counter in an attempt to intercept him, Jack McCall ran out of the No. 10 Saloon. Considering how easily the whole affair had proved, he was wondering why he had had the slightest qualms over setting out to kill Wild Bill Hickok. After he had overcome his fear and forced himself to enter, he had not ex-perienced the slightest difficulty. Stepping behind the gun fighter as if meaning to do no more than kibitz on the game, he had brought the revolver around and, saying 'Take that!' had sent a bullet into the back of the long haired head.[12] Such had been the element of surprise that none of the other players had tried to impede his departure. Even Young had dropped back behind the bar as he turned the Colt in that direction.

Reaching the sidewalk, McCall turned in the direction of the Silver Wheel Saloon. Not only did he want to report his success and collect the promised reward, he expected to find allies willing to stand by him against any of Hickok's friends who came seeking revenge. Before he covered half the distance, causing the people using the street to scatter hurriedly as the news of what he had

---

[11] Although the author had not learned Solomon Wisdom 'Solly' Cole's full name at the time of writing, his first meeting with Calamity Jane is described in: *Calamity Spells Trouble*.

[12] Passing through Wild Bill Hickok's head, the bullet emerged under his right cheekbone and ended its flight in Captain Massey's left forearm.

done was shouted by Young and passed along via other voices, he heard shooting from his destination. Then somebody burst through its front doors. Despite his *strabismus*, he was soon able to identify the swiftly approaching figure as Calamity Jane. Nor did he need to see the Colt in her right hand to deduce her intentions; the expression on her face supplied all the clues he needed.

Bringing up the Colt without stopping, McCall squeezed its trigger and, once more, was rewarded with nothing more than a click. Alarmed by the second failure of the weapon,[13] he dropped it and ran to the nearest horse tied to a hitching rail. Snatching free the reins, without thinking his actions could be construed as theft, he grabbed the horn and put his foot in the stirrup. Having been loosened by its owner, the girth slipped under his weight and the saddle turned from the animal's back. Now thoroughly alarmed, he managed to catch his balance and dashed across the street. Expecting at any moment to feel a bullet drive into him, he entered an alley between two buildings and ran on without shots being fired at him. Instead, he became aware of footsteps rapidly drawing closer from his rear. Although he guessed it was the girl coming, all his previous elation had been driven out by fear and he did not even glance to the rear much less turn to fight.

Exceptionally fit and always fleet of foot, the red head's rage added speed to her movements. Already overhauling him by the time she reached the alley, she noticed that McCall no longer held his gun as they were crossing the street at the other end. Revulsion assailed her at the evidence of his cowardice. Ignoring the sight of the big knife flapping in its sheath at his side, she dropped her Colt. Throwing herself forward, she tackled him around the waist and the pair of them plunged through the open door of Shurdy's butcher shop, causing the owner—who was about to emerge to investigate the disturbance—to leap aside and drop his meat cleaver as they entered and crashed to the floor. Just how it happened, she could not decide; but a brief scuffle ended with McCall supine and held down by her left knee rammed into his chest. Her next conscious realization was staring into his

[13] A subsequent examination of Jack McCall's revolver established that, apart from the one which killed Wild Bill Hickok all the bullets in its cylinder were defective and would not fire.

terrified face as he begged for mercy and finding that, somehow, she had picked up the cleaver which was now raised ready to be driven into his skull.

'No!' Calamity gasped, only just able to prevent herself from delivering the blow. Shuddering from the violence of her revulsion, she threw it aside and came to her feet. 'Get up, you bastard! You're going to live to stretch rope for killing Bill!'

Author's note: Jack McCall suffered the fate for which Calamity spared him, but circumstances prevented her from being present when it happened. There were suggestions that he should be lynched, but although Solomon W. Cole took no further official part in the proceedings at Deadwood, the presence of a U.S marshal in the town acted as a deterrent and it was agreed he would stand trial. Bringing this about proved difficult. There was neither a law enforcement agency, nor official judiciary in the community and the 'miners' court' before which he was brought on August the 3rd had no legal status. Utilizing their time to good advantage, the men behind Verity and Braskey not only organized a defence for him, but contrived to pack the jury with sympathizers ready to accept his plea that Hickok had threatened his life and he had also sought vengeance for a brother killed by the gun fighter. A verdict of 'Not Guilty' was returned.

When Calamity and other of Hickok's friends proposed inflicting a summary execution, Cole dissuaded them. He pointed out that to do so under the circumstances would sully Wild Bill's memory and promised justice would be done. So McCall was permitted to leave Deadwood unmolested. As Cole had anticipated, the killer could not resist boasting of his achievement. One night in Laramie, not knowing a deputy U.S. marshal had been assigned to follow him and await such a lapse, he admitted having lied to the jury and that the brother whom Hickok was supposed to have shot did not exist. Arrested, he was taken for trial before the Federal Court at Yankton and, on being found guilty, was hanged on the 1st of March, 1877. Also as Cole envisaged, the news of the blatant miscarriage of justice at the so-called 'miners' court' aroused such a wave of reproach and revulsion throughout the Dakota Territory that the honest citizens of Deadwood were able to establish effective law enforcement in their community. So, although Calamity may have regretted not having personally avenged Wild Bill Hickok, she eventually came to accept that in one respect he had not died in vain.

PART EIGHT

Belle Boyd in

AFFAIR OF HONOUR

With Martha 'Calamity Jane' Canary established, I turned my attention to another female protagonist whose acquaintance I had made in the course of my reading. As far as I am aware, Belle Boyd has never been made the subject of a movie;[1] although some of her Civil War activities may have been attributed to the other famous bearer of the Christian name in the 1941 film Belle Starr, *which had Gene Tierney and her co-star, Randolph Scott, playing 'Jim Starr', a Confederate officer, fighting the Yankees and so being driven to a life of crime.*

From the first time I came across information regarding Belle's career, in James D. Horan's Desperate Women, Book One 1861–1865, *Part Two, The Siren Of The Shenandoah',[2] I decided she offered great scope. As she had genuinely been a very capable Confederate States Secret Agent, she would be able to meet and work in close co-operation with Dusty Fog and other of my protagonists in the Civil War series. However, I felt the sobriquet attributed to her in Mr. Horan's book was a trifle too cumbersome for regular use and so she became 'The Rebel Spy'.[3]*

At the period of Belle's introduction, the 'gadget' spy movies

[1] Considering the current trend of the movie and television industry, wherein almost every 'baddie' speaks with a Southern accent—including an actress in one episode of *A Man Called Ironside* who did not start using one until *after* she was exposed as the villainess—I hope Belle Boyd will continue to be ignored. If not, she will in all probability be portrayed in a completely unfavourable light.

[2] James D. Horan's *Desperate Women* also introduced me to Rose Greenhow and Pauline 'the Major' Cushman, who served as spies respectively for the Confederate States and the Union.

[3] For the benefit of new readers: details of Belle 'the Rebel Spy' Boyd's family background and special qualifications can be found in Appendix Seven.

*were becoming fashionable. However, while Belle was to be well
equipped with devices to help in her assignments, I refused to
allow her to have anything which could not have been manufactured at that time. Nor, as my searching through reference
books informed me, was there any need to exaggerate. As I
mentioned in the Introduction to the Civil War section, the War
Between The States could claim to be the first of the 'modern'
conflicts in which scientific development played an ever growing
part.*

Those of you who have read The Colt and the Sabre, *in which
Belle made her first appearance, may have noticed that apart from
a reference to the colour of her hair and the beauty of her features,
she was not described. This came about because, after I received
the proofs from the publisher, I discovered I had inadvertently
conveyed the impression she had similar physical attributes to
those of Belle Starr. Unfortunately, the realization came at a point
where it would have been too expensive to make the necessary
alterations. All that could be done was delete the majority of the
description and wait until her second 'starring' role, in* The Rebel
Spy, *to present the correct version. As I had only a photograph to
work from, I was uncertain of her true dimensions. A study of
the picture allowed me to estimate her height and build. These
corresponded with those of a good friend, Myrtle Molloy—who,
with her husband Bob, is currently managing the Oakdale public
house in the Sneinton Dale district of Nottingham—and she
kindly made her dimensions—height five foot seven, contours,
36"–25"–36"—available to me.*

*Although Belle has never attained the status of having her own
series, she has 'starred' in two books,* To Arms! To Arms! In
Dixie! *and* The Remittance Kid, *to add to her various 'guest'
appearances. Also, apart from a not too accurate portrayal of
Dusty Fog, Mark Counter and the Ysabel Kid, on the 1966 Brown
Watson edition of* Guns in the Night, *she followed Calamity Jane
in being the first of my protagonists to be illustrated on the jacket
of a book.*

*Here is Belle's participation in this volume. The incident being
recorded takes place after the War Between The States and while
she is serving as a member of the U.S. Secret Service. I have*

selected this particular episode of her career because it allows me to give 'guest' appearances to two of my protagonists whom space does not allow me to present with a section of their own.

AFFAIR OF HONOUR

'Begorrah!' a voice said loudly and truculently, its accent that of a well educated Irishman. 'And is it calling the O'Malley a cheat you are?'

Words of that kind were likely to form the prelude to the crash of shots when uttered in many places west of the Mississippi River. However, while they caused silence to fall throughout the elegant bar-room of the Cattlemen's Hotel, few of its occupants expected they would result in the immediate and impromptu gun play which might have followed them elsewhere. As the capital city of the State of Texas, Austin—that section of it, at any rate—had become too civilized for such unseemly behaviour.

Although the high standards set by the co-owners, Charles Gannon and Horace Wickstead, had fallen somewhat during the impoverished period which followed the War Between The States, things had changed for the better. In fact, the condition of financial stability attained by utilizing the enormous numbers of half wild longhorns roaming the ranges had allowed the Cattlemen's Hotel to surpass its earlier reputation for luxury and excellent service. It was now well deserving of the name it had acquired as the finest establishment of its kind in Texas and equal to the best offered in any Eastern city. On any given day, its bar and dining room would be graced by leading civic dignitaries, senior members of the State's Administration and anybody of importance who might be visiting Austin. There too would frequently be found the leading participants in the cattle business upon which the current prosperity of the Lone Star State depended.

So, in such exalted company, the possibility of an altercation over a card table ending with hands reaching for revolvers was unthinkable.

That was particularly true under the prevailing circumstances.

After having been disenfranchised for supporting the Confederate States, the population of Texas was on the verge of having its right to vote returned. The man to whom the question had been directed was one of those named as being a candidate for office in the Legislature which would almost certainly replace the hated Reconstruction Administration when elections were held in the near future.

Tall, slender without being puny, Warren Chapter was in his early forties and had the carriage of a military man. There was just a trace of grey in his brown hair, but his handsome features were unlined. They showed strength of will, but also hinted at a spirited nature. Bare headed, he was clad in a new, well cut brown three piece suit, a white shirt with a celluloid collar and a plain blue tie. However, his tanned face and work roughened hands indicated that he spent much of his time out of doors and his footwear was a pair of black, sharp-toed, high heeled cowhand boots.

Equalling Chapter's height, Seamus O'Malley was slimmer in build and about ten years younger. Sun-reddened and good looking, his face appeared jovial except for its cold dark eyes. He had shortish curly black hair and a neatly trimmed moustache. Stylishly dressed in the height of Eastern fashion, there was nothing about him to supply a clue to how he earned his living.

'I didn't say any such thing,' Chapter answered, his Texas drawl even.

'Your comment could be construed as implying it,' O'Malley declared, his bearing redolent of arrogance and challenge. 'Perhaps you'd be after explaining it?'

'All I said was that luck seemed to be favouring you,' Chapter obliged, but a red flush was creeping into his cheeks and, to anybody who knew him, it was a sign that his temper was rising. 'What's wrong with *that*?'

'Well now, me bucko,' O'Malley replied, his offensive attitude doing nothing to lessen the rancher's growing annoyance. 'It's either the bad loser you are, or you're thinking it's cheating I've been.'

Perturbed looks came to the faces of the other three players. Well dressed, of late middle age, they were alike in having the pomposity of demeanour which characterizes a certain class of professional politician. None of them cared for the trend of the conversation. While they too had noticed how consistently the young Irishman had been winning, being aware of how delicate the situation was in Texas at that time, they had a mutual disinclination towards becoming involved—no matter how innocently —in what might develop into an unpleasant and unseemly scene.

'I don't think Major Chapter meant anything untoward by his remark,' the oldest of the trio put in placatingly, glancing up and waving for the bearer of the round of drinks he had ordered to go away although he realized that what was being said could not be kept a secret with everybody in the room listening.

One of the innovations brought to the Cattlemen's Hotel since Texas' return to solvency was service by waitresses in the barroom. To avoid any suggestion of them having the free and easy function of similar female employees in lesser establishments, they were attractively yet decorously clad in high necked, frilly bosomed mauve blouses, white aprons and long black skirts. Carefully selected for looks and deportment, they were trained to carry out their duties in a way which was praised by all who received their attentions and their behaviour on the premises was exemplary. One of the strictest rules imposed upon them was that they must carry out a customer's orders instantly.

While the waitress to whom the signal was made had up to that moment exhibited all the requisite qualities required by her employment, instead of walking away immediately, she remained standing by the table. Five foot seven in height, while nobody would call her skinny, she was more slender than the other girls. Very beautiful, with brown hair done in the fairly severe and sleek Cadogan style[1] which was *de rigueur* like the costume, she had a carriage and grace second to none.

'Well now, Senator,' O'Malley answered, showing no sign of having noticed the gesture of dismissal and ignoring the girl's continued presence. 'With all respect to you, I'm thinking its him-

---

[1] 'Cadogan' style: with the hair drawn into a large bun at the back of the neck, which reached the crown of the head and hung in a plait on to the shoulders, being held in place by a net or chignon.

self who should be doing the apologizing for such ungentlemanly conduct.'

'*Apologizing!*' Chapter barked angrily.

'This's the way I'm seeing it,' O'Malley asserted, before the rancher could continue. 'Either you're man enough to come right out and say you think I'm cheating, or you stand up and make a public apology for giving the notion that you think I am.'

'I'll be damned if I'll do *either*!' Chapter snapped, his voice brittle with barely controlled rage.

'Then I'm thinking we'll take the matter to somewhere that we can settle it like men,' O'Malley suggested. 'If you've the stomach for it, that is.'

'Settle it—— How?'

'I'm thinking *that'd* be plain enough to a *man*.'

'You mean fight a *duel*?'

'If it's the stomach for it you have.'

Listening to the muted rumble of excited talk which was welling up, and without noticing that—after glancing across the room—the waitress was walking away, Chapter began to appreciate the gravity of his position. Duelling was prohibited by law in Texas, but was still practised in a semi-clandestine fashion. Nor, as any injury would be accepted as having been inflicted in self defence even if fatal, would the survivor of an 'affair of honour' be likely to face arrest and trial. For all that, he was under no illusion over how his political opponents would capitalize on the issue no matter whether he took or refused the challenge. He was equally aware of the adverse effect a refusal to defend his honour would have upon the majority of the voters. There was, however, only one course left open to him. His own pride and upbringing as a Southron gentleman would not allow him to back away from such a challenging of his courage, no matter what the result or consequences of accepting might be.

'This is something we can't settle here,' the rancher said, shoving back his chair and standing up. 'I'll have my friends call on you to make the arrangements.'

***** *****

'Excuse me, sir,' the waitress said, her voice that of a well bred

255

Southron. She had crossed the room hurriedly, but without giving the impression of haste, to where Charles Gannon was entering from the kitchen. 'There's going to be serious trouble between Major Chapter and the young man with whom he and the Senators have been playing poker.'

'What kind of trouble—Miss—?' asked the plump, jovial featured co-owner, realizing that he did not know the girl's name.

When Gannon had looked into the bar-room earlier and noticed the girl, but did not recognize her, he had decided his partner must have hired her. Watching the deft yet unobtrusive way in which she kept her shapely bottom clear of the reaching thumb and forefinger of a prominent elderly local politician, he had approved of Wickstead's choice.

Curiously, the first time the other partner had seen the girl, there had been a similar lack of recognition and conclusion drawn. Studying the calm way in which she had warded off the advances of a rich young customer without causing embarrassment or offence, he had told himself that Charlie's good taste was not restricted to selecting food for the kitchen.

'It looks as if the young man is trying to provoke the Major into fighting a duel,' the waitress replied.

'A *duel*?' Gannon repeated, speaking louder than he intended in his surprise and alarm.

'Yes,' the girl confirmed. 'I'll go and fetch the marshal for you.'

Turning before her employer could comment upon the suggestion, the waitress set off in a similar swift, apparently unhurried, fashion towards the kitchen door. Staring and opening his mouth with the intention of calling her back, Gannon thought better of it. While he had no desire for the town marshal to be brought into the matter, he concluded that such an official presence might bring the participants to their senses. So, letting her depart without interruption, he started to walk towards the table where the altercation was taking place and hoped he might be able to sooth down the two men before the peace officer arrived.

Although the majority of the bar-room's occupants were fully engrossed in the centre of attraction, the by play between the girl and Gannon had not gone entirely unnoticed. Two young men who were standing at the bar close enough to hear what was being said had clearly found the conversation of considerable interest. Well dressed in Eastern fashion, there was such a close physical resemblance that it seemed certain they were related. Tall and slim in a gaunt way, with mousey brown hair longer than was fashionable in Texas, their sullen features were red and peeling, suggesting that they spent little of their lives in the sun.

'Come on!' ordered the older of the pair, his accent New England and educated, as the waitress went into the kitchen unfastening her apron.

'What about O'Mal——?' the younger began.

'He doesn't need us yet,' the first speaker hissed. Stepping forward he continued in a commanding manner: 'Come on!'

'The marshal won't be there,' Henry Tilletson protested as he too moved forward, having a dislike for receiving orders from anybody, even his elder brother.

'We don't want *anybody* connected with the law involved!' Richard Tilletson pointed out, leading the way to the door which opened into the reception lobby. 'So we're going to make sure that by the time they hear, it will be too late for them to do anything to stop the duel.'

On leaving the hotel's front entrance, the brothers hurried to the appropriate corner of the building. Looking along the alley, there was sufficient light from a three-quarters' moon for them to watch the waitress going by at the other end. She had removed her apron, collected a furled parasol and a reticule, but had not donned either a coat or a hat. Showing no indication that she realized she was under observation, and without offering to come to the front of the buildings, she walked on.

'You go along the street until you're ahead of her,' Richard instructed, as the girl passed out of sight. 'I'll get behind her so she can't get away. Between us, we'll scare her out of the idea of fetching the marshal.'

'All right,' Henry assented, far from displeased at the prospect of frightening a member of the opposite sex and confident that, as she was only a glorified saloon worker, there would be no repercussions if she should complain to the authorities about her treatment at their hands.

Passing through the alley, Richard followed the girl without at

257

first attempting to close the distance. Pleased that the street they were on was otherwise deserted, he walked as quietly as he could. In addition to wanting to prevent her from introducing a possibly obstructive element into a plot which had already proved effective on three previous occasions, he had an added inducement for wanting to deal with her. She had rebuffed him earlier that evening when he had suggested he escorted her home after she finished work. Although it had been done politely, his ego was hurt and his antipathy towards Southrons had done nothing to make him feel better disposed towards her.

After passing a few buildings, Richard saw his brother emerging at the other end of the one which the girl was approaching. So he increased his speed until he was almost within arms' length of her. Still giving no indication of being aware that he was behind her, she appeared to be devoting no more than a casual attention to Henry either.

'And where do you think you're going?' the younger brother demanded, as the girl came to a halt as unconcernedly as if they had the street to themselves.

'I hardly think *that* is any of *your* concern, *sir*,' was the reply, uttered with a haughty disdain hardly becoming a waitress; even if she was employed at the elite Cattlemen's Hotel. The final honorific expressed more contempt than respect.

'You're going to tell the marshal what's happening,' Henry accused, annoyed by the way in which he had been addressed.

'And what if I am?' the girl inquired, her left hand tugging in what might have been a nervous gesture at the waistband of the skirt while the right held both parasol and reticule.

'Don't you think you're poking your nose into something that doesn't concern you?' Henry demanded, watching his brother and preparing to spring forward and avenge himself for the disrespect with which he had been treated.

Even as his sibling was speaking, counting upon the words drowning the sound of his approach, Richard stepped forward. His right hand reached out to sink into the bun of brown hair with the intention of jerking her back to be encircled around the waist by his left arm. As he began to put his plan into operation, two *very* surprising and remarkable things happened.

258

Opening out as her tug liberated its retaining strap, the girl's skirt fell down. At the same moment, instead of being jerked into Richard's grasp, what proved to be a wig covering black hair cropped very short came away in his hand. Even before his mind could start to assimilate either development, she was stepping rearwards from the descending garment. Twisting at the hips to add impetus to it, her left elbow drove back to strike his *solar plexus* with considerable force. All the air burst from his lungs and, folding at the waist he stumbled away from his potential victim and collapsed to his knees.

Equally startled by the sight of the skirt being discarded and the loss of the 'hair', Henry forgot his intention of advancing. His gaze followed the garment as it fell, but not to be greeted by the sight he expected. Instead of being exposed in some form of feminine undergarments, the girl's slender yet shapely hips and legs proved to be clad in skin tight masculine black riding breeches and matching Hessian boots.

Having disposed of Richard, the girl stepped forward. Giving his sibling no time to recover from the surprise, she whipped up her right leg. Its movement was as graceful as might have been performed by a trained ballet dancer, or—considering its purpose—by an expert in the Gallic form of foot and fist fighting known as *savate*. The toe of her boot caught Henry in the portion of the male anatomy most susceptible to such an attack and it was propelled by a leg which, although slim, had powerful muscles. Giving a croaking wail of agony, he collapsed with his hands clutching involuntarily and ineffectively at the stricken area.

'Well, yes,' the girl said, in a belated answer to the younger brother's question, looking from him to his sibling—neither of whom was in any condition to listen—as she retrieved and donned the skirt. 'I suppose *you* might think I am.'

***** *****

'Howdy, ma'am,' greeted the man who rose from the desk in the town marshal's office. 'Can I help you-all?'

'Is the marshal here?' the waitress asked, glancing around the otherwise deserted room.

'No ma'am,' the man drawled, directing a look filled with speculation at the visitor. 'He took him the night off to go ...

259

fishing ... along the Colorado River some place. There's only me here.'

Returning the speaker's scrutiny, the girl decided he could only just have reached twenty. Yet there was an air of confidence about him which suggested he was not alarmed by being alone in a responsible position. Rusty red hair and a tanned rugged face with its nose having been broken and badly set, topped a wide shouldered, lean waisted, powerful six foot two frame. He wore the clothing of a working cowhand, but had a deputy town marshal's badge pinned to his dark blue shirt. A Colt 1860 Army revolver which had been converted to fire metal case cartridges rode on the fast draw holster at the right side of his gunbelt.

Considering the examination to which she was being subjected, the girl formed the impression that the deputy found her of more than usual interest. Nor, she concluded, did it merely stem from her being an attractive member of the opposite sex. Although she could not imagine why, she decided he was puzzled by her. Yet she had replaced her skirt and wig, so there was nothing out of the ordinary about her appearance. On the other hand, she doubted that the Tilletson brothers would have reported their treatment at her hands. For all that, she was convinced he was curious about her. What was more, she was intrigued by the slight pause and sardonic note which had crept into his laconic Texas drawl while he was explaining his superior's absence.

'There's nobody in the sheriff's office either,' the girl commented, hoping for enlightenment.

'No, ma'am,' the young man answered. 'Cap'n Schule come to ask him and all his deputies to go over to Travis Manor's word'd come in that "Smokey" Hill Thompson 'n' his boys're there and that they might come in more peaceable was they asked by the local law rather than the good ole State Police we all trusts and loves so dearly. So, minding the word he'd been passed, the sheriff said he'd do it.'

'I see,' the girl said soberly, having heard that all municipal and county law enforcement agencies had been requested to co-operate with the disliked State Police during the period of the return to the rights of franchise.

'What's up, ma'am?' the deputy asked.

'Something bad,' the girl replied and, after describing the incident at the hotel, concluded, 'Is there anything you can do?'

'Not unless I find them starting the duel in the city limits,' the young man confessed. 'I've no jurisdiction beyond 'em. Blast it, I sure wish Uncle Brady was here. He might've been able to figure a way to stop them, only the marshal sent him over to San Antone[2] on the afternoon stage to pick up a feller the marshal there's holding in jail for us.'

'It's as I expected,' the girl remarked cryptically.

'My name's Jefferson Trade, ma'am,' the deputy introduced, having continued to study his visitor in the same speculative fashion. 'Mind telling me who you-all are?'

'Clarice Dillwater——,' the girl commenced.

'Would that be your "summer name"?' the young man inquired.

'It would,' the girl admitted with a smile, knowing that to be asked such a question was a polite way of casting doubt over the name she had given. Opening her reticule, she took out and showed the deputy a small leather wallet's contents. 'I wouldn't want *this* mentioned, Mr. Trade.'

'It won't be by *me*, Col—ma'am!' the peace officer affirmed, requiring all his self control to prevent showing the surprise he had experienced on reading the card in the wallet and delighted to find he was correct in his assumption that the visitor was more than just a waitress from the Cattlemen's Hotel. 'Don't you reckon's they'd see sense and call it off was *you-all* to ask 'em personal-like?'

'I only wish it was *that* easy,' the girl replied, as pleased by the deputy's tribute as he had been over her decision that he could be trusted to learn her true identity and relied upon not to disclose it. 'But I'm afraid it won't be. Unless I'm mistaken, O'Malley is determined to make it take place.'

'Happen he is, he's likely to wind up sorry he got the notion,' Trade stated. 'What I've heard tell, Major Chapter handles a gun, or a sword, real good.'

***** *****

Crouching concealed behind a clump of bushes at the edge of a clearing in the woodland about three miles north of Austin, the

[2] 'San Antone': colloquial name for San Antonio, Bexar County, Texas.

slender girl realized that—as she had feared—the young deputy had been over confident the previous evening when referring to the rancher's chances. Having fired on the signal and missed, Chapter was spinning around with the back of his skull shattered open by the bullet from the English made single shot duelling pistol in Seamus O'Malley's right hand.

Despite having presented and identified herself to the rancher after leaving the marshal's office, the girl had been unable to dissuade him from going through with the duel. Her warning that three other men with his political background and aspirations had died in similar 'affairs of honour' had not changed his mind any more than the other arguments she put forward. He had claimed that his career would be ruined if it became known he had backed out after accepting a challenge, but she had also suspected his pride would not allow him to see reason.

Although the girl had drawn what little consolation she could from knowing he was as competent with weapons as Trade had claimed and his assurance that he would have friends present to ensure there would be no trickery on the Irishman's part, she had still been ill at ease. So that morning, clad in a boy's jacket, shirt, Levi's pants and a Stetson, she had followed him and his seconds to the rendezvous. Leaving the horse she had hired at the edge of the trees, she had arrived at the clearing in time to see the preliminaries being carried out and the duel take place.

A soft footstep behind her caused the girl to swing around swiftly with her right hand going to the ivory butt of the old Dance Brothers Navy revolver thrust into her waist band. Instead of drawing it, a look of relief came to her face as she saw who had approached so quietly that she had been unaware of his coming.

A wide brimmed, low crowned white Stetson rested on short, gingery hair. In contrast, the eyebrows, neatly trimmed moustache and chin beard of his tanned, strong face—an unlit crooked cigar thrusting from between its grim-looking mouth—were black. A tightly rolled, multi-coloured bandana trailed its long ends over a costly grey shirt and his brown trousers were tucked carefully into the tops of black Justin boots which still retained some of their shine despite his having walked through the woodland. His black gunbelt hung just right to permit the very rapid withdrawal of a recently introduced ivory handled Colt Civilian Model Peace-maker from its slightly forward raked, contoured and tied down holster. He had the appearance of a prosperous rancher who was still willing to turn out and help with any chore that came up on his spread. Most people in Texas would acknowledge that John Slaughter not only qualified for such a description, but could perform whatever the task might be as well as any top hand. They were also likely to comment upon his ability in handling a gun.[3]

'Great day in the morning!' the newcomer ejaculated, but *sotto voce* despite his surprise, his right hand having risen swiftly from the proximity of the revolver to snatch the cigar from his mouth at the first sight of the beautiful face. 'It's *Belle Boyd*!'

'Hello, John,' the girl replied, just as quietly. 'You didn't arrive in time.'

'So I see,' Slaughter growled, peering over the bushes. 'What happened?'

'Shall we talk about it on the way back to town?' Belle suggested. 'There's nothing we can do here.'

'Whatever you say,' the rancher assented without hesitation, being aware that—although the slender girl had earned the sobriquet 'the Rebel Spy' during the War Between The States—she was now a member of the U.S. Secret Service and held a rank equivalent to a full colonel in the Army.

'I didn't know you were in town, John,' Belle remarked, after she and Slaughter had withdrawn, collected their horses and were riding towards Austin.

'I arrived late last night.'

'How did you find out where the duel was being held?'

'Young Jeff Trade told me when I dropped by this morning. Didn't say how he found out and he didn't mention that *you* were involved. Or doesn't he know?'

'He knows,' Belle admitted. 'But I'd asked him not to mention me.'

'Then he wouldn't, his Uncle Brady trained him right,' Slaughter commented. 'Anyways, knowing Warren Chapter, I

[3] For the benefit of new readers: some details of John Slaughter's career are given in *Slaughter's Way* and he makes a 'guest' appearance in *Trigger Fast*.

figured I should come out and see if I could talk some sense into him; or back him up should he need it. I thought you might be a bushwhacker out to help that Irish feller when I come across your horse. Then, after I got a look, I figured you wasn't but a fool kid from town who'd sneaked out to see it. Was *everything* square and above board?'

'Have you *any* reason for thinking it might not have been?' Belle inquired. She sat astride her borrowed mount with a similar effortless-seeming ease to that with which her companion rode his fine dun gelding.

'I know how well Warren could handle a gun,' Slaughter stated. 'And I've heard about the other three who've been killed in duels recently.'

'It certainly all *looked* to be fair,' Belle asserted. 'His seconds were men he knew and could trust and the Director of the Duel, who would be more likely to favour him than O'Malley, did everything convention demanded. The pistols belonged to the Irishman, but he was allowed to fire the one he chose at a mark to see how it held before they started and he said he was satisfied with it. Then on the shot, he missed, but I couldn't see anything was wrong and, although they were surprised, neither did his seconds as far as I could tell.'

'So it could have been a fair duel,' Slaughter said bitterly, having no doubt that the girl was competent to make such a judgement and willing to accept her summation, which was no small compliment to her acumen.

'As far as appearances went it was. But I'd like to have a gunsmith take a look at those pistols.'

'There's a better than fair one in Austin.'

'Is he a *friend* of yours?'

'We've ridden a few trails together,' Slaughter admitted, having noticed the emphasis on the word 'friend'. 'But there's some might say that neither of us have any *legal* right to make O'Malley show them to him.'

'Well now,' Belle replied, looking so innocent that butter would have had difficulty to melt in her mouth. 'I wasn't really thinking of *asking* for his permission.'

*****   *****

Although the Tilletson brothers—who had recovered sufficiently to act as O'Malley's seconds for the duel—passed the Rebel Spy on their way to the front door of the Cattlemen's Hotel, they did not give her as much as a second glance. Yet, despite the circumstances under which they had last seen her, there was nothing surprising about their behaviour. So effective had been the changes she had made to her appearance that they never suspected the white haired, apparently aged woman in the heavily veiled mourning attire was the same person who had treated them so roughly the previous evening. She still carried the parasol, but it was covered with black cloth and the reticule dangling from her other wrist was of the same sombre hue.

On their return to Austin, while Slaughter went to visit the gunsmith, Belle had contacted Jefferson Trade. As she had surmised, the young deputy proved to be both helpful and competent. Anticipating something of her needs, he had ascertained in which rooms at the Cattlemen's Hotel the Irishman and the brothers were staying. He had also said that the sheriff had not returned, but sent a message asking the marshal to attend to any business which arose affecting his office. However, the latter official had taken to his bed with what he claimed to be a sudden attack of the grippe.[4] Learning of this and being disinclined to accept the responsibility of dealing with the complexities of the duel, the other deputies had found pressing business requiring their attention elsewhere and left Trade in charge, a factor which he was willing to turn to the Rebel Spy's advantage. On being told what she hoped to do, he suggested how he could be of the greatest assistance. Using the authority which had been thrust upon him, he had asked all the men involved in the 'affair of honour' to come to the marshal's office and give statements. Pretending he wanted to avoid the chance of trouble between the two factions, he had insisted that they came separately. By doing so, he not only was able to tell Belle when O'Malley's room would be unoccupied, but promised to ensure she had sufficient time to carry out her scheme.

Hobbling slowly up the stairs, the Rebel Spy continued to

[4] 'Grippe': colloquial name for the contagious, infective, sometimes epidemic disease generally caused by a filtrable virus, called 'influenza'.

convey the impression of advanced age. A glance over her shoulder as she reached the top informed her that O'Malley and the Tilletsons were going out of the front entrance to report to Trade. She noticed with relief that, as he had not been requested to take them, the Irishman was not carrying the case containing his pistols. So the way was open and everything now depended upon whether she could carry out her assignment.

Reaching the passage which gave access to the rooms on the second floor, Belle found to her satisfaction that it was deserted. Making at a more lively pace for the door of O'Malley's accommodation, she gave another glance around to ensure she was unobserved. Then, pushing back the veil, she bent to examine the lock. She gave a low sigh of relief on discovering it was of the type known as a 'lever' and felt sure that it was made for master-keying, which would allow her to gain admittance with comparative ease. Inserting a piece of metal shaped like a miniature golf iron into the key hole, she ignored the first little plates, called 'levers' that fitted into the lock's bolt and stopped it sliding until depressed by the corresponding notches on the key. Locating the final plate, which was the 'master lever' (when it was operated, the rest followed suit), she manipulated it after the fashion of the extra-long 'master' key that was supplied to certain members of the hotel staff so they could enter without the need to carry one for each respective room.

There was a click and the door opened to the Rebel Spy's push. Entering, she closed and used her 'pick' to relock it. Crossing to the window, she opened it and looked into the alley which separated the hotel from the adjoining building. Slaughter strolled forward, accompanied by a small, wizened man in town dweller's clothing and waited underneath as if they were doing no more than making casual conversation.

Returning to the wardrobe, Belle looked inside to find it held only clothes and two suitcases which proved to be empty. An examination of the dressing-table was more fruitful. In its bottom drawer was not the single mahogany gun case for which she was searching, but two. They were identical in appearance, even to a jagged scratch running across their highly polished lid, and their contents were duplicated just as exactly.

Reaching into the waistband of her skirt, the Rebel Spy extracted a canvas bag which was wrapped around her midsection. From this, she produced a coil of cord and a roll of soft cloth. Folding the two single-shot, percussion fired pistols from the left side case in it, she noticed that they seemed wider at the breech than appeared necessary. Having placed them in the bag, she used a towel from the wash-stand to cover their mates and hoped it would not be missed. With the second pair also protected against accidentally being marked, they joined the others in the bag. Securing its neck with the cord, she went and lowered it to the waiting men.

Belle was not kept in suspense for very long. Barely ten minutes elapsed before she heard a whistle from the alley. Closing and locking the door, having spent the time keeping watch with it ajar in case O'Malley returned, she retrieved the bag. Working swiftly, but refusing to allow herself to become flustered or overlook anything, she closed the window and, having examined them, replaced the pistols in their cases. With the bag, cloth, cord and towel—which was stained with oil—concealed upon her person, she ensured that there was no sign of her visit. Satisfied that all was as she had found it, with the exception of the missing towel, she took her departure.

'Well?' the Rebel Spy inquired, on joining Slaughter and his companion in the alley, thankful that Trade had carried out his part of the scheme.

'There's going to be another "affair of honour" real soon,' the rancher replied cryptically, his grim face set in lines of deadly determination.

*****   *****

'Mr. O'Malley asked me to say that, as you have agreed to use his pistols, it's only fair you should fire your choice at a mark and see how it holds,' Richard Tilletson announced, in the manner of one who was repeating a well learned speech. 'Would you care to do so?'

'I reckon it'd be as well if I did,' John Slaughter replied, as had each of the four men to whom the offer was made during the past few weeks.

Contriving to insult the Irishman in public the previous evening, the rancher had paved the way for himself to be challenged and leave the choice of weapons in the other's hands. Sent to act for him, Jefferson Trade had apologized for being alone and assured the Tilletsons there would be another second at the meeting as convention demanded. The deputy had also stated he would be off duty and acting in the capacity of a private citizen, not a peace officer. Being aware that Slaughter was another probable opponent for the political faction they represented, neither of the brothers had objected to the arrangement.

Because Belle Boyd was acting as the rancher's other second, she and her two companions had set off for the rendezvous ahead of the appointed time. Once more demonstrating her skill at disguise, she wore a black Stetson and, including a voluminous Confederate Cavalry cloak-coat, other masculine attire which completely concealed her feminine contours. A well made false beard completed the illusion that she was a man, but arriving before the opposition avoided the chance that her movements might give the truth away. When O'Malley's party, the Director of the Duel and the generally obligatory doctor[5]—a newcomer to Austin, according to Trade—reached the clearing in which the previous 'affair of honour' had taken place, restricting herself to the gruff monosyllabic affirmative or negative response which seemed appropriate, she had allowed the deputy to conduct the negotiations.

Accepting O'Malley's assurance that he had no familiarity with fencing, Slaughter had raised no objection to pistols being selected as the weapons. Nor had he complained when, in the interests of 'fair play', it was proposed they used the matched pair produced by the Tilletsons. On the surface, everything had appeared open and above board. He was allowed to take first choice, the other being left for his opponent and now he was being offered the chance to try it out. To a man of his known expertise in handling firearms, the concession apparently did much to lessen any advantage offered by the Irishman's familiarity with the pistols.

Hefting the weapon he had picked, the rancher found its balance

[5] As is described in *Ole Devil at San Jacinto*, the services of a doctor were dispensed with on occasion. This volume also goes into detail about the conducting of a duel in which pistols are the nominated weapons.

excellent in spite of the bulk of its woodwork and breech section. Cocking the hammer as he adopted the typical side-on stance of a duellist, he raised the pistol at arm's length to shoulder height and took sight at the blaze carved in the trunk of a cottonwood tree thirty yards from his position, the same distance over which the combat would take place. Squeezing the trigger, he found it was neither too light nor too heavy and dispatched the bullet. An examination showed it had struck exactly where he had aimed it.

'Do you want another shot?' Richard inquired.

'Nope,' Slaughter replied, sounding almost disinterested. 'Load her up and let's get to it. I'm satisfied.'

'One of your seconds can reload if you wish,' Richard offered and, in contrast to his brother's restless—almost worried—demeanour, he seemed relieved by what had been said.

'They're not used to such fancy hawg-legs,' the rancher drawled. '*You* do it. I reckon I can trust you to see she fires when I squeeze off.'

Despite being puzzled by the laconic comment, Richard charged and returned the pistol to Slaughter. Followed by his seconds and holding it negligently in his left hand, he strolled to where the Director of the Duel—a prominent Austin businessman —and the doctor were standing. Looking smugly satisfied, Richard joined his brother and O'Malley at the other side of the two officials.

'Is everything understood, gentlemen?' the Director asked, after explaining how he would conduct the duel.

'Why sure,' Slaughter agreed, a wolfish grin twisting his grim features and his eyes staring mockingly at the Irishman's party. 'Only I won't be lining straight at you-all, *hombre*. No sir, I'll be pointing this fancy gun at thigh level and to the right.'

'God in heaven, Seamus!' Henry screeched, led to indiscretion by the worries which had assailed him since it had been suggested that the 'waitress' he and his brother had accosted might be Belle Boyd, who was now a member of the U.S. Secret Service. He had tried to persuade the others to leave Austin instead of coming to the clearing, but to no avail and now it appeared that he had been correct. 'He knows about——!'

Spitting out a furious oath, O'Malley began to raise the pistol with his right hand and the left flew across to cock its hammer. Equally aware of his sibling's folly, Richard grabbed for the ·32 calibre Smith & Wesson No. 2 revolver in his jacket's right side pocket. Near the Director, convinced that his association with the other three was not suspected, the doctor reached for the compact British-made Webley Royal Irish Constabulary revolver he was carrying in a spring retention shoulder holster against his left side.

O'Malley might already be holding his weapon, but he was caught unawares. What was more, he was up against an authority in duelling frontier fashion. Dropping like a flash, Slaughter's right hand scooped the Colt from its carefully designed holster. Roaring when only just clear of the lip, it sent a bullet into the centre of the Irishman's forehead and killed him instantly.

Although Jefferson Trade could not compete with the rancher as far as speed went, he proved adequate for the occasion. Leaving his rig, the long barrelled Army Colt roared and, an instant after O'Malley died, his ·44 calibre ball ploughed into the centre of the doctor's chest. Its arrival spun the medical man round and his weapon slipped unfired from his grasp as he went down.

Showing an equal state of preparedness, Belle brought the Dance from where she had been carrying it concealed in the voluminous right sleeve of the cloak-coat. Lining it at Richard and deftly thumb-cocking the hammer, she brought his attempt to arm himself to a halt. Seeing what was happening, Henry threw his hands into the air and wailed that he surrendered.

***** *****

'O'Malley had the pistols custom built for his kind of duelling,' the Rebel Spy informed the group of dignitaries who had been assembled secretly by John Slaughter, concluding her description of the events which had led to them being gathered together. 'One pair is normal and produced for examination if there should be a formal complaint about the result. But he always used the other pair. The end of their barrels are seated in a sloping cavity at the base of the breech. When the barrel is at the forward end, it lines straight ahead. The recoil of the shot forces it back so that it halts at an angle. Not enough to be noticeable, but O'Malley made sure every victim was a very good shot. As the rear sight is on the breech and not the barrel, it makes a difference of several inches at thirty yards; sufficient for a good shot who thinks he knows how it holds to miss when O'Malley, who wasn't very broad, was standing sideways. And that was how he killed his victims.'

None of the men in the room at nine o'clock on the day of the second duel were connected with the Reconstruction Administration. In fact, most could confidently expect to help replace it after the forthcoming election. Having heard how Belle had got on the trio's trail after learning of their activities,[6] they wanted to know who else was involved.

'You say those three were hired to kill men who the carpet-baggers didn't want to be elected for the State Legislature,' remarked the Senator who had tried to avert the duel which cost Chapter's life. 'Were Captain Schule, the sheriff and marshal working with them?'

'Schule definitely was,' Belle declared. 'He tricked the sheriff into leaving with all the deputies so there would be nobody with the authority to stop the duel taking place outside the city limits. I think the marshal's just an opportunist who didn't intend to become involved in an affair where he could antagonize one or the other faction.'

'Is Governor Davis in it?' demanded one of the influential Texans who were present.

'Not according to Henry Tilletson and I believe he's too scared to lie,' Belle replied. 'He claims that only a few minor officials and carpet-baggers are involved.'

'How soon will those he named be arrested and brought to trial?' asked the man who had served as Director of the Duel, furious at the thought that he had been tricked.

'They aren't going to be,' Belle stated and, waiting until the rumble of indignant protest died away, elaborated, 'to do that will bring the whole affair into the open and would cause trouble which might lead to Congress reconsidering the return of the franchise.'

'But they might try something else!' the first Texan warned.

[6] Belle Boyd had arranged to take the place of a waitress at the Cattlemen's Hotel so that she could keep an eye on the trio. While she was unable to prevent Warren Chapter's death, because of his stubbornness, she had contrived to bring an end to O'Malley's career and helped pave the wave for the election which swept the corrupt Reconstruction Administration of Governor Davis out of Texas.

'They know their kind are through in Texas once the franchise is returned.'

'I don't reckon they'll be staying around to try,' Slaughter drawled, but his tone was hard and his demeanour charged with menace. 'I've passed word to every last son of them Tilletson named that, happen they're still in Texas by the end of the month, I'll be calling and there'll be some more "affairs of honour"—fought *my* way.'

'And that, gentlemen,' the Rebel Spy went on, 'takes care of *that*, I'd say.'[7]

[7] As the men who received the warning knew it was not John Slaughter's way to deliver idle threats, the mass exodus of 'carpet-baggers' which followed justified Belle Boyd's confidence and the rancher was not compelled to engage in any of the threatened 'affairs of honour'.

PART NINE

Brady Anchor and Jefferson Trade in

BRADY

When I was setting out the plot for Two Miles to the Border, *I concluded it was not suitable for the members of the Floating Outfit and turned my attention to the creation of two new protagonists. I decided that their motivation for becoming involved would be a desire to improve their lot in life. However, I had no intention of producing 'anti-heroes'. So, although they were now free-lance operators, they had served in the Texas Rangers and retired honourably. Also, while their aim in life was trying to 'earn enough to live in a manner to which they had always been too poor to become accustomed', they would stay within the law to bring this about.*

I can't remember the exact process by which I arrived at the names Brady Anchor and Jefferson Trade. All I know is that, when they came, they seemed to have a nice ring and to flow together. Nor can I think why I made Brady's description the way I did, but it too seemed to work. Having decided upon these points, I turned my attention to their equipment. I had read of a shoulder holster which was designed to hang horizontally instead of vertically. Having checked to make sure press-stud fastenings were available at the period, I had such a rig made and found it was almost as easy to use as the spring retention variety. So Brady carried his Colt Thunderer that fashion. Although Jeff's Colt Civilian Model Peacemaker was a more conventional weapon, his mode of carrying it was not.[1] Again my reference library supplied the requisite information, but so far I must confess I

---

[1] When making their 'guest' appearances in *The Quest For Bowie's Blade*, Brady Anchor and Jefferson Trade had not yet acquired their distinctive armament and holsters.

have not had such an attachment fitted to a belt, or converted one of my Japanese replica Peacemakers to be used as Jeff does.

With my heroes selected and armed, my next task was to create the other leading characters. I was very pleased with the Widow Snodgrass and the beautiful, innocent-seeming, yet very capable Sybil Cravern. While I'm not willing to go further at this point, I will say one thing. Unlikely as it might appear to those of you who read Two Miles to the Border, eventually they will both return. When it happens, you will find that Jeff is justified in asking, 'Who Do You Trust, Uncle Brady?'

BRADY

'I'm looking for the Triangle D ranch, ma'am,' the stocky man told Mrs. Rosie Maddox as he reached the bar. 'Which way would it be?'

Slowly, in a calculating manner gained by years of studying men and estimating their financial potential, Rosie looked him over before offering to reply.

Five foot eight inches in height, the newcomer to the Old Crooked Horn Saloon was a red-faced, cherubic-looking man in his early forties. There was an aura of guileless innocence about him. It made him look like a lamb just asking to be led to the slaughter. He conveyed an impression of well-fed, corpulent naivety that might have aroused motherly instincts in a less mercenary woman.

A wide-brimmed, low-crowned white 'planter's' hat was perched on the back of his head, to display a thinning thatch of soft, curly brownish hair. His grey linen suit, white shirt, sober blue cravat fastened in the fashion of a bow-tie and Hersome gaiter boots hinted that he did not belong to the range country. Most likely he hailed from one of the more civilized, pampered counties in East Texas. The fact that he did not wear a gunbelt and displayed no hint of carrying a weapon on his person suggested that he was not a regular denizen of Scurry County. Apart from the local preachers, no man in the county seat walked the streets without first buckling on his gunbelt and ensuring that a loaded revolver rode its holster.

There was something unusual about the man Rosie decided and, after a moment's thought, she realized what it was. The left flap of his jacket had the buttons instead of the right.

Nothing about the man served as a clue to his station in life. He dressed well and his clothing was expensive. Maybe he was a travelling salesman, except that he did not have a bag of his wares. Or he could be a speculator, looking for an investment in the thriving cattle industry. Ranching was booming wide open in Texas in 1879 and showed every sign of growing more lucrative with each succeeding year. It was a situation that caused businessmen to move in and offer financial backing to ranchers for a very reasonable share of the profits.

Although less obviously, the newcomer was returning Rosie's scrutiny. He saw a woman maybe an inch taller than himself, well-built, in her late thirties and still good looking. Her hair, piled on her head, was stiffly blonde; but her olive skin, high cheekbones and slightly slanted brown eyes hinted at Indian blood. Large loop earrings glinted brassily in the bar's lights as she moved her head. She wore a glossy, sleeveless white blouse with a décolleté that left no doubts of what lay underneath—and it was not clothing. Her black satin skirt was tight enough to emphasize rounded and full hips, buttocks and thighs.

There was a woman it would not pay to tamper with, the newcomer shrewdly concluded. She could hold up her end in any man's game and any class of male society, that was for sure.

'Joey!' Rosie called, glancing around the room and her eyes coming to a halt on a tall, gangling, heavily-moustached cowhand who had just come in through the rear entrance.

'Yes'm?' the cowhand answered, frowning as if he had not wished to call attention to his arrival.

'This gent's asking the way to the Triangle D,' Rosie explained, indicating the newcomer despite him being the only customer at the bar. 'I reckon you and Sandy can show him how to get there.'

'Howdy, mister,' Joey Bugler greeted and slouched to the bar instead of going to where several cowhands were playing a rowdy game of black jack at a table.

'Good afternoon, sir,' replied the newcomer, in a soft, mild and gently drawling voice. He extended his right hand languidly. 'I'll be obliged if you can escort me to the ranch.'

'Be easy enough happen you're not set on going straight away,' Bugler declared, taking the offered hand.

Although something of a practical joker in normal times, the cowhand did not give way to his sense of humour. Figuring that it might be inadvisable to take liberties, until he had discovered just who the stranger might be and what influence he wielded, he restrained an impulse to crush the other's hand. Besides which, he did not feel particularly humorous at that moment.

'I'm not in any desperate rush,' the newcomer admitted.

'You-all joining the outfit, mister?' Bugler inquired, releasing the hand.

'You might say that,' the newcomer admitted. 'My name's Brady. Mr. Ilfracombe asked me here for a vacation.'

'This's a real good section to be sinking your money into, Mr. Brady,' Rosie commented, watching for a reaction to the words.

'I'm not thinking of doing that, ma'am!' Brady declared, just a touch too hurriedly. His gentle, amiable drawl had taken on a worried note, like that of a man who suddenly realizes he might be saying too much. 'I'm merely down here for a vacation. Learn to ride and chase cows and all that sort of thing.'

'Like I said,' Rosie replied, directing a wink at Bugler. 'This's a real good neck of the woods for doing it.'

'I'm sure it is,' Brady conceded, his manner showing an eagerness to please which amused the hard-boiled lady owner of Snyder's toughest saloon. 'Er—Could I offer your good self and this gentleman a drink, ma'am?'

'We've neither of us never been known to refuse,' Rosie assured him and scooped up a bottle. 'How about you?'

The question went unanswered. Crashing hurriedly through the batwing doors, a short, lean cowhand entered. He was breathing heavily and looked very disturbed. A dozen pair of eyes swung in his direction, while hands in almost as many cases reached towards holstered Colts.

'Somebody's killed Ed Grass, boys!' the new arrival croaked hoarsely.

'Wh——!' Bugler gasped. 'What's that?'

'Sheriff found him down on the trail through Screech Owl Bosque,' the informant elaborated, while the card players and other occupants of the room gathered about him. 'Shot in the back.'

'Oh, lord!' Bugler groaned. 'I——'

Watching the cowhand, Brady noticed that he was deeply shocked by the news and had made an effort to prevent himself from finishing whatever he had meant to say.

'What happened, Joey?' demanded the big, bearded Sandy Sands, who also rode for the Triangle D. 'Why'd Ted pull out without us, you reckon?'

'I dunno,' Bugler answered hoarsely.

'He knowed what the boss allus said,' Sands went on. 'He come in for the payroll, with two of us riding shotgun on him. We could wait in here while he went to the bank for it, but we all had to ride back together.'

Once more the batwing doors opened. Moving in a loose arrowhead formation, three peace officers stepped in. They came cautiously, like men expecting, or at least ready to meet, trouble. In the lead, clad in expensive range clothes and with a nickel-plated, pearl-handled Colt Civilian Model Peacemaker in his tied-down fast draw holster, was the sheriff of Scurry County. A handsome man in his middle thirties, he looked hard, tough and capable.

Slightly behind him were his two deputies. They wore cowhand gear, with low hanging Colts and were obviously brothers. Dark-faced, black-eyed, there was more than a touch of Indian about them. The younger brother was clean-shaven and slightly taller than the moustached elder. Taken individually, or as a pair, they looked a tough handful.

Folks around Scurry County knew Sheriff Abel Higgins to be bad medicine, especially with the backing of Jack and Vic Hawk.

'Bugler,' Higgins said quietly, halting with his right hand hanging apparently negligently close to the fancy butt of the Colt Artillery Model Peacemaker. It was the attitude of an efficient lawman facing a potentially dangerous suspect.

'Yes, sheriff?' the cowhand asked, gulping nervously.

'I'm taking you in,' Higgins declared.

'What for?' Sands inquired, leaving the table and starting to move in the direction of the bar.

'Murder and robbery,' Higgins replied.

'Murder!' Bugler yelled, tensing and his right hand moving spasmodically in what might have been the direction of his gun.

278

Out flashed Higgins' Colt, flame licking from the barrel. Bugler was hit in the centre of the chest, whatever move he had been planning to make ending uncompleted. Flung backwards, he collided with the bar. Agony etched itself on his face and his right hand once more clawed in the direction of the holster.

Cocking his Colt on its recoil, Higgins responded in the manner of a trained gun fighter. Again he fired, taking a split second in which to aim, and the ·45 bullet ploughed between the stricken cowhand's eyes. Bugler twirled around and measured his full length on the floor.

On the heels of their superior's first shot, moving so swiftly that they might almost have been expecting it, the Hawk brothers fetched out their weapons. Fanning across to his left side, Jack's right hand slid the Remington 1875 Army revolver from its cross-draw holster. Almost as quickly, his younger brother, to the right of the sheriff, turned his off palm outwards and snaked the Smith & Wesson Schofield revolver from its low cavalry twist-draw rig. Knowing their law enforcement agency was not popular with that particular section of the community they lined their guns on the cowhands.

'What the hell, Higgins?' growled Sands, looking from the body to the Sheriff.

'He was going for his gun, Sands,' Higgins replied, returning the Colt to its holster.

'It looked that way to me, Sandy,' Rosie commented, having watched the whole affair without any display of distress or concern.

'Joey wasn't no gun slick,' Sands protested.

'He'd maybe never killed and robbed nobody afore either,' Higgins pointed out, eyes flickering around to pause briefly on Brady then moving away as if dismissing him as of no special importance.

'You know for sure he'd done it?' Sands challenged.

'Everything pointed to it,' Higgins answered. 'You and Bugler come in with Grass to fetch back the payroll, same as usual——'

'Yeah. And we come here to wait——'

'Only Bugler didn't wait,' Higgins said quietly.

'Nope. He allowed that he'd got to take his hoss to the blacksmith's,' Sands admitted.

'What'd the hoss need doing to it?' asked the sheriff.

'Nothing's I could see,' Sands replied. 'He went off and I come in to show the boys how to play black jack. Only, Joey wouldn't kill nobody.'

'Not even for money, if he needed it bad enough?' Rosie put in.

'How's that, Rosie?' the sheriff inquired, turning towards the woman.

'He's been coming in here regular and losing heavy at poker,' Rosie explained, reaching into the cash-drawer behind the counter. 'I've got some of his notes here. They total up to a fair sum. Almost a thousand dollars.'

'Joey never said nothing about this to me,' Sands declared. 'But, come to think of it, he's been acting a mite strange lately. Quieter, like something was bothering him.'

'Now we know what it was and what he aimed to do about it,' the sheriff drawled.

'Has he got the money on him?' Brady asked.

'Hell, yes!' Sands growled. 'Maybe we'd best take a look.'

A search of the corpse's pockets failed to yield anything like the sum of money that had been stolen. Nor, when the sheriff and his deputies, Sands and Brady, investigated, did they find it on Bugler's horse.

'He must've stashed it away afore he came into town,' Higgins decided. 'I'll have Jack and Vic go take a look.'

'I'll do it on the way back to the spread,' Sands stated, in a tone which brooked no refusal.

'If you don't mind, I'll come with you,' Brady offered.

'Who are you and how do you get sat in on this deal, mister?' Higgins challenged suspiciously.

'My name's Brady,' the stocky man introduced. 'I'm out here to visit with Al Ilfracombe for a spell on vacation.'

'Huh huh,' the sheriff grunted. 'All right, you tend to it, Sands. Only I want to know whether you find the money or not.'

'I'll see you hear about it,' the cowhand promised. 'Happen you don't have a hoss, Mr. Brady, you can use Joey's. It belongs to the spread.'

'Is it all right?' Brady asked. 'Your friend said he was going to take it to the blacksmith's.'

'Nothing wrong with it,' Sands decided, after checking the *bayo-cebrunos* gelding's hooves.

'I wasn't expecting there would be,' sniffed the sheriff. 'Take it back, if you're so minded, Sands. And tell your boss I'll ride out to see him comes morning.'

'I'll do that,' the cowhand promised. 'You reckon you can handle the hoss, Mr. Brady?'

Clearly Brady had handled horses before. Although the *bayo-cebrunos* was a good cowpony, it needed firm treatment. Showing calm competence, the stocky man tested the double girths and swung into the saddle. The gelding fiddle-footed, but he controlled it without any difficulty. When he was sure that the visitor could stay aboard the dead cowhand's mount, Sands swung afork his roan. They rode side by side along the main street.

'You've picked a helluva time to come visiting, Mr. Brady,' Sands declared as they reached the outskirts of Snyder.

'You mean with your foreman getting robbed and murdered, and the cowhand being killed?'

'Not only that. There's trouble all over this damned section.'

'What sort of trouble?'

'Accidents. Barns getting burned. Cattle and hosses've been poisoned, things like that.'

'Who's behind them?' Brady asked.

'Nobody knows, that's the hell of it,' Sands replied, watching how the other sat the horse. He was not merely just used to riding, he knew plenty about all aspects of it. 'Could be Farron.'

'Who'd he be?'

'There's plenty in Scurry County'd pay good money to learn the answer to that. He's been around here for maybe six months, but nobody's ever seen or met him, 's they knows of that is.'

'Then how——?' Brady began.

'How do we know about him?' Sands finished. 'He allus leaves a note after an accident. It says something like, "This land's mine. Get off, or else. Farron".'

'Anybody got off?'

'A couple of the smaller spreads' owners sold out. Some East

281

Texas syndicate bought the places. Nothing to tie them in with Farron, or to say he's been causing trouble for them to be able to buy.'

'Can't the sheriff catch this Farron feller?' Brady wanted to know.

'He's tried,' replied the cowhand. 'But he hasn't done nothing yet. The Hawk boys are part Kiowa and better'n fair at reading sign, but they haven't managed to trail him down.'

'Maybe the Rangers would have better luck,' Brady commented.

'Maybe they would,' Sands agreed. 'Only they have to be sent for by the local law and Higgins won't do it. We'd best start looking around, see if Joey did kill Ed and hide the money!'

Although the men searched along both sides of the trail between the town and the fair-sized clump of post oak trees known as Screech Owl Bosque, they failed to find any trace of the missing money. They examined the area around where the body had been found, but with no greater success.

'Won't have time to go through the whole damned bosque tonight,' Sands declared, turning towards Brady. 'So we'll get to the spread and I'll come back in the morning with the rest of the boys.'

'Huh?' Brady grunted, jerking up his gaze from where it had been directed with fixed intensity at the ground. 'Oh sure. That's what we'd best do.'

*****   *****

Night had fallen when Brady and Sands reached the headquarters of the Triangle D ranch. The grizzled, thickset owner, Al Ilfracombe, listened to his employee's story of what had happened. Then he looked at Brady and appeared to be on the point of asking a question. To Sands, it seemed that the stocky man gave a slight shake of his head and the words went unspoken. Ilfracombe confirmed the cowhand's decision to use more men and make a thorough search in daylight. Telling Sands to take over as segundo, the rancher allowed him to go for his supper.

After Sands had left, Ilfracombe led Brady into the room which he used as a combined study and office. Crossing to the window, the rancher looked out at where the moon was playing hide-and-go-seek with the clouds which scudded through the heavens.

'Sit down, Brady,' Ilfracombe offered and raised the bottom half of the window. 'It's hot tonight.'

'Real hot,' the stocky man agreed, watching his host.

Ilfracombe was anything but his usual brash, cheerful self. Obviously the murder of his foreman and apparent treachery of a trusted cowhand had been a great shock to him. However, his perturbation ran even deeper, or Brady missed his guess.

For several seconds neither man spoke. Ilfracombe passed an open box to Brady, who accepted and lit a cigar. With their smokes going, they watched the moths, drawn through the open window by the light, fluttering and banging into the glass of the lamp on the table at which they were seated.

'Farron's after me,' Ilfracombe finally said, thrusting a big hand into his hip pocket and hauling out a sheet of paper which he placed before his visitor. 'I found this on the back of the barn this afternoon.'

It was a page torn from an ordinary notebook, such as could be purchased in any general store. The only distinguishing feature was a small red number '31' in the upper right side corner.

' "Sell out, Ilfracombe," ' Brady read aloud. ' "If you don't, you'll have more trouble than enough and're likely to wind up dead. Farron." Writes a neat hand, Cousin Al.'

'*Real* neat,' Ilfracombe conceded, scowling and looking as if he had expected some far more constructive comment. 'That all it means to you, Cousin Brady?'

'It's just ordinary paper. Written in ink, which most likely means it was fetched here ready to be put up. Unless one of your crew did it.'

'They wouldn't.'

'You sure?'

'They've all been with me for years.'

'Huh huh!' Brady grunted. 'How about that Bugler feller?'

'He's worked here for maybe two years. A good hand.'

'Him and your segundo get on?'

'Sure. Ed got on with most folks.'

'Gal at the saloon allowed that Joey'd been losing money heavy and regular in a poker game there. Was holding some I.O.U.s he'd signed.'

'Could be,' Ilfracombe admitted. 'Ed and him used to go into Snyder two, three times a week.'

'Together?' Brady asked.

'Sure,' the rancher replied and looked evasive. Then he shrugged and continued, 'This's 'tween you and me, but I reckon Ed was a-courting and used to ride in with Joey so's the boys wouldn't cotton on to his game.'

'Who was the lady?' Brady inquired, still looking as impassive as a stone cherub on a rich man's lawn.'

'I dunno for sure. There's a young widder-woman been around town for maybe three, four months. Come to think on it, that's about when Ed and Joey started going to town regular.'

'Did any of your boys see any strangers sneaking around today?' Brady said, changing the subject and indicating the sheet of paper.

'Nope,' replied the rancher. 'Wasn't but the cook and his louse around the house from sun-up. The rest of us were working the north range. Cookie didn't see nobody. Know one thing, though.'

'What's that?' Brady drawled, eyes flickering towards the window.

'Whoever brought it was slick. I'm a pretty fair hand at reading sign, but I couldn't find nothing to show who'd come and put it on the wall.'

'I s——' Brady began, then he sent his chair skidding behind him and lunged to his feet. 'Drop!'

There was good cause for the last, shouted, word. A figure, the face masked by a bandana so that only the eyes showed between it and the brim of a Stetson, clad in a yellow 'fish' slicker, appeared at the open window. It held a nickel-plated Colt Civilian Model Peacemaker, the barrel slanting in Ilfracombe's direction.

Showing surprising speed for so bulky a man, and a real smart judgement of the situation, the rancher pitched sideways from his seat. He missed death by inches. Flame licked from the muzzle of the Peacemaker, but its bullet passed just above the intended

284

victim to slam harmlessly into the wall at the opposite side of the room.

Fast as Ilfracombe moved, his chubby-looking visitor was far swifter. Before the overthrown chair had struck the floor, Brady was facing the window and adopting what was already known as a gun fighter's crouch. His left hand stabbed like lightning under the right side of his jacket. It closed on something, reversed with a tugging motion and emerged almost immediately grasping the ivory butt of a two-and-a-half inch barrelled Colt Thunderer revolver.

Standing on spread apart feet, with legs slightly bent and torso inclined forward, Brady held the handgun at waist level and aimed by instinctive alignment. Unlike its predecessors, the Thunderer had a double action mechanism. Twice he squeezed the trigger, controlling the recoil between shots. Two Long Colt ·41 bullets sped through the air. Each found its mark in the centre of the yellow 'fish's' chest. Jerking backwards, the figure fell from sight.

Brady darted across to the window, dropping to his right knee and peering cautiously around its edge. Nothing moved or stirred for a moment, apart from the sound of shouts from the bunkhouse as the crew were disturbed by the shooting. Then hooves drummed and a rider approached, leading a second horse. Even as Brady prepared to line his weapon, the horseman swung away and galloped off into the darkness.

Men came boiling out of the bunkhouse. Some of them might not have been attired in a manner suitable for mixed company, but every one held a firearm. Not that they needed the guns. Long before they were in a position to shoot, the hoof-beats of the intruders' horses had faded into the distance.

'You all right in there, boss?' yelled Sands.

'Sure!' Ilfracombe assured him and stood up. 'What the hell, Brady?'

'I downed one of them,' the stocky man answered and returned his weapon to leather. 'Killed him, likely. It didn't seem to be the time, nor place, for fancy shooting.'

The holster was unusual, differing from the normal shoulder rig in that it hung horizontally instead of vertically. Cut to the shape

285

of the Thunderer, it had been equipped with straps which passed around the trigger guard and were fastened together by a press-stud. While these held the gun in place securely, a forward jerk on the bird's head handle snatched it free without delay. It was a carefully designed, well-made rig and he had proved to be exceptionally competent in its use.

'Let's go take a look at who he is,' Ilfracombe suggested.

'Be as well,' Brady admitted and ducked his head to climb out of the window. He knelt by the motionless figure and watched members of the ranch's crew arrive carrying lanterns.

'Hell's fire!' ejaculated Ilfracombe, leaning out of the window and staring as Brady pulled down the masking bandana. 'It's the sheriff.'

'Sure,' agreed the stocky man. 'I'd a notion it might be.'

'Sheriff Higgins!' the rancher gasped. 'I never took to him, but this——.'

'Sure,' Brady drawled and picked up a piece of paper which lay alongside the corpse. 'Number thirty-two,' he read. 'It's the mate to the one you found behind the barn. I reckon we've downed "Farron".'

'Was anybody with him?' demanded Sands.

'Somebody rode off like a bat out of hell,' Brady replied.

'It was one of them sneaking 'breed deputies——!' yelled a cowhand.

'Maybe it was,' Brady drawled, coming to his feet. 'And maybe it wasn't——.'

'We'll know soon enough when we get to town,' Sands growled. 'Let's saddle up, boss——.'

'Not tonight!' Brady ordered and, much to the crew's surprise, their boss backed him up without hesitation.

***** *****

Shortly after dawn the following morning, Brady left his borrowed horse standing ground hitched in Screech Owl Bosque close to where Grass had been murdered. He took the shovel which he had brought from the ranch and moved slowly through the trees. Carefully he scanned the ground ahead of him, following some very faint marks which he had noticed the previous afternoon. As he walked, he kept his ears working and sought to detect any slight sound that might warn of danger. He was dealing with desperate, dangerous men and did not intend to take unnecessary chances.

After covering about a hundred yards, he found himself on the edge of an overgrown ravine. Peering into it, he detected a splash of rich blue which did not look natural and was at odds with the greens and browns of the foliage.

'Guess I won't be needing this after all,' Brady mused and sank the blade of the shovel into the soil. 'Sure wish young Jeff was here. He's built for climbing and I'm not.'

With that sentiment, Brady climbed down into the ravine. He found what he had been expecting to see. On returning to his waiting horse, he looked like a cherub who was in grim and deadly earnest. Mounting, he rode towards Snyder.

Leaving the horse tied to the hitching rail outside the Old Crooked Horn Saloon, Brady crossed the sidewalk. Finding the front doors open, he went in. Rosie Maddox was sitting at a table, wearing a kimono and little else that he could make out, eating her breakfast. There was a sour, watchful look on her face. Brady looked around, discovering that he and the woman appeared to have the place to themselves.

'Seen the sheriff this morning, ma'am?' Brady asked.

'No,' Rosie answered in a flat, emotionless tone. 'Should I have?'

'Likely not, Mrs. Farron,' the stocky man drawled and saw a flash of shock cross her face before it returned to being a wary, expressionless mask. 'Why'd they have to kill the girl?'

'I don't know what you——!' Rosie began.

'Let me make a stab at guessing,' Brady offered. 'You and the sheriff wanted to get into the ranching business, only there's no land for sale hereabouts. You'd tried your game on two places, but lost out because the East Texas Syndicate jumped in afore you could get the deeds. So you figured on nailing the Triangle D this time.'

'Mister,' Rosie gritted. 'You've been walking out in the sun without your hat. I haven't a no——.'

'You got that widow-woman working in with you some way,' Brady interrupted. 'Who was she, Bugler's daughter?'

287

'Sister,' Rosie corrected, before she could prevent herself. 'You bastard!'

'No ma'am. My mammy and pappy was married, I can remember the wedding real good. Let me see if I can "remember" the rest of your game. You got Bugler and his sister working for you, maybe through him losing at poker. She had to make up to Grass and get him so's he'd come a-running when she asked. Then, when the time was ripe, she'd help you rob him.'

'It wasn't that way at all,' Rosie growled bitterly.

'She got on to your game, then, and was fixing to warn him. What I saw in the ravine, she was carrying his child. Anyway, she got her brother to ask him to meet her in Screech Owl Bosque and one of your 'breed deputies was laying for them. He killed 'em both and dragged her body to the ravine. Did a right smart job of hiding the tracks. It took me all my time to follow what was left. Then the sheriff comes to the saloon and kills Bugler "resisting arrest" and lays all the blame on him. Bugler being the one man who might give the whole snap away.'

'Smart son-of-a-bitch, ain't you?'

'It's been said, truthfully enough, that I am,' Brady confessed, exuding modesty. 'Anyways, your bunch got her and him out there. Figured that you'd lift the pay roll. Maybe even get rid of her, if she was in cahoots with you but hoping to change her sides.'

'You're living in borrowed time,' Rosie warned savagely.

'That's been said afore,' Brady drawled.

'My coming along didn't make things easier for you. You'd just started working on Cousin Al, but you got spooked 'cause you thought I was a buyer for the Syndicate. Your other 'breed had left a warning note at the spread. He hid his tracks real good, too. The loss of the pay roll was to be the start of Cousin Al's troubles. Only, with me out there, maybe trying to talk him into selling, you allowed you'd have to move fast. Higgins sneaked up to the house, aiming to gun Cousin Al and me down, only he didn't get the opportunity.'

'Who the hell are you?' Rosie croaked. 'Not that you're making sense.'

'Ma'am, you-all gave yourselves away with killing Bugler. It'd

288

all been arranged aforehand, that showed in everything that happened. The 'breeds got their guns out so slick they had to know the sheriff'd be shooting and you wasn't even surprised when it happened.'

At that moment, the rear door opened and the two deputies walked in. They halted, scowling at Brady, then strolled forward.

'You got breakfast, Ros——,' Jack began.

'He knows it all!' the woman snarled.

'Do he now?' Jack grinned wolfishly. 'Well, that ain't going to do him no good at all. Is it, Brother Vic?'

'Nary a bit of good,' Vic Hawk agreed, hand starting to turn palm outwards.

'Just start screaming Rosie and jerk open your dressing-gown,' Jack advised.

'It looks like you boys're planning to do something violent,' Brady said, sounding nervous and his right hand lifted towards his hat.

'Watch his le——!' Rosie screeched, suddenly realizing the reason for his jacket's buttons being on the 'wrong' side.

Ignoring the warning, the brothers commenced their draws. They were fast, but Brady did not stop at merely being fast. Out lashed the Thunderer, roaring and kicking in his left hand as rapidly as he could operate its double-action mechanism. Angling the barrel around, he poured three shots into Jack's chest. The fourth bullet passed between the stricken deputy and his brother. An instant later, the fifth and sixth loads were ploughing their lethal way into Vic and sending him sprawling across the room, the revolver slipping from his hand.

Letting out a screech, Rosie rocketed to her feet. She hurled the table over and sprang at Brady with her hands like talons ready to claw. Removing his hat, for he was always a gentleman, Brady weaved aside. Up and around whipped his left fist, slamming the bottom of the Thunderer's butt on to the top of the blonde head. Rosie went down as if she had been poleaxed.

'Who are you?' Rosie repeated, half an hour later as she sat nursing her sore head and surrounded by a hostile crowd of Triangle D cowhands and townspeople.

'The name's Brady Anchor,' replied the stocky man. 'I'm a

sergeant in Company G of the Texas Rangers.'

'Higgins didn't send for you!' Rosie protested, knowing that the services of the Rangers could only be obtained if the local law enforcement officers made a request.

'No, ma'am,' Brady conceded. 'But Cousin Al here did. I wasn't here in my official capacity. Fact being, I told you the truth. I had come for a vacation.' He looked at Ilfracombe and grinned. 'Next time you write and ask me, I'll be inclined to say "no". It sure hasn't been restful so far.'

PART TEN

Alvin Dustine 'Cap' Fog in

A CHORE FOR COMPANY 'Z'

*Shortly after the first of the Rockabye County series appeared
in the bookshops, I received what was to be the first of many
letters asking about the descendants of other members of the
Floating Outfit. So I gave thought to how I might introduce them.
I decided that I did not want them to be regular associates of
Woman Deputy Alice Fayde and Deputy Sheriff Bradford
Counter and, if any of them should arrive in Gusher City, it would
only be to make a 'guest appearance'. The solution eluded me
for a long time, but—as I always try to comply with my readers'
requests—I never forgot the problem. It remained in the back of
my mind to make sporadic reappearances for further consideration.*

*When I was given permission by Edgar Rice Burroughs Inc.
to branch out with the Bunduki series, I began to see a way in
which I might be able to revive another character for whom I
had developed a great affection over the years. One of my
favourite non-Western authors was Edgar Wallace and, to my
mind, his greatest creation was the gentle-seeming yet dangerously efficient Mr. J. G. Reeder.[1] From the first of the many
times I read* Terror Keep, *I had speculated upon what would
have happened if old 'Mad' John Flack escaped instead of
having been killed during the collapse of the underground laby-
rinth which formed the climax of the story. One thing was
certain, the malevolent criminal genius would neither forget*

---

[1] Details of Mr. Reeder's career prior to his organization's participation
in the events recorded in *'Cap' Fog, Texas Ranger, Meet Mr. J. G. Reeder*
are recorded in Edgar Wallace's *Room 13, The Mind of Mr. Reeder, Red
Aces, Mr. J. G. Reeder Returns* and *Terror Keep.*

nor forgive the man responsible for his downfall. So I began to work on this assumption. Having come up with a basic plot, I contacted Edgar Wallace's daughter Penelope and she kindly gave me permission to produce it for publication. With this received, the way was opened for Alvin Dustine 'Cap' Fog to be introduced.

Remembering how Flack could call upon the top experts of every criminal field from all over the world and bring them together quickly, my original idea was to have the best 'hit man' in the United States given a 'contract' to kill Mr. Reeder. Then 'Cap', a Texas Ranger who was hunting the man for murdering a friend, was to follow him to England and become involved. Those of you who have read 'Cap' Fog, Texas Ranger, Meet Mr. J. G. Reeder *will know the plot did not follow those exact lines. Incidentally, arriving at the title took some doing. My first idea was to call the book,* Kill Mr. J. G. Reeder, *but Penelope Wallace said she would prefer to have one of my characters mentioned also. I suggested* Mr. J. G. Reeder, Meet 'Cap' Fog. *Then Transworld's Sales Department asked for something which pointed to the 'Western' aspect and the title was arrived at. My interpretation of Mr. Reeder was based upon an excellent article,* Aureus Harundum,[2] *by John A. Hogan, A.M.I.M.I., arguable the world's foremost serious researcher of Edgar Wallace.*

That Alvin Fog should have a strong physical resemblance to his paternal grandfather, although he inherited his grandmother's black hair, allowed him to achieve a similar element of surprise when coping with larger, heavier and stronger men. He followed the example of his deceased grand-uncle Danny Fog[3] by enlisting in the Texas Rangers and, in addition to being arguably the finest combat pistol shot of his generation—some authorities claim the honour for Ed McGivern[4]—became the youngest man

[2] *Aureus Harundum*: to quote John A. Hogan, 'It is the nearest I can get, with my memories of Latin, to "Golden Reader", which seemed rather apt in this case.'

[3] Some details of Danny Fog's career as a Texas Ranger are given in: *The Bad Bunch* and *A Town Called Yellowdog*.

[4] See *Fast And Fancy Revolver Shooting And Police Training* by Ed McGivern. Follett Publishing Company, Chicago, 1938.

ever to hold the rank of captain in that force,[5] from which arose his sobriquet, 'Cap'. The story in this volume takes place early in his career and before he received his promotion.

Finally, if any of my readers doubt that the Hardin–Fog–Blaze clan existed, I would make a suggestion. The next time you are in Houston, Texas, contact my good friends Ellen and Chuck Kurtzman. They have not only put me up at their home on two visits, but listened to my horrible 'Swiss' jokes and supplied the 'wheels' so necessary for sight-seeing in the Lone Star State. If asked politely, they will show you the chair in which 'Cap' sat while giving me the information upon which several new books about the Floating Outfit, Belle Boyd and Calamity Jane were derived.[6]

[5] Formed mainly to fight Indians after Texas won its independence from Mexico in 1836, the Texas Rangers became a law enforcement agency with State-wide jurisdiction and continued in that capacity until being disbanded on October the 17th, 1935. Their duties were absorbed by the Texas Department of Public Safety and the Highway Patrol.

[6] These include: *Beguinage, Beguinage Is Dead!, The Remittance Kid* and *The Whip and the War Lance.*

A CHORE FOR COMPANY 'Z'

Bawling in alarm, the steer on the gravel spit at the north side of the Rio Grande struggled to rise and stared to where the tawny shape of a large male cougar was crouching ready to charge. Under normal conditions, having descended from the at best semi-domesticated longhorn cattle upon which the ranching industry had been founded in Texas and Mexico, the steer would have had little to fear from the predator. However, with its right leg broken, it was unable to either flee or fight. Despite being full grown and hungry, the cougar would have hesitated to tackle such large prey if it had not been incapacitated. In the circumstances, the attack could be made without too much danger.

Even as the predator's rear claws were digging into the ground as an aid to propulsion for the charge, there was a sharp hissing crack just in front of it. Something struck and flung several chips of gravel to strike its snarling face with some force. Letting out a startled squawl, it sprang backwards instead of towards its intended prey. Then another sound reached its ears. One which it recognized from past experience as heralding the presence of its kind's arch enemy, or which at least suggested that human beings might be close to its source. With the bawling of a hound ringing in its ears, albeit from a distance, the cougar instinctively concluded discretion to be the better part of valour. Spinning around, it raced along the spit and, crossing the man-made trail which ran parallel to the river, headed for the open range beyond.

'God damn you, Lightning!' roared the tall, lean, leathery

faced and white haired man at the right side of the dark green 1924 Oakland 6–54 car, grasping the collar of the straining and still baying big bluetick coonhound which had been a contributory factor to the cougar's flight. 'Leave be, you *loco* ole son-of-a-bitch. Way he's lit out, you'd be away a day and a half chasing him. Tain't's if he's wounded, or anything.'

'I for sure scared him, though,' the driver of the vehicle pointed out, lowering his Winchester 1894 Model carbine without offering to try a second shot. Lacking some six inches of his companion's six foot height, and much younger, he was tanned and good looking—if not too eye-catching—and black haired. The physique of a Hercules in miniature was set off by a waist-length brown leather jacket, open necked dark blue shirt, tight rolled scarlet bandana, faded Levi's pants and tan Justin boots. He too spoke with a Texas drawl, but his tone implied he had had a better formal education than his passenger. 'Which, at close to a quarter of a mile, was about all I counted on doing.'

There was nothing in the external appearance of either speaker to suggest their true status, which was how they wanted it to be. Their attire was that of South Texas' cowhands and had changed little from that worn when Ole Devil Hardin's legendary Floating Outfit were helping the Lone Star State to grow from hide and horn out of the poverty left in the wake of the War Of Secession. Nor did the fact that one of the low horned, double girthed range saddles on the vehicle's back seat had an old Winchester 1873 Model rifle in its boot—the carbine in the smaller man's hands having come from the other—offer a clue. Most people who had cause to travel through the border country in the vicinity of the Rio Grande carried similar firearms as a basic precaution and means of self protection. This was still as necessary on occasion in 1924 as it had been for at least the previous hundred years.

Neither the driver nor the passenger gave any indication that he carried a handgun and the star-in-the-circle badge of a Texas Ranger concealed upon his person. It was not the policy for officers of that very efficient law enforcement agency to disclose their connection with it unless the situation warranted.

This was particularly the case where members of the recently formed and little publicized Company 'Z' were concerned.[1]

Summoned to join their commanding officer in El Paso, the two Rangers were travelling along the river road so as to visit a peace officer friend of the older man at Chuckville. Seeing the steer being threatened by the cougar, they had stopped to prevent it meeting its end in a painful manner.

'That's the trouble with them non-smoking itty-bitty "Thirty-Thirty"[2] saddleguns you young jaspers tote,' Sergeant Jubal Branch declared, as the bluetick[3] obeyed his command and slumped into a somnolence which was a complete contrast from the vigour it had been displaying. His laconic Texas drawl was amiable and did not express any resentment over the fact that, despite the disparity between their ages and lengths of service, they were both the same rank[4] and he was sure the other was marked for early promotion. 'They can't hit sic 'em 'cept when it's close up.'

'I notice you didn't fetch out that charcoal burning old relic to show me how it was done,' Sergeant Alvin Dustine Fog answered, glancing with apparent disdain at his companion's rifle.[5] The choice of weapons each preferred had become a source of friendly controversy between himself and the experienced old Ranger appointed by Major Benson Tragg to be his mentor during these early and vitally important days of his career as a peace officer. 'I'd best go down and put the steer out of its misery.'

'You-all for sure couldn't do it from up here,' Branch sniffed, although he had good cause to know how accurately his partner could shoot. Releasing the dog's collar, he went on, 'I'd best

[1] Because of the unconventional nature of its duties, Company 'Z' has never been mentioned in any history of the Texas Rangers. Even to this day, the State Legislature refuses to admit that such a Company existed.

[2] 'Thirty-Thirty': a ·30 calibre cartridge powered by a thirty grain powder charge.

[3] A full description of a bluetick is given in: *Hound Dog Man*.

[4] To enhance his authority, every member of Company 'Z' was given the rank of sergeant.

[5] Although the ·44·40 Winchester Model of 1873 fired a forty grain charge of black powder, the ·30·30 Model of 1894 was powered by smokeless powder which created a stronger propellant force and had a greater effective range.

come down with you, just in case you run out of shells afore you've managed to do that poor critter to death. Get back in the car, Lightning.'

'*Lightning!*' Alvin snorted, watching the lethargic way in which the big bluetick did as it was told. 'You-all surely picked the wrong name for him.'

'I figured calling him by it, he just might take the hint and start acting that way,' Branch explained, contriving to sound defensively defiant and as if wishing to exculpate himself for what had been an error in judgement. 'Anyways, who-all wants a hound dog's's allus rushing about wild-like?'

'One thing's for sure,' Alvin said dryly, turning his gaze from where Lightning was already curling up on the back seat between the two saddles as if tired beyond endurance. 'If *you-all* did, anybody'd figure you'd got a mighty big disappointment.'

Continuing their friendly bickering while walking down the fairly steep slope towards the gravel spit, the Rangers also studied the injured animal. It was medium sized, scrawny and showed little of the blood imparted by the whitefaced Hereford stock which had all but replaced the free-ranging longhorns on ranches in Texas. A large and complicated brand was burned into its winter thick brindle coat and the fork shaped gash in its right ear was clearly man-made but, apart from these marks of ownership, at first there did not appear to be anything out of the ordinary about it.

'I'd call that a greaser madhouse, or a map of Mexico,' Branch commented, looking down, after his companion had brought the steer's suffering to an end with a single bullet through the head. 'How'd you-all read it?'

'About the same, with a swallowfork earmark,' Alvin replied, being aware that ranchers in Texas employed smaller and more easily applied brands to identify their stock than the *hacienderos* south of the border. Having noticed something else while conducting the scrutiny at close quarters, he continued despite feeling sure it had not escaped his partner's attention, 'That's a mighty slick piece of iron work. Fact being, I don't reckon I've ever seen better hair branding.'

'It's pretty well done,' Branch conceded, with the air of a

297

connoisseur, pleased that the younger man had justified his faith by observing how the brand had only been burned into the hair and, when the winter coat was shed, would not leave a mark on the hide. 'Next thing being, how'd this critter get over here. 'Less I miss my guess, he's scrub stock from up in the Mexican high country.'

'One thing's for sure,' Alvin decided. 'He didn't come over of his own accord. Nor before dawn, the way the coat's dried out. I know cattle don't have a whole heap of good sense, but they've got enough savvy not to start swimming after dark when the river's high as this unless they're forced to it.'

'Which they wouldn't be easy forced,' Branch pointed out, glancing across the river at the high and sheer cliffs which rose from the water's edge for as far as he could see in either direction.

'Well now,' Alvin countered, still looking down at the dead steer. 'I'd say that depends on how the forcing's done.'

'You-all seen something I've missed?' the older Ranger inquired, swinging his gaze in the same direction.

'This burn mark here,' Alvin affirmed, pointing to a circular patch of singed hair by the side of the animal's tail. 'Have you-all ever seen anything like it?'

'Nope,' Branch confessed, without admitting he had previously overlooked the mark. 'Closest is when somebody's jabbed a red hot poker on to a piece of wood. Only that don't strike me's real likely to have happened. A cow thief having a red hot poker on hand, I mean.'

'It wasn't a red hot *poker*,' Alvin stated. 'But something mighty close to it.'

'How's about making that a lil mite plainer so a poor half-smart ole cuss like me can read the sign?'

'Back on the OD Connected, just before I joined the Rangers, a drummer brought along the damnedest cattle goad you ever did see. It looks and works like a flashlight, except there's a round metal plate instead of a bulb and it gives off heat, not light. Told us that, was you-all to use it on a steer bogged down in a mud hole, that old steer would come out like he'd backed his butt on to a cactus after just one jab from it.'

'Was that ole plate hot enough, it could happen.'

'Why sure,' Alvin drawled. 'Except that, like you-all figured and daddy told him, a man would have to get behind the steer before he could do the jabbing and then you'd have the man and the steer bogged down. Thing being, though, using one of those goads would sure make a steer lose his reluctance to go swimming even in high water—unless getting jabbed with it caused him to jump and bust a leg.'

'Wouldn't be just this 'n' whoever done it was bringing across, though,' Branch commented pensively.

'It's not likely,' Alvin agreed. 'And they didn't cross anywhere close by.'

'Nope,' Branch replied, then gave a shrug. 'Anyways, any rustling that's being done don't concern us. It's being done in Tim Whalen and Jose Colon's bailiwicks 'n' one or t'other of 'em'll likely have it well in hand.'

***** *****

'Hey, Jubal *amigo*,' greeted Captain Jose Colon, coming to his feet lethargically as the two Texas Rangers entered his office. 'Is good to see you. I give you the keys to the city in welcome.'

Matching Branch in height, the commanding officer of the Mexican *Guardia Rurales* based in La Guaira was massively built. His khaki uniform might be wrinkle, but it was spotless and his dark eyes were alert for all the sleepy look on his face. All in all, he struck Alvin Fog as being as deceptive as the big bluetick lying asleep on the back seat of the Oakland.

On arriving at Chuckville, the Rangers had been informed that Deputy Sheriff Timothy Whalen was out of town conducting an investigation. So they had driven across the Juarez Bridge to inform the head of the *Guardia Rurales* about their discovery of the steer about six miles down the Rio Grande.

'*Gracias, amigo*,' Branch answered and, after introducing his partner, went on, 'only it ain't a socializing visit. We've done come on duty.'

'Something tells me I may have to take back the keys,' Colon sighed, sinking on to his reinforced chair in a languid fashion. 'What can I do for you?'

'Tell us who-all hereabouts runs a brand like this,' Branch requested and laid a sheet of paper on the desk, ' 'n' uses a swallowfork earmark in the off ear.'

'That is the *hacienda* of Don Phillipe Gonzales-Rodriquez,' Colon stated, studying the sketch Alvin had made of the steer's brand. 'He is a most important man, runs maybe twenty thousand head of cattle in the high country.'

'He's only got nineteen thousand, nine hundred 'n' ninety-nine head at most now,' Branch corrected. 'We found one of 'em on a gravel spit down the river a ways. It's dead.'

'So is one of Don Phillipe's *vaqueros*,' Colon said quietly, but his languorous words did not fool either of the visitors. 'I have just come back from seeing the body. He was shot in the head sometime around midnight last night.'

'What was he shot with?' Branch inquired, something in the captain's attitude and tone leading him to assume the weapon was out of the ordinary.

'The bullet was a seven point six-three millimetre and, providing his horse threw him off when he was hit, had been fired from some fifty yards away,' Colon replied, taking a spent cartridge case from his tunic's left breast pocket. 'I found this. From a pistol, I would say.'

'I'll float my stick along of you-all on that, *amigo*,' Branch drawled, studying the smallish brass tube for a moment. Then he swung his gaze at his partner and went on in a tone of dry derision, 'Seeing's it don't have a rim to hold it in the cylinder of a *decent* gun, it's pretty near certain to have come from one of them 'auty-matic' shooting irons *some* folks're loco enough to tote. So that *vaquero* must've been unlucky, they're all the time jamming up on a man.'

'At least they don't spray fire out from the sides of the cylinder like revolvers,' Alvin replied, aware of what had provoked the comment and springing to the defence of the Colt Government Model ·45 automatic pistol in the spring retention shoulder holster under the left side of his jacket. Then he put aside the levity and addressed the man at the other side of the desk. 'He was shot from around fifty yards, you said, captain?'

'All the signs point to it,' Colon confirmed, making a shrewd

300

guess at what had provoked the previous exchange between the Rangers.

'There wasn't much moonlight even when it wasn't raining last night,' Alvin said pensively. 'A man would have to be lucky, or a better than fair shot with a handgun, to make a hit at fifty yards under those conditions. Has there been much rustling around here recently?'

'Not that I've heard about,' Colon answered. 'Mostly it starts after the hair has grown out in the spring and taken the brand with it, so there is nothing to show who owns the animal. There's not much of a market for cattle down here and most are just sold for their hides. Which means it is advisable not to offer something that can be identified as belonging to somebody else.'

'That's about how I figured it to be,' Alvin stated. 'That steer we found had been hair branded.'

'Just about the only place in Texas you could sell scrubby stock like that would be the dog food canning plant at Del Rio,' Branch put in. 'Word has it, happen the price is right, they don't look too careful at the brands when they're buying.'

'They'll even take the butchered out meat,' Alvin supplemented. 'And that means there won't be any brands for them to look at. So why go to all the trouble of hair branding in the first place?'

'I dunno,' Branch replied, sounding bored and disinterested. 'Anyways, finding out's not a chore for Company "Z". All we 'n's do is find the son-of-a-bitching crime. Then we leave the local John-Laws to solve it.'

'You see what I meant, amigo?' Colon inquired plaintively of Alvin Fog. 'Every time he comes down here, I wind up having to go to work. That's why I said something told me I might have to take back the keys to the city.'

***** *****

'Blast the luck!' Jubal Branch grumbled sotto voce, watching the three riders—two were leading pack horses which had no loads—who were making for the small cluster of buildings about half a mile from where he and Alvin Fog were concealed in a cottonwood grove. 'Some folks just don't have no consideration for hard working peace officers. Happen they'd held off coming back for a while longer, we could've gone down and looked around to our hearts' content.'

'*Some* folks want everything too easy,' Alvin answered, also studying the horsemen with the aid of a pair of binoculars.

Despite the elderly Ranger's comment to Captain Colon, he and his young partner were far too conscientious to ignore a serious crime. However, while Company 'Z' were less subject to the restrictions,[6] in general the Texas Rangers were only supposed to involve themselves in an investigation if requested to do so by the county or municipal law enforcement agency in whose jurisdiction it occurred.

Returning to Chuckville at the conclusion of their interview with the commanding officer of the *Guardia Rurales*, Alvin and Branch found that Deputy Sheriff Timothy Whalen was still absent. It had been after midnight before he was brought back, having sustained a broken hip during a chase after a criminal. Hearing that not only had cattle been stolen in Mexico and in all probability driven over the border, but there was possibly a murder involved, he had asked for the Rangers assistance as he was incapacitated. A telegraph message to Major Tragg in El Paso had been answered promptly, giving his authorization for them to offer their services.

Although the rain during the night of the suspected theft had wiped out any tracks that might have been left, Whalen's knowledge of the surrounding district had allowed him to select the only crossing place in the vicinity of the gravel spit at which the injured steer could have been carried down to it by the current. A similar experience of the region and its residents had led him to conclude who would be the most likely suspect. Despite his ranch being small and run to seed, Paul Helmuth and his hired hands always appeared to have a fair amount of money considering how little work and effort was put into it. Furthermore, his was the nearest property to the crossing.

Accepting Whalen's summation, Alvin and Branch had studied

[6] An example of this is given in Part Three, 'The Deadly Ghost', of *You're a Texas Ranger, Alvin Fog.*

a large scale map of the county to get their bearings. Then, borrowing two horses, they had set off accompanied by Lightning to conduct an investigation. Selecting a route which would allow them to approach their destination without it being obvious they had come from Chuckville, they had halted in the cottonwood grove to examine their surroundings before going closer. As Whalen had informed them, they observed that the ranch's living quarters, barn and corrals were in need of attention. However, there were two new Moreland three-ton trucks with their loads concealed beneath lashed down tarpaulin sheets parked in front of the house and a smaller Ford with a canopy stood in the lean-to alongside the barn. Although there had been no sign of life when the Rangers came into view, this favourable state of affairs had not continued long enough for them to take advantage of it.

'Going by what Tim told us, the short runt on the pinto's Helmuth,' Branch decided, ignoring his companion's comment. 'The big unshaven cuss afork the dun's Tinhan, which means t'other 'n' must be Whit Gollicker. Can't say's how I've ever run across any of 'em afore, so they'll likely not know we 'n's're Rangers.'

'The hired help's got belt guns on,' Alvin supplemented, being able to see that the two larger men were armed although their employer did not appear to be and knowing why his companion had made the latter part of the comment. 'There's no call for us to worry about *that*, though. They're only toting *revolvers*.'

'I'd worry a whole heap less was they fool enough to be toting "auty-matics",' Branch sniffed. 'Let's sort of drift on down and say, "Howdy you-all" perlite like.'

'Seems almost a shame to wake that fool critter,' Alvin remarked, returning the binoculars to his saddlebag and glancing to where the bluetick, having flopped down the moment they halted, appeared to be sleeping. However, as they set their horses into motion, it lurched up and advanced between them. 'Damned if he didn't spit out of the corner of his mouth at me for disturbing him. And it wasn't *me* who said we should do it.'

'You-all didn't expect him to spit at me, now did you?' Branch asked, also having replaced his field glasses and reaching behind his back under his jacket to ensure there was nothing to impede him drawing the Colt Civilian Model Frontier revolver from the horizontal holster attached to his waist belt. 'I'm the owner he loves 'n' respects.'

For all the comments they were making, the Rangers were alert and watchful as they rode slowly from the grove. That Helmuth's hired hands were each carrying a revolver in plain view struck them as being most significant. While possession of handguns was too common in Texas to arouse comment, they were only worn openly when the owners anticipated they might be needed. Such a precaution could be considered necessary by men who were, or had been, engaged upon an illegal enterprise.

It said much for the skill by which Alvin and Branch had selected their route that their presence in the vicinity was not detected until they were about a hundred yards from the buildings. By that time, Helmuth and his men had left their horses hitched to the corral near a water trough and were walking towards the barn. Swinging around as the sound of hooves reached their ears, they stopped in line with the rancher at the centre. Short, foxy-featured, wearing an untidy three piece town suit and collarless shirt, he took a pace forward hooking thumbs into the armholes of his vest. Looming menacingly behind him, Tinhan and Gollicker had on dirty and blood stained cowhand clothes. Both their right hands dangled close to the butts of their low hanging Colts.

'Howdy, gents,' Branch called, as he and Alvin reined in their mounts fifty yards from the trio. 'Mind if me 'n' me nephew water our hosses?'

'Come ahead,' Helmuth authorized, after glancing from one to the other Ranger and taking a swift look all around.

'*Gracias,*' Branch drawled, swinging from the saddle.

Dismounting, Alvin followed his partner as they led their horses to the trough. While doing so, he studied the animals which were hitched to the corral. Although he had not been able to see the left flanks earlier, he was now able to do so. The two which had been ridden by the hired hands each had a Winchester carbine in a saddleboot. However, his main attention was directed towards the pinto. Something which looked like the wooden butt section of a rifle was suspended from the near side of the saddlehorn.

Having a very thorough knowledge of firearms, Alvin was aware of the device's true purpose. A quick glance informed him that his partner had seen it and was cognizant of what the sight might imply. However, as always, he waited for Branch's guidance in how they were to behave.

'Right obliged, friend,' Branch remarked, stepping clear of the horses as they started to drink and stretching, then reaching under his jacket as if to rub a sore back. 'Been hunting up along Bull Crick all night.'

'Have any luck?' Helmuth inquired, throwing a disdainful look to where the bluetick had flopped down almost as soon as its owner stopped.

'Not a whole heap,' Branch confessed, aware without needing to look that his partner was positioned a few feet to his left and ready to back whatever play he made. As he went on, he noticed—although Whalen had claimed Helmuth employed only two men—a figure wearing cowhand's clothing stepping out of the barn. 'Reckon that fool ole——!'

'Look out!' the emerging man yelled, after staring for a moment at the newcomers then spinning on his heel to leap back through the door. 'That old bastard's a Ranger.'

Hearing what was being shouted brought Branch's words to a halt. The warning had also reached the men for whom it was intended.

While the elderly Ranger was unable to recall when and where he had made the acquaintance of his betrayer, he realized that the lack of recognition was not mutual. Equally apparent was that the three men in front of him were willing to accept the inelegant identification by their companion. Nor did they show the slightest hesitation over acting upon it. Of them, Helmuth proved to be the fastest. Flashing across, his left hand disappeared beneath the suit's jacket to emerge holding a Colt Officer's Model ·38 Special revolver which had had its barrel cut down to a length of two inches since its purchase to make it more easily concealed.[7] Armed with Colt Artillery Model Peacemakers, Tinhan and Gollicker were somewhat slower which did not imply they were drawing at a snail's pace.

Responding with the instincts and alacrity acquired by almost a lifetime spent facing similar threats to his well being, Branch began to pluck the Peacemaker from its holster behind his back. Even as he was doing so, he became conscious of the fact that three of the participants in the developing situation were exceeding him in the rapidity with which they were responding.

Fortunately, two of the three were allies!

At the first hint of trouble, all the somnolence left the big bluetick and it began to act more in keeping with its name. Coming to its feet, it landed upon them already in motion. Bounding forward with a roaring snarl, it hurtled into the air at the nearest of the three men it realized were threatening its master.

Displaying an equal appreciation of the way in which the situation was developing, the younger Ranger demonstrated that he had inherited more than just the physique of a Hercules in miniature from his illustrious paternal grandfather, Dusty Fog. Realizing that his partner might make the precaution necessary, he was already standing with his feet spread to about the width of his shoulders and knees flexed slightly. At the first warning of danger, working in smooth co-ordination, his left hand rose to grasp and draw open the near side of the leather jacket, his torso inclined forward and the right fist passed across to grasp the butt of the Colt Government Model automatic pistol.

By the time Helmuth had begun to bring the snub-nosed Colt into view, he found he was already confronted with a dilemma and his first summation had been erroneous. The smaller of the visitors, who he had scarcely noticed until then, was moving with an even greater rapidity than the man identified as being a Texas Ranger. However, even as he was deciding to send his

[7] The shortening must have been done privately. It was not until 1926 that the Colt Patent Firearms Mfg. Co., of Hartford, Connecticut put their first revolver with a two inch barrel on the market. This was the 'Detective Special' which started out production merely as a 'Police Positive Special' with a shortened barrel to allow it to be employed as a concealment weapon; but the Company decided it should be given a more distinctive and individual name.

306

bullets into the youngster—who he suspected was also a peace officer—leaving his employees to deal with the older man, he was made aware of a further factor which he had failed to take into consideration. Discarding its slothful appearance, the large dog was behaving in a manner which was alarming to say the least.

Unfortunately for Helmuth, before his mind could fully assimilate the changed conditions, it was too late to take any effective action. A set of powerful jaws closed on his left wrist, with teeth sinking in to crush and grind painfully. Struck by the leaping bluetick's one hundred pounds of solid bone, muscle and sinew, he lost his grip on the Colt and was knocked from his feet. Going down under the dog, the back of his head struck the ground with considerable force. Blackness descended upon him, preventing him from discovering what was portended by certain sounds which reached his ears even above the savage snarling of his attacker.

Trained from childhood by experts in every aspect of gun handling pertaining to a peace officer's duties, Alvin felt no qualms over the way in which he intended to act. His grandfather and father[8] had taught him that the kind of situation he was facing justified shooting to kill. Nor did the behaviour of either hired hand lead him to assume they would hesitate over taking his or Branch's lives if granted an opportunity. What was more, unless his judgement was in error, there was another element which might preclude any hope of persuading the pair to surrender instead of fighting.

On liberating the automatic from the retention spring of the shoulder holster, Alvin waited until its muzzle was turning outwards before allowing his forefinger to approach the trigger or thumbing down the manual safety catch. For all that, aligned at waist level, the weapon roared just ·6 of a second after his hand began to move towards it. Having noticed Tinhan was the faster of the hired hands, although standing in front of Branch, his bullet was directed accordingly. Struck between the eyes and

[8] Although Jackson Marsden Fog has not received the acclaim accorded to his father, Dusty, or son, Alvin, records of his exploits during World War 1 and as the sheriff of Rio Hondo County prove he was equally proficient in handling weapons.

killed instantly, the burly man was flung from his feet and the revolver which had just cleared leather fell unfired as he sprawled supine to the ground.

During the period they had been working together, Branch and Alvin had developed into a smoothly functioning team. Each was aware of the other's capabilities and could guess how he would react under any given set of circumstances. So the older Ranger knew which of their antagonists would be taken by his partner. Consequently, when his Frontier came out, he kept its barrel turning towards Gollicker. It was still moving when the automatic thundered. Then flame and the white smoke of ignited powder belched from the muzzle. A ·44·40 bullet, which would have been interchangeable with those in his Winchester, was sent into the second hired hand's left breast sufficiently quickly to prevent him from being able to throw down on the younger peace officer.

Having dealt with Tinhan, Alvin did not relax his vigilance or readiness. His estimation of the situation had alerted him to the possibility of another source of peril. Sure enough, the man who had recognized Branch reappeared. As Alvin had suspected, he had returned to the barn to arm himself. What was more, the weapon he had collected was well suited to his needs. Swinging the butt of the Winchester Carbine to his shoulder, he clearly assumed he had little to fear with at least fifty yards separating him from the Rangers.

This would have been the case with most men, but Alvin Fog was not one of them. Without straightening from his slightly crouching posture, he raised the Colt. Leaving the jacket, his left hand joined the right on the butt and gave added support as he took rapid sight. Four times, as quickly as the cocking slide could ride back and, having ejected an empty case, advance to feed a live round from the lips of the magazine, the automatic cracked. Between each shot, controlling the recoil aided by the double-handed hold, he turned the barrel slightly. Although the first bullet missed, the next three all struck home and any one of them would have proved fatal. For all that, the man by the door managed to reply and sent Branch's hat spinning away before he was hit and sent reeling. Colliding against the wall of the barn, he bounded from it and went down.

'*Now* what do you have to say about automatics?' Alvin challenged, looking around and relieved to discover his partner was unharmed.

'If you-all'd been using a revolver, I wouldn't've had a good hat spoiled,' Branch replied, walking to where the bluetick was standing over but not continuing to attack the unconscious rancher. 'Leave be, you fool dog.'

'Looks like we've got the right men,' Alvin commented, as Lightning moved clear of Helmuth and settled down to look as docile as before the trouble erupted.

'Looks like,' Branch conceded, glancing around. 'Know something, boy. I reckon I was wrong back in La Guaira. This just could be a chore for Company "Z".'

***** *****

'Now just lemme get this straight, Mr. Helmuth,' Jubal Branch said slowly. 'You still reckon's how you took us for owlhoots's was concluding to rob you-all?'

'That's what I thought,' the pallid-faced rancher admitted, sitting with his back to the wall of the barn and nursing his bandaged left wrist. Darting a frightened look at the bluetick which sprawled close by, he went on, 'You pair started throwing lead and that dog jumped me afore I could find out who you was for sure.'

In the half hour which had elapsed since the shooting, the two Rangers had been busy. While Branch was attending to Helmuth's injury, Alvin collected the object which they had noticed from the pinto's saddle. It was, as they had guessed, a combined butt-stock and holster made to carry a Mauser pistol. On being extracted carefully to avoid smudging any fingerprints, the weapon it held had proved—by the lack of the figure 9 carved on the butt to indicate a calibre of 9mm—to be of the 7·63 millimetre model. Examining the two Moreland trucks, the peace officers had found they were loaded with meat. While a search of the immediate area had failed to locate the hides of the slaughtered animals, there were sufficient signs to suggest they had been carried off for disposal on the pack horses. The search had also produced two of the electric cattle goads Alvin had guessed were responsible for the injury sustained by the steer they had found.

'Then there's nothing to what Whit Gollicker told us just before he died?' Branch inquired. 'He allowed's how you-all done shot a *vaquero* over in Mexico while you was widelooping some of Don Phillipe Gonzales-Rodriquez's cattle, using that fancy Mauser "auty-matic" with its butt-holster fastened on to turn it into a pretty accurate carbine.'

'He was lying!' Helmuth yelped, starting to move and freezing immediately as the dog looked up with a low, rumbling growl.

'We've got the Mauser with your fingerprints on it and likely can find folks in Chuckville who knows it belongs to you,' Alvin pointed out. 'I don't know if you've heard, but there are ways it can be proved a bullet, or a spent shell, came from a particular gun. So I don't reckon it'll be too hard to find out who-all of you's lying.'

'So take me to court and prove it!' Helmuth challenged defiantly, but keeping a wary eye on Lightning. 'I'll stand trial *anywhere* in *Texas* you care to name.'

Having regained consciousness while the Rangers were conducting their search, the rancher had been prevented from taking advantage of their absence by the presence of the big bluetick. Any movement he had made was greeted by a menacing growl and a tensing of the powerful body which he had discovered was capable of far more rapid movement than he had believed possible at first sight. With flight precluded, he had given thought to his predicament. By the time his captors returned, he had concluded that the situation was not as desperate as it appeared on the surface.

Seeing the blanket-covered bodies of Tinhan, Gollicker and the man he had recently hired to help with the extra cattle stolen in Mexico, Helmuth had realized they could not be produced to testify against him. Nor, as the brands had been cut out and burned before the hides of the latest batch were buried in lime, could it be established that the meat in the trucks was other than his property. Using the excuse he had given, the shooting might be explained away by the unscrupulous lawyer he would hire to conduct his defence. He had heard about the science of ballistics and did not doubt his Mauser could be identified as having killed the *vaquero*, but the crime had been committed on the other side of the international border. He could not be tried for the crime in Texas. Nor could he, as an American citizen, be extradited by the Mexican authorities from the land of his birth. So, taking everything into consideration, he believed he had little to fear.

'Get up and climb into the back of your truck,' Branch ordered, nodding to the Ford which Alvin had brought from the lean-to.

'Are you *arresting* me?' Helmuth demanded, rising slowly without taking his gaze from the dog.

'Shucks, no,' Branch replied, in a resigned tone. 'Like you've figured, there's nothing we can prove again' you-all. So we're taking you to let a doctor 'tend to that bite.'

'I'm obliged,' Helmuth stated, barely able to conceal his triumph, walking over and climbing into the truck. 'Just so it's understood I'm coming along voluntarily.'

'Why sure,' Branch confirmed. 'We respect your rights as a tax-paying 'n' law-abiding citizen of the Sovereign State of Texas. You're *not* arrested and can get out of there any time you take a mind. Neither Alvin nor me'll stop you—Lightning!'

At the mention of its name, the big bluetick rose and bounded into the truck, causing the rancher to retire hurriedly to the end. Then he stared with something close to terror at the dog as it lay down and watched him.

'Sit down 'n' make yourself at home,' Branch suggested, raising and fastening the truck's tailgate. While Helmuth was carrying out his instruction, he let the rear flaps of the canopy fall, continuing in a voice which had become charged with thinly veiled menace, 'Was I you-all, though, I wouldn't make any move to get up, nor cause no loud noises like maybe yelling. You'll wake ole Lightning here up should you do either 'n' he gets close to mean's a well boiled owl should it happen.' Stepping back so the flaps closed, he went on, 'Hitch our hosses to the back here, *amigo*, so's we can get moving.'

*****   *****

311

A sense of perturbation began to replace the fear which had assailed the rancher all through the journey. The truck had come to a halt a few minutes previously and its driver, having quit the cab, had unfastened his horse to lead it away. However, neither he nor his companion—who had ridden ahead earlier, announcing he was going to inform the doctor that an injured man was being brought in—had offered to come and open the flaps. Nor had the big bluetick moved from its place by the tailgate. Yet, as various sounds which reached Helmuth's ears informed him that he was in the proximity of other human beings, the worrying ideas he had formulated during the ride seemed unlikely to eventuate.

The rancher had made the journey from his house to Chuckville in the Ford on numerous occasions, but he had always sat in the cab and been able to see where he was going. Carried in the back with the flaps closed, he had been unable to estimate how far he had travelled. When he had tried to move close enough to lift the edge of the canopy and see, an unmistakable threat from the apparently somnolent dog had brought him to an immediate halt. It had also left him in no doubt of what would happen should he disregard the older Ranger's advice. What was more, he had begun to suspect that his captors hoped he would either move or shout to provoke an attack. Unable to bring charges against him, or being disinclined to participate in a trial which they might lose and result in themselves facing charges over the shootings, they were trying to produce a version of what the Mexicans called *ley fuego*.[9] Except that he was to be killed by the bluetick instead of being shot on the pretext that he had tried to escape.

Even as the rancher was trying to decide what the Rangers were up to, he heard a whistle from a fair distance away. Coming to its feet, the dog bounded over the tailgate and he could hear it running off. Waiting a few more seconds in case it returned, he finally plucked up sufficient courage to rise. Walking to the rear, he eased open the flaps cautiously. For a moment, he

[9] *'Ley fuego'*: translated literally, 'law of fire'. Said when a prisoner was told to run away and then shot on the pretence that he was trying to escape.

thought he was in an army barracks of some kind. There was an open area like a parade ground surrounded by a high adobe wall with a parapet from which rifles could be fired. To his left was a building that might have been the guard house, some of its windows having bars at them. However, he knew there was no such establishment in Chuckville.

A realization of where he must be began to assail Helmuth, sending a chill of apprehension through him. As if wishing to confirm his suppositions beyond any shadow of a doubt, three men clad in the khaki uniforms of the Mexican *Guardia Rurales* emerged from the building. Not only did he recognize the big and bulky figure of Captain Colon, he identified the object which dangled in a hand the size of a ham.

'*Saludos, senor,*' Colon greeted, making a gesture with the Mauser's wooden butt-stock holster he was holding. 'Would you come out, please. I wish to hold you until tests can be made to find out whether this weapon found in your possession is the one which killed a *vaquero* earlier this week.'

'But—But——!' Helmuth gasped.

'You will find our prison very crowded, *senor,*' Colon went on. 'It seems some of Don Phillipe Gonzales-Rodriquez's *vaqueros* had been hair branding his cattle, but somebody else started stealing them before the hair could grow out and another brand applied. There was shooting between the two parties last night and I have arrested the survivors of both.'

'Y—You can't hold *me*!' Helmuth protested, having no doubt that one of the men who had helped him steal the cattle would betray him or the friends of the *vaquero* he had murdered would try to take revenge. 'I'm an American citizen——'

'Who is being detained on suspicion of having committed crimes in Mexico,' Colon pointed out, but was not allowed to say any more.

'Where're those god-damned Rangers?' the rancher howled, staring around as the full understanding of his position drove home with a chilling effect.

'*Rangers?*' Colon repeated blandly. 'There are no Rangers here.'

Which was true.

First Alvin Fog had arrived, bringing the Mauser with him and explaining how it had come into his possession. Then he waited for Jubal Branch to come with the prisoner. At that moment, accompanied by Lightning, they were leaving the Juarez Bridge on the Texas bank of the Rio Grande.

Having accepted that there was no *legal* way by which Helmuth could be brought to trial for his crimes in Mexico, the two Rangers had set about ensuring he would not escape the consequences. Nor had the fact that they would not be acting within the letter of the law deter them. They were aware that there were frequently circumstances in which ordinary peace officers were prevented by the rules from taking appropriate action. When that happened, it became a chore for Company 'Z'.

PART ELEVEN

THE ROCKABYE COUNTY SERIES

PREVENTIVE LAW ENFORCEMENT

During the early 'Sixties, in addition to establishing my traditional, Civil War and 'off-beat' Western books, I was also producing a short story and artists' scripts series on a variety of subjects for Victor *boys' paper. To keep up my flow of three or four episodes a week, I was constantly on the lookout for any fact which could be converted into the base on which to build a story. Among my sources, I found American firearms magazines,* Guns *and* Ammo *in particular, were fruitful in their supply of material. This particularly applied to a three-part article about the rapidly growing sport of combat pistol shooting written in March, April and May, 1964, by Jeff Cooper.*

I had already read descriptions of the 'fast draw' competitions which became popular in the wake of the great action-escapism-adventure Western television series such as Cheyenne, Bronco, Gunsmoke[1], Wagon Train, Bonanza, Sugarfoot,[2] *etc., but I discovered combat shooting was a vastly different proposition. In fast draw, speed alone counted and the revolver—almost always a variation of the Colt Peacemaker—was loaded with blank cartridges or wax bullets. Developed mainly by law enforcement officers, with the intention of improving their skill, combat shooting placed considerable emphasis upon speed, but just as much was devoted to attaining accuracy over various distances and in as near actual fighting conditions as could be arranged. The*

---

[1] *Gunsmoke* starring James Arness, was screened in Britain as *Gun Law* and each episode commenced with U.S. Marshal Matt Dillon outdrawing and shooting holster and gunbelt maker Arvo Ojala.

[2] When *Sugarfoot*, starring Will Hutchins, was transferred in Britain from Independent Television to the British Broadcasting Corporation's network, its title was changed to *Tenderfoot*.

weapon employed by most of the leading contenders was the Colt Government Model of 1911 ·45 automatic pistol accurized as I was to describe in The Professional Killers, *although any other kind of handgun with a calibre of not less than ·38 Special—the official round for almost every law enforcement agency in the U.S.A. at that time—was permissible. Whatever the weapon, it had to be carried in a rig capable of being worn for every day duty.*

While I was considering how to put my information regarding combat pistol shooting to use, I began to see a television series, The Sheriff of Cochise, *which was a Western in a modern setting and I bought one of my sons a Corgi Toys' Oldsmobile Super 88 sheriff's patrol car. From then on, the Rockabye County series became a distinct possibility. The next problem was to sell the idea to my publisher and this proved far more difficult than producing the first manuscript. The editor of Brown Watson Ltd. at that time refused to even consider the idea. So, rather than waste it, I brought off a series of twelve short stories which eventually appeared in* Victor *under the title of* The Sheriff of Rockabye County. *Jack Tragg and Gusher City were involved, but Bradford Counter became 'Mike' as the editor said there might have been confusion with the 'Brad' in the* Braddock *series about the Royal Air Force, and Woman Deputy Alice Fayde had to wait until the books were published before making her appearance. Nor, due to the limitations of working to between three and four thousand words, could I introduce too many of the Sheriff's Office staff in* Victor.

Having a somewhat stubborn streak, I never forgot my ambition to write the Rockabye County books. A change of editorial staff at Brown Watson appeared to be offering me the chance to do so. I was on excellent terms with the new editor, Brian Babani and he was receptive to the idea. By that time, I had written some forty-seven titles and, with all undue lack of modesty, was a main earning factor for the company. So Brian said he would take the opening Rockabye County volume after I had written my fiftieth standard western, which he suggested should be a one hundred thousand word 'special'. Before either project got under way, Transworld Publishers Ltd. took over my contract. While I was delighted by the prospect of working for a much larger company, I also thought I would be compelled to start from scratch in my struggle to persuade them to publish the 'modern day Westerns'. This did not happen. I was asked to send the first manuscript along. It was read by Corgi Books who liked it sufficiently to launch the series.

I had already decided, when contemplating the series, that to have a tie-in with my established work would be beneficial. My reason for selecting Mark, rather than Dusty, the Kid or Waco, to have a descendant stemmed from the way in which some elements in the television and movie industries portrayed any man with a good physique as a dim-witted moron. So I decided to do a bit of counter-publicity. That's how Brad was born, along with his Colt Government Model automatic pistol, Hardy-Cooper spring shoulder holster and Bianchi Cooper-Combat rig in which to carry it when in plain clothes or uniform.

Although Alice Fayde was not allowed to tread the pages of Victor, she emerged at the same time as Brad. This happened long before Chief Ironside had a female assistant—but the first volume did not reach the bookshop shelves until after Raymond Burr climbed into the wheelchair and on to our television screens —or Policewoman and the, in my opinion, far superior Dog and Cat series were shown. There had been a few other detective series in which the hero had a female partner, of course, but none of them took such an active part in the proceedings as Alice was destined to do.

Finally, the modern law enforcement techniques and procedures employed in the Rockabye County series could not have been produced without the help given by the Sheriff's Association of Texas, the Federal Bureau of Investigation, the Enforcement Branch of the Inland Revenue Service's Alcohol And Tobacco Tax Division and the various municipal police departments in the United States with whom I corresponded. They all willingly sent me, by airmail and without delay, all the information I required and much more detail I had not requested. This was something of a contrast with the one occasion when I asked for information from the Leicestershire Constabulary. They took longer to answer than any American agency and gave only a *couple of short paragraphs which just covered the points I had raised.*[3]

[3] I must, in all fairness, admit that while working on *'Cap' Fog, Texas Ranger, Meet Mr. J. G. Reeder*, the Public Relations Department of Scotland Yard were most helpful in supplying information pertaining to the late 1920s.

PREVENTIVE LAW ENFORCEMENT

'Remember it's on the hip!' Deputy Sheriff Bradford Counter informed himself mentally, as he stood waiting for the signal that he was to draw and start shooting. 'Forgetting could get you killed!'

If Dusty Fog, the Ysabel Kid, Waco, or any other of Mark Counter's friends had been alive and in the basement shooting range of Gusher City's Department Of Public Safety Building, they would not have doubted for a moment that the young peace officer was one of his descendants.

Brad had the same golden blond hair, exceptionally handsome features, six foot three of height, width of shoulders and slender waist indicative of Herculean strength. What was more, although manufacturers who were not in existence during the Nineteenth Century had supplied his clothes, he had inherited his great-grandfather's predilection for dressing well. He had on a silver-grey Resistol Rancher 125 hat shaped with a Luskey roll crease, a black leather vest to which was attached his badge of Office, a beige Klopman Ultressa shirt and Levi's pants whose legs hung outside a pair of Luskey Ropers 'Center Cut Ostrich' boots which had cost more than two hundred and fifty dollars.

The most noticeable difference was in the blond giant's armament and means of carrying it. Instead of wearing a *buscadero* gunbelt with twin low hanging holsters tied to his legs, he had on a black Bianchi Deluxe Sam Browne belt to which was attached a pouch for spare ammunition, a handcuff case and key ring. His single Colt Government Model ·45 automatic pistol, action cocked and manual safety catch applied, was held by an Elden Carl 'Fly Off' strap in a somewhat skimpy, forward-raked

Bianchi Cooper-Combat rig set high on his right hip and from which an Old West gun fighter might have felt it could not be drawn swiftly.

As the red light on top of the target fifteen feet away glowed, Brad employed a gun fighting technique which had not been developed in his great-grandfather's day. Standing with his feet slightly apart, he bent his knees and inclined his torso to the rear. While doing so, he brought up his right hand and the left arm bent to act as a counter-balance. Hooking under the long tang of the 'Fly Off' strap, his right forefinger broke open the press-stud securing it and it lived up to its name by leaping into the air. While it was still rising, he 'speed rocked' the pistol from the holster. Thumbing down the manual safety catch as the barrel was turning away, he fired from waist level and by instinctive alignment. There was a clang of lead striking metal and the light went out.

'Point twenty-nine of a second!' the range master announced, reading the electronic timer which was activated at the same instant as the red light and stopped when the bullet hit the target. 'That's the best you've done today.'

'Why sure,' Brad agreed. 'I didn't start by reaching up and across this time.'

'Do you want to——?' the range master began, but the buzzing of the telephone on his desk brought the question to an end and he scooped up the receiver. 'Range. Sure, Mac. Hey Brad, Mac McCall says can you go up to his office straight away.'

'Yo!' the big blond assented, removing the ear plugs which broke up the concussion of the shot's detonation without preventing him from hearing what was being said.

Having set the safety catch, holstered the Colt and replaced the 'Fly Off' strap, Brad left the range. As he was making for the elevators, he wondered why First Deputy McCall wanted him. He also decided that his decision to come in early and visit the range might have been a wise precaution. There were times, even in jet-age Texas, when a peace officer needed to be able to draw and shoot with lightning speed and even a split second's fumble could prove fatal. Such a thing might have happened under the current situation if he had not taken the time to condition his reflexes to the way in which he would be wearing his Colt for the next few days.

Normally, serving in the capacity of the town's homicide investigation detail, the deputies in the Sheriff's Office at the Department Of Public Safety Building carried out their duties in civilian clothes and with their weapons concealed. However, during Frontier Week—which had just commenced—they were called 'deputy town marshals' and dressed in the fashion of their Old West predecessors. While they were expected to wear the appropriate attire, prudence dictated that they carried their handguns on regulation belts. So Brad had been making sure he was accustomed to having the Colt on his right hip instead of at his left side in the Hardy-Cooper spring shoulder holster he normally used.[1]

Arriving at the third floor, the big blond went straight to the Watch Commander's office. He found that both the Day and Night Watch Commanders were present.[2] However, although the time was only five minutes to four, First Deputy Ricardo Alvarez[3] allowed his opposite number to do the talking.

'Seeing that Tom's down in Brownsville and, if I know him, will make sure he doesn't get back before Frontier Week's over,' the craggy-faced First Deputy McCall said without preliminaries and in a pronounced Scottish burr, 'you'll be teamed up with Sam Cuchilo.'

'*Bueno*,' Brad assented, being on good terms with the man who had been named although they were on different Watches. He was confident that they could work together harmoniously in the absence of his regular partner, Deputy Sheriff Thomas Cord.[4] 'Is Sam on anything?'

'You both will be this evening,' McCall replied. 'It's what you might call a piece of preventive law enforcement.'

Without asking the big blond to sit down, the Scottish First

[1] How the training paid dividends is told in: *The Sheriff of Rockabye County*, Part Four, 'Walt Haddon's Mistake'.
[2] Details of the Rockabye County Sheriff's Office routine and of how Bradford Counter became a member of it are given in Appendix Nine.
[3] Due to a printing error in *The ¼ Second Draw*, First Deputy Ricardo Alvarez was referred to as 'First Deputy Ricardo'. It is hoped that the error will be rectified in future editions of this work.
[4] What happened when Deputy Sheriff Thomas Cord returned by train from Brownsville is told in: *The Professional Killers*.

Deputy elaborated upon the assignment. A carnival had arrived as part of the Frontier Week's festivities. Being aware that the often justified suspicions of having been cheated was frequently a source of friction between townspeople and the 'carnies', Sheriff Jack Tragg had warned the manager that such activities would not be tolerated. Having worked in carnivals before becoming a peace officer, Deputy Sheriff Sam Cuchilo had an extensive knowledge of the various dishonest tricks which might be pulled. So, wanting to find out whether his orders were being obeyed, the sheriff had said that the deputy would conduct an investigation and, as his temporary partner, Brad would be accompanying him.

'I don't reckon we'll learn much if we go there dressed any way that will let the carnies know what we are,' Brad commented.

'Aye,' McCall conceded. 'That's what Sam said. So go down to see Corey Haynes and he'll fix you up.'

***** *****

'Do you-all know what that rumbling is, good buddy?' Brad inquired, as he and his temporary partner were walking along the sawdust covered midway of the carnival at shortly after nine o'clock in the evening. 'It's Great Grandpappy Mark turning over in his grave at the thought of me being seen in public looking this way.'

'Why I reckon you cut a mighty fine figure, paleface brother,' Deputy Sheriff Sam Cuchilo declared with a grin. 'Don't change a *thing*. It's *you*!'

Although Sergeant Corey Haynes normally worked in the Gusher City Police Department's Records & Information Bureau, he was also an expert in make-up and disguises.[5] As a result of his specialized abilities, there was little danger of the deputies' true status being discovered accidentally.

Brad now sported a very natural looking shoulder long blond wig, with a matching droopy moustache and beard. While nothing could be done to reduce his height, a loose fitting and multi-hued *caftan* which hung almost to knee level and had full length wide sleeves, added to some padding around his slim waist, did much

---

[5] Other examples of how the Sheriff's Office availed themselves of Sergeant Corey Haynes' specialized training are given in: Part Three 'Cat-Catching Cop' of *The Sixteen Dollar Shooter* and *Point of Contact*.

to conceal his magnificent physique. He completed his attire with a pair of faded and patched blue jeans and his oldest, most scuffed hunting boots. However, the way he was dressed did not allow him to carry his Colt.

Barely exceeding the five foot seven minimum height for male peace officers employed in Rockabye County, Cuchilo had the coppery brown, somewhat Mongoloid features and thick-bodied, powerful build of a *Kweharehnuh*, 'Antelope', Comanche. Although he was dressed in the same general fashion as the big blond, the long black wig he had on emphasized that he was a pure blood Indian. Like his companion, he was unarmed. Arrangements had been made, however, if the need for weapons should arise. What was more, even without having firearms, he and Brad possessed sufficient fighting skill to be a formidable proposition in a brawl.

'What do you reckon?' Brad asked, having watched the way in which his companion had been studying the various concessions they were passing.

'Going by the "slum" they've put out,' Cuchilo answered, 'most of the "joint men" are taking the manager's warning that the "grift" is off seriously.'

'I hate a feller who uses "in" words to show off how much he knows,' the big blond sniffed, although he was aware that 'slum' was the carnival term for cheap prizes and 'grift' meant to employ a cheating technique or device. Nodding towards half a dozen citizen's band radio sets prominently displayed among the other clearly much cheaper items offered by a dart throwing concession, he commented, 'But those c.b.'s look mighty expensive to be called slum.'

'They would be, *if* they were won. But you'd have to look for a long time before you find *anybody*, other than a "stick" working for the joint man, who's done it. The "marks", non-carnies like *you*, always wind up winning something a whole heap less valuable and not necessarily because the game's grifted, but because that's the way the rules are.'

'So there might not be any grifting going on then?'

'I wouldn't count on it. Not many of these "flat joint" owners can make more than a bare living when the grift is off and that's *not* what they've come to make. So I'm betting there'll be at least one who's doing a number and the rest waiting to see how he makes out with it. Which's why we're here. If we can nail him the first night, the rest will keep the grift off and no townie can cause trouble because he's been cheated. That's why they call this preventive law enforcement.'

'I'd never have guessed,' Brad said dryly, then indicated a concession they were approaching and at which a woman who had been walking a short distance in front of them was about to start playing. 'How about that one? It's offering cash prizes instead of slum.'

'You've been reading up on the subject,' Cuchilo accused. 'Trouble being, a "roll down joint" isn't grifted in a way that's easy to expose. Let's take a look, anyway.'

The concession about to be subjected to the deputies' scrutiny exhibited a sign with bright red lettering reading:

'FOLKIN'S PREMIER SIX BALL ROLL DOWN
Tonight's BIG SPECIAL—6 Balls For Only One Dollar!
CASH PRIZE OF $100.00 For A Score Of 6–8–10–32–34–36
Consolation Prize of $5.00 If Score Is 7–9–11–31–33–35'

For all the grandiloquent name, the stall was narrow and allowed only one competitor to participate at a time. About two foot in width, the sloping playing surface was six foot in length. Its edges were surrounded by a ledge about four inches high to prevent the hard rubber balls from falling off when they were rolled towards the thirty-six pockets arranged in a two foot square at the bottom of the incline. There were six holes for each number from one to six and no two with the same number were adjacent to one another. The six balls, each about two inches in diameter, rested in the chute of a triangular rack mounted on a swivel at the top of the slope and were held in place by a small lever.

'This is a game combining skill and chance, lady,' the tall, sharp-featured joint man was saying as the deputies strolled up and halted. He flickered a glance in their direction without stopping speaking, or showing any sign of suspecting their true status and purpose. 'Just pull the lever and turn the rack as the balls start to roll.'

Not much over five foot four in height, the woman's buxom

figure was made even more dumpy by a loose fitting, full length, multi-hued Hawaiian *mumu* dress. The garment clashed badly with upswept orange-red hair that was all too obviously a wig. Apparently the latter and the heavy make up plastered over what would otherwise have been pleasant features were intended to conceal any suggestion of her true age. Instead, they tended to imply she was older than she hoped to appear. Hitching the strap of an equally colourful—if far from complimentary—bag higher on her left shoulder, she carried out the instructions.

When describing how to play, the joint man had omitted to mention one important point. After the lever had been pulled to release the foremost ball, there was no way by which the contestant could prevent the others from following it immediately. However, as the rack turned smoothly on its pivot, they trickled away in slightly different directions instead of running down the board in single file. Rolling in such rapid succession, they began to settle in various holes in a way which rendered it exceedingly difficult for the average person to be able to watch each in turn and find out what was the value of the hole. What was more, on entering a pocket, the ball effectively concealed its number.

Brad was not an average person!

Two of the qualities which helped to make the blond giant—aided by the modern combat pistol shooting techniques and equipment—an even more effective gun fighter than his great-grandfather and others of that era were his superbly attuned reflexes and exceptionally keen eyesight. They allowed him to duplicate the feat of reading the printing on a gramophone record while the turntable was rotating which has been attributed to the deceased comedian W. C. Fields, boxer Jack Dempsey and various other sporting champions.[6]

Taking full advantage of his ability, Brad watched carefully. He felt sure that five of the balls had rolled into holes marked 'six' and the other entered one scoring four to give the contestant a total of thirty-four which qualified her for a one hundred dollars 'Grand' prize.

[6] See Chapter Twenty-Four, Page 212, *W. C. Fields, His Follies And Fortunes,* by Robert Lewis Taylor; Cassell & Co., Ltd., London, Toronto, Melbourne, Sydney, Wellington.

Glancing at Cuchilo, the big blond found he was staring intently at the bottom of the board. The Comanche deputy's face showed nothing of his thoughts. Nor did he speak or do anything to suggest he had reached a similar conclusion with regards to the woman's score.

'Here's a six, another six for twelve and a third making eighteen,' the joint man counted, before Brad could return his gaze and attempt to check on the value of the higher scoring unoccupied holes. Listing the balls swiftly in what appeared to be random grabs with alternate hands and tossing them against the bottom ledge, his movements ruined any chance of an onlooker being able to say for sure from which each was plucked. 'And six is twenty-four and six more, thirty. By golly though, lady, this *is* hard luck. The last's a five. One more, or less, and you'd've won a hundred dollars. As it is, you get a consolation prize of five. Better luck next time.'

Almost before he had finished speaking, the operator of the concession was offering a five dollar bill. Accepting it with a cheery word of thanks, the woman turned and walked away tucking it into her shoulder bag.

'How about you, gents?' the joint man asked, darting a malevolent scowl at the winner's departing back as she carried off the money instead of offering him an opportunity to reclaim it and setting the balls back on the rack as he was speaking. 'You saw how close the lady came and how easy it is to win.'

'Why sure,' Brad drawled, after having thrown a quick look at Cuchilo and received a negative head shake. 'But anything *that* easy doesn't have enough of a challenge to interest lil ole me.'

Having lost his original contestant and failed to attract either of the deputies, although he regarded them as nothing more than a couple of unproductive marks, the joint man swung his gaze to a young woman who was approaching. Despite his primary interest in her being as a potential customer, he decided she was well worth the look. She had shoulder long straight blonde hair and a very attractive face. A sleeveless black and white candy stripe blouse with an extreme décolleté and a pair of brief blue denim shorts set off a very curvaceous figure. Black cross-strap sandals and a sizeable brown leather shoulder bag completed an ensemble which was both eye-catching and revealing. However, ignoring the man's lascivious gaze and 'grind' explaining how easily winning numbers could be rolled in his game, she continued on her way.

***** *****

'Damn it, Sam!' Brad ejaculated, after he and the other deputy had walked a short distance from the roll down joint. 'I could have sworn the score was thirty-four.'

'It was,' Cuchilo declared, glancing over his shoulder. 'Five sixes and a four.'

'I *thought* I was right,' Brad stated, having concluded from his partner's lack of response that he had been mistaken about the score. 'I'll say one thing, though, that joint man's got good eyes.'

'It goes with the job,' Cuchilo replied. 'Every grifter working a roll down joint can add up quicker than a pocket calculator, but he doesn't just count on that. He knows his layout so well he can tell at a glance where every ball's gone and knows even before he starts to count whether or not he's got to "hype" the score up or down a point to save paying out a hundred.'

'I'm only a half smart lil ole Texas boy,' Brad pointed out. 'So you'll have to spread that out a mite thinner on the ground before I can see through it.'

'It plenty easy, paleface brother,' Cuchilo explained, speaking like Tonto addressing the Lone Ranger. 'All-um heap big win numbers even. So, when bad white-eye grifter see-um all balls had landed in even number holes, him know must hype the score by calling "five" instead of "four" to make-um score consolation prize.'

'I bet you don't even know how to speak *Comanche*,' Brad grunted and, realizing why his companion had kept quiet at the concession, went on more seriously, 'and I can see what you meant about the grift being hard to prove, the balls follow each other so closely that most folks couldn't watch every one of them dropping into its hole. Once they're there, they hide the numbers and, before you can look around to find out which are empty, he's taking them out in a way which stops you being able to say for sure where each came from. Once they're out, it's your word against his what they scored.'

327

'You read-um sign like *Nemuneh tuivitsi*, paleface brother,' Cuchilo praised, impressed by the way in which the big blond had grasped the situation. Losing the accent, he continued, 'And, should the mark complain when the word's been passed that the grift is off, he'll lift them out slowly enough for you to do the counting yourself. Which means there's no way you can make the grift stick.'

'So the only hope is to catch some other joint grifting and use it to have the manager make him lift the balls slowly all the time,' Brad suggested.

'That's the only——!' Cuchilo commenced. Pausing, he gazed ahead like a bird dog pointing at a bush in which a covey of bob-white quail were sheltering. 'I think we've got a live one, Brad!'

For a few seconds as he looked in the same direction, the big blond was at a loss to decide what had provoked such a definite comment. Then he saw that what he had taken for no more than an empty space between a 'ten in one'—which offered several acts including a sword swallower and a mind reader in a single large marquee—and a 'Hall Of Mirrors', was occupied by a small gambling concession. Comprised of a wheel on a table, behind which was a vertical board bearing a painted map of the United States, each State having a little electric light bulb in its centre, it was set back a short way from the midway almost as if to avoid attracting attention. Spinning the wheel, the portly, jovial faced and loudly dressed joint man caused the lights to flicker on and off in rotation until it stopped and only one remained lit.

'Why that one?' Brad inquired, watching the woman in the *mumu* approaching the concession and coming to a halt himself.

'Those canvasmen aren't standing around to enjoy breathing in all this good Texas air, or to watch the local girls going by,' Cuchilo replied, indicating several burly men wearing open necked shirts and jeans who were standing apparently in a casual fashion not too far from the game. 'And they're not toting those umbrellas because they're expecting rain.'

'You're leaving me behind again,' Brad confessed, having noticed and been puzzled by the furled umbrellas some of the carnival's canvasmen were holding. 'Tell me all, big chief.'

'The grift'll probably go this way,' Cuchilo obliged and, after making the explanation, suggested the means by which proof might be obtained, concluding, 'How about it, paleface brother?'

'I'm damned if I know how we got Manhattan Island off you Indians so cheaply,' the big blond answered sardonically, for his companion had not minimized the risks he would face while carrying out the scheme. 'But I'll give your fool notion a whirl. The County will pay for my hospitalization.'

***** *****

'I'll have me a buck on Texas!' Brad announced, teetering on his heels and slurring the words slightly as if somewhat the worse for drink. 'Give her a whirl, *amigo*.'

'One moment, sir,' the joint man boomed jovially, glancing from the thick wad of bills the big deputy was holding to the attractive blonde who came up. 'Perhaps this charming lady wishes to participate.'

'I'll take a dollar on Arizona,' the newcomer offered in a pleasant Texas drawl, without as much as a glance at Brad or the plump red head standing beyond him and betting on Wisconsin.

'Here we go!' the joint man said, spinning the wheel. 'Bet a dollar, win ten!'

'Damn the luck!' Brad ejaculated, with what appeared to be drunken annoyance, scowling at the light bulb which remained lit in the centre of New Mexico after the wheel stopped.

'Hold hard there, sir,' the man requested, as the blond giant made as if to turn away. Tossing down two ten dollar bills from an even thicker wad than the other had displayed, he went on, 'As this is the first night in your fair metropolis, I'll give you a sporting chance. Bet again and I'll let you select not one, but *two* States. The same goes for you lovely ladies, I might add.'

'Gimme Texas again,' Brad selected. 'And Montana.'

'Darn it! Once again I'm forced to be generous!' the joint man protested, tossing down two more ten dollar bills as Oregon won without having been chosen by any of his customers. 'For the paltry sum of five dollars, I will allow you to select not two— but *four* States.'

'You're on, god damn it!' Brad accepted, showing no sign of having noticed the owner surreptitiously controlling the wheel and lights by means of a button hidden under the table. 'Go to her again! I'll have Texas, Montana, Illinois and New Jersey.'

Neither of the women bet again. Instead, they stood and watched the wheel being twirled. It halted with the light of Alabama glowing. Another twenty dollars joined those already laid down by the joint man and he informed the big blond that the wager of another five would permit the selection of six States. Continuing to act in a completely convincing fashion, Brad accepted. When he displayed annoyance at losing again, a further twenty dollars were added to the pile and he was told that if he was willing to stake another ten, he could pick eight States.

'Hey though!' Brad growled in suspicious tones, after putting down his money and stating his choice. 'What do you-all keep reaching under the counter for?'

'Merely an accidental gesture, sir,' the joint man answered, his head making what could have been a slight jerk to the rear. 'But, to allay your suspicions, I'll go and stand at the other end and allow you to control the wheel yourself.'

Although the big blond appeared mollified, Cuchilo had told him there would almost certainly be at least two concealed controls and he was certain that the man could still stop the wheel at will from the new position. Furthermore, he had been warned by his partner that his question would provoke a signal for the waiting canvasmen to move closer in case they were needed. So, without offering to look, he guessed they were carrying out their instructions.

As the game continued, with the owner adding to the heap of bills at each succeeding win and allowing Brad to bet on even more States, but for increasing amounts, the audience changed. Two of the largest canvasmen were hovering just behind him and another four holding umbrellas formed a half circle which blocked the entrance from the midway. Apparently neither of the women had cared for being in close proximity with the newcomers. As the men arrived, they withdrew. Now the blonde was standing at the corner of the Ten In One and watching some of the entertainers trying to draw custom for the next show. At the other side of the gap, the red head stood as if contemplating whether to go into the Hall of Mirrors. Lounging against the side of a Dodgem car arcade, Cuchilo watched all that went on without making his interest obvious.

At last, Brad was betting on every State except Washington, Rhode Island and Connecticut and he sensed that the game would not be allowed to continue beyond that point. His suspicion was confirmed by the joint man insisting upon him putting the rest of the money he was holding against the not inconsiderable pile on the counter.

'Right on!' Brad agreed and, after setting the wheel in motion, went on, 'Only this time you come around here so you can't do *anything* to interfere with where the light stops.'

'Whatever you wish, sir,' the owner replied, still in the amiable tone. He raised his voice a little as he went on, 'But it looks like rain!'

Hearing the last words, the four canvasmen opened their umbrellas in such a way that the canopies blocked off the view of the concession from the midway. At the same moment, the owner began to scoop the money from the table so it fell into a wooden box placed on the floor for such a purpose and the other two of his helpers began to carry out their instructions. For his part, despite being aware of the response his comment would evoke and guessing what was coming, Brad was standing with his arms hanging by his sides.

'All right, you turkey!' growled the larger of the canvasmen, catching the blond's right wrist and bicep while his companion duplicated the action with the other arm .'You're coming——.'

Before the speaker could finish, or fully appreciate just how massive a bicep he had grasped, Brad went into action. Bowing his shoulders inwards, he straightened them while suddenly raising and spreading his arms. His acting had been so competently performed that his captors were taken completely unawares. Up to that point, they had believed themselves to be dealing with an unsuspecting, slightly drunk and rather overweight victim who could be hustled behind the Ten In One's marquee to be beaten up prior to removing him from the vicinity of the carnival. Instead, they were up against a man who was not only cold sober and exceptionally powerful, but who was anticipating their intentions.

Such was the big blond's strength that, aided by their being

331

unprepared for such a response, he flung the pair away from him like a hound dog shaking off flies. Nor were they able to prevent themselves crashing into and through the quartet holding the umbrellas on to the midway. Seeing what happened, more canvasmen showed signs of intending to participate. Letting out a startled exclamation, the joint man made a grab for the heavy wooden mallet which lay on a shelf under the table.

Even as Cuchilo started to go to his partner's assistance, a canvasman on each side of the gap displayed similar intentions; except that they intended to help the owner. Neither was to achieve his purpose.

Advancing from the front of the Ten In One, one of the canvasmen had to pass the attractive blonde. As he was doing so, without taking her right hand from inside the shoulder bag, she thrust her left foot between his legs and tripped him. Before he had sprawled to the ground, her hand emerged grasping a snub-nosed Colt Cobra revolver from the triggerguard of which was suspended a deputy sheriff's badge.

At the other side of the gap, the buxom 'redhead' moved into the path of the second carnival employee. In his haste, he tried to shove by her. Showing surprising speed, she swivelled at the hips and propelled her left elbow into his solar plexus. Such was the force of the impact that he went backwards a few steps, folding at the middle and gasping in a winded fashion, to sit down involuntarily. Without as much as a glance at him, she too brought her right hand from her bag and it proved to be holding a similar weapon and indication of official status. However, she immediately dipped her left hand into the bag to extract a Smith & Wesson ·41 Magnum revolver which was also embellished with a deputy's badge.

'Here Sam!' the woman called, tossing the weapon to the approaching deputy who caught it deftly and turned it to menace a couple of canvasmen who were coming from the arcade.

Remembering Cuchilo's warning that the joint man would almost certainly have some form of weapon available. which could also pass as a legitimate adjunct of his work, Brad did not hesitate on seeing what he was doing. Bringing up his right leg, the big blond kicked over the table with such vigour that it struck the owner and sent him reeling backwards.

'Peace officers here!' the 'red head' was shouting, as Brad turned ready to continue defending himself against the six canvasmen if the need should arise. 'Everybody stand fast.'

***** *****

'Well now,' Brad drawled, eyeing the manager of the carnival sardonically, having gone with the other deputies at his request to his mobile office. 'I can't say for *certain* that the joint man intended to cheat me on that last spin, but he'd got the means to do it and tried to sic the canvasmen on me when I asked him to come where he couldn't use either the button or the lever to stop the wheel.'

'They *might* only have meant to take Brad off the lot and ask him not to cause trouble,' the buxom woman continued, holding her wig and proving to have blonde hair. 'But, even though I believe in fairies and Father Christmas, I don't really buy that.

Having been making his rounds to check his orders were being carried out by the joint men, the manager had arrived on the scene quickly. He had found the peace officers had everything under control. Like their male counterparts. Women Deputies Alice Fayde, who had red hair under the wig supplied by Sergeant Haynes, and Joan Hilton, might have been disguised so they could carry out their duty as back ups in case of trouble, but they all had the means to establish their identities and official status. Ordering the canvasmen to disperse and telling the joint man to come along, the manager requested that the peace officers accompanied him to the privacy of his living quarters. Leaving the grifter with his assistant managers, he had taken the deputies into the office section for what he sensed would be anything but a friendly interview.

'I passed the word the grift was off,' the manager answered. 'And I was looking for anybody who hadn't heard, or wasn't doing it, when the fuss started. What are you going to charge him with?'

'Nothing,' Joan replied, being the senior deputy present. 'But he'd best be long gone from Rockabye County by noon tomorrow.'

'I'll see he is,' the manager promised.

333

'And tell Mr. Folkin and any of his good buddies on the roll downs to lift the balls slowly enough to let the marks count the scores themselves,' Joan went on. 'He hyped the score on *me*, but I'm not holding a grudge so long as *you* make sure none of the County's law abiding, tax paying citizens get shortcaked that way.'

'You sound like you've been "with it",' the manager commented, meaning the woman had worked with a carnival.

'I have and so has Sam,' Joan admitted. 'So we'll be looking around all the time you're here. It's what the sheriff calls preventive law enforcement.'

PART TWELVE

Bunduki in

THE MCHAWI'S *POWERS*

As I mentioned earlier, one of my favourite authors was Edgar Rice Burroughs and I consider him to be the greatest action-escapism-adventure writer the world has ever known.[1] *Of all the characters he created, none caught my attention as much as his best known, Tarzan of the Apes. I must admit, however, that I did not start reading his books until after I had seen the first of the Johnny Weissmuller's series of Tarzan movies.*[2] *I immediately discovered there was a vast difference between the character E.R.B. had created and the way he was portrayed on the screen. Instead of being the illiterate, far from fluent or loquacious white savage who travelled through the jungle by swinging on a sequence of conveniently positioned vines,*[3] *Tarzan in the books was the son of an English peer who—although raised by the 'Great Apes' after his parents' death—had taught himself to read and write before discovering others of his kind existed. Then, his true identity having been established, he became a cultured and well-educated gentleman without losing touch with his primitive way of life.*[4] *I found the stories interesting and entertaining, but felt that some of the possibilities for action which were presented had been neglected. Jane was, I considered, never exploited to the full in any of the stories.*

---

[1] Edgar Rice Burroughs also wrote science fiction, Westerns and detective novels.

[2] Tarzan had previously been played by Elmo Lincoln, Gene Pollar, P. Dempsey Tabler, James Pierce (who married E.R.B.'s daughter, Joan), and Frank Merrill. He was later played by Buster Crabbe, Herman Brix (who later changed his movie-name to Bruce Bennett), Glenn Morris, Lex Barker, Gordon Scott, Denny Miller, Jock Mahoney (television's Range Rider), Mike Henry and Ron Ely.

[3] There is no suggestion that Tarzan uses vines as a means of travelling

With my career as a writer in the Western field firmly estab-lished and the Rockabye County series finally launched, I started wondering how I could branch out. Obtaining a copy of Gabe Essoe's definitive work, Tarzan of the Movies, *suggested a way of doing so. I had the plot for a Tarzan story worked out and I wrote to Edgar Rice Burroughs Inc., at Tarzana, California, re-questing permission to produce it as a tribute to E.R.B.'s memory. I was refused courteously, with the explanation that it had been his instruction for no other author to be allowed to take over his character.*

Although it appeared the matter was closed, I never forgot the idea of the story. Then coming across a copy of Philip Jose Far-mer's magnificent Tarzan Alive, A Definitive Biography Of Lord Greystoke, *I saw a way in which I might be able to put it to use as I hated to see a good plot going to waste. Contacting Edgar Rice Burroughs Inc. again, I explained how I would like to intro-duce Tarzan's adopted son and adoptive great granddaughter. This time, to my delight, the permission was granted with the proviso that Tarzan was not brought into the story.*

And that is how James Allenvale 'Bunduki' Gunn and Dawn Drummond-Clayton were born.

Since then, partly as the result of the publication of Bunduki *in the United States, I was refused permission to mention the family links with Tarzan in future books despite generous sug-gestions made by me and despite the fact that I had always made a point of referring to various of E.R.B.'s books in footnotes. But as Bunduki and Dawn are my characters, I have decided to con-tinue the series without the Tarzan tie-in and the next title.* Fearless Master of the Jungle, *will be appearing shortly. I regret having to take this step but there was no other solution.*

---

through the treetops in any of the twenty-three books Edgar Rice Burroughs wrote about him.

[4] An even greater divergence between book and film occurs with Max Brand's *Destry Rides Again*. In the book, having been 'framed' and sent to prison for a crime he did not commit, Destry comes back in search of revenge on the men he holds responsible. The 'Destry' in the movie is the son of a famous town-taming marshal who, although an expert at using one, doesn't believe in wearing a gun. The 1939 version starred James Stewart and Marlene Dietrich and was re-made in 1955 as *Destry* with Audie Murphy and Mari Blanchard in the leading roles.

As has been requested by a number of readers, the following story is set in Africa prior to Dawn and Bunduki being transported to Zillikian. I must apologize to those of you who are Dawn's fans for the small part she plays in it. This will be rectified, I promise, in a future book.[5]

[5] See: Part Two, Dawn Drummond-Clayton in 'Death to Simba Nyeuse', *J.T.'S Ladies*.

THE *MCHAWI'S* POWERS

'Good *pombe* for a bunch of *nugu!*' Old M'Bili snorted, his time-wrinkled black face showing indignation at the thought. 'I know a much better way to use it.'

'I don't doubt *that*,' retorted James Allenvale Gunn, who was known throughout much of Africa, Asia, Australia, Europe and the New World as 'Bunduki', the Swahili word meaning a hand-held firearm of any kind. He spoke his companion's native tongue, Wa-Kamba, fluently and this was only one of a dozen tribal languages in which he was more or less conversant. 'You'd probably drink a gallon or so and decide to come out to capture them with your bare hands. Except that you'd fall asleep for a week before you set off and wake up with a hangover that would make you even worse tempered than usual for the next month.'

As was the case with his look-alike cousin. Deputy Sheriff Bradford Counter of Rockabye County, Texas, Bunduki's six foot three height, tremendous muscular development of a 'Mr. Universe', golden blond hair and tanned, exceptionally handsome features were inherited from their paternal great-grandfather.[1] He had on a wide brimmed bush-hat with a leopardskin band around its crown. A tightly rolled, scarlet and blue silk scarf was knotted about his throat. Open at the neck and with the sleeves rolled up to display powerful biceps and forearms, his khaki drill shirt was tucked into matching trousers which ended in the calf high legs of brown hunting boots. Hanging in its well-made sheath on the left side of the belt encircling his slender waist was a massive Randall Model 12 'Smithsonian' bowie knife with a

---

[1] For the benefit of new readers, details of James Allenvale 'Bunduki' Gunn's background and special qualifications are given in Appendix Ten.

concave ivory handle, but he was otherwise unarmed.

'Getting drunk and going to sleep is about all that's left to do at nights when you get to be my age.' the old Wa-Kamba pointed out, showing no sign of being abashed by the accusation. Small, grey-haired, but still sprightly and sturdily built, he wore a red, brimless felt *tarbush* with a buffalo head cap badge, clean and neatly pressed khaki bush-jacket and shorts and a pair of sandals. There was a bandoleer of ammunition around his waist and he carried a large calibre double barrelled rifle slung over his right shoulder. At the end of his comment. he glared around and bellowed in the variety of Swahili which is the *lingua franca* throughout much of Africa,[2] 'Pour it on the ground, in the cage, or on the wheels, you *shenzi*,[3] but not down your throat.'

Although the vehicle which had towed it there was nowhere to be seen, an open trailer was standing on the banks of a small stream. Half a dozen Africans were gathered around it and, if any uninformed observer had come upon them, he would have been surprised and puzzled by what they were doing. They were busily engaged in splashing quantities of the native brewed beer known as '*pombe*' on the ground, the tyres, bed and floor of the wire mesh cage which the trailer was carrying .

All around the area of activity as far as the eye could see was a typical expanse of what white settlers had jokingly and, generally, lovingly referred to as the M.M.B.A.A.: the Miles and Miles of Bloody Awful Africa. It was comprised of rolling, grass covered savannah speckled by occasional clumps of bushes and trees, with knob-like *kopjes*[4] rising here and there as if to break the monotony. While the region was not as thickly populated by wild animals as it was before Ambagasali was opened up by white settlers, having been given the status of a national park in good time, it was saved from human occupancy. What was more, despite some diminution, the Ambagasali Wild Life Reserve could still claim to be able to offer as many kinds and numbers of

[2] Derived from Ki-Swahili, a very complicated language native to Zanzibar and the coastal belt of East Africa, the *lingua franca* was referred to as 'Up-Country Swahili' or, derisively, 'Ki-Settler'
[3] '*Shenzi*': Up-Country Swahili name for a unrefined or uncivilized, barbarous. makeshift person or object.
[4] '*Kopje*': a rocky outcrop, from the Afrikaans word meaning a peak.

creatures as in any other such area on the continent. It was as a result of this proliferation that the unusual activities on the bank of the stream were being carried out.

As was the case with every such sanctuary, there was a limit to how many animals could live inside its boundaries without destroying the habitàt. Natural predation could rarely maintain the balance, so the various populations had to be controlled by artificial means. Appointed as Chief Warden by the ruler of Ambagasali, Prince Simba Nyeuse,[5] Bunduki was making preparations to carry out the second of this kind of task since he had taken office a week earlier.

Because poaching of leopards had reduced the numbers which would otherwise have preyed upon them, a band of Ambagasali baboons—the 'nugu' to which M'Bili had referred, although the correct Swahili word would have been 'nyani'—had increased to the point where a reduction had become a matter of urgency. They had started raiding the *shambas* of a village just beyond the boundary of the Reserve, doing great damage to the growing crops which they ate. Although as yet no official complaint had been made by the villagers, Bunduki had considered it advisable to act without delay. Once protests were made, they could be used by vote-seeking political opportunists to support demands that the area's status as an animal sanctuary be revoked and the land thrown open to human occupancy.

Shrewd, progressive and well-liked, Simba Nyeuse was a stout supporter of the Reserve. Aware that there were those in his Government who would like to gain acclaim by having its land made available to the voters, he had laid down rules for its operation which were calculated to ensure it would continue to exist. Being a practical conservationist, rather than one whose views were based upon conforming to a modern trend of 'animals first' as a means of acquiring acclaim and financial benefits, the Prince accepted the need for controlling the population. With this and the political situation in mind, he had stipulated—and Bunduki was in complete accord with him—that where possible any animals it became necessary to cull should be put to some kind of

[5] *'Simba Nyeuse'*: Swahili for Black Lion, literally Lion Black.

340

gainful use. There were religious *tabus* which prevented the meat from any baboons that were killed from being presented for consumption by the local population, which would otherwise have avoided waste, but two reputable zoological gardens had asked to be allowed to purchase sufficient of them to establish breeding colonies and this would allow the reduction of the band to be carried out in an acceptable manner.

Although the blond giant had not been informed of the baboons' depredations, he had felt sure that there would be no difficulty in capturing the specimens required by the zoos. The family into which he had been adopted, following the murder of his parents by Mau Mau terrorists while he was a very young child, were acknowledged as the world's greatest authorities on animals and survival in the wilds. All their vast store of knowledge, which had been gained under far more exacting and dangerous conditions than sitting in the safety of a Land Rover in a National Park where the animals were used to the presence of human beings, had been passed on to him and he had shown a great capacity for retaining what he was taught. Something he had been told about the habits of baboons had led him to assume the task would be easy.

While he had not brought one very important ingredient of the far from sophisticated equipment he required with him, Bunduki had been able to procure it on the spot. He had known that he would need more help than could be supplied by M'Bili, the three young Ambaga tribesmen they were training as game scouts and his adoptive cousin, Dawn Drummond-Clayton—who was spending her vacation helping him settle into his duties. However, he had not doubted extra assistance could be obtained locally. Not only was he backed by the authority of Prince Simba Nyeuse, but he had already demonstrated his prowess in a way which he considered would have put him in the villagers' good books. Summoned to deal with a pair of young lions which had taken to living off the villagers' goats and cattle, he captured the first. It was now in a lightweight travelling cage at his base-camp and when Dawn, who was attending to the matter helped by two of the Ambaga trainee game scouts, brought in the other, they would be transferred to an area where they would be compelled to hunt more natural and acceptable prey.[6]

Much to the blond giant's surprise, he had found a marked reluctance towards co-operating from the villagers. Although the men who were selected had accompanied him, it had been apparent that their hearts were not in the task. As they were not showing the eagerness he would have expected over being involved in an interesting, novel and, as they were to be well paid from public funds, lucrative as well as beneficial enterprise, he had asked M'Bili and the three Ambagas to try to discover what was causing the reaction.

'Have you found out what's wrong with the villagers, *mzee*?' Bunduki inquired, using the Swahili word for an elderly person as he knew his good friend did not care for such a reference to age.

'No,' M'Bili replied with a sniff. 'But, if you want the opinion of an *old man*. you'll find there's witchcraft behind it.'

Having been born and raised in Africa, the blond giant neither laughed at nor dismissed the suggestion as ludicrous. He knew all too well that, as it had been since the earliest days of what was then known as the 'Dark Continent', witchcraft was still a very potent and active force as far as Africans were concerned. All the efforts during years of white rule and on the part of the governments which had come to power after the various countries had gained independence had not succeeded in eradicating the belief in its efficacy among the majority of the population. So he was aware that the villagers would not give him their willing assistance in any task which might infringe one of the local tabus of witchcraft.

'Is that true, Shotu?' Bunduki asked the senior of the Ambagas, who had remained to learn the technique of baboon catching, which he intended to employ, speaking the tribal dialect almost as fluently as he had used Wa-Kamba.

'I'm afraid it may be, Mr. Gunn.' was the reply in excellent English. 'But, if it is, I have no idea what it is all about. These Gasali villagers are very secretive where their primitive tribal

---

[6] What the result of Dawn Drummond-Clayton's hunt was is told in Part Two, 'Death to Simba Nyeuse', *J.T.'s Ladies*.

superstitions are concerned.'

'So Abu and Kioti aren't likely to know anything about it either?' Bunduki guessed, referring to the other two trainee game scouts.

'I would be inclined to doubt it,' Shotu declared, just a trifle smugly. 'Although, unlike myself, they have not attended college, they have been to mission school and are Christians as I am and don't believe in such things as witchcraft.'

'See if you can find out if that's what is involved, will you,' Bunduki requested, knowing that not only his present assignment but his future relations with the villagers could be affected adversely if he was acting against some tabu with which he was unacquainted.

'I will,' Shotu promised, but he sounded neither hopeful nor enthusiastic.

Tall, slender in build, with the reddish-brown pigmentation and delicate features suggestive of Nilotic origins,[7] which contrasted with the dusky-black, generally shorter and invariably more thickset physique of the Bantu-descended Gasali villagers,[8] the young man had had a good formal European-style education and a Christian upbringing. Yet, while he tended to look down upon the more backward members of his nation, if in a less objectionable and snobbish way than some who had acquired similar backgrounds, he still could not throw off the inborn and culturally inspired beliefs of generations where such a vital force as witchcraft might be involved. In fact, having heard numerous stories of how lethally effective the possession of such powers could be, his acceptance of the Christian faith and the teachings of the college he had attended could not dispel the thought that he might be treading on *very* dangerous ground if he should display too much curiosity over whatever local beliefs might have been transgressed.

'Huh!' M'Bili grunted, as the young Ambaga walked away.

[7] Nilotic: possessing the physical characteristics of the people native to the Nile basin. The Masai of East Africa are probably the best known examples of this ethnic group.
[8] Bantu: pertaining to one of the many Negroid tribes such as the Zulu, Bechuana, Xhosa, Damara, Swahili, Kikuyu, Wa-Kamba, etc., of Central and Southern Africa.

'Much good *that* will do!'

'I haven't heard anything more constructive from *you*,' Bunduki objected, with the candour of one who was addressing an old and respected friend who he knew would take no offence. 'Are you saying we are up against witchcraft?'

'It doesn't worry *me* if we are,' M'Bili declared, exuding the lofty disdain of a Wa-Kamba warrior who had served as a sergeant with the King's African Rifles during World War II and through the fight against Communist terrorists in Malaya. Not only was he a Moslem but had little fear of witchcraft unless it was being practised by a member of his own nation. 'I heard some of them saying we wouldn't catch the *nugu*, but none would bet on it and *that's* unusual. Every Gasali I've met was always ready to gamble on anything.'

'Perhaps *your* reputation had already reached here before you arrived,' the big blond suggested with a grin, being aware of the Gasali tribesman's proclivity for indulging in games of chance.

'Nobody ever *accused* me of cheating,' the old man protested with what sounded like a mixture of injured innocence and righteous indignation.

'That could be because nobody ever *caught* you at it,' Bunduki countered, remembering the instruction in how to cheat at various gambling games which he had received from his companion. 'Anyway, let's get on with it. When they see how the baboons behave, they'll soon decide we have the right kind of *dawa*[9] to deal with whatever of their customs we might be offending.'

Seeing that the men had finished dousing the trailer and ground around it with the *pombe*, which was the name given to the locally brewed beer, the blond giant told them to place the remaining liquid in the open containers on the floor of the cage. Leaving the sliding door open when this was done, he took them to a place of concealment which also offered a point of vantage. Warning them to keep quiet, particularly when their quarry came into view, he settled down to await the next developments.

***** *****

'Here they come!' M'Bili hissed, after almost two hours had gone by and the sun was sinking low over the western horizon.

[9] *'Dawa'*: Swahili word meaning 'medicine'.

Looking in the direction indicated by the old Wa-Kamba chief game scout, Bunduki repeated his order for complete silence. He noticed that, although they still showed signs of being worried and sceptical, all of them were continuing to obey his instructions. Since taking up their position, there had been none of the chatter which normally went on when a group of Africans were together without some form of activity to keep them occupied. Now those who had fallen asleep were awakened without noise or disturbance. Satisfied that there was nothing to spoil his preparations, he gave his attention to the reason for his being in the area. What he saw increased his belief that he would have no difficulty in carrying out the necessary culling.

Coming in size between the chacma (*Papio Ursinus*) and smaller western baboons (*P. Papio*). the Ambagasali species (*P. Ambagasalii*) looked like a cross between the former and the forest dwelling drill (*P. Leucophaeus*). It had the chacma's dark olive brown colouration and less elevated head carriage, but its hindquarters showed the large bright blue, violaceous and scarlet calliosities—in the male only—and tiny stump of a tail peculiar to the drill. Their habits were not noticeably different from those of the other plains-dwelling baboons and even when they had been hard hunted, which did not apply in this case, shared the trait which the blond giant intended to utilize as the means of reducing their numbers.

Having spent the day foraging for food somewhere within the fifteen square miles they claimed as their territory, the troop was returning to their sleeping area on the steep, bare rocky walls of a near by *kopje*. After the fashion of their kind, despite being at least a hundred strong, they were moving with a strictly enforced, almost militaristic style of discipline and formation. In the centre strode the dominant males with the females which were on heat or carrying babies and the young close to them. They were surrounded by the rest of the females and juveniles. Ahead, on the flanks and to the rear were the socially inferior males. They were the scouts and had the responsibility for raising the alarm if any kind of danger should occur to threaten the safety of the troop.

Making its way towards the stream, at the open area clear of the thick bushes which coated most of the banks and could har-

345

bour predators waiting to attack while the troop were engaged in quenching their thirsts before retiring for the night, the leading scout caught sight of the trailer. Coming to a halt, it gave its barking alarm signal. Instantly, the orderly advance erupted into purposeful and far from disorganized action. With their subordinates scattering from their path, the half a dozen dominant males dashed forward and those of inferior status followed to help fight off whatever intruder was ahead. The females, juveniles and very young bunched together and stood ready to flee to the safety of the *kopje* if the need arose.

Knowing the efficiency of the baboons' social structure, which allowed the species to survive upon the open plains, Bunduki had expected such a development and was neither surprised nor concerned when it took place. He was confident that, having ascertained the trailer posed no threat, the dominant males would conclude it was safe to resume the interrupted march to the stream and, unless anything happened to disturb them, bring his plan to fruition.

Sure enough, on detecting no sign of movement from the cause of the alarm and, being upwind, prevented from picking up any warning odours, the dominant males began to move forward. They were still alert and wary, but their confidence was increasing. Once they were completely satisfied there was no danger, they would signal for the rest of the troop to follow them.

In spite of his belief in the method he was employing, Bunduki could not help feeling a trifle apprehensive as he watched the troop resuming its advance. He had seen it work with chacma, western and yellow baboons and his adopted father had claimed it to be equally effective where drills and their forest inhabiting cousins, mandrills,[10] were concerned. However he had had no experience with *P. Ambagasalii* and, although they showed little difference in their behaviourism patterns from the other plains-dwelling species, there was a chance that they had not developed the one vitally important taste upon which his plan depended. He knew that, particularly now that it seemed there was some

[10] The mandrill, *Papio Mandrillus*, differs most noticeably from the drill by the face of the full grown male being bright scarlet and blue, with deep ridges and an orange beard. Its buttocks, however, are bright scarlet and violaceous, but have no blue.

witchcraft or local custom involved, he would never again be able to obtain the co-operation of the villagers in the event of failure and his ability to do so throughout the country would also suffer. In fact it could be said that his future career as the Chief Warden of the Ambagasali Wild Life Reserve hung in the balance.

Nearer and nearer to the trailer stalked the dominant males, the largest and most powerful of them a few feet in the lead. Although there was no movement from the strange object which was blocking the path to the watering place, it was still displaying caution. Taking each step with its mane of hair bristling to convey the impression it was even larger and more dangerous, it was ready for instant flight at the slightest suggestion of hostility on the alien thing's part.

To the blond giant, it seemed that the big baboon was deliberately delaying the moment upon which would depend the success or failure of his scheme. Nor, for all his appreciation of the correctness of its behaviour, could he produce the usual sympathy it would have evoked by such cautious hesitancy, when his own career was hanging in the balance.

'Come on, you ugly, scar-faced, evil-looking old bastard!' Bunduki ordered, without realizing that the words were just loud enough to reach one keen pair of ears. 'The bloody thing can't move and isn't going to hurt you.'

'Us *old men* have more sense than to take foolish chances when there's no need for them,' M'Bili whispered, but still managed to convey a feeling of superiority which could only have been produced out of the wisdom acquired by age. 'That's why we've lived as long as we have.'

'Is that so?' the blond giant challenged, also *sotto voce*, glaring with what appeared to be savagery at the man who had carried him to safety during the attack, which had cost his parents their lives and had taken a major part in the pursuit which had avenged them. 'Well, if he's no wiser than a certain old Machakos[11] goat-eater I know, we've as good as caught all of them. Come on, damn you, make up your mind!'

'That's what's wrong with the world,' M'Bili complained,

[11] Machakos: Kenya town which is in the heart of the Wa-Kamba tribal territory.

knowing the banter was helping to relieve his companion's tension as he too was aware of how much was at stake. 'You *mutu kijana*[12] not only don't have enough respect for age and wisdom, you haven't any patience either. Let a *mzee* show you how to do it. Come on, good old *nugu* friend. You know it's safe to take a look and you'll like what you find.'

'If that works,' Bunduki breathed, 'this *mutu kijana* will buy a certain *mzee* all the *pombe* he can drink.'

Almost as if it had overheard and wished to repay the support its actions had received from another elderly person, the big, scar-faced male rushed forward as the blond giant concluded the offer. It was equally ready to attack or flee should the strange object make a movement calling for one or the other response. Before either course could be required of it, the male's keen nostrils were assailed by an odour which brought it to a halt. Lowering its head, it sniffed curiously for a moment and then began to lick eagerly at the ground.

Having followed on their leader's heels, the other dominant males displayed a similar interest in the smell and taste of the pombe which had been spilled around the trailer. In fact, such was their enthusiasm that they ignored first the subordinate males, then the juveniles and females who came up to investigate. Nor did it take long for one of them to climb a wheel and discover the bounty which was waiting inside the cage. Entering, it began to drink noisily from one of the containers. The sound of its delighted gulps, belches and lip smacking brought more and more members of the troop to join in.

The effects of the very potent liquor rapidly began to take a hold on the baboons. By the time ten minutes had gone by, all the older animals were in an advanced stage of intoxication. Some reared up and tried unsuccessfully to fight with their closest neighbours. Others stumbled and staggered from the cage, allowing room for those which had not yet managed to reach the *pombe* to do so. One took a flying leap from the trailer, landed in an undignified sprawl and went to sleep. Reeling after a wobbly-legged male which had contrived to return to the ground, a

[12] *'Mutu kijana'*: Swahili term meaning 'young men', but literally 'men young'.

drunken young female knocked him down and made a determined attempt to mount him. As the male squealed in outraged protest, but was too befuddled to resist, another female dragged off his assailant and they rolled over briefly in a tussle before subsiding helplessly in each other's arms.

Having seen the kind of hilarity elicited from other Africans over the antics which ensued when primates had on previous occasions been induced to participate in a drunken orgy as a prelude to their capture, Bunduki had been interested in his present company's reactions. Even though M'Bili had witnessed similar events many times, he still guffawed heartily at what he was seeing. Forgetting his usual prim, sober and correct demeanour, Shotu was soon howling with unrestrained merriment. However, it was to the Gasali villagers to whom the blond giant directed most of his attention.

When the baboons had come into sight, the local men had been restless and darted nervous glances about them as if expecting something unpleasant or frightening to take place. They had watched without comprehension as the dominant male had discovered the *pombe*. Then, as they began to appreciate what was happening, the prospect appealed to their gamey and unrefined sense of humour. One after another, they had burst into laughter. Soon each was pointing out the pieces of behaviour he found most amusing and the attempted rape of the young male provoked such a hearty response that tears of merriment poured down almost every villager's cheeks. Watching them, the big blond decided that for the moment at least they had forgotten their earlier misgivings over the work they were engaged upon.

At the end of an hour, there was not a single fully grown baboon awake and many of the juveniles had also contrived to join their elders in the drunken stupor. What was more, towards the end, even a few of the youngsters had been able to get into the cage and there had been sufficient *pombe* left to cause them to succumb to its potency.

'That's that,' Bunduki stated with satisfaction, coming to his feet. Looking to where the trainee game scout was mopping away tears with a large silk handkerchief, he went on, 'Well, Shotu, what do you think now?'

349

'I didn't believe it would work when you told us how you planned to capture them,' the Ambaga confessed frankly, making an effort and regaining his composure. Having no desire to let the still laughing villagers discover he had shared their enjoyment, he continued, 'Shall I go and fetch the lorry, Mr. Gunn?'

'If you would,' the big blond answered. 'Come on, M'Bili. Let's go down and sort out the ones who'll be going to the zoos.'

'I wish *he'd* been so sure it wouldn't work that he'd taken a bet on it,' the old Wa-Kamba commented, watching Shotu walking away. 'But, anyway, I seem to remember something a certain *mutu kijana* said he'd do if that a scar-faced old one did as the *mzee* asked.'

'I hoped you'd forgotten *that*,' Bunduki sighed, accompanying the words with a well simulated look of disgust. 'All right! All right! I'll never hear the end of it if I don't keep my word. But I just hope I've enough money in the bank to pay for all that bloody *pombe* you'll be guzzling.'

*****   *****

'That's not *Memsaab* Dawn's *gari*,'[13] M'Bili decided, staring across the savannah in the direction in which the party had come from the village.

'No,' Bunduki agreed, then nodded towards the villagers. They had gathered together when one of their number had seen and drawn the rest's attention to a Land Rover which was approaching. Although up to that moment they had been in high spirits, there was already a marked change in their demeanour. 'But they know who it belongs to and, going by the way they're acting, they don't like or they're scared of whoever it might be.'

Aided by the effects of the *pombe*, the work of culling had been completed without any difficulties or a resumption of the villagers' earlier reluctance towards helping. They had not mentioned what had caused it, nor had Bunduki offered to make inquiries. Not only did he consider it would be unwise to show interest in their private affairs, particularly if some form of witchcraft was involved, he had wanted everything finished before darkness descended.

Normally, to have attempted to handle even a half grown

[13] *'Gari'*: the Swahili term for a wheeled vehicle no matter what kind.

juvenile male baboon would have been a very hazardous undertaking and to have gone among such a large troop suicidal. Attacking as a group, the big dominant males were sufficiently strong and aggressive enough to tear a leopard or a man to pieces with their grasping hand-like front feet and powerful, well equipped jaws. However, having imbibed not wisely but too well, none of them were in any condition to resist when Shotu arrived with the big lorry which had towed the trailer from the village. It was then hidden to prevent it from frightening the animals away. With the sturdy collapsible wire mesh cages it carried assembled, the blond giant pointed out the members of the troop he wanted to remove. Not one had woken up while being placed in the cages and the task had been completed without interruption.

Knowing how delicately the social structure of a baboon troop was balanced, Bunduki chose with the intention of disrupting it. His choice included all the dominant males and such senior females as had babies or young infants dependant upon them, in addition to enough of the others to create breeding groups in the two zoos. Deprived of the control previously exerted by their superiors, the largest of the subordinate males would contest the leadership. Each would break away from the main body with as many followers as it could acquire, then set about establishing its own territory, scattering over a larger area than the original terrain they had occupied. Even if one or more led its party from the Reserve, or tried to continue the crop-raiding, lacking the cohesive guidance and sheer weight of numbers which had allowed the big troop to do so with impunity, they would easily be driven away by the villagers

There was another benefit which the blond giant was confident would accrue from the scattering of the remaining baboons. The region given over to the Reserve had always been noted for the number of leopards which inhabited it One of the things which had helped the poachers to take such a toll of them was their taste for the flesh of *Papio Ambagasalii*. No matter how many were killed, there had always been others attracted by the proliferation of their favourite food. These in turn would be trapped before they could effect any reduction in the size of the troop. With its remaining members scattered in smaller bands, the spotted carnivores would also be compelled to spread out instead of congregating in a clearly defined and comparatively restricted area. Consequently, in addition to encouraging a more equitable balance between the predators and the hunted to be resumed, this would make the poachers' task of locating their quarry more difficult and increase the game scouts' chance of catching them in the act.

'My old eyes aren't what they used to be,' M'Bili went on, after a few seconds. 'But I think it belongs to the *Wa-Hindi*[14] who runs the *duka* in the village.'

'You *could* be right, *mzee*,' Bunduki admitted, contriving to sound as if he thought such a contingency unlikely, although he too had identified the approaching vehicle as the Land Rover he had seen under a lean-to at the rear of Ghamba Patel's Bar and General Store. 'How about telling me what he's after?'

'I can only do miracles once every other week,' the Wa-Kamba stated calmly. 'So I'm not going to waste this fortnight when we can learn the answer soon enough by just waiting for it.'

Giving an apparently disdainful sniff at the excuse, the big blond turned his gaze to the vehicle. As it drew closer, he could make out that there were two men—a very large Asian and a much shorter African—on the front seat, with at least two more male passengers in the back. He discovered that his summation was correct when it came to a stop half way between where he, M'Bili and Shotu were standing and the now clearly perturbed villagers.

Two fairly tall and brawny Gasalis jumped from the rear of the Land Rover, going immediately towards the front passenger door. They were far better dressed than any of the villagers, wearing respectively a bright red and green and an orange and white striped shirt which clashed badly with their electric blue trousers and two-tone white and ox-blood red shoes. Each had a long hunting knife hanging sheathed on his waist belt. There was an arrogant swagger to their movements. Yet, despite the disdainful way in which they glanced around, they displayed a remarkable respect for the person they hurried to help alight.

[14] '*Wa-Hindi*': derogatory Swahili name for an Asian whether of Indian or Pakistani origins.

Going by first impressions, there did not appear to be any reason for the garishly dressed pair's subservient behaviour. Clad in a dirty old khaki army overcoat which was now buttonless and hung open, the man they were assisting was of medium height, skinny and of a considerable age. White haired, apart from his piercing dark eyes, his face was crumpled and wrinkled like a walnut. Under the coat, he was naked except for a filthy loincloth and had a thick necklace of small animal skulls and bones suspended around his scrawny neck. He was grasping a fly-switch made from the tail of a wildebeest in his claw-like right hand. Rancid lion fat glistened on his body, its odour carrying to Bunduki's keen nostrils. Yet, for all his unprepossessing appearance, he carried himself with a truculent demeanour and his attitude towards his helpers seemed more impatiently demanding than grateful for their aid. Without as much as a glance in the blond giant's direction, he started to walk with surprising vigour towards the huddled and once more nervous-looking villagers.

'Who is he, Shotu,' Bunduki inquired.

'I believe his name is Wakata, Mr. Gunn,' the Ambaga replied, looking worried. 'He is the local *mchawi*.'

The answer confirmed the big blond's suspicions. There were two Swahili names for a witch-doctor. If one was called a *mganga*, it meant he was a good man employing primitive methods and remedies, often quite successfully, for the benefit of those who sought his services. A *mchawi* was a very different proposition. In fact, he was what the average European always expected a witch-doctor to be. The *mchawi* dabbled in evil, especially at putting on curses which could also produce surprisingly effective results.

Before Bunduki could continue the questioning, the owner of the *duka* and Land Rover opened the right front door and extricated himself, with some difficulty it seemed, from behind the steering wheel. Just over six foot in height from his grubby off-white turban to his sandal-covered otherwise bare feet, Ghamba Patel was fat to the point of grossness. Nor was his bulk improved by a violently-hued Hawaiian *aloha* shirt which hung outside rumpled grey flannels that ended just above his ankles. Clean shaven, he had what might have passed as a hearty and jovial face if it had not been for his eyes. Muddy-brown and close-set, they were cold and would never meet another person's gaze for more than a couple of seconds at a time. On first having met him, the blond giant had thought that if they did not indicate the possession of a shifty and untrustworthy disposition, he could sue them for libel. Having emerged, he waddled ponderously around the front of the vehicle and approached the three Reserve officials.

'Goodness me, Bunduki!' the Asian boomed in excellent English and with what could have been enthusiastic amiability. 'You *have* been lucky. But, by golly, I don't think old Wakata there will be any too pleased.'

'Why?' the big blond inquired, giving no sign of knowing the old man's status. 'Does he like having his crops ruined?'

'He doesn't grow any,' Patel answered. 'There's no need for him to. He's the local witch-doctor and the baboons are his big medicine totems. You know what these *munts* are like where things like that are concerned.'

'I've an idea,' Bunduki admitted, refraining from stating his abhorrence for the word '*munt*' which was a derogatory term for an African.

'More than just an idea, being related to the *Bwana Mkubwa*,' Patel corrected, using the tribesmen's name for the big blond's adoptive father.[15] 'So you can see that you've given the old boy a problem. He's said nobody has to interfere with them and here you are, treating them like this.'

'Hum!' the big blond said, looking what passed as pensive. 'So he's come out here to complain, has he?'

'Most stringently.'

'And I'll have to do something to sooth his feelings?'

'They most assuredly will have to be soothed.'

'With *money*?'

'Unfortunately, the days when the *munts* could be bought off with trade beads, mirrors and bits of cloth are over.'

'How do *you* come into this?' Bunduki inquired almost mildly, noticing that the Asian's manner suggested a regret for the pass-

[15] The circumstances recorded in the Introduction to this section prevent us from disclosing the true identity of Bunduki's adoptive father. The Swahili name, '*Bwana Mkubwa*' means 'Big White Master', or literally, 'White Master Big'.

ing of such unsophisticated times.

'*Me?*' Patel replied, oozing harmless innocence which was *almost* convincing. 'Oh, he just hired my Land Rover to come out here and, knowing how these *munts* treat vehicles, I decided to act as chauffeur. I tell you, though, it was amazing the way he knew just where to come. All he did was sit there as if he was half asleep and point first one way, then another and, the next thing I knew, there you were with the *gari* and trailer loaded with his bloody *nugu*.'

'It's amazing the powers of these witch-doctors,' the big blond stated, contriving to sound impressed and without commenting that the tracks left by the lorry and trailer had been clearly discernible.

'This one's are!' Patel confirmed and the sincerity with which he spoke struck Bunduki as being close to genuine. 'They do say the local *mchawi* and he had a big row one day and, that same night no less, the *mchawi* got out of bed, walked from his hut and fell into the *donga*[16] at the back of the village and broke his neck.'

'Wasn't *that* a coincidence?' Bunduki said drily, as he had not overlooked the implication that Wakata's rival was the *mchawi* and he also observed the way in which the Asian was watching M'Bili and Shotu rather than himself.

'It couldn't have been anything else, could it?' Patel replied. 'Although there are *some* who believe the *mganga* have remarkable powers and can do terrible things when they are crossed. Anyway, you'll soon find out what he's wanting. Here comes his nibs now.'

Turning his attention from the stolidly indifferent old *Wa-Kamba* and the clearly disturbed Ambaga, Bunduki glanced around. Followed by his burly young attendants and—a few paces to the rear—the villagers, Wakata was approaching. It was apparent that he too was directing his attention to the two Africans rather than the blond giant as he came to a halt in front of them.

'*Hu jambo*, Bunduki?' the old man asked grudgingly, after several seconds had gone by without the big blond, M'Bili or Shotu offering to open the conversation.

[16] '*Donga*': Swahili for a dried-up watercourse.

'*Si jambo*,' Bunduki replied, but his response to the question, 'Are you all right?' was literally, 'I have no affairs' and, spoken with the tone he employed, could be taken as meaning, 'Mind your own business'. Normally he would have made the first greeting as a sign of respect for the other's age and social position, but he knew on this occasion he must not show anything which might be construed as fright or weakness. 'What can I do for you?'

'Why are you going to kill my children?' Wakata demanded, his voice as creaky as a rusty hinge.

'I'm not,' Bunduki corrected. 'There are too many of them around here and they are doing great damage to the village's *shambas*. So we're taking those in the cages to be sold to foreign zoos. The money will be used to repay the people for the damage they have suffered and the rest of the troop will still be here.'

'Is that your word too, Ambaga?' the old man challenged, having heard a mutter of pleasure from the villagers when the matter of being recompensed for the damage was raised.

'Y—Yes!' Shotu answered. 'All who suffered damage will be paid for it.'

Despite the bold front he was trying to put up, the young Ambaga was perturbed by the way Wakata was staring at him. The piercing eyes seemed to be probing into his mind and reading his thoughts. However, he had been encouraged in his defiance by the ease with which the baboons—allegedly under the *mchawi*'s protection—had been caught. Nor had he wished to let Bunduki and M'Bili, for both of whom he had formed a great respect, or the villagers, think that a college graduate and Christian like himself believed in the supernatural powers of witchcraft.

'So be it!' Wakata spat out. 'But who knows what evil will befall unless my children are released?'

*****   *****

'*Bwana* Bunduki!'

Hearing his name, the blond giant turned from where he had been about to feed the goat killing lion in its sturdy lightweight travelling cage. While its as yet uncaptured consort was said to have a jet black mane, this one—a large young adult in the prime of life and peak of physical condition—had a flowing mass of yellowish-blond hair on its head and shoulders to indicate its masculinity.

After having delivered his cryptic utterance the previous evening, Wakata had taken his departure before anything more could be said. Wise in such matters, Bunduki had not played up his importance by trying to ask questions which he would refuse to answer. The blond giant had sensed that, as with Shotu, the villagers were uneasy over the *mchawi's* visit; but less than they would have been before they saw with how little difficulty baboons were captured. They were, he had guessed, less impressed by Wakata's potential powers than previously and willing to wait and see if the warning produced any effect.

For all the lack of opposition from his assistants, the big blond had been puzzled. He had suspected that the old man had come, possibly at Patel's instigation, to demand money as a means of soothing the 'spirits' which were supposed to inhabit the baboons. Such a trick would not have been unprecedented as *mchawi* in general used their *dawa* as a source of financial gain. So Bunduki wondered why the imposition had not been delivered. Discussing the matter with M'Bili during the return journey to the village, after the remaining members of the baboon troop had been carried away or driven to the safety of the *kopje*, he had formulated a theory for the untypical behaviour. As yet, however, he had not been able to find a way of proving whether it was correct.

Having recognized the Wa-Kamba's voice, Bunduki was not surprised to see him approaching. He was accompanied by the leader of the local men who had helped deal with the baboons the previous evening. What was more, they were followed by a growing group of villagers.

'What's wrong, *mzee*?' the big blond demanded, knowing that only something of a serious nature could be causing the obvious agitation the two men and the crowd were showing.

'It's Shotu,' M'Bili said hoarsely.

'What's wrong with him?' Bunduki asked, realizing he had not seen the young Ambaga that morning.

'When he didn't come for breakfast, I went to look for him,' the Wa-Kamba replied, for once losing his air of cheerful impertur-

357

bability. 'He wasn't in his tent. From the look of things, he'd torn open the flaps at the back instead of just unfastening them and left.'

'When?' Bunduki barked as the words trailed away.

'Some time during the night!' M'Bili answered. 'I followed his tracks——.'

'He'd gone to and fallen into the *donga* just like the *mganga* after the quarrel with Wakata!' the Gasali interrupted, his broad and strong shoulders appearing to have shrunken and his features seeming more grey than black.

'Show me the body!' Bunduki ordered.

Directed by M'Bili and the Gasali, with the crowd on their heels keeping uncharacteristically quiet, Bunduki examined the ground between the rear of Shotu's tent—which had been opened in the manner described by the Wa-Kamba—to the edge of the *donga*. Well trained and competent in such matters, he studied the various marks on the ground detected by his keen eyes. He found the story they told increased rather than cleared up the mystery. There was evidence of only one human being's passage. It was made by bare feet which, as was established by the tightness of the toes imprinted clearly in a patch of soft ground, normally wore shoes. The maker of the tracks had walked, apparently unhurriedly, in an almost straight line. Nor had he shown any sign of noticing when one of the dogs which roamed the village had darted towards him from behind a hut. Yet, although there was nothing to suggest he had caused the reaction, the marks of the animal's paws indicated it had suddenly skidded to a halt when very close and then had taken flight.

Arriving at the *donga*, Bunduki found himself even further from a solution than when he had left the tent. Nothing he could see inferred other than that the motionless shape in the bright red pyjamas sprawled face down at the bottom had walked straight over the edge. It could not have been done by accident, but equally there was no sign of it being anything else. The night had not been so dark he would be unable to see where he was going. Yet, apart from the tracks left by M'Bili and the villager as they followed—but stayed clear of—the single set of footprints, he could detect no trace of any other human beings having been in the vicinity.

Finding a place at which a man with his superlative agility could negotiate the sheer forty foot high side of the *donga*, the blond giant descended and turned the body over. His examination proved no more informative than the story, or lack of it, he had deduced from the tracks. There was nothing to suggest Shotu had not walked to his death deliberately and of his own free will. All his injuries, from the abrasions on his body to the broken neck, were such as would have been caused by coming through the thorn bushes which fringed the lip of the *donga* and tumbling to crash on to the stony bottom.

'This is beyond me!' M'Bili declared, after the blond had emerged from the *donga*. 'He just seems to have got up, ripped his way out of the tent and came here. Nobody forced him. Or, if they did, it was without them leaving any tracks or signs.'

'You're right about that, old friend,' Bunduki confirmed, with none of the banter which he would have used in less perturbing circumstances, as he could never remember having seen the Wa-Kamba so shaken. 'But there *has* to be a solution. Where did he go after we got back to the village last night?'

'Nowhere!' M'Bili stated vehemently. 'All he did was eat his supper, have his hair cut and go to bed. So how did this happen?'

'I'm damned if I know!' the big blond growled, trying not to let his thinking be influenced by the crowd's muttered—but clearly audible—references to the *mchawi*'s warning. Having made the declaration in English, he reverted to Swahili and went on, 'Where's Wakata?'

'At the *Wa-Hindi's duka*,' a villager called back.

Swinging on his heel, Bunduki strode forward without saying or waiting for any further information. There was an expression on his face which caused the crowd to scatter from his path like impala being charged by a lion. Frightened, but curious, the people formed a silent procession as he went past closely followed by M'Bili and the villager.

Looking neither left nor right, the blond giant returned to the village. Striding along the main street, he arrived at the front entrance of the *duka*. The double doors were locked, but a kick from his right foot burst them open as if they were secured with nothing stronger than a solitary piece of cotton thread. Stepping across the threshold, he saw Wakata seated at a table in the far left corner. The two young men who had been in the Land Rover and another pair—one their age, the other in his mid-forties—equally as gaudily dressed, were positioned in a rough half circle between him and the newcomer.

'Good morning, Bunduki,' Patel greeted from behind the bar, his fat face wet with perspiration. 'I'm not open yet, but if you're *that* impatient for a bottle of beer, I suppose I'd better serve you.'

Showing no sign of having heard the words, the big blond continued to advance until his path was blocked by the oldest of the quartet. Lacking two inches of Bunduki's height, but so thickly set that he had a few pounds' advantage in weight, the man had short, crinkled hair with a touch of grey. His face was brutal, with a nose that had been broken and badly set and the left ear having acquired the condition known as a 'cauliflower'. Reaching out, he laid the palm of his massive right hand on the chest of the khaki bushshirt. Apparently as a result of its pressure, the blond giant came to a halt.

'You heard, *mzungu*!' the man said loudly. His employment of the derogatory term for a European was, when used in such a fashion, filled with deliberate offence. 'So get out of h——.'

'Move your hand!' Bunduki said and, gently though the words had been spoken, they were clearly given as an order.

Darting a quick glance at the villagers who were gathered outside and able to witness everything that was being said and done, the man did not hesitate. He was aware of how much the future was dependant upon the awe in which they regarded himself and his men. It went beyond having the backing of the *mchawi*, at least as far as his pride was concerned. With that in mind, he removed his hand and, having folded it into a fist, swung it with a sharp, hard outward jerk of the elbow. The knuckles hit the big blond hard at the side of the jaw, eliciting an excited exclamation from the onlookers.

But no other discernible effect!

The blow had been well thrown, with the shoulder dropped and the weight of the blocky body behind it. For all that, Bunduki's head did not move more than an inch. Instead, having taken it, he shook himself briefly and his left hand closed with the power of a bear-trap's jaws on the man's throat. Sliding his feet apart before the other could contemplate any form of defensive action, the blond giant turned and bent him backwards. Placing his other hand against his assailant's spine, Bunduki shoved. Thrown across the room with his arms flailing, spinning helplessly, the man went over a table and collided against the wall with a crash which was like music to more than one of the onlookers' ears.

Leaping forward to take advantage of the white man's preoccupation, the taller of the Land Rover's passengers learned painfully that he had not acted swiftly enough as the back of a hard left hand swung with great rapidity to meet him. Bright lights seemed to be bursting inside his skull as he was knocked in an uncontrollable twirling sprawl in the opposite direction to his leader. Then blackness engulfed him as he landed on the floor.

More successful in his endeavours to take part in the attack, or at least so it seemed in the first instance, the other young man who had accompanied Wakata darted in to enfold and pinion Bunduki's arms from the rear. Showing an equally quick grasp of the situation, the last of the quartet advanced eagerly upon what he assumed to be a trapped and partially innocuous victim. Much to his alarm, before he could do anything positive, two hunting boots were raised and placed against his chest to thrust with irresistible force. Even as he was propelled across the room to crash into the door of the gentlemen's toilet, which burst open under the impact, he saw that his companion was in difficulty as great as his own.

Thrown off balance by having the blond giant's weight placed suddenly and unexpectedly upon him, the fourth African was given not the slightest chance of recovering his equilibrium. Bringing down his feet, Bunduki wrenched free his arms and, turning swiftly swung a punch which sent its recipient, spitting blood and a couple of teeth through crushed lips, to land supine and stunned near the bar.

'Raise your hands empty, *Wa-Hindi*!' a voice yelled in Swahili.

Watching the four Africans' abortive attempts to deal with the blond giant, Patel was grabbing for the sawed-off shotgun he kept on a shelf under the bar when the shout reached his ears. Looking in the direction from which it had originated, he had not the slightest hesitation over obeying despite his usual disdainful regard for '*munts*'. The muzzles of the double barrelled elephant gun M'Bili was lining at him seemed far larger than their not inconsiderable ·600 calibre and, although he had had little cause to hold the average African's marksmanship in high esteem, he was disinclined to gamble on this being the case where the little Wa-Kamba was concerned; not with his own life as the stake.

'Well, white man,' Wakata said, remaining seated and showing no sign of alarm as the blond giant came across the room to confront him. He raised his voice so that the words would carry to the assembled people, using Swahili. 'I warned you that the spirits of my children would be angry——!'

'Rubbish!' Bunduki thundered.

'Perhaps the Ambaga would not have met his very unusual—accident if you had set my children free,' the old man hinted, giving not so much as a glance at his immobilized bodyguard or the Asian standing with hands raised behind the bar.

'An accident is all it was,' Bunduki scoffed, sounding contempt-uous and also speaking loudly to permit all he said to be heard by the crowd. 'Shotu got drunk, went for a walk and fell over the *donga* in the darkness. That's all there was to it.'

'Are you sure? Wataka challenged.

'Are you saying that it was *your* witchcraft that caused his death, *mchawi*?' the blond giant countered.

'I——!' Wakata began, but he paused as he contemplated the results which might accrue from his answer. To deny responsibility could lose the effect created upon the villagers by the Ambaga's death, but to claim it would offer the white man an excuse to have him arrested for an admission of murder. Even if he was not charged, or was found not guilty, there would be a delay which could ruin his lucrative business. Cagily he inquired, 'Do you say that it did not?'

'I do!' Bunduki confirmed without hesitation. 'I say you have no powers, old man. If you had, the baboons would never have let themselves be trapped as they should have been under your protection. There is only one way you can prove you have powers.

Use them to put a death curse on *me*.'

'Black man's witchcraft won't work on a *mzungu*,' Wakata protested warily. '*Everybody* knows that!'

'But I'm *not* a *mzungu*,' the blond giant answered. 'All my life has been spent in Africa. My adoptive father is *Bwana Mkubwa* himself. I am a circumcision brother in the Waziri Year of the One Tusked Elephant.[17] M'Bili of the Wa-Kamba and Kira-Kangano the Masai *melombuki*[18] have each taken me as his brother-in-blood and sworn to it by all the sacred oaths of his people. Do you still call me a *mzungu*?'

'That is so!' M'Bili shouted, forgetting his adoption of the Moslem faith for the moment and, lowering his rifle, looking over his shoulder. 'By every sacred oath of the Wa-Kamba and all the gods of my people, every word Bunduki says is true. He is no *mzungu*, but a true *African*!'

'Now listen to me well, *pretended mchawi*!' the blond giant commanded in ringing tones, bringing silence to the rumble of concurrence which had followed his companion's pronouncement. 'Put your death curse on *me* today and, if it has not worked by dawn tomorrow, look to yourself, old eater of the dung left by the *nyangau*.[19] As surely as I'm still alive, I'll come and make you wish you'd never listened when the *Wa-Hindi* there told you keeping so many baboons together would attract leopards for your poachers to kill, which is the *only* reason you don't want the troop broken up and wouldn't let the villagers defend their *shambas* from the *nugu*.'

With that, Bunduki turned his back contemptuously upon the old man and strode from the bar-room. Holding the rifle with both hands at arms' length in front of him so it could be brought into use rapidly, M'Bili backed out after the big blond. Neither Wakata nor Patel spoke or moved, but if looks could have killed Bunduki and the Wa-Kamba would never have reached the door alive. Having parted to let them through, the crowd followed them

[17] As with other tribes, all Waziri boys born in a year are circumcised at the same time in a religious ceremony and classed as 'brothers' as a result of it. Although Bunduki was circumcised in the hygienic European fashion, he was put through the rest of the ceremony and so qualified as a 'circumcision brother' for that particular year.

[18] For the benefit of new readers: see Appendix Ten, Footnote 6.

[19] The more generally used Swahili name for the hyena is '*fisi*'.

away from the *duka*.

'Did you hear what he said?' the Asian demanded worriedly, after waddling across to make sure nobody was listening outside and closing the front doors. 'He *knows* what we're up to with the baboons.'

'Much good will it do him,' the old man replied, spitting out the words as if they were burning his mouth and showing just as little concern as Patel for his henchmen's condition. He was quivering with rage caused by the way he had been treated, particularly over receiving the ultimate insult for a Gasali; to be accused of eating the hard whitish droppings of the hyena. 'By dawn tomorrow, he will have gone the way of the *mganga* and that so called Christian Ambaga.'

'Can you do it to a white man?' the Asian asked dubiously.

'You heard what he and the Wa-Kamba, who will follow him soon, said. More's the pity I can't take them both at the same time,' Wakata answered, sounding completely confident if annoyed by his inability to cope with the whole problem at once, 'Any man with that background can't be *white*. He's an African, no matter what the colour of his skin and, before morning, he will have felt the powers of the *mchawi* although he thinks I have none.'

*****   *****

The rending of wire mesh being torn apart, followed by a masculine bellow of alarm, shattered the silence of the night!

Lying fully dressed—even to having the big bowie knife sheathed at his side—upon the camp-bed in his tent, Bunduki woke instantly and without even a brief interim period of dull-witted somnolence. It was a trait with which he had been born, then was honed to perfection by time spent in situations where any delay in becoming in full control of his faculties might have proved fatal.

While he could not imagine how Shotu had been induced to walk over the edge of the *donga*, being aware that he had issued a challenge which Wakata dare not refuse to accept, the blond giant had been alert against attempts upon his life since leaving the *duka*. In spite of his background and the knowledge that witch-doctors could produce remarkable effects upon those who believed in their powers, he had not considered he had anything to fear from that source. So it had been with the efforts of human agencies rather than supernatural forces in mind that he had taken his precautions. From the reports he had received via M'Bili during the day, none of the *mchawi*'s henchmen had suffered serious or incapacitating injuries in the brief fracas. Although he was told that they and Patel, but not Wakata, had left the village in the Land Rover once they recovered, he had not relaxed his vigilance.

Bringing in the second of the goat-killing lions, Dawn Drummond-Clayton had arrived shortly after the five men had taken their departure and provided Bunduki with three extra pairs of completely reliable eyes. On hearing of Shotu's death, the other two Ambaga trainee game scouts had been furious and had had to be restrained from their stated intention of seeking out and avenging themselves upon the witch-doctor.

From all appearances, the villagers had been content to await developments before deciding what action to take with regard to the captured baboons. There had been a constant stream of visitors to the blond giant's camp. They came ostensibly to see the animals, but he had suspected also to find out if there had been any manifestations of the *mchawi*'s powers. Yet none of them had mentioned the matter and such reminders were usually a necessary adjunct to the infliction of any kind of curse, being made to induce a condition in which the intended victim became convinced it would work.

Wanting to show how little he cared for the possibility of having brought down the malevolent wrath of a *mchawi* upon him, Bunduki had carried on with his normal tasks; even to the extent of yielding to Dawn's comments that he was starting to look like a 'bloody left wing hippy' and having his hair cut. Although the local barber had been nervous, the task was performed to the girl's satisfaction shortly before she served the dinner which she had prepared. With the meal over, having arranged a rota for a guard to be kept, they had retired to their respective sleeping quarters to spend what they all had hoped would prove to be an uneventful night.

As he was rising swiftly and wondering what was causing the

disturbance, Bunduki reached for the extra weapons he had placed ready in case of an emergency. Without needing to light the lamp, his left hand closed upon the smooth, carefully contoured hardwood handleriser of his bow. A black Fred Bear Super Kodiak, although custom built to his own specifications, which had stipulated that the draw weight of the recurved fibreglass limbs was increased to one hundred pounds, it was sixty inches long and already strung. There was a bow-quiver holding eight fibreglass arrows with Bear Four-Blade Razorhead hunting points attached to its right side, but he left them in position and plucked the ninth from where it was sticking in the ground. Nocking it to the double-loop, braided black Dacron string as he advanced, he went from the tent prepared to use it if the need should arise.

Rapidly as the blond giant had moved, he found Dawn and M'Bili were also emerging from their sleeping quarters. They too were armed, the Wa-Kamba with his rifle, ready for action. The beautiful, tawny haired girl was clad in a khaki bushshirt and slacks—which set off her magnificent figure to its best advantage —and hunting boots. An eight inch bladed Randall Model 1 'All Purpose' fighting knife hung from the left side of her waist belt. In her hands, she held her Ben Pearson Marauder Take-Down bow. Drawing seventy pounds, it too had an eight-arrow quiver attached and she was carrying it with a ninth nocked to the string.

'What was——?' Dawn began, but did not get the opportunity to finish the question.

'*Bwana, memsaab!*' gasped the younger of the Ambagas, dashing up. He had been on guard and the fright he received caused him to employ words his generation had tended to consider unnecessary when addressing white people since their country was granted independence. 'The—the white haired lion has escaped!'

'How?' Bunduki asked.

'I—I don't know!' the clearly terrified Ambaga confessed. 'It—it just got up and crashed through the side of the cage!'

'Come on!' the blond giant ordered.

Even as he was setting off to investigate, Bunduki felt puzzled. While unsuitable for long term incarceration, the travelling cage was sturdily made and he would have sworn it could retain the lion. However, on reaching the scene, he found that it had been incapable of withstanding what must have been an exceptionally violent and determined effort to break out. One side had been burst open to let the big animal escape. Yet, in spite of being disturbed by the commotion, the other, which was equally as large and powerful, had not been able to follow its example. That could be, he told himself, because it had not yet fully recovered from the effects of the tranquillizer drug which had been injected via one of Dawn's arrows to bring about its capture.

'Which way did it run, Kioti?' Dawn inquired, as the big blond was wondering what had induced the lion, which had been well fed to keep it comparatively reconciled to captivity, to make such an obviously determined effort as had been required to escape.

'T—towards the v—village, *memsaab*!' the young Ambaga replied, sounding as if he could hardly credit the statement he was making. 'B—but it did not run. It w—walked—slowly.'

'*Walked?*' Bunduki asked, diverted from his unproductive speculations.

'V—very slowly!' Kioti confirmed.

'Come on!' the blond giant snapped, sensing that Dawn and, even more so, M'Bili were matching his thoughts about the lion's strange behaviour. 'Stay and help Atu guard the camp, Kioti.'

'*Ndio,*[20] *bwana!*' the young Ambaga assented, only too willing to be excused from such an inexplicable set of circumstances and the other trainee game scout, who had arrived in time to hear the conversation, showed signs of sharing his sentiments on the matter.

Hurrying towards the village, Dawn, Bunduki and M'Bili were guided by the barking, then frightened yelps of its dogs. Yet, for all the commotion, not one of the people who must have been awakened in the houses offered to look outside and investigate the cause of the disturbance.

'Do you see which way we're going?' M'Bili asked, in a perturbed tone, as he and his companions were approaching the last of the buildings.

'I see!' Bunduki agreed, feeling as if he was being touched by an ice cold hand.

[20] '*Ndio*': literally, 'It is so', but in Up-Country Swahili employed as 'Yes'.

As on the previous night, the visibility was reasonable. It was sufficient, in fact, for the blond giant to have become aware that they were going in almost the identical direction taken by Shotu when walking to his death.

Starting to tell himself that the route must be nothing more than a coincidence and trying to prevent himself from considering it in conjunction with the lion's peculiar behaviour, Bunduki was interrupted. From the woodland a short distance ahead rose a shout which turned into a yell of fear and was followed by the roaring snarl of a lion as it was launching an attack.

***** *****

Ghamba Patel was a very worried man as he stood between Wakata and the oldest of their four henchmen among the bushes. Despite having had a successful demonstration where the young Ambaga was concerned (he had previously thought the death of the *mganga* was no more than a propitious accident) he was far from convinced that the *mchawi*'s powers would prove efficacious against a white man no matter how well connected with various African tribes the intended victim might be. Nor was he certain that causing Bunduki to die would end their problems. It could easily add to them. From all accounts, the big blond was on terms of close acquaintance with Prince Simba Nyeuse. The ruler was noted for loyalty to his friends and would insist upon an investigation when the news reached him. Furthermore, the *Bwana Mkubwa* was sure to come in search of the truth on hearing of what had happened to his adopted son and he was far more to be feared than anybody the Prince sent.

Taking all the points into consideration, the Asian felt the time was coming when he should not only bring to an end what had proved a lucrative business, but also leave the country. Although there had never been the pressures exerted upon members of his race in Ambagasali that had occurred in other emergent African states, he had taken the precaution of acquiring the passport which endowed him with British citizenship. He had also transferred the majority of his ill-gotten gains to a Swiss bank and would have the means to start a new life in England.

'Our *Wa-Hindi* friend looks nervous, Hitani,' Wakata remarked quietly.

368

'It's like always,' the senior of the henchmen replied, fingering the Short Magazine Lee Enfield rifle he was carrying. 'He hasn't the stomach for doing anything except paying others very little for doing all the work and taking all the risks.'

Startled by the *mchawi*'s comment, which had come just as he was deciding to start making arrangements for his departure, Patel's alarm grew even greater as he listened to the answer. That both had been made in Swahili, instead of Gasali which he did not understand, struck him as menacingly significant. Turning his gaze to Wakata, he found he could make out little of the wrinkled black face in the gloom of the woodland and felt uneasy as he envisaged the piercing eyes studying him. Wondering if the old man's powers extended to reading other people's thoughts, he was not sorry that he had brought along his sawed-off shotgun.

'There's no call for such talk among friends,' the Asian protested, trying to prevent the fear he was experiencing from showing in his voice. 'I didn't object when I was asked to come and see Bunduki walk to his death.'

Although the statement was far from truthful, something happened to distract the two Africans before either could contradict it.

'Where's Njarbi?' Hitani hissed, having suddenly become aware that only three of the younger men were present.

'He was boiling mad over having those teeth knocked out this morning,' the tallest of the trio answered. 'So he said he was going to take his *panga*[21] and pay the *mzungu* back for doing it.'

'What's that you say?' Wakata spat out and the evidence of his furious disapproval produced a more frightened response than had been evoked by the bigger man's question.

'He went to——!' the informant commenced, pointing nervously.

'Come on!' the *wachawi* commanded. 'We've got to stop him before he makes it obvious what's happened.'

Sharing Wakata and Patel's appreciation of how well connected their intended victim was, Hitani had no reason to have it explained how undesirable such a clear indication of the cause of

---

[21] *'Panga'*: a heavy, long chopping knife generally used as an agricultural implement, but also employed as a weapon.

death would be. So he led the others through the bushes in the direction that had been indicated. Coming to the edge of a small clearing, they saw their errant companion at the other side. Unfortunately, it was obvious that they were going to be too late to prevent him from behaving in the ill-advised manner the trio had hoped to avert.

The bushes towards which Njarbi was staring were being agitated by something as yet unseen pushing through. Raising the *panga* with which he was armed, he sprang forward.

'Die, you——!' the young man shouted in his native tongue.

At the discovery of the terrible error he had made with regards to the cause of the foliage shaking, Njarbi's words became a scream of horror and he staggered backwards. His involuntary, although basically well advised, attempt at withdrawal was to no avail. Letting out a snarling roar, the lion, which he had discovered was approaching instead of the expected white man, attacked. Launching itself into the air, it knocked the screaming young man into the centre of the clearing. Its jaws closed upon the woolly haired skull, bringing the cries to an abrupt end, as its front claws ripped into the belly to perform a disembowelment. Then it began to shake at the lifeless body with such vigour that it turned in the direction from which it had come.

Yells of alarm burst from the other three young men as they saw what had arrived instead of their intended victim. Filled with superstitious dread at the thought that in some way the white man had overcome the *mchawi*'s spell and transformed himself into a lion, they discarded their weapons and fled from the clearing as fast as their legs would carry them.

Although Wakata was showing similar signs of panic, Hitani was made of sterner stuff. He too might have suspected some form of counter-witchcraft had he not seen and recognized the three human beings who were emerging from the bushes from which the lion had appeared. Deciding nothing more than pure chance had brought the carnivore on the scene at such an inopportune moment, he also concluded that Bunduki must have evaded being brought under the old man's control. The big blond was behaving in a far different fashion to their previous victim. With that thought in mind, ignoring Wakata who was turning to run away,

Hitani started to raise his rifle. What was more, fear rather than courage providing the incentive, Patel also began to lift up his weapon towards a firing position.

Already having anticipated what he would find, Bunduki was drawing his bow as he reached the clearing. Much as he hated what he must do, he was aware that he had no other choice. Sighting swiftly as the lion released its victim and raised a snarling face to glare at him, he loosed the arrow. Flying forward faster than the human eye could follow, the point, equipped in a fashion which justified its trade name 'Four-Blade Razorhead,' sank into the lion's skull to cut a quadruple swathe of destruction through the brain. Killed as instantaneously as Njarbi had been, it collapsed as if it was boned across the body of its victim.

Allowing the bare minimum time for the fletching of the shaft to pass beyond the handle-riser and while the bow's limbs were still vibrating from supplying the propulsive force, the blond giant's right hand reached for another arrow. He realized that he could not liberate it from the bow-quiver, nock and release it sufficiently swiftly to deal with the two human threats to his life. Even if he should be able to fell one, the other man was sure to open fire at him. His survival, he knew, depended upon his adoptive cousin and M'Bili.

Bringing up the heavy rifle, the old Wa-Kamba sighted along the rib of the twin barrels as if aiming a shotgun. For all the urgency, knowing his weapon, he was aware that he had to make the first bullet count. If he missed, the Gasali would be in action before he could try again. Flame erupted from the right hand muzzle to the accompaniment of a thunderous roar and the rifle rose in an uncontrollable recoil kick. Although his instincts informed him correctly that he had held true, they could not guess just how effective he was to be.

Struck in the chest by a ·600 calibre bullet driven by the propellant power capable of stopping a full grown bull elephant in its tracks, Hitani was flung backwards. The lead emerged, shattering his spine in passing, to fly on and pass through Wakata, who had the misfortune to be passing behind the stricken man at that moment, with little or no loss of velocity and ended its flight by striking down the last of the fleeing trio of young Gasalis.

Showing an equal appreciation of her adoptive cousin's peril, Dawn had drawn the correct conclusions as to what was required of her. Nor did she hesitate as she identified the type of weapon in Patel's hands. Making the draw, aim and loose with the speed which told of excellent training and considerable practice, she sent an arrow into the right side of his chest as he was vacillating between which of them should become his first target. A howl of pain burst from him. Reeling, he discharged both barrels' charges involuntarily and, as the buckshot balls flew harmlessly into the air, without effect.

***** *****

'The *mganga* was a good man, *bwana, memsaab*,' the barber declared, scuffling his feet on the ground and not looking at either Dawn or Bunduki. 'He cured my daughter when she was very ill and the white doctor in Ambaga said she must die. That is why I did what I did.'

It was the morning after the fight in the clearing. While the girl and the blond giant were eating their breakfast, prior to going to the capital city and reporting what had happened, the Gasali had come with a request to speak to them.

'What was that, my friend?' Bunduki prompted, remembering something M'Bili had mentioned about Shotu's activities on the night of his death.

'I had never believed the *mchawi* caused him to die,' the barber explained. 'So, when he told me to fetch him some of the Ambaga's hair, I did as I was told. Hitani had told me what would happen to me and my family if I did not, or warned you, so I didn't dare do anything else. But I never guessed what the old one would be able to do.'

'Who could have guessed?' Dawn said sympathetically.

'When he told me to bring some of your hair, *bwana*,' the man went on, showing relief at the response his confession was eliciting, 'I knew what he must want it for. So, hearing Hitani telling the *Wa-Hindi* this time they would take him to watch it happen, I saw a way to have my revenge. Instead of *your* hair, I gathered some from the bars of the light-maned lion's cage. The old one never knew the difference and used it. Do you blame me for what I did, *bwana*?'

372

'I don't,' Bunduki declared, realizing why the man had insisted on only himself and Dawn being present. 'And your secret is safe with us.'

'It *can't* be!' Dawn ejaculated, but without any great conviction, after the barber had taken his departure.

'Maybe not,' Bunduki replied. 'All I know is that a witch-doctor is supposed to need some part of his victim's body to work with when casting a spell and hair's the favourite for it. Wakata was given some from Shotu and, without knowing it, from that lion. Then both of them walked in the same direction, after breaking out of where they were sleeping. I'll tell you one thing, Dawn. It's unlikely we'll ever learn the truth, or how whatever it was could be done, but I'm pleased that for once the *mchawi*'s powers went wrong.'

PART THIRTEEN

Dan Hollick in

THE DOGS OF KWANG

I had tried to sell work to the D. C. Thomson & Co., Ltd., group of boys' papers when I first started writing with the idea of publication. In fact, I had offered them a sample chapter of Trail Boss *(the one in which the Ysabel Kid recovers the stolen sourdough keg) believing it might be acceptable for publication in the form of a serial. I knew that Western serials were published on occasion,[1] but instead of being received with exclamations of acclaim, I was sent a rejection slip. However, with my career set into motion by Brown Watson Ltd., I decided the time had come for another attempt to break into what I felt sure would prove a fruitful market.*

Having decided to expand, the problem was how to bring this about. One of the very few useful hints I accrued from the short story writing correspondence course to which I referred in my Introduction was the advisability of studying the market before putting pen to paper. I did and found the main subjects covered were war or traditional British sports—football, cricket, boxing, athletics, etc.—neither of which had any particular appeal to me, but I realized that my Army service had supplied a vast potential source of knowledge on one particular military subject. The training of war dogs.

So Sergeant Dan Hollick of the Royal Army Veterinary Corps was born.[2]

---

[1] One example I remember was *Solo Solomon*, a U.S. Marshal who worked undercover as a drifting cowhand and, being a ventriloquist, used to turn the tables on the 'baddies' by throwing his voice and making his horse, Gasbag, appear to be speaking.

[2] As originally written, Dan was called by the traditional Army nickname 'Diab', but the editor made the substitution without telling me.

374

Dan's first series was set at the No. 5 Army Guard Dog Unit, Hong Kong—actually the kennels were in the Kowloon suburb of Sham Shui Po, on the mainland—and he was already a sergeant. I would like to disclaim any responsibility for the title The Dogs of Kwang. *My own idea had been* The Guard Has Pointed Ears. *Much to my satisfaction, the first episode—which you are about to read—was accepted and the other eleven followed suit. They not only paved the way for four more series, but they opened up another outlet for writing which I will describe in the Introduction to Part Fourteen of this volume.*

In the course of time, I told how Dan transferred into the R.A.V.C., as so many of us did, was trained as a dog handler and won promotion to lance corporal (Dan Hollick, Dog Handler), *next came his work with specialist dogs—i.e. tracking; infantry patrol, trained to locate hidden persons by wind borne scent or sound; liaison, message-carriers; red cross, finding wounded on the battlefield and fetching stretcher bearers to them; mine detection—promotion first to corporal and, in the last episode, sergeant, and acquiring his big doberman pinscher, Kano* (The Dogs of Dan Hollick). *Having described how Dan was taught the trade of dog trainer, I decided to carry on his career after he had served in Hong Kong and, as in my own case, took him to Kenya during the Mau Mau Emergency. I called the first series in the new location* Tracker One, Shambulia, *which was based on the call sign given over the unit's tannoy system—'shambulia' being the Swahili word meaning 'attack'—when Dan's combat team was being turned out to investigate an incident.*[3] *This did not meet with the editor's approval and he name it* Dan Hollick, Dog Handler *again, although by this time our hero was a fully qualified sergeant dog trainer; quite a distinct difference to any member of the Corps. The final series, still in Kenya, was* The Saga of the Samburu Scouts, *telling how Dan was posted there and covering*

[3] In *The Saga of the Samburu Scouts*, the work of ambush breaking dogs was described. Although these were never needed in Kenya, they had considerable success in Malaya and Cyprus. The 'Hitter' teams comprised a heavily armed squad and an exceptionally large, aggressive dog which was trained to attack anybody who discharged a weapon in its presence. The group rode in a vehicle along a road which the terrorists were known to be attacking. If they were ambushed, the dog was released to attack and create a diversion allowing the men to get into action.

incidents involving other members of the unit.

In all the five Dan Hollick series, the training methods and other aspects of working the dogs were based on genuine Army practices. I also covered other aspects of service life, including the black market which used to operate in Germany from the end of World War II to the early 1950s—the second and third series being set at the War Dog Training Wing in Sennelager—I also managed to work in stories about my favourite pastime, fishing.

Although Dan Hollick established me in the writing field for the boys' papers, I did only two other series and one short story in the text format for the Thomson Group. The series were The Sheriff of Rockabye County, *to which I have already referred in Part Thirteen and* Son of a Yellow Cop, *about a young Federal Bureau of Investigation agent's hunt for a criminal who could clear his dead father, a policeman, of a charge of cowardice and which, although I was paid on acceptance, has not yet been published. My short story, which had its title changed to* Finnegan Flew the Black Phantom *was about the special service pilots who flew Westland Lysander aircraft in clandestine missions to supply the various Resistance groups in Europe during World War II with arms. Although one of the heroes was a South African, his name was changed from van Rensburg to Finnegan for some reason which the editor never did explain.*

Finally, to settle a long standing debate among my fellow members of the R.A.V.C., Dan Hollick was not *modelled on any member of the Corps. Nor was anybody else who appeared in the five series, although W.O.II William Knight may possibly have had his origins in my revered superior W.O.II 'Bill' Day, to whom I dedicated* The Bad Bunch.

THE DOGS OF KWANG

Hop Chan, a Hong Kong Chinese, decided that the easiest way of making a living in the Kwang area was by robbing the Army stores depots, where the sentries patrolled in full view of anyone who was outside the perimeter wire.

The soldiers' khaki drill uniforms showed up well in the light and their brasses gleamed out a warning. So too did the heavy studded boots they wore, sounding loud on the road.

A man need only stay reasonably alert to avoid them. He could either see or hear them coming, then fade silently into the shadows of the lines of big store huts, or slip back out of the hole cut in the fence to the safety of the teeming tenements which backed on to the depot.

Even if he were seen, a man could easily escape, for the sentries were not allowed to fire their rifles. They could only run in pursuit and their heavy boots slowed them down.

That was why Hop Chan never worried when he received orders to rob such a depot, even this one which was attached to an Army camp at Kwang. His tong, the Seven Teeth of the Dragon Tong, was one of the largest and best organized of all the criminal secret societies of Hong Kong and Kowloon. They maintained members in every Army depot, members who were installed to locate and mark the buildings where a robbery would be most profitable.

This night, Hop Chan found a place in the perimeter fence which was cut ready for him to make an entrance. This had been done by one of the inside men, who had also left a sign which told Hop Chan which hut held the most easily transportable loot. This time the sign read third hut, fourth row.

Hop Chan lay in the shadows just inside the fence, listening for the sentries. Hearing nothing, he darted across the lit area, moving fast into the shadows.

He halted there for a moment, getting his bearings. He went to the fourth row of huts and went by the first hut, moving on silent feet. He felt safe now, for the sentries never came in between the buildings, and Hop Chan was used to moving in the darkness.

'Halt!'

The voice came from the blackness ahead of Hop Chan. It brought him to a stop right away. He did not speak any English but understood what that word meant. He saw something blacker than the darkness looming ahead of him. A large black shape with a smaller one by its side.

From the smaller shape sounded a deep and bloodchilling snarl which terrified the Chinaman. He spun around and raced away, feet flying over the ground as he headed for the gap in the fence.

From behind Hop Chan came other shouted words but he ignored them. It was not the first time he had been spotted and challenged. Now he expected to hear the heavy, slow-moving clopping of the pursuing man's boots. This time, there was no such sound, only a rapid pattering noise which he could not explain to himself.

He was approaching the lighted road now. From behind him sounded a sudden deep snarling growl, some heavy, living weight crashed into him, teeth sinking through the thin black coat he wore, numbing the arm below. Even as he felt the pain and screamed, Hop Chan was brought crashing down to the ground.

Being only a poor and simple Chinese coolie, Hop Chan was filled with terror at this sudden attack. He could not see what was attacking him, only feel those powerful jaws crushing his arm and hear the savage snarling noise.

He staggered under the impact and was knocked forward into the light, going down hard. Still he fought against whatever it was which held him, his mind filled with thoughts of demons and evil spirits. He hit down on the hard tarmac of the road, his arm still held while a heavy weight crushed down on him from above and two thin, yet strong legs gripped him, claws digging into his flesh.

It was no demon which held Hop Chan down, although in the

perimeter lights it could have passed for one. It was a dog. A big, black and tan coloured Doberman Pinscher, short coated, stumpy tailed and with the cropped ears which told the dog was bred in Germany.

The dog still held Hop Chan down, not savaging him, just holding the arm between its jaws. When Hop Chan lay still the dog relaxed its hold slightly, if the man struggled, the grip tightened again. The Chinaman was hurt and scared but he realized that as long as he did not move the demon or whatever it was would not hurt him any more.

A man came from the shadows of the huts, a tall man with an enormous black moustache. Now it was easy to see why Hop Chan had not seen the sentry. The usual Army sentries wore khaki drill, a blue beret, heavy boots and showed shining brasses. This man's uniform consisted of a cap comforter such as the Commandos used to wear on operations. His shirt and trousers were of a material coloured jungle green. His boots were also green, made of canvas, calf high and with very thick rubber soles. His waistbelt, with a revolver holster, was the new 1948 type with gunmetal fittings.

The man moved forward. All the time he called encouragement to the dog. Coming closer, he called for the Chinaman to be still, so he could get the dog off.

Hop Chan heard the voice and panicked still more, trying to get up. He rolled over but the dog never relaxed, changing the grip with its legs and hanging on grimly with its jaws. The Chinaman flung himself back in a desperate attempt to break free. His head struck the ground with a sickening thud and his body went limp. The instant Hop Chan's body went limp the dog relaxed its grip once more.

'Kano, leave!' the big man snapped, in a more normal tone than the excited note with which he'd encouraged the dog.

At the word of command the dog released its hold on the man, leaping clear to avoid any attack. Turning, the big Doberman loped back to its master, going past his right side, straight around his back to sit with its shoulder almost touching his left knee.

Dropping his hand to the dog's sleek head, the big sergeant praised it, rubbing its ears. To Sergeant Dan Hollick of the Royal

379

Army Veterinary Corps, it was the most natural thing in the world to praise his dog for a job carried out correctly.

'Kano, down!' Hollick said, and the dog dropped its front legs to lie by his side, but it did not take its eyes from the still form on the ground. 'Stay!'

Leaving his dog, Hollick went forward and looked down at the Chinese coolie he had captured. Taking a whistle from his pocket he blew loudly on it, then returned to the dog. Taking a five foot dog rope lead from his shoulders, Hollick clipped the quick-release fastener on to the D string of the dog's collar and waited.

COOLIE MISSING

Four men came running up, brought by the whistle. They were led by a medium-sized, dapper-looking Captain of the R.A.V.C.

The others were a Major and two warrant officers of the R.A.O.C., who controlled and operated the Depot. The Major was a large, heavily built man with a moustache almost as large as Hollick's luxuriant growth.

'Got one, sergeant?' the Major asked unnecessarily. 'Good show, good show.'

'Nice going, Dan' one of the warrant officers agreed.

Captain Hornsby winked at his training sergeant and stood back. The two warrant officers picked up the groaning Hop Chan and carried him off to the guardroom where he could be treated for his injuries, then taken to the civilian police. As the men went towards his prisoner the big dog gave a low growl and started to move. Hollick snapped out a command for the dog to leave and stay. Kano sank down again to lie once more without a move.

'Well, Keith, how about the dogs now?' Hornsby inquired.

'Humph!' Major Baker stroked his moustache and looked at Dan Hollick, taking in the way he was dressed without any great signs of approval.

'Have to admit you caught the chap alright. But dash it, Tony. Look at him, cap comforter, J.G. uniform, 48 webbing, jungle-boots. Sneaking around in the dark there like an owl. I like to see a sentry patrolling under the lights—gives me confidence. A smart sentry out there gives the Chinese a show, scares them off.'

Hollick and Hornsby exchanged glances, both were thinking the same thing. Dan hoped his C.O. would hold his temper, for Hornsby was inclined to say what he thought, particularly where his dogs were concerned. They had run across this type of thinking before.

The officers of the army often could not see how dogs should be used correctly, in some cases they did not even think dogs should be used at all. However, for once, Hornsby did not lose his temper, but explained, or tried to explain, exactly how dogs should be used and worked for guard duties.

Dan Hollick listened to Hornsby while looking around. The perimeter lights were badly arranged. They should shine on the outside of the fence, not on the inside. That should be left in partial shadow.

That way the sentry would be patrolling unseen while anyone approaching the fence would be clearly lit up. Dan was also wondering how a man could have confidence in a normal sentry after the losses which were being sustained from every Depot around Kwang.

'You've seen what the dogs can do, Keith,' Hornsby was saying as they started to walk back to the guardroom. 'I could lay on a full scale demonstration in the daylight for you, but I haven't enough trained men yet and my training staff are working day and night. The first batch of handlers will be ready for duty on Monday morning. We could start work the same night'.

'I'll let you know later in the week, old chap. Like to think it over first. I don't suppose your chaps could move around in the centre and let my blokes do the beat around the fence?'

Hornsby raised his eyes to the sky as if searching for strength to carry on. Patiently he explained, although he knew he was not getting through, that the idea of guard dogs in addition to security, was to release other men from guard duties.

Also a dog located hidden men by either scent or sound. To have a sentry wandering up and down a road, wearing heavy boots, would distract the dog. It would also be very dangerous for the sentry, for an Army dog knew only one friend, its master.

'I'll let you know on Monday, old chap.'

With that, Hornsby knew he would have to be satisfied.

Major Blake sat at his desk on the Saturday after the capture. He was thinking, not about the use of guard dogs but about his golf that afternoon. He looked up as the R.S.M. of the Depot entered, halted in front of the desk and saluted.

'We've a coolie missing, sir. I think he's still in the Depot somewhere. '

Blake came to his feet, moustache bristling. It was an old game for a coolie to hide in the Depot, chancing being missed when the others left after work. Then when the Depot was deserted except for the Security patrol, the coolie sneaked out to steal some easily transported loot and slip out through a hole ready made in the fence.

It was very annoying for Major Blake, for all the main store buildings were locked up. Unless the man was found in one of the unlocked buildings it meant going to the trouble of opening each hut to make a thorough search.

'Are you sure about it, Mr. Saunders?' the Major asked.

'Yes sir, we checked one hundred and twenty-three in this morning and only one hundred and twenty-two went out.'

JOB FOR A DOG

Blake growled angrily and left his office. The Depot staff were on parade waiting for orders. They started searching the Depot, going into every unlocked building.

The search lasted for an hour without the missing coolie being found. The men were late for their lunch now and it looked as if their afternoon off was going to be spent searching. Blake was about to order the buildings opened when R.S.M. Saunders came up with a suggestion.

'Dogs!' Blake snorted. 'Dogs? Ah. You mean Hornsby's lot. Might be an idea, sort of try out for them. Dog's supposed to locate a hidden man and all that.'

Captain Hornsby was seated in his office, hat hanging behind the door and feet elevated on to the desk top. He was listening to Sergeant Hollick making a new squad of handlers welcome to the Unit.

The phone on the desk buzzed and Hornsby removed his feet as he picked up the receiver.

'Hornsby here. What's that, Keith?' Hornsby grinned, as he listened to Blake's spluttered story.

'I'll give it a try, Keith. Be down there in fifteen minutes with Sergeant Hollick. Get all your bods cleared out ready for me.'

Dan Hollick came in answer to Hornsby's yell. The big Doberman walked by his left side, loose yet staying close to him.

It was not the normal thing for an Army guard dog to be allowed to walk loose like this but Hollick knew Kano well. They had been a team for six years and the big dog was completely trustworthy. Hollick had trained Kano not only in guard work but almost every other kind of job an Army dog was called on to perform.

'How are the new men?' Hornsby asked.

'Very good, from the looks of them sir. All volunteers and I think they'll make the grade.'

'Good, now we've just had a job dumped on our plate.'

Hollick listened as Hornsby explained about the man hidden in the R.A.O.C. Depot. Dan thought it over. He could see the difficulty of making a search. He also knew they must try.

'It won't be easy, sir,' he said.

'I agree. There's just a chance it might work, though. Major Blake says they only just found out the bloke was missing. I know they've been searching for over an hour. If we find him it'll be one in old Keith's eye.'

SEARCH SUCCESS

Dan Hollick and Kano stood at the gates of the Depot outside the guardroom. Blake, Hornsby and the same two warrant officers were on the porch of the building watching him.

With the eye of an expert, Dan studied the situation. A road which ran around the inside of the perimeter fence was clear and he knew it would be no use searching it. The unlocked buildings did not need searching either. That left the seven rows of big stores sheds in the centre of the depot. The man would be hidden in one of them.

'Kano, heel!' Hollick ordered and stepped forward, the Doberman walking at his left side. 'Watch 'em!'

At that command, Kano tensed. It was the warning that he was on guard work. He was alert for either scent or sound of a hidden man. That was how a guard dog was trained.

With a less well trained dog, Hollick would have been constantly on the watch, encouraging it to work. With an old hand like Kano it was better to leave him alone to work his own way. The dog knew what he had to do. Locating a man hidden in a closed building was an exercise he had done often before. This time, however, there were a lot of distractions not found in training areas.

At each door, Kano halted, sniffing and pricking his ears for some sound. All along 'A' line he moved without success, then 'B' line. Half way along 'C' line the dog came to a halt. The neck hair rose and a deep snarl rumbled from his throat as he looked at the door of the building.

Reaching into his pocket for his whistle, Hollick knew his dog was on to something. Before he could get out the whistle, Kano was leaping forward, hitting the end of the lead, barking and pulling towards the corner of the building.

Dan Hollick followed the dog, allowing Kano to pull him towards the edge of the building.

Rounding the corner, Kano began to pull harder and bark even louder than before, straining to get at the Chinese coolie who was climbing from the window at the side of the building. The man gave a startled yell, reaching back inside to pull out a bulging sack.

When the coolie saw Dan follow his dog around the corner, he dropped the sack and belted for the perimeter fence and freedom. Kano was tugging at the lead, now raging as he tried to get after the man.

Hollick hauled on the lead hand over hand, gripping Kano's collar and unclipped the spring release.

'Halt!' he shouted. 'Halt! Halt, or I release my dog.'

The Chinaman was not travelling slowly and did not even break his stride as he heard the shouts. Hollick gave his next order, releasing the dog.

384

'Kano, Attack!'

Kano hurled forward as if he were jet propelled, travelling so fast he overhauled the fast running coolie as if he were standing still. Between the buildings he raced, with Kano after him closing the gap at every stride. They burst into view of the watchers at the guardroom, racing across the gardens and towards the road.

Gauging the distance, Kano left the ground in a smooth leap, a deep snarl rumbling in his throat. The powerful jaws clamped on the man's arm as it swung back, then Kano's lithe muscular body struck against the legs of the running man.

The coolie was knocked sprawling by the weight of the dog, brought down hard on to the road and winded by the fall.

He lay still and Kano left in a bound, moving backwards to lie on the ground watching the man.

NARROW ESCAPE

On the veranda of the guardroom Hornsby and Blake watched all this. The Major, seeing the thief knocked down, forgot what Hornsby had told him about dogs.

The Major jumped from the veranda and hared towards the prisoner. Ignoring the warning shouts of Hornsby and Hollick, who had run up and could see what was happening, Blake ran to the coolie who was on his hands and knees.

Hollick was running flat out but he dived the last few feet, grabbing Kano's collar even as the big dog came up to attack this other stranger. Even as he did so, Hollick saw the coolie roll on to his back, a knife in his hand.

The coolie looked up, saw a face above him, a face with a bristling moustache and made a mistake. He had seen Hollick as he came out of the window and thought this was the same man. His hand shot up to grip the front of the Major's jacket, dragging him down.

Blake was taken by surprise. He lost his balance and fell over the coolie's body, landing flat on his back. He saw the coolie kneel up, the knife lifting above him. Even as he tried to grab the man's wrist Blake knew he would be too late to save himself.

Kano tore loose from Dan Hollick's grip, hurling himself up

into the air. The dog's jaws closed on to the Chinaman's wrist, and Kano's weight dragged him over backwards.

Hollick did not wait this time. He hurdled Blake and landed by the struggling coolie and the dog. He did not wait to tell the man to lie still this time, but just grabbed Kano and pulled the dog off. The coolie was scared now and could see no chance of escape so he lay still.

Hollick kicked the knife to one side than watched Hornsby and the two warrant officers running towards him. He wiped his face, feeling the sweat running down his brow. It had been close, very close, to being a nasty accident. He had not been sure, when Kano leapt forward, which of the two men the dog was going to attack.

Hornsby came to a halt. He too was looking worried, for he knew the danger Blake was in.

'Don't ever do a fool trick like that again,' he rapped out bluntly. 'When you ran up the road there, I thought we'd be taking you and the coolie to the hospital.'

Blake sat up, gasping and looking like an elderly walrus, with his huge moustache drooping.

'What?' he gasped. 'Does the dog not know I'm a friend?'

Hornsby laughed.

'Kano's only got one friend, and that's Sergeant Hollick. Now, how about the dogs for guard duties here? Kano found and caught that man after ten minutes, where your men were looking for him for over an hour and didn't find him.'

Blake's face turned even redder as he got to his feet. Blake was a good enough sport to admit he had been beaten and was now sure the dogs would be of use to him.

'Well,' he began.

'When do we start?' Hornsby asked.

'Tonight, if you want to.'

'Not likely. I want the fence repaired completely and the lights fixed so that they shine outside the fence, not in. We'll be ready to start when we see the lights changed. Fair enough?'

'Fair enough, Hornsby, you drive a hard bargain,' Blake smiled.

'How about the handler's dress?' Hornsby went on.

Blake looked at Dan Hollick's jungleboots and green uniform.

Another broad grin slit his face.

'If they go on catching thieves at this rate, I don't mind if they go on guard in bathing costumes and bowler hats.'

PART FOURTEEN

JOHNNY ORCHID

While I was writing the first series of Dan Hollick, sending in three episodes a week, I was brought into contact with a fascinating branch of an author's work. The editor of Victor *sent me a specimen strip cartoon and the script from which the artist produced it, asking if I could do this kind of story. Thinking about the prospect, which offered a most satisfactory financial remuneration, I decided to try with a series covering the work of a modern white hunter. There had been other such characters in the boys' papers, but I intended to be closer to the real thing.*

Creating Johnny Orchid was easy enough, but I soon discovered producing artist's scripts was a very specialized task. It was as different from writing 3,000 word Dan Hollick text episodes as creating them was from writing a fifty to sixty thousand word book. In a script, the plot had to be set down in thirty or forty separate frames, with not more than three 'forties' in a twelve episode series. There was a limit to how much written explanation was permissible. Speech was restricted to two or rarely three balloons per frame—and then only if not more than a couple of short words were involved. The action had to be kept flowing and the amount of people, or background detail, one could use was not great. As far as the latter was concerned, how much appeared depended upon the artist assigned to illustrate the strip. With a few exceptions. I was fortunate in having my work given to excellent illustrators.

After I had finished the first Johnny Orchid series, I was asked for more and I decided producing artist's scripts was a worthwhile pursuit. It allowed me to branch out into other action-escapism-adventure fields. My reading upon various subjects suggested numerous plots and my series were generally 'faction', fiction based on fact. However, I did very few Western scripts. The Town Tamers, *which D. C. Thomson & Co., Ltd. kindly permitted me to turn into the book of the same name, was one. Others were* The Guns Which Won the West, *stories about various types of firearms (with Dusty Fog and the Ysabel Kid making 'guest' appearances),* The Building of the Albemarle, *in which Dusty also 'starred' (although Ole Devil became General 'Bull' Hardin) and two series about the early days of the Royal Canadian Northwest Mounted Police,* The Boot and the Saddle *and* The Queen's Cowboys. *For the remainder of my career as an artist's script writer, which lasted a few years, I covered a number of subjects.*[1] *In fact, on occasion, I had two and sometimes three series running concurrently and was, I've been told, one of the very few authors to have achieved this.*[2]

[1] The following are the series for which I produced the scripts:

Johnny Orchid, White Hunter; The Guns that Won the West; The Making of the Albemarle; The Boot and the Saddle; The Queen's Cowboys; The Town Tamers; Cottrell of the Rangers (a ranger in a U.S. Wildlife Park); *The Catchem Company* (animal trappers based in Asia, Africa and America); *The Dawson of Dumballa* (White hunters in the old foot safari days, originally entitled *Fungua Safari*, Swahili for Start The Journey); *Duke Farlow, Big Game Fisher* (about a professional deep sea fishing guide in Florida, which had a *Jaws* type episode years before the movie); *The Hounds of the Hunter* (a predator hunter and his big game hounds in the U.S.A.); *It's a Dog's Life* (working dogs of various kinds through the ages); *Johnny Boyes of Kenya Colony* (stories about a legendary character); *Lord of the White Highland* (a tribute to Lord Delamere, who did much to open up Kenya for white settlement); *The Making of a White Hunter* (how Johnny Orchid learned his trade); *The Rifle and the Rod* (adventures of a roving reporter for an American hunting-fishing magazine); *The Rebel of the Iron Road* (about Lee Christmas, an engine driver who became involved in a revolution in Central America); *Steamboat Jim* (Technically a Western, being the adventures of Jim Bludso, a riverboat engineer on the Mississippi River in the early 1800s); *Long Bow* (again technically a Western, being the story of a pioneer in America who used a bow and arrows instead of a Kentucky rifle. This series appeared in *Hotspur*, all the others being in *Victor*);

As with *Son of a Yellow Cop*, a series about building the railroad from Mombasa to Lake Victoria, *The Lunatic Line*—which was the name its would-be detractors in England gave to the project—was accepted, paid for, but never appeared.

[2] A further claim to fame is that I contrived to introduce *girls* into the generally completely masculine preserves of the boys' papers. Not only did *Johnny Orchid* have the pretty receptionist, but in one episode of *The Town Tamers*, Calamity Jane—portrayed wonderfully by artist Macabich, another of my favourites—took a *very* active part in the proceedings, although *not* in the kind of relationship she has with Mark Counter.

This then is an example of my work as an artist's script writer. It was illustrated by Arnau, one of my favourites.

(Don't blame me. Transworld said they didn't believe they would get the full script in.)

Then Mendoza broke one of the strictest rules of the Park. He got out of his car, armed with his Garand service rifle.

BAH! RULES, THEY ARE MADE TO BE BROKEN. I WILL PAY ANY FINE. I HAVE PLENTY OF MONEY.

IT'S NOT THAT EASY. THEY DON'T FINE YOU FOR SHOOTING IN THE PARK. THEY PUT YOU IN JAIL, AND WE'D LOSE OUR LICENCE TO HUNT. AND YOU CAN'T USE ANY SEMI-AUTO-MATIC RIFLE LIKE THIS FOR HUNTING EITHER.

Later, we pulled up when we sighted a pride of lions.

THERE HE IS, OLD M'KUBWA SANA HIMSELF, MR MENDOZA. HE'S ALWAYS AROUND THIS PART OF THE PARK.

LET GO! I WANT THAT LION. IT IS A BETTER ONE THAN HENRANDEZ BROUGHT BACK.

THAT'S M'KUBWA SANA, 'OLD VERY BIG.' HE'S THE PRIDE OF THE NATIONAL PARK. BESIDES, IT'S ILLEGAL TO SHOOT HERE.

PUT UP YOUR GUN, YOU FOOL!

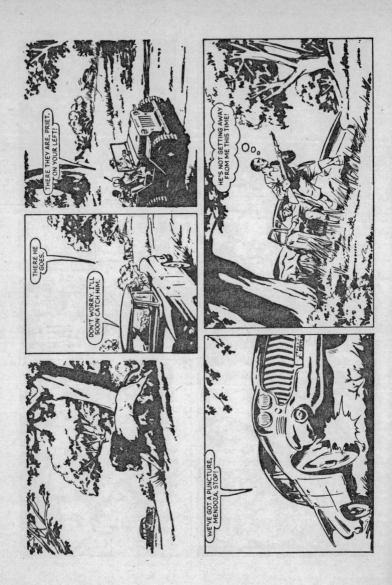

PART FIFTEEN

Johnny Boyland in

JOHNNY BOYLAND AND THE QUAIL HUNTERS

In 1968, shortly after Transworld Publishers had taken over my contract from Brown Watson Ltd., I was contacted by the editor of Boys' World Annual *and asked if I could write a Western story for the next year's edition. I accepted as thinking up a plot presented no difficulty. In fact, I already had one which would be suitable. Some time before, I had written what I hoped would be the first four episodes of a 'factional' artist's script based on the early life of arguably the world's best and certainly the most prolific designer of firearms, John Moses Browning.[1] For some reason which was never explained, the editor of* Victor—*to whom the manuscripts were submitted—did not care for the project and it was rejected.[2] However, I never forget an idea. So I dug out the scripts from the files and selected one which I transformed into the requested short story. The hero was changed into Johnny Boyland, who—like John Moses Browning—had been trained by his gunsmith father and, as the following story proves, had learned his trade very well.[3]*

[1] John Moses Browning makes a 'guest' appearance in: *Calamity Spells Trouble*.

[2] This was one of my very few rejections. Another was *Bring Law to Kenya Colony*, a 'factional' artist's script about the formation of the Kenya Police. Regrettably, the latter was submitted at a time when—to a certain section of the community, anyway—anything which showed how beneficial aspects of colonialism had been was highly unpopular and this may have been why the series was rejected.

[3] Finally, there are numerous derogatory comments made by 'intellectuals' in interviews about the 'Boys' World' heroics of various action-escapism-adventure movies. Personally, I fail to see what is wrong with exhibiting courage, loyalty to one's country, decency and a willingness to stand by one's friends and that is what so-called 'Boys' World' heroics is all about.

JOHNNY BOYLAND AND THE QUAIL HUNTERS

The crack of the shotgun split the lazy morning silence like a bullwhip. Johnny Boyland slapped the butt of his rifle angrily and gritted his teeth.

'Dogonne it!' he muttered. 'I spend half an hour tracking that mule deer, then some trigger happy cowboy lets off a shot and ...'

He drew a coloured neckerchief across his moist brow as the big buck mule deer bounded farther down the slope and, reaching the stream running through the valley, leapt across and began loping up the other side.

Suddenly Johnny saw another chance and raised his Winchester again. Instantly the speeding animal was in his sights. His finger curled round the trigger and squeezed ... then he let the rifle drop to his side.

It was no good ... the gun was perfect for close range rapid fire—but at two hundred yards it lacked the power to kill the buck. He could only hope to wound it at this distance, leaving it to die slowly and painfully. And he didn't want that.

The tall, well-built youngster picked up a stone and cast it down into the shallow stream. He waited until it had plopped into the water, then said: 'Dang the luck!'

He turned and walked slowly back towards his horse. He was still a good way from it when another shotgun blast ripped the air. Then another, and another ....

He spun round in the direction of the shots. 'What're them fellers playing at? They'll spook every mule from here to Idaho and back the long way!'

He reached the horse and slid the carbine into its saddleboot. There seemed no point in continuing to hunt in that area, so he rode back along his tracks. He felt annoyed at the men with the shotguns for frightening the buck. With his parents leaving that afternoon on a tour of the surrounding ranches, he would be left in charge of the family's gunsmith business and unable to go hunting until they returned. He had hoped to collect a buck, but with those fellers banging off their shotguns down Saw Ridge way he figured the chances of doing so were slight.

At noon, after a fruitless search for another buck, Johnny was riding along the westbound trail to Walkerville. Suddenly a large pointer dog dashed yapping and barking from the woods flanking the trail. Two men followed it. They wore deerstalker hats, loose jackets over turtleneck sweaters, demin pants tucked into stout canvas leggings, and heavy walking boots.

Johnny recognized them as Cyrus Orzy and Rudolph Eggars, visiting sportsmen who had arrived in Walkerville earlier that week. They had come to Wyoming in search of better sport than was obtainable back East. Although the short, slim Orzy smiled, his taller, heavily-moustached companion scowled at the sight of the youngster.

'Hello, young feller,' Orzy greeted amiably. 'Looks as if you haven't had any luck either.'

'No, sir,' Johnny replied. He judged from the shotguns they carried and the direction from which they had appeared that they must have been responsible for disturbing the buck. 'Didn't you get anything?'

'Nope. 'Cept mebbe a sore finger from pulling this darn trigger.' He chuckled and held up a fine looking shotgun. 'We've been after bobwhite quail. P'raps you heard us shooting?'

'I heard.'

'They're sure hard little guys to hit,' Orzy went on. 'In fact, we haven't dropped a single bird all day. Still, that's hunting.'

'It sure is,' Johnny grinned, then remembered the time. 'Well, I'd best be getting back home.'

He held his horse to a fast trot and soon reached Walkerville. He rode along the main street. The County Sheriff and a tall, smartly dressed townsman were coming from the bank, followed by Deputy Town Marshal Vic Stirton.

The tall, lean young Deputy shook hands with the two men,

they went to their horses and mounted, the townsman swinging astride with almost military precision. After speaking quietly but urgently to Vic, the Sheriff accompanied the other man along the trail leading to the County Seat.

'Did you finish cleaning the barrels of my shotgun, Johnny?' Vic asked the youngster.

'It's nearly done ... but you said you didn't want it back in any hurry.'

'I don't,' Vic said, just a shade too quickly. 'Only I—I feel sort of undressed without that old pacifier around.'

Johnny looked at the Deputy for a long moment. He knew there was more to Vic's concern than he had revealed—but that was none of his business.

Dressed in cowhand clothes, Vic carried an 1860 Army Colt revolver in the contoured holster of his gunbelt and was very good with it. Normally he performed his duties with no other weapon and only produced the shotgun in the event of serious trouble. With payday for the local ranches two weeks away, the town was peaceful. Sufficiently so for Vic to take the opportunity to have the weapon overhauled. At the time of handing it over, he had told Johnny there was no immediate rush for its return.

'Come on,' smiled Johnny, 'I'll finish it now. Hey though, what did the Sheriff want?'

'Oh, he was just passing through,' Vic answered in a matter-of-fact tone.

Johnny asked no further questions and went with Vic to his father's shop. After saying goodbye to his parents and stabling his horse, Johnny joined Vic in the front of the shop and produced the shotgun. Ever since he had been old enough to handle tools, Johnny had helped his father. At sixteen, he was a competent gunsmith. Certainly Vic, whose life occasionally depended on their correct functioning, did not hesitate to let the youngster carry out repairs on his weapons.

Sitting on the counter, Vic watched the deft manner with which Johnny completed his work and reassembled the shotgun. Just as the youngster handed over the weapons, Cyrus Orzy entered the shop.

'Hello, Deputy. Well, it's you, young feller,' the dude beamed,

402

laying his magnificent shotgun on the counter. 'Is the gunsmith here?'

'Pa's out of town, sir,' Johnny answered. 'Is something wrong?'

'The barrels are leaded,' Orzy explained. 'Darn it! Now I'll not be able to go hunting in the morning.'

'I can fix it for you,' Johnny offered.

'He can do it alright,' Vic broke in, holding his own shotgun as proof. 'This old scatter was so badly leaded that you'd've thought the barrels were two calibre instead of ten gauge. Look at them now.'

'A most satisfactory piece of work,' Orzy declared after examining the gun. 'By all means do mine young feller. They're not so badly leaded, but I like clean barrels for quail hunting. Can you have it ready for me by ten o'clock tomorrow?'

'It'll be ready,' Johnny promised.

'Fine, fine!' Orzy boomed. 'I think the leading's why I kept missing today.' He winked at Johnny and chuckled. 'At least, that makes as good an excuse as any.'

Laughing and talking animatedly, the dude left the shop with Vic. Johnny took up the shotgun, broke it open and looked down the barrels. Instead of finding two smooth tubes, he saw a number of small protuberances and, even without Orzy's explanation, would have known what caused them.

Softened by the heat of the exploding powder charge and friction raised during the bullet's passage along the barrel, fragments of lead adhered to the inside of the tube. Subsequent firings added to the mounds. Although the leading had not been sufficient to reduce the ·729 inch of the twelve gauge barrel to ·22 calibre, it would be enough to ruin the shots' trajectory; an important factor when bird-hunting.

But something nagged at Johnny's subconscious as he examined the shotgun. He put it from his thoughts and concentrated on the job in hand. As Orzy had shown the good sense to bring the gun in the early stages of leading, Johhny found no great difficulty in removing the debris.

Working hard, he had both tubes cleared of the protuberances by nightfall. With his parents away he had to do his own house-keeping, so he left the gun on the bench and did not bother to clean away the leading before going to cook his supper.

At nine o'clock the next morning, Johnny opened the shop and gave the shotgun a final check. Just as he was about to start tidying his work-bench, he heard a wild screech and the sound of a shot rang out along the street.

'Yahoo!' howled a squeaky voice. 'Yahoo! I've done it!'

Johnny left the shop and saw Vic Stirton burst from the jailhouse carrying the ten gauge shotgun. Other Walkerville citizens appeared from their homes, staring at the man responsible for the noise.

Short, dirty, bewhiskered, he looked a typical old desert-rat prospector. Leading a mule carrying his pick, shovel, gold-pan and other property, he stumped along the main street and fired a big old Colt Dragoon revolver into the air.

'Gold!' screeched the old-timer. 'I done found gold!'

Hearing the good news, people flocked forward. They gathered around the old man, jostling each other and firing questions at him.

Johnny ran up, following on Vic's heels as the Deputy thrust unceremoniously through the crowd. They arrived in time to see the prospector holster his Dragoon and haul a leather pouch from his trouser pocket. From it, he poured a small pile of gold nuggets into his left hand.

'There she be!' the old man cackled triumphantly, his toothless mouth falling apart with awe. 'And there's plenty more where these came from!'

'Where'd that be, old timer?' asked one of the crowd.

Neither Johnny nor Vic—nor even the man who asked—expected the prospector to answer. Even if he did, they doubted whether he would tell the truth. But he let out a chuckle and waved his right hand in the direction from which he had come.

'Out on Saw Ridge! I hit me a big vein there ... now I's on m'way to register ma claim.'

'Saw Ridge!' yelled a dozen excited voices. 'There's gold on Saw Ridge!'

'It's open range out there!' another speaker went on.

'Hey now!' Vic barked, seeing what was happening and wanting to check it if he could. 'Don't let's go off half-cocked . . .'

He might have saved his breath for all the effect his warning had on the crowd. Already gold-fever gripped them. Thoughts of the big gold discoveries in California and Montana filled every head. Under law, the precious metal belonged to whoever discovered it and staked a claim with the local Land Office. Nobody owned the Saw Ridge area, so all who wished could go there, select, mark out and register a claim. Much the same thoughts raced through the heads of the crowd. The quicker one reached Saw Ridge the better the chances of staking a good claim.

Ignoring the Deputy's words, the crowd split up. Some headed for their homes to collect digging implements. Others dashed straight out of town, hoping to pick a site and return after marking it to collect the means of tearing a fortune from the hard rock of the ridge. In five minutes a rush of men, women and children left town. The street was deserted except for Johnny, Vic and the old prospector.

'Waal I'll be!' the old timer snorted, returning his nuggets to the pouch. 'I never figured on nothing like this!'

'What did you expect?' Vic countered. 'Yelling you'd found gold that way!'

'Ain't never found none before, sonny. So how'd I kn——' the old man cut himself short, fury twisting his leathery old face. Thrusting the pouch into his pocket, he reached for the butt of the Dragoon. 'Dang 'em! They ain't gonna jump ma claim. I'll git out there and . . .'

'If you try, I'll toss you into the jail-house!' Vic warned. 'Go stake your claim. I'll ride out there and make sure nobody steals it from you.'

'I trust you, sonny,' the prospector decided. 'Ye've got an honest face.'

'Have a box of bullets waiting for me, Johnny,' Vic requested as the old man walked away. 'I'll pick them up after I've collected my horse.'

'Can you fetch mine along?' Johnny asked. 'I'll come and lend a hand.'

Vic frowned, then nodded. If serious trouble developed he could use Johnny as his messenger to take word to the County Seat.

There was a worried expression on the Deputy's face as he looked at the bank. Then he turned and headed in the direction of the livery barn to get the horses.

As Johnny reached the shop he saw Orzy's shotgun on the work bench. He wondered, as he crossed the room, why the two dudes had not arrived to investigate the disturbance. Then something caught his eye, a glinting among the leading chipped from the barrels. He bent down and made a closer examination. A low whistle broke from his lips. Thoughts flooded into his head, including the one which had nagged at him the previous afternoon while preparing to clean the gun.

For a moment Johnny stood looking down ... he then reached a decision and picked up one of his tools.

'Is my gun finished, young feller?' Orzy called as he entered the shop some five minutes later.

'Just done now, sir,' Johnny replied, handing it over. 'I'd've fetched it sooner, but I was watching the folk ...'

'Oh that,' Orzy smiled, breaking open and inspecting the gun. 'Darned if I didn't nearly go myself. But my partner reminded me we're here for a holiday. You've done a first rate piece of work here, I must say.'

At that moment Vic entered the shop. 'Come on, Johnny,' he said. 'I reckoned I'd best go out to Saw Ridge and keep the peace, Mr. Orzy.'

'A sound decision!' boomed the dude. 'There might be fighting over who owns which claim if you don't.'

'Vic,' Johnny said as he and the Deputy rode fast out of Walkerville. 'When did you last shoot any bobwhite quail around here?'

'Never,' Vic replied. 'You should know there aren't any out this way.'

'Orzy said he was hunting them, and missing them, yesterday.'

'He must've meant sage-grouse.'

'Nope. He said they'd been after bobwhite quail. Say ... is Mr. Orzy rich?'

'I reckon so,' said Vic, wondering what the youngster was driving at.

'Rich enough to use gold shot in his gun? Because that's what it was leaded with!'

406

'Gold!' the Deputy spat out stopping his horse.

'Sure,' agreed Johnny, 'It was mostly gold I dug out of the barrels. When I saw it, I remembered that Orzy was up on Saw Ridge yesterday.'

Vic's eyes flamed. 'Then instead of hunting, they must have been salting a mine!'

Salting a mine was an old trick. A small amount of gold would be put into an otherwise worthless property to make a victim believe he had a valuable mine. One way of introducing the gold was to fire nuggets from a shotgun into a cliff face or rocky slope.

'Why'd they do it?' Johnny asked.

'Because of what's in the bank, I reckon!' Vic growled, turning his horse back towards town. 'That feller you saw with the Sheriff is an Army pay-master. He deposited twenty thousand dollars in the bank ready for the Army's remount buyer when he comes on Friday. Only it's supposed to be a secret. There's a plot to steal the money on its way here. That's why it came early and we haven't brought in any extra guards, to avoid attracting the attention of would-be bank robbers.'

'Now I know why you wanted your shotgun in a hurry.'

'Yeah,' Vic agreed, drawing the weapon from his saddleboot. 'I figured it'd be best to have old Betsy here on hand. Come on. Orzy must have rigged that gold-rush to clear the town while he robbed the bank.'

Instead of going along the main street, Johnny and Vic left their horses behind a house on the outskirts of the town. They advanced by the back streets towards the rear of the bank. Cautiously they moved along the alley by the bank. There were no windows in that side of the building so they could not see if their suspicions were correct. Vic peered carefully around the corner. Three good horses stood in front of the bank, their reins hanging over—but not tied to—the hitching rail. It was an old outlaw habit, allowing for an even quicker getaway should one become necessary.

'Don't turn, Deputy!' Orzy's voice ordered from behind them. 'Straighten up slow, then both of you toss your weapons into the street.'

Looking back over his shoulder, Vic knew that he must obey.

Orzy stood at the rear opening of the alley, lining his shotgun with both hammers drawn back to full cock. To argue or resist would be fatal. Vic tossed his shotgun into the centre of the street and Johnny flipped his Winchester after it.

'That's better,' sniggered Orzy. 'Now turn and back into the street before you take your gunbelt off. That corner's too close for my liking.'

'You won't get far before the law. . . .'

'Shut up!' Orzy snapped. 'The Sheriff and Army are making a big thing of guarding the bank at the County Seat, after the rumours I started about an organized attempt to steal the remount purchase money. So they'll not be around to stop us!'

'You were lucky they thought of this notion of bringing the money here,' Vic commented playing for time.

'Lucky nothing Deputy! Until recently I was a trusted member of the Treasury Department and in a position to offer a smart method of safeguarding the money. Hence its, and my, arrival here.

'And you can't expect help from the citizens either ... as we planned, they're all rushing up to Saw Ridge to get in on my prospector friend's imaginary gold-strike. So I ask you, who can stop us?'

'I say Vic can,' Johnny retorted.

'I admire your faith in the Deputy, young feller,' Orzy laughed and gestured with his weapon. 'But I'm afraid it's misplaced as long as I'm pointing this shotgun at him.'

'Don't let that worry you, Vic,' Johnny said confidently. 'After I found that the barrels were leaded with gold and remembered they'd been hunting up at Saw Ridge yesterday, I took out the firing pins.'

That was all Vic needed! Such was his faith in the young gun-smith that he fell to one knee and stabbed a right hand at his Colt. Orzy reacted with equal speed. He levelled the shotgun against his shoulder ... squeezed the triggers ... and two dry clicks told him that Johnny had done what he said.

Instantly he tossed the shotgun aside and jabbed his hand to-wards a holstered pistol. But Vic was ready—his revolver spat flame, and a bullet smashed into Orzy's shoulder, spinning him

408

round. The pistol leapt from his fingers and he crumpled to the dust.

A second later the doors of the bank burst open and Eggars came flying out, pistol in hand. He saw the Deputy and swung up his weapon. Vic threw himself to one side as the dude fired. Two bullets slashed the air inches above Vic's head as he landed in a rolling dive. He angled two swift shots upwards ... Eggars caught both bullets in the chest and reeled. Desperately he squeezed off another round. It went wild and he measured his length on the sidewalk.

Johnny snatched up his carbine and pivoted towards the bank door. He sank to his left knee and cradled the Winchester's butt against his shoulder just as the old prospector—carrying two bulging saddlebags—appeared from the bank.

'Enough!' choked the old timer, dropping the saddlebags and raising his hands. 'Don't shoot! I'm tricky, not tough!'

At noon the first of the dejected gold-seekers began to trickle back into town. They learned of the attempted hold-up from an irate bank manager who had remained at his post and been tied to a chair while the robbery took place.

In the jail, Orzy sat on a bed, his shoulder bandaged. As usual, he was in a talkative mood. After explaining that he had been keeping watch to make sure everybody had left town when he saw Vic and Johnny return, he went on: 'I don't see how you came to suspect me.'

'You gave yourself away,' Johnny explained. 'There are no bob-white quail around here. This is sage grouse country.'

'Such a small mistake,' Orzy sighed. 'I didn't want to ruin the shotgun, even though I suspected the leading might be gold. That's why I brought it to you. I knew your father would be away and, while satisfied you could clean the barrels, I never expected you to identify the lead as gold.'

'Johnny's a whole heap smarter than you figured,' Vic pointed out.

'That he is. He suspected me and made sure the gun wouldn't fire.'

'I could always say it was a mistake later, if I was wrong,'

Johnny remarked.

'Well,' Orzy sniffed. 'You'd better have that shotgun of mine, young feller. Guess I won't be needing it for some time. There's only one thing though ...'

'Yes, sir?' Johnny asked. 'What's that?'

The dude grinned. 'Don't go shooting any bobwhite quail ... they lead the barrel too quickly.'

AUTHOR'S LAST WORD

Well, that's all we have room for unfortunately!

I've enjoyed writing this, my one hundredth book, probably more than any other and I hope that you all have found it just as enjoyable. I apologize, however, for not having been able to include Waxahachie Smith and Amanda 'the School Swot' Tweedle, but space was not available. They will be back in the future, that I promise you.

Once again, I would like to extend my thanks to all of you for having bought and read my books in the past. I also hope you will continue to do so. This is essential, as I am far too idle to start working for my living again.

As they say in Texas:
Best wishes, you-all,
Come back again now, mind.
Yours sincerely,

(Already busily working towards J.T.'s Two Hundredth, but please don't start trying to order it just yet).

APPENDICES

APPENDIX ONE

During the War Between The States, at the age of seventeen, Dustine Edward Marsden 'Dusty' Fog had won promotion in the field and was put in command of Company 'C', Texas Light Cavalry.[1] Leading them during the Arkansas Campaign, he had earned the reputation for being an exceptionally capable military raider and a worthy contemporary for the South's other leading exponents, John Singleton Mosby and Turner Ashby.[2] In addition to preventing a pair of pro-Union fanatics from starting an Indian uprising which would have decimated most of Texas,[3] he had supported Belle Boyd, the Rebel Spy,[4] on two of her most dangerous assignments.[5]

When the War had finished, he had become the segundo of the Great OD Connected ranch in Rio Hondo County, Texas. Its owner and his uncle, General Jackson Baines 'Old Devil' Hardin had been crippled in a riding accident,[6] placing much responsibility—including handling an important mission upon which the good relations between the United States and Mexico had hung in the balance[7]—upon his young shoulders. After helping to gather horses to replenish the ranch's depleted *remuda*,[8] he had been sent to assist Colonel Charles Goodnight on the trail drive to Fort

[1] Told in: *You're in Command Now, Mr. Fog.*
[2] Told in: *The Big Gun*; *Under the Stars and Bars*; *The Fastest Gun in Texas* and *Kill Dusty Fog!*
[3] Told in: *The Devil Gun.*
[4] Further details of Belle Boyd's career are given in: *The Hooded Riders*; *The Bad Bunch*, *To Arms, to Arms in Dixie*; *The South Will Rise Again* and *The Whip and the War Lance.*
[5] Told in: *The Colt and the Sabre* and *The Rebel Spy.*
[6] Told in the 'The Paint' episode of *The Fastest Gun in Texas.*
[7] Told in: *The Ysabel Kid.*
[8] Told in: *·44 Calibre Man* and *A Horse Called Mogollon.*

Sumner, New Mexico, which had done much to help the Lone Star State to recover from the impoverished conditions left by the War.[9] With that achieved, he had been equally successful in helping Goodnight convince other ranchers it would be possible to drive large herds of cattle to the railroad in Kansas.[10]

Having proven himself to be a first class cowhand, Dusty went on to become acknowledged as a very capable trail boss,[11] round-up captain,[12] and town taming lawman.[13] Competing in a revolver handling competition at the Cochise County Fair, he won the title, 'The Fastest Gun In The West', by beating many other experts in the *pistolero* line.[14] In later years, following his marriage to Lady Winifred Amelia 'Freddie Woods' Besgrove-Woodstole,[15] he became a notable diplomat.

Dusty Fog never found his lack of stature an impediment. In addition to being naturally strong, he had taught himself to be completely ambidextrous. Possessing perfectly attuned reflexes, he could draw either or both his Colts—whether of the 1860 Army Model[16] or their improved successors, the 'Peacemakers'[17] —with lightning speed and great accuracy. Ole Devil Hardin's

[9] Told in: *Goodnight's Dream* (Bantam edition title *The Floating Outfit*) and *From Hide and Horn.*

[10] Told in: *Set Texas Back on her Feet* and *The Hide and Tallow Men.*

[11] Told in: *Trail Boss.*

[12] Told in: *The Man from Texas.*

[13] Told in: *Quiet Town*; *The Making of a Lawman*; *The Trouble Busters*; *The Small Texan* and *The Town Tamers.*

[14] Told in: *Gun Wizard.*

[15] Their grandson, Alvin Dustine 'Cap' Fog became the finest combat shot of his generation and the youngest man ever to become a captain in the Texas Rangers, see: *'Cap' Fog, Texas Ranger, Meet Mr. J. G. Reeder.*

[16] Although the military sometimes claimed derisively that it was easier to kill a sailor than a soldier, the weight factor of the respective weapons had caused the United States' Navy to adopt a revolver of ·36 calibre while the Army employed one of ·44. The weapon would be carried on a seaman's belt and not—handguns having originally and primarily been developed for use by cavalry—on the person or saddle of a man who would be doing most of his travelling on the back of a horse. Therefore, ·44 became known as the 'Army' calibre and ·36 the 'Navy'.

[17] Introduced in 1873 as the Colt Model P 'Single Action Army' revolver, but more generally referred to as the 'Peacemaker', production was continued until 1941 when it was taken out of the line to make way for more modern weapons required in World War II. Over *three hundred and fifty thousand* were manufactured in practically every handgun calibre—with the exception of the ·41 and ·44 Magnums, which were not developed during the production period—from ·22 Short rimfire to ·476 Eley. However, the majority fired either ·45 or ·44·40; the latter allowing the same

valet, Tommy Okasi,[18] was Japanese and a trained *Samurai* and from him Dusty learned *ju-jitsu* and *karate*.[19] Neither had received the publicity they were given in later years and were little known in the Western Hemisphere at that time. So the knowledge was very useful when he had to fight bare-handed against larger, heavier and stronger men.

---

ammunition to be used in the Winchester Model of 1873 rifle.

The barrel lengths were from three inches in the 'Storekeeper' Model, which did not have an extractor rod, to the sixteen inches of the so-called 'Butline Special'. The latter was offered with an attachable metal skeleton butt stock so it could be used as a carbine. The main barrel lengths were: Cavalry, seven and a half inches; Artillery, five and a half inches; Civilian, four and three-quarter inches. Popular demand, said to have been caused by the upsurge of action-escapism-adventure Western series on television, brought the Peacemaker back into production in 1955 and it is still in the line.

[18] For further information about 'Tommy Okasi', see Appendix Six.

[19] As is told in: *Kill Dusty Fog!*, *The Bad Bunch*, *McGraw's Inheritance*, *The Rio Hondo War* and *Gunsmoke Thunder*. General Hardin's 'granddaughter', Betty, was also given instruction in *ju-jitsu* and *karate* by Tommy Okasi and gained considerable proficiency.

APPENDIX TWO

With his exceptional good looks and magnificent physical development, Mark Counter presented the kind of appearance which many people expected of Dusty Fog. It was a fact of which they took advantage when the need arose[1] and at least once was almost the cause of Mark being killed in mistake for Dusty.[2]

While serving as a lieutenant under General Bushrod Sheldon's command in the War Between The States, Mark's merits as an efficient and courageous officer had been overshadowed by his taste in uniforms. Always a dandy, coming from a wealthy family, had allowed him to indulge his whims. His clothing, particularly a skirtless tunic, had been much copied by the other young bloods of the Confederate States' Army despite considerable opposition and disapproval on the part of hide-bound senior officers.

When peace had come, Mark followed Sheldon to fight for Emperor Maximilian in Mexico. There he met Dusty Fog and the Ysabel Kid, helping with the former's mission.[3] On returning to Texas, he had been invited to join the OD Connected's floating outfit.[4] Knowing his elder brothers could help his father, Big Rance, to run the R Over C ranch in the Big Bend country—and suspecting life would be more exciting with Dusty and the Kid— he had accepted.

[1] One occasion is described in: *The South Will Rise Again.*

[2] One incident is told in: *Beguinage.*

[3] Told in: *The Ysabel Kid.*

[4] 'Floating outfit: a group of four to six cowhands employed by a large ranch to work the more distant sections of the property. Taking food in a chuck wagon, or 'greasy sack' on the back of a mule, they would be away from the ranch house for long periods. Because of General Jackson Baines 'Ole Devil' Hardin's prominence in the affairs of Texas, the OD Connected's floating outfit were frequently sent to assist his friends who found themselves in trouble or endangered.

An expert cowhand, Mark was known as Dusty's right bower.[5] He also gained acclaim by virtue of his enormous strength and ability in a roughhouse brawl. However, due to being so much in the small Texan's company, his full potential as a gun fighter received little attention. Men who were competent to judge such matters stated that he was second only to the Rio Hondo gun wizard in speed and accuracy.

Many women found Mark's appearance irresistible, including Miss Martha Jane Canary,[6] who was better known as 'Calamity Jane'.[7] In his younger days, only one—the lady outlaw, Belle Starr—held his heart.[8] It was not until several years after her death that he courted and married Dawn Sutherland[9] who he had first met on the Goodnight trail drive to Fort Sumner, New Mexico.[10]

[5] 'Right bower': second highest trump card in the game of euchre.
[6] Mark's main meetings with Miss Martha Jane Canary are told in: *Troubled Range*, *The Wildcats* and *The Fortune Hunters*.
[7] Books in which Martha Jane Canary takes a leading role are: *Cold Deck*, *Hot Lead*; *Calamity Spells Trouble*; *Trouble Trail*; *The Cow Thieves*; *White Stallion*, *Red Mare* (co-starring the Ysabel Kid); *The Big Hunt* (in which Mark Counter makes a guest appearance); *The Whip and the War Lance* (co-starring Belle Boyd).
[8] How Mark's romance with Belle Starr commenced, progressed and ended is recorded in the 'The Bounty on Belle Starr's Scalp' episode of *Trouble Range*, *Rangeland Hercules*; the 'The Lady Known as Belle' episode of *The Hard Riders* and *Guns in the Night*. She also appears in *Hell in the Palo Duro* and *Go Back to Hell*, assisting Dusty Fog, the Ysabel Kid and Waco and in *The Bad Bunch* and *The Quest for Bowie's Blade*.
[9] Two of Mark's great grandchildren, Deputy Sheriff Bradford Counter and James Allenvale 'Bunduki' Gunn, achieved considerable fame on their own behalf. Details of the former's career as a peace officer are given in the Rockabye County series covering various aspects of modern law enforcement in Texas and the latter's life story is recorded in the Bunduki series.
[10] The first meeting is described in: *Goodnight's Dream* and *From Hide and Horn*.

APPENDIX THREE

Raven Head, the only daughter of Chief Long Walker, war leader of the *Pehnane*—Wasp, Quick Stinger, or Raider—Comanches' Dog Soldier lodge and his French Creole *pairaivo*,[1] married an Irish Kentuckian adventurer, Sam Ysabel, but died giving birth to their first child. Baptized with the name, Loncey Dalton Ysabel, the boy was raised in the fashion of the *Nemenuh*.[2] With his father away on the family's combined business of mustanging—catching and breaking wild horses—and smuggling, his education had been left largely in the hands of his maternal grandfather.[3] From Long Walker he had learned all those things a Comanche warrior must know: how to ride the wildest, freshly caught mustang, or when raiding—a polite name for the favourite *Nemenuh* sport of horse stealing to subjugate domesticated mounts to his will; to follow the faintest tracks and conceal traces of his own passing;[4] to locate hidden enemies and keep out of sight himself when the need arose; to move in silence through the thickest cover, or on the darkest of nights and to be highly proficient in the use of a variety of weapons.

In all the subjects, the boy had proved an excellent pupil. He had inherited his father's Kentuckian rifle shooting skill and, while not real fast on the draw—taking slightly over a second, where a top hand could practically halve that time—he performed pass-

[1] *Pairaivo:* first or favourite wife. As in the case of the other Comanche names, this is a phonetic spelling.

[2] *Nemenuh:* 'The People', the Comanches' name for their nation. Members of the other Indian races with whom they came into contact called them the '*Tshaoh*, the Enemy People'.

[3] Told in: *Comanche.*

[4] An example of the Ysabel Kid's ability to conceal his tracks is given in the 'The Half Breed' episode of *The Half Breed.*

ably with his Colt Second Model Dragoon revolver. He had won his *Pehnane* man-name, *Cuchilo*—Spanish for 'Knife'—by his exceptional skill in wielding one as a weapon. It was claimed that he could equal the alleged designer[5] in performing with the massive and special type of blade[6] which bore Colonel James Bowie's name.[7]

Joining his father on smuggling expeditions along the Rio Grande, the boy had become know to the Mexicans of the border country as *Cabrito*: a name which, although meaning a young goat, had come from hearing white men refer to him as the Ysabel Kid and was spoken *very* respectfully in such a context. Smuggling did not attract mild-mannered pacifists, but even the roughest and toughest of the bloody border's brood had acknowledged that it did not pay to rile up Sam Ysabel's son. The Kid's education and upbringing had not been calculated to develop an over-inflated sense of the sanctity of human life. When crossed, he dealt with the situation like a *Pehnane* Dog Soldier—to which war lodge of savage and efficient warriors he had been initiated and belonged—swiftly and in an effectively deadly manner.

During the War Between The States, the Kid and his father had commenced by riding as scouts for Dixie's 'Grey Ghost', Colonel John Singleton Mosby. Later, their specialized knowledge and talents were converted to having them collect and deliver to the Confederate States' authorities in Texas supplies which had been

[5] Some researchers claim that the actual designer of the knife was James Bowie's eldest brother, Rezin Pleasant. It was made by the master cutler, James Black, of Arkansas. (A few authorities state it was manufactured by Jesse Cliffe, a white blacksmith employed on the Bowie family's plantation in Rapides Parish, Louisiana).

[6] As all James Black's, q.v., bowie knives were hand-made, there were variations in their dimensions. The specimen owned by the Ysabel Kid had a blade eleven and a half inches long, two and a half inches wide and a quarter of an inch thick at the guard. According to W. D. 'Bo' Randall of Randall Made Knives, Orlando, Florida—a master cutler and authority on the subject—Bowie's knife weighed forty-three ounces, having a blade eleven inches long, two and a quarter inches wide and three-eighths of an inch thick. One thing they all had in common was a 'clip' point, where the last few inches on the back of the blade joins the main cutting surface in a concave arc to become an extension of it.

[7] What happened to James Bowie's knife after his death during the final assault at the siege of the Alamo Mission, San Antonio de Bexar, Texas, on March the 6th, 1836 is told in: *Get Urrea* and *The Quest for Bowie's Blade*.

run through the blockade imposed by the United States' Navy into Matamoros, or purchased elsewhere in Mexico. It had been hard and dangerous work, but never more so than on the two occasions when they had become involved on a mission with Belle Boyd, the Rebel spy.[8]

Soon after the end of the war, Sam Ysabel had been murdered. While hunting for the killers, the Kid had met Dusty Fog and Mark Counter.[9] When the mission upon which they had been engaged came to its successful conclusion, learning that the Kid no longer wished to follow the family business of smuggling. Dusty had offered him employment on the OD Connected ranch. It had been in the capacity of a scout, rather than a cowhand, that he was required and his talents were of great use as a member of the floating outfit. The Kid's acceptance had been of great benefit all round. The ranch obtained the services of an extremely capable and efficient man. Dusty had acquired a loyal friend who was ready to stick by him through any kind of danger. For his part, the Kid had turned from a life of petty crime—with the ever present danger of having his activities develop into serious law breaking—and became a most useful member of society. Peace officers and law abiding citizens might have found cause to feel thankful for that. His *Nemenuh* education would have made him a terrible and murderous outlaw if he had been driven to a life of criminal intent.

Obtaining his first repeating rifle while in Mexico with Dusty and Mark—a Winchester Model of 1866, nicknamed the 'Old Yellowboy' because of its brass frame, although at the time known as the 'New, Improved Henry'—the Kid had soon become acknowledged as a master in its use. At the Cochise County Fair in Arizona, he had won the first prize—one of the legendary Winchester Models of 1873 'One of A Thousand' rifles—against stiff competition.[10]

In part, it was through the Kid's efforts that the majority of the Comanche bands had agreed to go on to the reservation following the circumvented attempts to ruin the peace treaty meeting at Fort

[8] Told in: *The Bloody Border* and *Back to the Bloody Border.*
[9] Told in: *The Ysabel Kid.*
[10] Told in: *Gun Wizard.*

422

Sorrel.[11] Nor could Dusty have cleaned out the outlaw town of Hell without his assistance.[12]

[11] Told in: *Sidewinder*.
[12] Told in: *Hell in the Palo Duro* and *Go Back to Hell*.

APPENDIX FOUR

Left an orphan almost from birth by a Waco Indian raid, from whence had come the only name he knew, Waco had been raised as part of a North Texas rancher's large family.[1] Guns had always been a part of his life and his sixteenth birthday had seen him riding with Clay Allison's tough, 'wild onion' ranch crew. The C A hands, like their employer, were notorious for their wild ways and frequently dangerous behaviour. Living in the company of such men, all older than himself, he had grown quick to take offence and well able, even eager, to demonstrate his ability to draw at lightning speed and shoot very accurately. It had seemed to be only a matter of time before one shoot-out too many would have seen him branded as a killer and fleeing from the law with a price on his head.

Fortunately for Waco that day did not come. From the moment Dusty Fog saved the youngster's life, at considerable risk to his own, a change for the better had come.[2] Leaving Allison, with the Washita curly wolf's blessing, Waco had become a member of the OD Connected's floating outfit. The other members of this elite group had treated him like a favourite younger brother and taught him many useful lessons. From the Ysabel Kid he had learned to read tracks and generally act as a scout. Mark Counter gave him instruction in bare-handed combat. From a gambler of their acquaintance had come information about the ways of honest and crooked members of his profession. From Dusty Fog, he had gained the knowledge which—helped by an inborn flair for deduc-

---

[1] How Waco repaid his obligation to Sunshine Sam Catlin, his adoptive father, is told in: *Waco's Debt.*
[2] Told in: *Trigger Fast.*

tive reasoning—would help him to gain fame as a peace officer of exceptional merit.[3]

Benefiting from his education at his friends' hands, in later years Waco was to become an extremely competent and highly respected peace officer.[4] He served with distinction in the Arizona Rangers,[5] as sheriff of Two Forks County, Utah,[6] and finally held office as a U.S. Marshal.[7]

[3] Told in: *The Making of a Lawman* and *The Trouble Busters.*
[4] Early examples of Waco's ability as a peace officer are given in the 'The Hired Butcher' episode of *The Hard Riders*; the 'A Tolerable Straight Shooting Gun' episode of *The Floating Outfit* (*Corgi Books' edition title*); *The Small Texan* and *The Town Tamers.*
[5] Told in: *Sagebrush Sleuth, Arizona Ranger* and *Waco Rides In.*
[6] Told in: *The Drifter* and, by inference, *Doc Leroy, M.D.*
[7] Told in: *Hound Dog Man.*

APPENDIX FIVE

Although Jackson Baines 'Old Devil'[1] Hardin had been proven innocent of the murder which caused him to flee from Louisiana, the reasons outlined in *Ole Devil and the Caplocks* prevented him from returning. So, having accepted Texas as his permanent home, he had thrown himself whole-heartedly into the struggle for independence. Given the rank of captain and placed in command of Company 'C', Texas Light Cavalry—a regiment raised and equipped by the Hardin, Fog and Blaze clan—he had shown himself to be a very capable fighting officer. Not only had he an inborn flair for leadership, he was capable of enforcing his wishes by physical means when necessary. He was helped in this by having a thorough knowledge of *savate*, French foot and fist boxing, augmented with several *ju-jitsu* and *karate* tricks learned from Tommy Okasi, q.v.[2] In addition, he was superbly armed and expert in the use of weapons.

Made by the Arkansas master blacksmith and cutler, James Black, who produced the original for James Bowie, Ole Devil's knife was a copy of that famous weapon.[3] Sixteen inches in overall length, weighing forty-three ounces, it had a lugged brass hilt, a concave ivory handle and a scolloped brass butt cap. Its eleven

[1] The sobriquet came partly from the way in which he enhanced the mephistophelian aspect of his features, but mainly out of the reputation he gained among his contemporaries for being a 'lil ole devil' for a fight.

[2] Ole Devil Hardin never acquired the skill of another member of the clan to whom Tommy Okasi imparted the secrets of *ju-jitsu* and *karate*. This was Captain Dustine Edward Marsden 'Dusty' Fog, C.S.A., details of whose career are given in the author's Floating Outfit and Civil War series. Ole Devil's 'granddaughter', Betty Hardin, also acquired considerable ability in both the martial arts.

[3] Some researchers claim that James Bowie's oldest brother, Resin Pleasant, was the actual designer of the knife.

inches long blade was two and a quarter inches wide and three-eighths of an inch thick at the stock. Only the last five and a quarter inches of the back of the blade was sharpened. This made a concave arc to join the main cutting surface and form a 'clip' point.[4]

Although the knife, Old Devil's matched brace of percussion-fired, British-made Manton ·54 calibre single shot pistols and Haiman Bros. sabre were conventional arms, the same could not be said of his rifle. It was, in fact, a successful attempt by the Mormon gunsmith, Jonathan Browning,[5] to produce a weapon capable of firing several shots in succession without the need to reload in the usual manner after each one.

Fifty-eight and seven-eighths inches in length, the octagonal barrel accounting for forty and five-sixteenths of an inch of this, the Browning Slide Repeating rifle weighed nine pounds fourteen ounces. The 'Slide', a rectangular iron bar with holes to accommodate the powder, shot and percussion caps—generally five in number, as this was the size which could be carried most conveniently, but longer slides could be had as a special order—was placed through an aperture in the rifle's breech. A thumb-operated lever on the right side of the frame caused the slide to advance until each chamber moved into line with the barrel's bore, then rammed it forward to obtain a gas tight seal. The hammer was underneath the frame, in front of the triggerguard, within easy reach of the forefinger, so the piece could be cocked without removing it from the shoulder.

In spite of the difficulty in transporting the rifle with the slide in position, it was simple in design and operation, as well as being capable of continuous fire far in excess of any contemporary weapon. However, during the period when he was manufacturing it, between 1834 and '42, he lacked the facilities to go into large scale production. He would have been able to do so in later years,

---

[4] The dimensions have been duplicated by master cutler William D. 'Bo' Randall, Jnr., Orlando, Florida, in his Model 12 'Smithsonian' bowie knife, one of which is carried by James Allenvale 'Bunduki' Gunn, see: *Bunduki, Bunduki and Dawn* and *Sacrifice for the Quagga God*.
[5] Jonathan Browning's eldest son, John Moses (1855–1926) became the world's most prolific and, arguably, finest designer of firearms. He makes a 'guest appearance' in: *Calamity Spells Trouble*.

but the development of self-contained metallic cartridges and more compact, if less simple, repeating arms made it obsolete.[6]

[6] While engaged in manufacturing the Slide Repeating rifle, Jonathan Browning also developed a rifle which could be discharged six times in succession. The ammunition was held in a cylinder similar to that of later revolvers, but there was no mechanism and it had to be rotated manually after each shot. While the same calibre—approximately ·45—and almost ten inches shorter, it was more bulky and weighed twelve pounds, two ounces. It was not offered for sale until he had settled in Council Bluffs, Utah, in 1852. By that time, due to the ever increasing availability of Samuel Colt's mechanically superior rifles and revolvers, it too had become redundant.

APPENDIX SIX

The author regrets that he is unable to say why Tommy Okasi, a trained *Samurai*,[1] should have been compelled to leave Japan with no possibility of ever returning.[2] Even his true name cannot be divulged. The one he used was an Americanized corruption of that which he had been given when taken as the sole survivor from a derelict vessel in the China Sea by a ship under the command of Ole Devil Hardin's father. His only possessions were a *daisho* of matched swords[3]—comprising a *tachi* with a thirty inches long blade and a *wakizashi* about half of the former's length—made of an exceptionally high quality steel,[4] a six foot long bow of a

[1] *Samurai:* a member of the Japanese lower nobility's elite warrior class, who usually served as a retainer for the *Daimyos*, the hereditary feudal barons. A masterless *Samurai* who became a mercenary was known as a *Ronin*. From the mid-1800s, increased contact with the Western Hemisphere brought an ever growing realization that the retention of a hereditary and privileged warrior class was not compatible with the formation of a modern industrialized society. Various edicts issued by the Emperor between 1873 and '76 abolished the special right of the *Samurai* and, although some of their traditions, concepts and military skills were retained, they ceased to exist in their original form.

[2] The various members of the Hardin, Fog and Blaze clan with whom I discussed the subject while visiting Fort Worth, Texas in 1975 said that, because of the circumstances and the high social standing of the people involved—all of whom have descendants holding positions of influence and importance in Japan at the time of writing—it is inadvisable even at this late date to make public the facts concerning the reason for Tommy Okasi's departure.

[3] Traditionally, the *daisho* was carried thrust into the sash about the *Samurai*'s waist in which case, the longer sword was called a *katana*. As Tommy Okasi spent a considerable amount of his time on horseback after he arrived in the United States, he found it more convenient to wear his suspended by their bamboo sheaths on either side of a leather belt.

[4] After the blade had been shaped by fusing together numerous layers of steel, it was ready to be tempered. A clay-like material, for which every master swordsmith had his own secret recipe, was applied to the whole of the blade apart from an inch or so at the tip and along the entire cutting

style peculiar to his nation[5] and a selection of different kinds of arrows.[6]

In addition to being an expert with the weapons and a reason-

---

edge after heating the blade to the correct temperature—which by tradition was commenced in the half light of the early morning. It was plunged into a tub of cold water. The exposed metal cooled instantly and became very hard. Being encased in the clay sheath, the rest of the metal lost its heat more gradually and, remaining comparatively soft, was given a greater pliancy. To prove that the finished product was capable of carrying out the work for which it was intended, the smith beat it against a sheet of iron and hacked to pieces the body of a dead criminal before handing it over to the owner. This is, of course, only a simplified description of the process.

[5] Unlike Occidental 'self' bows of the period, with the stave formed from a single length of timber, the Japanese weapon was built of three bamboo strips sheathed on two sides with mulberry wood. This formed a core which was encased by further lengths of bamboo, the whole pasted by fish glue and painted with laquer. By laminating the bamboo and the softer, more pliable, mulberry wood, a great strength and flexibility was achieved.

How Tommy Okasi strung his bow is described in: *Ole Devil and the Mule Train* and a comparison with the Occidental method when using a modern recurved (where the ends of the limbs are bent back from the straight line) composite hunting bow (with some form of fibreglass limbs and a wooden handle-riser) can be made by reading: *Sacrifice for the Quagga God.*

[6] The traditional Japanese arrow was made from *mashino-dake*, a very hard, straight and thin species of bamboo. After being cut in the winter, the bamboo was left to dry out of doors until spring. After it had been further dried and hardened by being placed close to a fire, the joints were carefully smoothed down. When the shaft had been polished with emery powder and water, it was once more exposed to the fire. Finally it was fletched with three feathers from a hawk, falcon or eagle and had its nock and some form of metal arrowhead affixed.

The *karimata*, 'forked arrow' point—which Tommy Okasi did not find cause to use on the assignment described in *Ole Devil at San Jacinto*—was a two-pronged design with extremely sharp cutting edges. Originally intended to sever ropes and leather armour lacings, it was also an extremely potent weapon. The width varied from one to six inches between the tips of the prongs. Because of the terrible injuries they were capable of inflicting, the larger sizes—none of which Tommy had in his possession—were also called 'bowel rakers'.

In conclusion, the author feels that a brief description of the Japanese technique called *yabusame*—translated literally, 'shooting from a running horse'—may be of interest. In competition, the mounted *kyudoka* rides at a gallop over a course two *chen*—roughly two-hundred-and-thirty-eight yards—in length, along which are placed at approximately thirty-eight, one-hundred-and-eighteen and one-hundred-and-ninety-three yards, two foot square wooden targets on posts between thirty-six and forty-eight yards, two inches high. Passing them at a distance of around thirty yards, the *kyudoka* discharges an arrow with a forked head that shatters on impact.

able shot with a pistol or rifle,[7] the latter skill having been acquired after his arrival in the United States, he was also a master of *jujistu* and *karate*. As these forms of unarmed combat were practically unheard of in the Western Hemisphere at that time,[8] they were useful in helping to offset any disadvantages in height and weight when he found himself in conflict with larger or heavier men.

[7] Although early types of firearms had been known in Japan since the arrival of Portugese explorers in 1543, the *Samurai* had small regard for them as weapons and spent little time in learning how to use them.

[8] Until the visits by a flotilla under the command of Commodore Perry, United States' Navy, paved the way in 1853–'54, there was little contact between Japan and the Western World.

APPENDIX SEVEN

Wanting a son and learning that his wife, Electra, could not have any more children, Vincent Charles Boyd had given his only daughter, Belle,[1] a thorough training in several subjects not normally regarded as being necessary for a wealthy Southron girl's upbringing. At seventeen, she could ride—astride or side-saddle—as well as any of her male neighbours, men who were to help provide the Confederate States with its superlative cavalry. In addition, she was a skilled performer with an *epée de combat*[2] or a sabre, an excellent shot with any kind of firearm and an expert at *savate*, the French form of foot and fist boxing. All of which were soon to be very useful accomplishments for her.

Shortly before the commencement of the War Between The States, a mob of pro-Union supporters had stormed the Boyd plantation. Before they were driven off by the family's Negro servants, they had murdered Belle's parents and set fire to her home. She was wounded in the fighting and, on recovering, joined her cousin, Rose Greenhow,[3] who was operating a successful spy ring. Wanting to find the leaders of the mob, Belle had not been content to remain in one place. Instead, she had undertaken the dangerous task of delivering other agents' information to the Confederate authorities. Adding an ability at disguise and dialects to her accomplishments, she had gained such proficiency that she won the sobriquet, the Rebel Spy. She had also graduated to handling more important and risky assignments. On two, she had

[1] According to the researches of fictionist-genealogist Philip Jose Farmer, q.v., Belle Boyd was the grand aunt of Jane, Lady Greystoke, née Porter, whose biography is recorded in the *Tarzan of the Apes* series of biographies by Edgar Rice Burroughs.

[2] An *epée de combat* is used mainly for thrusting when on foot and the sabre primarily for slashing from the back of a horse.

[3] Some details of Rose Greenhow's career are given in: *Kill Dusty Fog!*

worked with Captain Dustine Edward Marsden 'Dusty' Fog, q.v.,[4] and a third had brought her first contact with the Ysabel Kid.[5] However, she had not concluded her quest for vengeance upon the murderers of her parents until shortly after the War ended.[6]

While the 'Yankees' might have had reason to hate the Rebel Spy when she was engaged upon her duties against them, the majority had had no cause to feel other than gratitude towards her after peace was reached at the meeting in the Appomattox Court House. On signing the oath of allegiance to the Union, she had been enrolled in the United States' Secret Service. Despite all the trouble she had given that organization during the hostilities, she served it loyally and with efficiency. Her participation in thwarting a plot to assassinate President Ulysses Simpson Grant had prevented friction, possibly another war, between the Northern and Southern States.[7] Assisted by Martha 'Calamity Jane' Canary, q.v., and the lady outlaw, Belle Starr, she had brought an end to the reign of terror created by a murderous gang of female outlaws.[8] With the aid of General Jackson Baines 'Ole Devil' Hardin, C.S.A.'s[9] floating outfit, she had broken up the Brotherhood For Southron Freedom.[10] After having helped avert diplomatic difficulties with the Republic of Haiti in the same company,[11] and wrecking two attempts by European anarchists to create hostility between the U.S.A. and Great Britain,[12] assisted by Capt. Patrick 'The Remittance Kid' Reeder[13] and Lieut. Edward Ballinger[14] of the Chicago Police Department in one case

[4] Told in: *The Colt and the Sabre* and *The Rebel spy*.
[5] Told in: *The Bloody Border*.
[6] Told in: *Back to the Bloody Border*.
[7] Told in: *The Hooded Riders*.
[8] Told in: *The Bad Bunch*.
[9] Details of General Jackson Baines 'Ole Devil' Hardin, C.S.A.'s younger days are given in Part IV of this book.
[10] Told in: *To Arms! To Arms! In Dixie!*
[11] Told in: *Set A-Foot*.
[12] How the first plot was foiled is told in: *The Remittance Kid*.
[13] The researches of fictionist-genealogist Philip Jose Farmer, q.v. have established that Captain (Later Major General) Sir Patrick Reeder (K.C.B., V.C., D.S.O., M.C. and Bar) was the uncle of the celebrated detective, Mr. Jeremiah Golden Reeder, see Introduction to Part Twelve Alvin Dustine 'Cap' Fog's first footnote.
[14] The researches of Philip Jose Farmer, q.v., suggest that Lieutenant Edward Ballinger's grandson, Frank, held a similar rank in the Chicago Police Department at a later date and his exploits formed the basis of the 1957 television series, *M. Squad*, starring Lee Marvin.

and Calamity Jane in the second, she had joined forces once more with Belle Starr and the Ysabel Kid when involved in the efforts of the international master criminal Octavius 'the Ox' Guillemot to gain possession of James Bowie's knife.[15]

[15] Told in: *The Quest for Bowie's Blade.*

APPENDIX EIGHT

Deserted by her husband, Charlotte Canary decided the best way she could assure a future for herself and her children was to leave them in a St. Louis convent and head west to seek her fortune. However, there had been too much of her lively, reckless spirit in her eldest daughter, Martha Jane. Rebelling against the strict life being imposed by the nuns, the girl had celebrated her sixteenth birthday by running away. Hiding on one of Cecil 'Dobe' Killem's freight wagons, she had been twelve miles from the city before she was discovered. She might have been sent back to the convent if the outfit's cook had not been too drunk to work. One of the things the girl had learned from the nuns was cooking. The meal she had prepared was so good that Killem had yielded to her request to be taken to Wichita, Kansas, where she claimed to have an aunt who would give her a home.

Before the outfit had reached its destination, raiding Sioux warriors who had wiped out two other trains failed to locate them. What was more, the goods they were carrying had been sold so profitably that the whole crew received a bonus. Regarding the girl as a good luck charm, they had prevailed upon their employer to let her stay with them when the aunt proved to be a figment of her imagination. Not that Killem, having taken a liking to the spunky youngster, had taken much persuading.

At first, Martha had helped the cook and carried out other menial duties. She graduated to driving and soon there was nothing she could not do in that line of work. Not only could she drive a six-horse team Conestoga wagon, she had learned to use a long lashed bull whip as an inducement to activity or a weapon, to handle firearms with skill and generally take care of herself on

435

the open ranges of the West. Nor did her self-reliance end there. Visiting saloons with the rest of the outfit, she had frequently been called upon to defend herself against the objections of the female denizens who resented her trespassing on their domain. Leading a much more active and healthy life than saloongirls, as well as having been taught the rudiments of unarmed combat, she had only once been beaten in a fight;[1] although the lady outlaw, Belle Starr, q.v., had held her to a hard fought draw when they first met.[2]

Courageous, loyal to her friends, happy-go-lucky and generous to such an extent that she had deliberately lost a saloon she inherited jointly with a professional gambler, Frank Derringer,[3] the girl had a penchant for becoming involved in dangerous and precarious situations. Visiting New Orleans, she had acted as a decoy to lure the Strangler, a notorious mass murderer, to his doom.[4] While helping deliver supplies to an Army post, she had fought with a female professional pugilist and rescued an officer captured by Indians.[5] In Texas, she had helped halt a wave of cattle stealing which was threatening to cause a range war.[6] What started out as a peaceful journey on a stagecoach ended with her helping to capture the criminals who robbed it.[7] Going to visit a ranch left to her by her father in the company of the Ysabel Kid, q.v., she had nearly been killed when a rival claimant had had her fastened to a log which was to be sent through a circular saw.[8] She also played a major part in preventing an Indian uprising in Canada in the company of Belle Boyd and Capt. Patrick 'The Remittance Kid' Reeder.[9]

Among her friends, she counted the members of General Jackson Baines 'Ole Devil' Hardin's C.S.A.'s legendary floating outfit, q.v.; being on exceptionally intimate terms with the handsome

[1] The story of how the defeat came about is told in the 'Better than Calamity' episode of *The Wildcats*.
[2] Told in the 'Bounty on Belle Starr's Scalp' episode of *Troubled Range*.
[3] Told in: *Cold Deck, Hot Lead*.
[4] Told in: *The Bull Whip Breed*.
[5] Told in: *Trouble Trail*.
[6] Told in: *The Cow Thieves*.
[7] Told in: *Calamity Spells Trouble*.
[8] Told in: *White Stallion, Red Mare*.
[9] Told in: *The Whip and the War Lance*.

blond giant, Mark Counter.[10] She had also, on one memorable occasion, posed as the wife of its leader, Captain Dustine Edward Marsden 'Dusty' Fog, q.v. and assisted him to deal with a band of land grabbers.[11] Later, she participated in a big game hunt during which she was kidnapped.[12]

Because of her penchant for finding trouble and becoming involved in brawls, the girl had acquired the sobriquet by which she was soon known throughout the west and beyond.

People called her 'Calamity Jane'.

[10] Calamity Jane's meeting with Mark Counter, other than those referred to in Footnotes One, Two and Eleven are told in: *The Bad Bunch, The Fortune Hunters, Terror Valley* and *Guns in the Night*.
[11] Told in the 'A Wife for Dusty Fog' episode of *The Small Texan*.
[12] Told in: *The Big Hunt*.

APPENDIX NINE

Unlike the other deputies in the Rockabye County Sheriff's Office, Bradford Counter had not served as a member of the Gusher City Police Department, or with some other law enforcement organization, prior to his appointment. Instead, after having been an honour graduate in the Police Science & Administration class at the University of Southern Texas, he had taken the Federal Bureau of Investigation's exacting twelve weeks training course for police officers at his own expense and passed it with distinction.

As a deputy sheriff, Brad had a rank equivalent to a lieutenant in the G.C.P.D.'s Patrol Bureau, or a sergeant in the Detective Bureau. Employing the modern combat shooting techniques perfected by such masters as Sheriff Jack Weaver of Lancaster, California, Elden Carl, Thell Reed and arguably, the dean of them all, Colonel Jeff Cooper, he was able to qualify as a Distinguished Expert on the very demanding Police Combat Shooting Course —which included other types of law enforcement weapons as well as his 'accurized' Colt 1911 Government Model ·45 automatic pistol[1]—and earned an extra sixteen dollars a week on his salary

---

[1] The 'accurizing', performed by the Pachmayr Gun Works in Los Angeles, California, comprised of: tightening the fit between the cocking slide and the receiver; installing an enlarged bushing; decreasing barrel slackness and increasing potential accuracy; working over the internal mechanism to encourage smoother functioning; polishing the feed ramp to an ice-like slickness and trimming the barrel's mouth, both of which would ensure a quicker and more certain transfer of the bullets from the magazine to the chamber, reducing the chance of jamming. Externally, the pistol was fitted with 'combat stocks' which were shaped to make certain the user's hand always closed upon them in the same manner. The butt's 'grip safety' mechanism was welded into the closed position and the manual safety catch's spur enlarged to facilitate changing it to a state of

by virtue of his skill.

The Sheriff's Office based in the Gusher City's Department of Public Safety Building worked a two-watch rota. The Day Watch commenced at eight in the morning and ended at four in the afternoon and the Night Watch continued from four until midnight. If deputies were required between midnight and eight, they would be called from their homes by the G.C.P.D.'s Business Office which was manned for twenty-four hours a day.

In addition to their other duties, the Sheriff's Office were responsible for the investigation of homicides and twenty-two other legal infractions, such as wife-beating, bigamy, train wrecking, assault, which might end in murder. The idea of handling the latter crimes was that, if a death should result from their commission, the officers in charge would have knowledge of the facts leading up to it. Unlike members of the G.C.P.D., who were confined to the city limits, the deputies had jurisdiction throughout the whole of Rockabye County.

---

readiness. A trigger-shoe spread the four pounds' firing pressure to give the impression of a lighter pull by the trigger-finger without reducing the safety-margin. The pistol was fitted with an adjustable rear sight, allowing an increased accuracy when shooting at comparatively long distances.

APPENDIX TEN

James Allenvale 'Bunduki' Gunn's tremendous physique and strength were hereditary. On his father's side, he was descended from an illegitimate son of Sir Henry Curtis who had accompanied the great white hunter, Allan Quatermain on two epic journeys of exploration in Africa.[1] His mother, Allison Dawn 'Tex' Gunn, was the granddaughter of Mark Counter, a Texan who in the mid-1800s had attained legendary status by virtue of his Herculean power as a cowhand, peace officer and all round fighting man.[2] Nor had his parents proved unworthy of such bloodlines. Along with Sir Armond John and Lady Hazel Drummond-Clayton, they had served in the little known but highly effective 'Group Thirteen' Special Missions Organization of British Military Intelligence all through World War II.[3]

When Bunduki's parents were murdered by Mau Mau terrorists, he had been adopted by a wealthy titled family who were related to Dawn. In their care, he had received the education which befitted him perfectly for survival on Zillikian. Arguably the world's foremost authority on wild life and wilderness survival, his adopted father had imparted much practical knowledge. He had been taught how to follow tracks which were scarcely discernible to less keen eyes, to move in silence even through dense undergrowth, to locate hidden enemies and conceal himself from them when necessary and to climb with great agility. He had the know-

[1] If Sir Henry Curtis's biographer, H. Rider Haggard, knew of the son, he was too tactful to mention the matter in *King Solomon's Mines* or *Allan Quatermain*.

[2] Mark Counter's history is recorded in the author's 'Floating Outfit' series of biographies.

[3] Even to this day, British Military Intelligence are reluctant to comment upon, or even acknowledge the existence of 'Group Thirteen'.

ledge to find or hunt for food, while his training in various forms of fighting allowed him to protect himself against predators or human foes.

In Bunduki's hands, the Randall Model 12 'Smithsonian' bowie knife—sixteen inches in overall length, weighing forty-three ounces, with an eleven inch long, two and a quarter inch wide, three-eighths of an inch thick clip point blade[4]—was an even more effective weapon than James Bowie had found the original.[5] Sir Armond Drummond-Clayton had taught him fighting techniques which were unknown in Bowie's day. In archery, he had acquired sufficient skill to duplicate most of the feats attributed to Robin Hood. From a Masai *melombuki*[6] he had learned to throw a *m'kuki*, that nation's traditional spear, and handle a shield. During visits to the United States, along with his Texas-born look-alike cousin Bradford Counter,[7] he had been instructed in the arts of horse handling and lariat throwing by a pure bred Comanche Indian. To round off his knowledge of martial arts, he was equally adept at fencing with a sabre or an epée[8] and had gained great proficiency at boxing, judo, karate and plain, old fashioned rough house brawling.

[4] 'Clip' point: one where the back of the blade curves to meet the main cutting surface in a concave arc. In the case of the Randall Model 12 'Smithsonian' bowie knife, the arc's 'false', or 'top' cutting edge is five and a quarter inches in length and sharp as the main cutting surface.
[5] What happened to James Bowie's knife after his death at the conclusion of the siege at the Alamo Mission, San Antonio de Bexar, Texas, on March the 6th, 1836, is told in *The Quest for Bowie's Blade*. Some authorities have claimed that Bowie's elder brother, Rezin Pleasant, was the actual designer of the knife which was made by the Arkansas' master cutler, James Black.
[6] *Melombuki: a* Masai *moran*—warrior—who has on four separate occasions grasped and held the tail of a hunted lion so that his companions could close in and kill it with their spears or *simis*—fighting knives. A man who attains the title is expected to be ready to fight anybody, or anything.
[7] Details of Bradford Counter's career as a deputy sheriff are given in the author's 'Rockabye County' series of treatise on modern Texas law enforcement.
[8] Generally a sabre is used for slashing and when mounted, while an epée's primary purpose is thrusting and fighting on foot.

APPENDIX ELEVEN

Always something of a tomboy, Dawn Drummond-Clayton had, with her parents' full approval, duplicated the lessons in martial arts and wilderness survival that her inseparable companion, Bunduki, was receiving. Even during her formal and conventional education, which had not been neglected, she had contrived to keep up her training and did not forget what she had been taught. In addition, while attending Roedean,[1] she had taken part in every permissible form of sporting and athletic activity, excelling in them all. However, like Bunduki, she had become completely disenchanted by the blatantly one-sided political bias and hypocrisy of the international sporting bodies and authorities. So in spite of being a world class athlete, gymnast, swimmer and fencer with either sabre or epée, she had refused to compete in their events. For all that she had always kept herself at the peak of physical condition.

As was the case with Bunduki, much of Dawn's perfect physical health stemmed from being allowed to share in some longevity pills obtained by his adoptive parents. Specimens had been given to Dr. Clark Savage, jr.,[2] for analysis and reproduction. He had

[1] Although Sir Armond John and Lady Hazel Drummond-Clayton served in 'Group Thirteen' with Miss A. P. (Amelia) Benkinsop, M.A., B.Sc.(Oxon), Honorary Member, Holloway Old Girls' Association—some details of whose career are recorded in the author's *Blonde Genius*, in collaboration with Peter Clawson—their family background did not meet the special qualifications for Dawn to be allowed to attend Benkinsop's Academy for the Daughters of Gentlefolk.
[2] Details of Clark Savage, Jr.'s life and adventures are recorded in Kenneth Robeson's extensive series of 'Doc Savage' biographies in *Doc Savage, His Apocalyptic Life* by Philip Jose Farmer. This latter also elaborates upon the source of the longevity pills.

discovered that, in addition to slowing down the ageing process in human beings— granting those who took them what amounted to immortality barring accidental death, suicide, or murder—they also gave immunity[3] from practically every tropical disease and destroyed all such harmful internal parasites as the various nematode worms—commonly called 'hookworms' of the genera *Necator* which might be ingested when eating the raw flesh of wild animals.

So, with such qualifications, Dawn was ideally suited to survive on Zillikian and made a fitting mate for the man who had been created the *Dapan-Dankara*, the Fearless Master of the Jungle.

[3] Unfortunately Doc Savage was unable to isolate the immunity element so that it could be reproduced without the added effect of increasing the recipient's life expectancy. The later factors, taken with the human race's ever multiplying birthrate, would have led to Earth becoming over-populated. So it was decided that the pills were unsuitable for general use and they were never released to the public.

DOC LEROY, M.D.

J. T. EDSON

Marvin Eldridge Leroy had been on the point of leaving home to attend medical college when bushwhack lead cut down his parents. Although he was forced to abandon his plans and take a job as a cowhand, he never forgot his ambition of following in his father's footsteps and becoming a qualified doctor. Working on ranches, or driving cattle over the northbound trails to the Kansas railheads, he took every opportunity to continue his medical studies—and gradually he earned a reputation as a doctor . . . people even called him 'Doc'. There were men, women and children alive who would have been dead without his assistance. There were also men who had died at his hands—experience had made him lightning fast with a Colt . . .

0 552 10406 X—**50p**

OLE DEVIL AT SAN JACINTO

By J. T. EDSON

In 1835, the oppressions of Presidente Antonio Lopez de Santa Anna had driven the colonists in Texas to rebellion. Major General Sam Houston, realizing that his small force could only hope to face the vast Mexican army when conditions were favourable, had ordered a tactical withdrawal to the east.

At last, on Thursday, April 21st, 1836, Houston decided that the time had come to make a stand. The Mexican Army, fifteen hundred strong, was on the banks of the San Jacinto river: Houston, with half that number, launched the attack that would decide the future of Texas.

0 552 10505 8—**60p**

SET A-FOOT

By J.T. EDSON

In the days of the open range, a cowhand's most vital possession was his horse. When a cowhand left a spread with no mount of his own, the rancher would usually allow him to borrow one from the remuda, but sometimes, if they parted on bad terms, this loan would not be made . . . There was no greater disgrace for a cowhand than to be set a-foot. It meant he was untrustworthy, and once the news got around, he would find it almost impossible to get another job. So when a cowhand was set a-foot, there was usually trouble—and often gun play!

Dusty Fog knew this, but he still set a-foot the man he blamed for the loss of an OD Connected trail herd and the injuries to some of the crew. He knew too that the cowhand he was disgracing was real fast with a gun—and knew that gun might be turned against him. The cowhand's only name was Waco . . .

0 552 10660 7—**65p**

SUDDEN—THE MARSHAL OF LAWLESS

By OLIVER STRANGE

'Being Marshal of Lawless is plain suicide!' That's what they told the young fellow who applied for the job. They figured that anyone who had hocked his horse, his saddle and his guns to get money for liquor, was not the kind of man who could hold down one of the toughest towns in the West.

But then the young stranger redeemed his guns and strapped them on. Lawless looked again. 'Gentlemen, hush!' said one inhabitant. 'A man has come to town!'

0 552 08906 0—**60p**

TO THE FAR BLUE MOUNTAINS
By LOUIS L'AMOUR

For some men, an acre of land and a cottage are enough: not for Barnabas Sackett—the wanderlust in his blood drove him from the peaceful fen country of England over the sea to the New World. The call of the West was strong, and with Abigail beside him—and a Queen's warrant for his arrest behind him—Barnabas turned his face to the far blue mountains of Virginia . . . He and his followers fought off wild beasts, shot buffalo and just about kept themselves alive—and at last they built their stockade on the James River. For a while, all was peaceful. Then one night, there were noises outside the stockade and, in a flare of torch-light, a dozen savage, painted faces . . .

0 522 10550 3—65p

WESTWARD THE TIDE
By LOUIS L'AMOUR

The wagon trains were pushing further West, carrying men in search of adventure, or in search of gold from the Black Hills. Matt Bardoul had craved—and won—both in his time, but now he needed more: one look at old man Coyle's daughter and he knew why he'd agreed to join the trek. Yet there was the lure of gold too—a fortune for the taking up in the Big Horns, where the Sioux still roamed . . . There would be trouble on the trail too, with Gunmen like Logan Deane along and the gold-lust in every man's mind. Matt figured there'd be a heavier price paid for that Big Horn Gold . . .

0 552 10483 3—60p

BEGUINAGE

By J. T. EDSON

To protect the life of a visiting European Crown Prince from threatened assassination, the Govenor of Texas could have called up the Texas Rangers, or even the United States Army. Instead, Stanton Howard obtained the services of Ole Devil Hardin's floating outfit. Dusty Fog, Mark Counter, the Ysabel Kid and Waco had handled many dangerous people in their time but they'd never met the like of the one employed by this band of conspirators to kill the Crown Prince. Acknowledged as Europe's premier assassin, Beguinage came and went unnoticed by all except the victims. And he never failed in an assignment. The only way Dusty saw of saving the Prince was to use himself as bait for a trap—knowing that when it was sprung either, Beguinage or he would be dead . . .

0 552 10769 7—**65p**

THE WHIP AND THE WARLANCE

By J. T. EDSON

Having thwarted one scheme to invade Canada from the USA, Belle Boyd, the Rebel Spy, and the Remittance Kid were hunting the leaders of the plot, who had escaped and were plotting another attempt. To help them, they called upon a young lady called Miss Martha Jane Canary better known as Calamity Jane . . . Belle, Calamity and the Kid made a good team, but they knew they would need all their fighting skills when the showdown came. For they leLoup Garou and the Jan-Dark, the legendary warrior maid with the warlance who, it had long been promised, would come to rally all the Indian nations and drive the white man from Canada.

0552 10964 9—**65p**

If you have enjoyed reading this book and other works by the same author, why not join

THE J. T. EDSON APPRECIATION SOCIETY

You will receive a signed photograph of J. T. Edson, bi-monthly Newsletters giving details of all new books and re-prints of earlier titles.

Competitions with autographed prizes to be won in every issue of the Edson Newsletter.

A chance to meet J. T. Edson.

Send SAE for details and membership form to:

The Secretary,
J. T. Edson Appreciation Society,
P.O. Box 13,
MELTON MOWBRAY,
Leics.